Günter Grass was born in Danzig in 1927. He is
Germany's most celebrated contemporary writer.
Though best known as a novelist – author of The
Danzig Trilogy (*The Tin Drum*, *Cat and Mouse* and
Dog Years) and *The Flounder* – he is also poet,
playwright, sculptor, graphic artist, essayist and
political spokesman.

Günter Grass

THE RAT

Translated by
RALPH MANHEIM

published by **Pan Books**
in association with
Secker & Warburg

First published in Great Britain 1987 by
Martin Secker & Warburg Limited
This Picador edition published 1988 by Pan Books Ltd,
Cavaye Place, London SW10 9PG
9 8 7 6 5 4 3 2 1
© Hermann Luchterhand Verlag GmbH & Co KG, Darmstadt und Neuwied 1986
English translation © Harcourt Brace Jovanovich, Inc. 1987
ISBN 0 330 30283 3
Printed and bound in Great Britain by
Richard Clay Ltd, Bungay, Suffolk

FOR UTE

Chapter One, *in which a wish comes true, there is no room for rats in Noah's ark, nothing is left of man but garbage, a ship changes its name frequently, the saurians die out, an old friend turns up, a postcard brings an invitation to Poland, the upright posture is practised, and knitting needles click vigorously.*

AT CHRISTMAS I wished for a rat in the hope no doubt of stimulus words for a poem about the education of the human race. Actually, I wanted to write about the sea, my Baltic puddle; but the animal won out. My wish came true. Under the Christmas tree the rat came as a surprise.

Not thrust aside, no, roofed over by fir branches, harmonized with low-hanging decorations, there lay, in place of the crèche and its well-known personnel, an oblong wire cage with white-enamelled bars and inside it a small wooden hut, a baby bottle and a feeding bowl. How self-assured my gift stood there, as though no objection were possible, as though nothing were more natural than a rat under a Christmas tree.

Only moderate curiosity when paper crackled. A creepy rustling in its litter of curly wood shavings. When after a short leap she crouched on top of her house, a glittering golden ball reflected the play of her whiskers. Surprising from the start: how long and naked her tail, and her human five-fingeredness.

A clean animal. Here and there a rat dropping or two, the size of a little-fingernail. The Christmas Eve smell, compounded, in accordance with an old recipe, of candlewax, fir tree, a bit of embarrassment and gingerbread, drowned out the effluvia of the young animal, purchased from a snake breeder in Giessen, who bred rats for snakefeed.

True, there were other surprises; some useful, some useless, spread out to the left and right. It's getting harder and harder to give presents. Who has room for anything these days? Oh, the misery of not knowing what to wish for. Every wish has come true. What's needed, we say, is need, as if that could be a wish. And mercilessly we go on giving. No one knows any more what came to him when and from whose generosity. Surfeited and needy, that was my state when, consulted about my Christmas wishes, I wished for a rat.

Of course there were facetious remarks. And plenty of questions: At your age? Is this necessary? Just because they're fashionable at the moment? Why not a crow? Or hand-blown glassware, like last year? – But never mind, a wish is a wish.

It should be a female. But please, not a white one with red eyes, not a laboratory rat like the ones used by Schering and Bayer-Leverkusen.

But does any dealer carry the grey-brown rats, commonly known as sewer rats?

As a rule, pet shops stock only rodents which are not ill-famed, which are not proverbial, about which nothing bad is written.

They tell me it wasn't until the fourth Sunday of Advent that word came from Giessen. The son of a pet dealer with the usual stock, who happened to be driving through Itzehoe on his way north to see his fiancée, was kind enough to bring the requested article; it didn't matter that the cage had been borrowed from a golden hamster.

I had just about forgotten my wish by Christmas Eve when the female rat surprised me in her cage. I spoke to her, said something idiotic. Later, gift phonograph records were played. A shaving brush occasioned laughter. Plenty of books, including one about the island of Usedom. The children happy. A cracking of nuts, a folding of gift wrapping. Scarlet-red and zinc-green ribbons, twisted at the ends, demanded – waste not want not – to be spooled for re-use.

Fleece-lined slippers. Odds and ends. And a present that I had rolled in tissue paper for my dearest, who had given me the rat: a hand-coloured map showing Vineta, the submerged city, off the coast of Pomerania. A handsome engraving, in spite of mould spots and a crosswise tear.

Candles burnt low, the condensed family circle, the wellnigh unbearable atmosphere, the holiday dinner. Next day, the first visitors called the rat sweet.

My Christmas rat. What else can I call her? Holding a nut kernel, an almond or a bit of pressed hamster food in her delicately articulated pink toes. Though queasy at first about my fingertips, I'm beginning to spoil her – with raisins, crumbs of cheese, egg yolk.

I've set her down beside me. Her whiskers take note of me. She plays with my fears, she can feel them. So I talk in self-defence. To begin with, plans from which rats are excepted, as though any future happening were conceivable without them, as though the She-rat could possibly be absent when the sea ventures to make little waves, when the forest dies by man's doing, and/or when, possibly, a humpback little man starts on a trip.

I've been dreaming about her lately: school problems, the dissatisfactions of the flesh, all the stuff that sleep foists on me, the happenings I'm involved in when wide awake, my daydreams, my night dreams are her staked-out territory. No imbroglio, to which she doesn't give bare-tailed form. Everywhere she deposits her scent marks. Whatever I put in her way – false bottoms, lies as big as houses – she nibbles her way through. Her incessant gnawing, her know-it-allness. It's not me speaking any more, it's her haranguing me.

Finished! she says. You people used to be, you're has-beens, a remembered delusion. Never again will you set dates. All your prospects wiped out. You're washed up. Completely. It was high time.

Nothing left but rats. Few at first, because practically all life came to an end, but even in the telling the She-rat multiplies while reporting our demise. Sometimes she squeaks regretfully, as though to teach future litters to mourn for us; sometimes there's derision in her ratgibber, as though hatred of our kind lingered on: You're through, through!

But I hold up my end: No, She-rat, no! We are still as the sands of the sea. Punctually, news items report our deeds. We dream up plans that promise success. At least in the medium term we're still here. Even that humpback little man who's dying as usual to butt in, said only recently, when I wanted to go down to the cellar to see how the winter apples were doing: Maybe mankind is on the way out, but in the last analysis it's us who'll decide when to shut up shop.

Rat stories! How many she knows! According to her, they inhabit not only the warmer zones, but even the igloos of the

Günter Grass

Eskimos. They settled Siberia along with the deportees. Side by side with the polar explorers, they discovered the Arctic and Antarctic. For them no wilderness was too inhospitable. In the wake of caravans through the Gobi Desert, in the train of pious pilgrims, they made their way to Mecca and Jerusalem. Rats in serried ranks were seen migrating with the migrations. With the Goths they reached the Black Sea, with Alexander India, with Hannibal they crossed the Alps, affectionately they followed the Vandals to Rome. To Moscow and back with Napoleon's Grand Army. With Moses and the children of Israel, rats scurried dry-shod through the Red Sea and tasted of heavenly manna in the desert of Zin; from the start there was plenty of garbage.

No end to what the She-rat knows. Loudly enough to make the rafters ring, she shouts: In the beginning was the don't. For when the God of humankind blustered: Behold, I will bringe in a floud of water apon the erth to destroy all flesh from under heaven, wherin breth of life is, we were expressly forbidden to go aboard. For us it was no admittance when Noah turned his ark into a zoo, though his ever-punishing God, in whose syghte he had found grace, had made himself plain from on high: Of all clene beastes take unto thee seven of every kynde, the male and hys female. And of unclene beastes a payre, the male and hys female. For seven days hence wyll I send rayne uppon the erth, forty dayes and forty nyghtes and wyll destroy all maner of thynges that I have made, from off the face of the erth, for it repenteth me that I have made them.

And Noah did God's bidding. He took of fowls after their kind, of cattle after their kind, of every creeping thing of the earth after its kind; only of our kind he was determined to take no pair, no male and no female, into his tub. Clean or unclean, as he saw it, we were neither one nor the other. Already, the prejudice had taken root. Hatred from the start and the urge to eradicate what gives people that retching sensation. Man's innate loathing for our kind prevented Noah from carrying out the orders of his stern God. He denied us, he crossed us off his list of all creatures wherein the breath of life is.

Of cockroaches and spiders, of wriggling worms, even of lice and warty toads and iridescent bluebottles, of each he took a pair aboard his ark, but not of us. We were supposed to go under like the numberless remnant of corrupt mankind, which the Almighty, that forever punishing, vengeful God, with his habit of cursing his own foul-ups, disposed of as follows: The wekednesse of man was encreased apon the erth, and all the ymaginacion and thoughtes of his hert was only evell continually.

Whereupon he made rain that fell for forty days and forty nights, until everything was covered with water, everything but the ark and its contents. But when the flood receded and the first mountaintops emerged from the waters, when the raven that Noah sent forth returned, followed by the dove, concerning whom it is written: She cam to hym agayne aboute eventyde; and lo, and beholde: there was in her mouth a lefe of an olyve tre which she had plucked. But the dove brought more than greenery, she also brought Noah a startling message: where there was nothing else that crept or flew, she had seen rat droppings, fresh rat droppings.

And then God, weary of His bungling, laughed, because Noah's disobedience had been foiled by our tenacity. Speaking as usual from on high, he decreed: Let the ratte henceforward be man's companioun on erth, and carrye all the promised playgues.

He prophesied still more, things that are not written. He made the plague our business and, as you might expect of the Almighty, claimed to be more almighty than he was. He personally, so he said, had saved us from the flood. An unclean pair, so he said, had been on his divine hand; the dove sent forth by Noah had seen fresh rat droppings on the divine hand; we owed our prolific survival to his paw, for it was on the palm of God's hand that we had brought forth ratlets, nine of them, and during the hundred and fifty days while the waters prevailed upon the earth, that litter multiplied into a nation of rats. So spacious is the hand of the almighty God.

After this speech, Noah remained stubbornly silent and thought wicked thoughts, as he had done from the days of his youth. But when the ark came, broad and flat, to rest on Mount Ararat, we had already occupied the wasteland round about; for it was not in God's hand that we, the tenacious nation of rats, had escaped the flood, but in underground passages that we had plugged with moribund animals, so forming air bubbles that served as safe nesting chambers. We of the long tails! We of the presentient whiskers! We of the perpetually growing teeth! We, the serried footnotes to man, his proliferating commentary. We, indestructible!

We had soon moved into Noah's tub. No countermeasures helped; his food was ours. More quickly than Noah's human entourage and his chosen fauna could multiply, we became as the sands of the sea. The human race has never got rid of us.

Then Noah, affecting to humble himself before his God, but actually setting himself in God's place, said: I hardened my heart, I disregarded the Lord's word. But God's will be done, the rat has survived with us on earth. It shall be cursed to grovel in our shadow, where our refuse lies.

That came true, said the She-rat of my dreams. Where man had been, in every place he left, garbage remained. Even in his pursuit of the ultimate truth and quest for his God, he produced garbage. By his garbage, which lay stratum upon stratum, he could always — one had only to dig — be known. For more long-lived than man is his refuse. Garbage alone lives after him.

How naked lies her tail, now this way now that way. Oh, how my pretty little Christmas rat has grown. Restlessly back and forth, then rigid except for her quivering whiskers, she takes up all my dreams. Sometimes she babbles casually, as though the world and its trivia deserved no better than gossiping ratgibber, and then again she pontificates, takes me as her pupil, gives me ratty, piping history lessons; and what certainties, as though she had nibbled her way through Luther's Bible, the major and minor Prophets, the Proverbs, the Lamentations, and while she's at it the Apocrypha, the chanting of the men in the fiery furnace, every one of the Psalms, and seal upon seal, the Revelation of St John.

Yea verily, ye have ceased to be, I hear her proclaim. As resoundingly as the dead Christ speaking from the top of the world, the She-rat speaks from atop the garbage mountain: If it were not for us, nothing would bear witness to you humans. It's we who inventory what the human race has left behind. Vast plains infested with garbage, beaches strewn with garbage, valleys clogged with garbage. Synthetic flakes on the move. Tubes that have forgotten their ketchup and never rot. Shoes of neither leather nor straw walk self-propelled with the sand and collect in pits full of garbage, where already yachtsman's gloves and droll inflatable animals are waiting. All these things speak of you, now and forever. You and your works wrapped in clear plastic, sealed into vacuum bags, moulded in synthetic resin, you in chips and clips: the human race that was.

What else is left; scrap-iron clatters over your roads. No paper for us to feed on, only torn awnings wrapped around pillars, around steel girders. Curdled foam. Jello shimmies as if it were alive.

The Rat

Everywhere hordes of empty cans. Liberated from cassettes, video tapes are on the move: *The Caine Mutiny, Dr Zhivago, Donald Duck, High Noon, Gold Rush* – all that in moving pictures was life for you, entertained you or moved you to tears.

Oh, your car cemeteries, in places where it was once possible to live. Containers and other warehoused goods. The boxes you called safes and strongboxes stand wide open: every secret vomited up. We know it all, all! And what you stored in leaky barrels, forgotten or misleadingly inventoried, we find it, your thousands on thousands of poison disposal sites, places that we delimit by depositing scent marks as a warning – warning to us, for by now there's no one else.

Granted: your very garbage is impressive. We rats are sometimes amazed when storms, along with glittering dust, waft structural elements over hill and dale. Look, there goes a fibre-glass roof. That's how we remember man and his hubris: always higher, always more boldly conceived . . . How crumpled is his fallen progress.

And I saw what I dreamed, saw gelatin shimmying and tapes on the move, saw truckloads of scrap and foil buffeted by storms, saw poison seeping from barrels. And I saw the She-rat on top of the garbage mountain, proclaiming that man is no more. This, she cried out, is your heritage.

No, She-rat, no! I cried. We're still alive and kicking. Appointments are made – by the Inland Revenue, by the dentist, for instance. Tickets are booked for holiday flights. Tomorrow is Wednesday and the day after will be . . . Moreover, a humpback little man stands in my path, saying: This and that remains to be written down, to the end that our demise, should it come about, will occur as planned.

My sea that stretches eastward
and northward, where Haparanda lies.
The Baltic puddle.
What else originated in the windy island of Gotland.
How seaweed took the air from herring
and mackerel, and triggerfish as well.

The story I'm going to tell
in an attempt to put off the end with words,

might begin with jellyfish, which are increasing
more and more, immeasurably,
until the sea, my sea, is becoming
one single jellyfish.

Or I could make picture-book heroes come sailing,
the Russian admiral, the Swede, Dönitz or whomever
until plenty of flotsam and jetsam
remains – planks and logbooks,
inventoried provisions –
and all sinkings have been commemorated.

But when on Palm Sunday fire from heaven
fell on Lübeck and its churches,
the whitewash burned off the inner brick walls;
once again Malskat the painter will have to climb high
on scaffolding, lest we should lose
our Gothic.

Or else, because I can't resist
beauty, the organist from Greifswald
will speak with her Rs rolled like pebbles on the beach.
She outlived no less than
eleven pastors and always
carried the cantus firmus.

Now she bears the same name as Witzlav's daughter.
Now Damroka refuses to say
what the Flounder told her.
Now on the organ bench she is laughing
in memory of her eleven pastors; the first was
a creep from Saxony . . .

Be my guests: for Anna Koljaiczek
from Bissau near Viereck near Matarnia
will soon be a hundred and seven.
They're all coming to celebrate her birthday
with head cheese and mushrooms and cake,
for the Kashubian plant has branched wide.

The overseas contingent: From Chicago they come.
The Australians take the longest route.
Those who are doing well in Western Europe

are coming to show those who
have stayed in Ramkau, Kartuzy, Kokoschken,
How solid the Deutschmark.

Five from the Lenin Shipyards form a delegation.
Blackskirts bring the Church's blessing.
Not only the State Post Office,
but the Polish state as well is represented.
And our Herr Matzerath is coming, too,
with chauffeur and gifts.

But the end! When will it be?
Vineta! Where is Vineta?
Sea-wise they heave in sight; for in the meantime
women have become active.
At the most, messages in bottles
give an idea of their itinerary.

All hope is gone,
for fairy tales,
it shall be written here,
are dying with the forests.
Neckties cut off just below the knot.
At last, with nothingness behind them, men are choosing retire-
    ment.

But when the sea showed the women Vineta,
it was too late. Damroka perished,
and Anna Koljaiczek said: It's all washed up.
Oh, what's to become of us if there's no more to come.
And I dreamed of the She-rat and wrote:
The New Ilsebill goes ashore as a rat.

In October 1899, when the *Dora*, a steel sailing barge with a
wooden bottom, was ordered from the shipbuilder Gustav Junge
and in 1900, when it was launched at the Wewelsfleth shipyard, the
owner Richard Nickels had no suspicion of all that lay in store for
his Alster barge, designed for the dimensions of the Hamburg
Graskeller locks, especially as the brash, loudly heralded new
century was born with bulging pockets, as though setting out to
buy up the world.

The barge measured exactly eighteen metres in length and four point seventy in width. Its displacement came to thirty-eight point five gross register tons, its capacity to seventy tons, though registered at sixty-five. A cargo ship, good for grain and cattle, lumber and bricks.

Not content with moving freight on the Elbe, the Stör and the Oste, Skipper Nickels also put into German and Danish ports as far north as Jutland and as far east as Pomerania. With a good wind his barge could do four knots an hour.

In 1912 the *Dora* was sold to Skipper Johann Heinrich Jungclaus, who brought it undamaged through the First World War and in 1928, at the time of the Rentenmark, put in an 18 hp diesel engine. The home port inscribed in white letters on the black-painted stern was Krautsand and no longer Wewelsfleth. That changed when Jungclaus sold his freight barge to Skipper Paul Zenz of Cammin on the Dievenow, a small town in Pomerania, now called Kamien.

There the *Dora* attracted attention. The coastal skippers of Pomerania ridiculed the barge as a 'clumsy bastard', when it was sailed through Greifswald Bay. It still carried cargoes of grain, winter cabbage and cattle, not to mention lumber, bricks, roofing tiles and cement, because plenty of building was going on until well into the Second World War: barracks, shacks for prison camps. But the name of the *Dora*'s owner was now Otto Stöwase, and the home port announced on the stern was Wollin; that is the name of a city and an island, which side by side with the island of Usedom is situated off the coast of Pomerania.

From January to May 1945, ships big and small, overloaded with civilians and soldiers, crossed the Baltic, though not all of them reached Western safety in the ports of Lübeck, Kiel, Copenhagen, and shortly before the Second Soviet Army broke through to the Baltic, the *Dora*, too, carried refugees from Danzig-West Prussia to Stralsund. That was when the *Gustloff* sank. That was when the *Cap Arcona* was consumed by fire in Neustadt Bay. That was when everywhere, even on the neutral coast of Sweden, innumerable corpses were washed ashore; all survivors thought they had truly escaped and for that reason, annulling everything that had gone before, referred to the end as zero hour.

A decade later, while armed peace prevailed on all sides, the barge, length and breadth unchanged, was fitted with a 36 hp Brons diesel engine by her new owner, the firm of Koldewitz in Rügen, who also changed its name from *Dora* to *Ilsebill*, no doubt in allusion to a Low-German fairy tale which was taken down at a time when fairy tales were being collected all over Germany, hence also on the island of Rügen.

Named after the fisherman's wife, who wanted more and more of the talking Flounder, and ended up wanting to be 'like God', the *Ilsebill* long continued to carry cargo in Greifswald Bay, in the Peene estuary and the Achterwasser, until in the late sixties, while armed peace still prevailed, its owners thought of dismantling it and sinking it in the harbour of Warthe in Usedom as a breakwater foundation. The steel hull, whose stern had last boasted the city of Wolgast as home port, was to be flooded.

This was not done, for in the wealthy West, to which the lost war had brought prosperity, a purchaser turned up, a woman from Greifswald, who had moved with detours to Lübeck, but retained a passion for junk from Western Pomerania, whether originating in Rügen or Usedom or, as in the case of the steel sailing barge with the wooden bottom, ending up there. Actually, she had been looking for one of the Baltic trawlers which had become a rarity.

At the end of the long-drawn-out negotiations, the purchaser, thanks to her truly Pomeranian tenacity, got her barge, because the last owner, the German Democratic Republic, was hungry for hard Western currency. As it happened, it cost her more to move the freight barge than she had paid for it.

For a long time the *Dora*, now the *Ilsebill*, lay in Travemünde. Black the hull and the foremast, blue and white the pilot house and the rest of the superstructure. On long weekends and during vacations, the new owner, whom I shall call Damroka because I am fond of her, cleaned, repaired and painted her barge. Then in the late seventies, though an organist by profession, who as far back as she could remember had devoted hands and feet to the service of God and Bach, earned her captain's certificate and licence for coastal navigation. Leaving organ, church and pastor behind her, she threw off the servitude of music, and will henceforth be called Captain Damroka, even though she sailed her ship less than she lived in it, and stood around meditatively on deck as though welded to her perpetually half-full coffee pot.

It wasn't until the early eighties that Damroka conceived a plan which, after a few trial runs in Lübeck Bay and across to Denmark, is to be carried out at the end of this year, which according to the Chinese calendar is the Year of the Rat.

A sailing barge built in 1900, which has several times changed its owner and home port, lost its mizzen mast but acquired a powerful diesel engine when last overhauled, has now, as though to embody a programme, been renamed *The New Ilsebill*. Soon to be manned by women, it has been converted in Travemünde harbour from a freight barge to a research vessel. In the forecastle a narrow sleeping compartment has been boarded off for the female crew. A locker built into the prow provides room for seabags, books, knitting materials and first aid equipment. Furnished with a long work table, the hold amidships will in future be devoted to research. Over the engine room with its new 180 hp engine, the pilot house, a wooden pergola with windows on all sides, has been extended on the stern end to form a kitchenette, more like a cupboard than a galley.

Overmanned with five women, the ship is cramped and only passably comfortable. Everything functional; the work table has to double as dining table. *The New Ilsebill* is expected to navigate in West German, Danish and Swedish waters, and if a permit is granted, in the coastal waters of the German Democratic Republic as well. Its mission has been specified: to make selective measurements of jellyfish density in the western Baltic, which is increasingly infested with these coelenterates. The beach resorts are suffering. Moreover, the aurelia jellyfish, which live on plankton and herring larvae, are impairing the fishing grounds. The Institute for Oceanology, with headquarters in Kiel, is therefore distributing research assignments. Of course there's the usual shortage of funds. Of course, the cause of the infestation is not to be investigated, but only its quantitative fluctuation. Of course it's known in advance that the findings will be catastrophic.

This is said by the women on board, who are all inclined to laughter and sarcasm, sharp-tongued, and when necessary poisonously abrasive; all are greying and no longer as young as they used to be. As the barge leaves the harbour – on the port side, the breakwater, occupied by waving tourists – the bow wave divides and churns up a superabundance of jellyfish, which reunite behind the stern.

For this expedition, the five women I've wished for have submitted to training. They can tie knots and hug the wind. They have no difficulty in handling cleats or coiling cables. They are pretty good at reading channel markings. They can steer a seamanly course. Captain Damroka has hung up her licence, glassed and framed, in the pilot house. Otherwise, no pictures, no ornaments; instead, a new Atlas sonar in addition to the old compass and a weather receiver.

True, it is well known that the Baltic is clogged with algae, bearded with seaweed, supersaturated with jellyfish, not to say, polluted with mercury, lead and heaven knows what else, but it must be established where more, where less, where not yet, where especially clogged, bearded, supersaturated, regardless of all the noxious substances inventoried elsewhere. For that reason the laboratory ship has been equipped with instruments of measurement, one of which is nicknamed 'the shark' and facetiously referred to as a jellyfish counter. In addition, the incidence of plankton, herring larvae and whatever else jellyfish eat, is to be measured, weighed and recorded. One of the women is a trained oceanographer. She has all the obsolete data at her fingertips and can compute the biomass of the western Baltic down to the nearest milligramme. In the present account she will henceforth be referred to as the oceanographer.

The research barge makes its way under a light northwesterly breeze. As calm as the sea and confident of their skill, the women go about their seamanly duties. Slowly, because that's how I want it, they get into the habit of calling one another by their functions. 'Hey, engineer,' or 'Where's the oceanographer keeping herself?' But though the oldest of the women does the cooking, she will be called, not Cookie but the Old Woman.

No need for the present to let out the 'shark'. There's still time for stories. Three miles from the Holstein bathing beaches, the captain talks to the helmswoman of olden times, when for seventeen years she kept faith with her congregation and outlived eleven pastors, one after another. For instance, she would cut short the first – he was a creep, he came from Saxony – whose sermons were always too long, with the chorale 'O Lord 'tis enough'. But as the helmswoman smiles only inwardly and displays only her native bitterness, Damroka shortens her tale and makes the first of her eleven pastors pass away after a sudden fall from the organ loft. 'And then there were ten . . .'

No, says the She-rat in my dream. We're sick of these stories. This Once-upon-a-time stuff. All the drivel that's put down in black and

white. The wisdom and the Church Latin. We rats have battened on
it, eaten our way to erudition. Oh, those mouldy parchments,
those leather-bound folios, those collected works bristling with
slips of paper, those clever-clever encyclopedias. From d'Alembert
to Diderot, we know it all: the holy Enlightenment and the
subsequent revulsion against science. All secretions of human
reason.

Even before that, as early as Augustine's day, we overate. From
St Gall to Uppsala, every monastery library contributed to our
erudition. We are decidedly well read; in times of famine we fed on
quotations, we know our belles-lettres and our philosophy inside
and out; the pre-Socratics and Sophists have filled our bellies. Not
to mention the Scholastics. Persistently gnawed, their involute
sentences have always agreed with us. Ah, footnotes! What
delectable condiments! Enlightened from time immemorial,
treatises, theses, digressions have provided us with button-bright
entertainment.

Oh, your cogitative sweat, your inkflow! What quantities of
paper have been blackened to further the education of the human
race! Polemics and manifestos. Words hatched and hairs split.
Poems scanned and interpreted. So much cleverness. Nothing was
immune to doubt. To every word seven were opposed. Your
polemic's shot from every pulpit; was the earth round, was bread
really the Lord's body? We especially relished your theological
quarrels. True enough, the Bible could be read in different ways.

The She-rat, who was bored with Damroka and her pastors, told
me what she remembered of zealotic times, before and after Luther:
monkish arguments and theological disputations. Always about
the true word of God. And naturally she soon came back to Noah,
thrusting the three-storied ark, which God had demanded, into my
dream.

Exactly! she cried. He should have taken us aboard his pinewood
tub. Rats, keep out. The book of Genesis doesn't even mention us.
Even the serpent who, as you can read in black and white, was
cursed above all cattle and every beast of the field, was admitted,
male and female, into the wooden tub. Why not us? That was an
injustice. Time and again we protested.

Whereupon I was obliged to witness, in fluid dream images, how
Noah caused seven pairs of clean animals and one pair each of
unclean animals to be led over the gangplank into the three-storied

tub. Like a circus director, he took pleasure in his menagerie. Not a species was missing. The lot of them stamped, trotted, hopped, tripped, scurried, crawled, fluttered, crept and slithered in, not excluding the earthworm, male and female. In pairs, they took refuge – camel and elephant, tiger and gazelle, stork and owl, ant and snail. And in pairs came dogs and cats, foxes and bears, followed by all the many rodents: voles and mice, yes, indeed, wood, field, harvest, and jumping mice. But always when the rats, male and female, tried to line up and escape with the others, the word was: Keep out! No admittance!

It wasn't Noah who shouted that. Noah stood silent and morose by the gangplank, checking arrivals against his lists – clay tablets in which he made notches. The shouting was done by his sons, Shem, Ham and Japheth, three big bruisers, who later got instructions from on high: Be fruitful and multiply and replenish the earth. Beat it! they yelled. No admittance for rats! They carried out their father's orders. It was pathetic to see the biblical rat couple being hunted out of the shaggy wool of long-haired sheep, driven with sticks from under the sagging belly of the hippopotamus, and chased away from the gangplank. Ridiculed by pigs and monkeys, they finally gave up. And if, said the She-rat, if God hadn't picked us up as the ark got more and more crowded, or rather, to play it safe, if we hadn't dug ourselves in, plugged our underground passages, and transformed our nesting chambers into salutary air bubbles – we wouldn't be here today. There wouldn't be anybody worth mentioning capable of outliving the human race.

We've always been around. We were definitely on hand during the Cretaceous; when man hadn't even been thought of. That was when here and elsewhere dinosaurs and suchlike monsters were razing the horsetail and fern forests. Stupid coldbloods who laid preposterously enormous eggs, that hatched out ungainly new monsters which grew to gigantic proportions until, fed up with nature's excesses, we rats – smaller than today, about the size of the Galapagos rat – cracked their gigantic eggs. Stupid, congealed by the cold night, the saurians stood helpless, incapable of defending their offspring. Caprices of capricious nature, they were obliged to look on out of tiny eyes, half-forgotten in the act of Creation, while we, who had always been warm-blooded, we, the first viviparous mammals, we of the incisors that never stopped growing, we restlessly mobile rats gnawed holes in the hard thick shells that were doing their best to protect those gigantic eggs. Just laid and not yet hatched, the eggs had to put up with hole after hole, through which they drained for our pleasure.

Poor dinosaurs! sneered the She-rat, showing her incisors that never stopped growing. And she listed: the brachiosaurus and diplodocus, two monsters weighing up to eighty tons, the scaly sauropods and the armoured theropods, an order including the tyrannosaur, a rapacious monster fifteen metres long, the bird-footed saurians and horned torosaur: and all these monsters appeared to me with dreamlike vividness, along with amphibians and flying lizards.

Good God, I cried, one monster more hideous than the next.

They didn't last long, said the She-rat. Bereft of their gigantic eggs, deprived of their future baby monsters, the dinosaurs dragged themselves into the swamps, there to perish uncomplaining and outwardly undamaged. That is how it came about that man, with his restlessly digging curiosity, would later find their skeletons in excellent shape and build spacious museums around them. Bone fitted to bone, the saurians were put on display, each exemplar filling a whole room. The diggers also found gigantic eggs with our tooth marks in their shells. These too were exhibited, but no one, no student of the late Cretaceous, no high priest of evolutionary theory saw fit to credit our achievement. It was held that the dinosaurs had died out for hitherto unelucidated reasons. The extinction of the monsters was attributed to multiple thickening of the eggshells, to a sudden drop in the temperature, to diluvial storms, and so on; no one wanted to give us rats credit.

Thus did the She-rat of my dreams lament after repeatedly demonstrating, with frantic biting motions, the cracking of the giant eggs. If it weren't for us, she cried, those ungainly creatures would still be around. We made room for new, unmonstrous species. Thanks to our industrious gnawing, new, warm-blooded mammals were able to develop, among them early forms of future domestic animals. Not only dogs, horses, and pigs, but man as well can be traced back to us, the first mammals; for which man has ill requited us since the days of Noah, when male and female rat were refused admittance to his tub . . .

Someone wants to be greeted. Someone introduces himself as an old friend and claims that he still exists. He wants to make a comeback. All right, let him.

Our Herr Matzerath, who will soon be sixty, has had his share of trouble. Even if we forget about his trial, his stay in a mental hospital, and the imponderable question of his guilt, a good measure of tribulation has piled up on Oskar's hump since his discharge – ups and downs despite slowly increasing prosperity. After all the attention he attracted in his early years, his obscure senescence has taught him to enter losses as small gains. Amid persistent family quarrels – always about Maria and especially about his son Kurt – the elapsed years have turned him into a common tax payer and businessman – visibly aged.

So he was forgotten, though we suspected that he must be alive, living somewhere in retirement. It would suffice to call him up – 'Hello, Oskar!' – and there he'd be, his garrulous old self, for there's been no word of his death.

I, at any rate, have not caused our Herr Matzerath to pass on, it's just that I haven't thought of anything special to say about him. Since his thirtieth birthday there's been no news of him. He's held aloof. Or was it I who shut him out?

Only recently, when with nothing special in mind I was going down to the cellar to see about the wrinkling winter apples, thinking at the most about my Christmas rat, we met, as though on a higher plane: there he was standing and not standing, claiming to exist and suddenly casting a shadow. He wanted attention, he wanted to be questioned. And already I'm giving him my attention. Why is he suddenly worthy of notice again? Is the time again ripe for him?

Ever since the hundred and seventh birthday of his grandmother Anna Koljaiczek turned up on the calendar, there have been inquiries – thus far in an undertone – after our Herr Matzerath. A postcard has reached him, inviting him to be among the guests when the festivities open in Kashubia. He has been asked not to Bissau, whose fields have been converted into concrete runways, but to Matern, a village nearby. Is he in the mood to travel? Should he ask Maria and young Kurt to go with him? Can it be that our Oskar is frightened at the thought of going back? And what of his health? How does the humpback little man dress these days? Should we, may we, resuscitate him?

As I was cautiously thinking it over, the She-rat of my dreams had no objection to the resurrection of Herr Matzerath. In the midst of further remarks about the garbage that will bear witness to us, she observed in passing: He'll be more modest, less excessive. He's beginning to suspect what has been so depressingly confirmed.

So I pick up the phone – 'Hello, Oskar' – and there he is. With his suburban villa and his big Mercedes. His firm and its branch offices. His surpluses and reserves. Outstanding debts, written-off losses and ingenious prefinancing plans. The whining rest of his family is with him, and so is his film studio, which thanks to his promptness in going into video is steadily increasing its share in the market. After an objectionable and now suspended porn series, it is chiefly his educational pictures, served up in vast numbers of cassettes, that have been giving more and more students food for thought. There he is with his ingrained obsession with the media and his weakness for anticipations and flashbacks. I just have to lure him, to throw him a few crumbs, and he'll be our Herr Matzerath again.

'What, Oskar, do you think about the dying forests, for instance? How do you feel about the threat posed by jellyfish to the western Baltic? Where exactly would you locate the sunken city of Vineta? Do you, too, believe that the end is imminent?'

Neither the dying forests nor the superabundance of jellyfish gets a rise out of him. But when I ask him what he thinks of the Malskat case – remember, Oskar, that was in the fifties – he shows signs of life and will soon, it is hoped, start talking.

He collects furniture from those days. Not just the kidney-shaped tables that were then modern. His white record player, on whose turntable he gently sets *The Great Pretender*, is an instrument manufactured by Braun, a concern preoccupied with beauty of form; in the days of the Malskat case, it was known, because of its colour and plexiglass lid, as 'Snow White's Coffin'.

Seeing that I'm there in his suburban villa, he shows me his basement rooms; all but one, which arouses my curiosity by being locked, are chockful of furniture from the fresh start period. A good-sized room is used for private showings of films. On tin canisters I read titles: *Sissi*, *The Forester of the Silver Forest*, *The Sinner*, and suspect that our Herr Matzerath is still a prisoner to the decade of illusions, even though his video production identifies him as a man who stakes his money on the future.

'Right,' he says. 'Basically, the fifties are still with us. We're still feeding on the flimflam of those days. That was honest deception. What came afterward was profitable entertainment.'

Proudly he shows me his Messerschmitt bubble car. Standing on a raised platform, it dominates a smaller basement room. It looks as good as new and invites two persons to be seated, one behind the other. Arranged in groups on the cream-coloured wallpaper: framed photographs, showing our Herr Matzerath in the back seat of the bubble car. He must be sitting on a cushion, because he appears to be as big as the glum-looking man at the wheel. A photo shows the two of them, now patently differing in stature, standing beside the car. 'Why, that's,' I cry out. 'Of course it is. I recognize him in spite of the chauffeur's cap.'

Our lilliputian Herr Matzerath smiles. No, he's laughing inwardly, because his hump jiggles. 'Right,' he says. 'It's Bruno. My former keeper, but also my friend in hard times. A faithful soul. After my discharge from the mental hospital, when I asked him to be my companion in the outside world and join me in taking advantage of the new mobility, he lost no time in taking out a driver's licence. A first-class driver, though stubborn. But why am I telling you this? After all, you know him.'

Our Herr Matzerath goes on to tell me how he and Bruno Münzenberg 'started from scratch' in 1955. The next thing after the Messerschmitt bubble car was a Borgward, a come-down, but then came a Mercedes 190 SL, which is now a museum piece, but which his chauffeur is still driving. If he should go to Poland – there are good reasons why he shouldn't – he would entrust himself to this indestructible witness to German craftsmanship. And, by the way, it was then, in the bubble car days, that the case named after the painter Malskat came to a head. But while he's still carping at the verdict, seeing Malskat as a kindred spirit and going so far as to speak of 'the great Malskat', our Herr Matzerath and his museum vanish from my sight.

Strapped into a wheelchair, I screamed as if a loudspeaker had been available in my dream. We're still here. Every last one of us. Who are you trying to kid? But she goes right on piping, first incomprehensible ratgibber – do minsher gripsh doomadosh – then more intelligibly: A good thing they're gone! They made a mess of everything. Always had to contrive something with those erect heads of theirs. Even when stifled in glut, they never had enough. When necessary, they invented shortages. Starving gluttons! Stupid know-it-alls! Always at odds with themselves. Scary in bed, they went looking for danger outside. Impatient with senior citizens, they spoiled their children. Slave-holding slaves. Pious hypocrites! Exploiters! Unnatural and therefore cruel. Crucified their God's only son. Blessed their weapons. Good riddance!

No, I screamed in my wheelchair, no. I'm here. We're all here. Alive and kicking and bursting with new ideas. Things will get better, that's right, more human. All I have to do is turn off this dream, this muddle, then we'll be back again, then we'll start upward and onward again; right after breakfast, as soon as the paper, I'll . . .

But her piping voice drowned out my loudspeaker. Good that they've stopped thinking, stopped getting ideas, stopped planning, projecting, setting themselves goals, never again will they want to transcend. Those fools with their reason, their oversized heads, their logic that brought results, brought results to the bitter end.

What good did it do me to shout No, I exist, I still exist; her voice won out, defeated me: They're gone! And good riddance. They won't be missed. Those humans thought the sun would hesitate to rise and set once they evaporated, dried up, or burned to a crisp, once an unviable species, the human race, died out. The moon and the stars didn't give a damn. Not even the tides suspended operations, though here and there the oceans boiled or went looking for new shores. Silence ever since. Their noise died with them. And time goes on as if it had never been counted and shut up in calendars.

No! I scream. Wrong! and demanded immediate rectification: It is now, I imagine, five-thirty a.m. Shortly after seven, I shall wake up with the help of the alarm clock, leave this damnably comfortable wheelchair in which I'm sitting as though strapped, and start my day – Wednesday, yes, it's a Wednesday – right after breakfast, no, after brushing my teeth, but before tea, rye bread, sausage, cheese and egg, and before the newspaper starts selling me a bill of goods, I shall tackle my untarnished resolutions . . . But she wouldn't listen; on the contrary, she increased in numbers. Several litters started piping and rushed into the picture. More ratgibber: Futsh midde minsher, stubbich geshemmele nuch! Which was supposed to mean: Dust and ashes, and a good thing they've stopped casting shadows.

Nothing left but radioactive garbage and their toxic chemicals leaking out of barrels. No one would know they'd ever existed if it weren't for us, piped the rat offspring and offspring of offspring.

Now that they're gone, it's possible to think of them kindly, even with indulgence.

I had only my wheelchair to sustain me, when the She-rat resumed her monologue: Oh yes, we admired their upright gait, their posture, that trick they've been doing down through the ages. For centuries, under the yoke, on their way to the scaffold, in lifelong treks up and down corridors, shown from anteroom to anteroom; always somewhere between erect and bowed, seldom crawling on all fours. Admirable bipeds: on the way to work, to exile, headed straight for death, singing rowdy songs on their way to battle, silent while falling back. We remember man's posture, whether piling up pyramids stone upon stone, building the Great Wall of China, cutting canals through malarial swamp land, cutting themselves down to smaller and smaller numbers at Verdun or Stalingrad. They stood fast in their positions, and those who fell back without orders were stood against the wall and shot. Many a time we said to ourselves: Whatever lunacy they let themselves in for, they will be distinguished by their upright posture. Strange were their pathways, but always they walked erect. And their processions, their parades, dances and foot races. Look, we said to our litters. There goes man. That distinguishes him. That makes him beautiful. Hungrily standing in line for hours, yes, even bowed, tormented by his fellows or by an imaginary burden that he calls God, groaning under the malediction of his avenging God, under the weight of the Cross. Look at those works of art, all colourfully different and all dedicated to suffering. He went through all that. Erect, he went on after downfalls, as though intent on setting us, who have always been close to him, an example. No longer in sibilants and ratgibber, no longer in anger, the She-rat spoke softly to me in my wheelchair, which hovered God knows where, more and more like the seat of a space capsule. Friend, she said to me. Later on, pal. Look, friend. We're starting to practise the upright gait. We stretch, we sniff at the sky. But it will take us time to master the human posture.

And then I saw rats, saw them singly, saw litters, saw multitudes of rats practising the upright stance. First in a no-man's-land, a treeless, shrubless desert; then all of a sudden their drill ground looked familiar to me. First I saw them scampering across squares, then through streets between tall-gabled houses, heading for church portals. Rats practising bipedalism. Finally, I saw the high-vaulted interior of a Gothic cathedral. At the feet of upward striving columns, they stood erect, if only for a few seconds, sagged briefly, rose to their feet again. I saw multitudes of rats pushing their way to the chancel over the stone floor of the nave, saw them in transepts, driving to the steps of the side altars. This wasn't Lübeck's Church of Saint Mary or any other brick Gothic edifice on the eastern shore of the Baltic, no, it was undoubtedly in Saint Mary's Cathedral in Danzig, which in Polish is called Kościół Najświętszej Panny Marii, that the multitudes of rats were practising the new posture.

Splendid, I cried. How splendid! Everything is still in its place, stone upon stone. Not a gable missing, not a spire expunged. How can we be extinct, She-rat, if Saint Mary's, that old brick hen, is still, how shall I put it, brooding?

It seemed to me that the She-rat smiled. Well yes, pal. That's the way it looks, like in a picture book, all faithfully present. There are reasons. Something special was planned for Danzig's or Gdańsk's, whatever you like to call your native place, Doomsday. Something that snatches away and at the same time preserves, that takes only the living but shows respect for dead objects. See for yourself, not a gable fallen, not a spire beheaded. Amazing how every arch still strives toward its keystone. Finials and rose windows, enduring beauty. Everything but the people was still intact. How comforting that something other than garbage bears witness to your existence.

Surprised me demolishing cocktail snacks,
pretzel sticks sticks disposed fanwise in glasses,
easy to grab hold of.

At first I nibbled them singly,
faster and faster till nothing was left;
then I exterminated them by the bundle.

That salty mash.
With a full mouth I cried out for more.
My hosts had plenty on hand.

Later, in my dream, I asked for advice
because avid for pretzel sticks I was still
bitingly out for destruction.

It's your rage that wants compensation,
compensation, by day and by night,

said the She-rat of my dreams.

But whom, I asked, do I really want
singly and in fistfuls
to destroy until nothing is left?

First of all yourself, said the She-rat.
In the beginning self-destruction
was practised only in private.

On the water, they knit. They knit at half speed and lying at anchor. Their knitting has a superstructure. It can't be overlooked because, when they are knitting, more happens than can be counted in knitting and purling stitches, for instance, how united they are in their work, though each wishes each the seven-year itch.

Actually, the five women on board *The New Ilsebill* should be twelve women. That many had applied for the expedition on the former sailing barge, and I at first recruited that excessive number in my head. But since a five-day congress was being held in Luxemburg and a three-week seminar in Stromboli, offering opportunities for collective knitting, my excessive figure was reduced; applications for the *Ilsebill* fell to nine, then to seven, because two women with their knitting were urgently needed in the Black Forest and two more with wool and knitting needles were called to the lower Elbe; for everywhere, and not only in my head, militant women were in demand, in Luxemburg to fight against dioxine in mother's milk, on the island of Stromboli to protest the insane over-fishing of the Mediterranean, in the Black Forest to highlight the dying forests, and on both banks of the lower Elbe to oppose the proliferation of nuclear power plants. Eloquent and never at a loss for expertises and counter-expertises, they militated knowledgeably, earning praise even from men. No one had an answer to their facts. They always had the last word. And yet their struggle, successful as it was in words, was in vain, because the forests went on dying, toxic chemicals went on seeping, no one knew what to do with the waste, and in the Mediterranean the last fish were caught in nets with undersized meshes.

It looked as if only the women's knitting would get results. Then something with a lozenge or hooked pattern was completed. Attractive articles were turned out in cable or combination stitch. Nay more: ridiculed at first and disparaged as a female quirk, knitting at congresses and protest meetings came to be recognized by male as well as female adversaries of the embattled *tricoteuses* as a source of mounting strength. Not that the women drew their arguments from their nimbly crisscrossing woollen threads; oppositional knowledge lay ready in files and statistical tables side by side with their work baskets. The process, the incessant, rigorous but seemingly gentle guiding of the yarn, the toneless counting of stitches, served rather as a framework to the knitter's persistently repetitive argument; though this relentless knitting process failed to convince the adversary, it impressed him, and would have worn him down in the long run, if as much time and wool had been available.

But also for and among themselves, without opponents to confront, the women knitted as though determined that their yarn should never break off; for which reason, in my head and in actual fact, the remaining five who had resolved to ply the western Baltic aboard the research ship *The New Ilsebill* and measure its jellyfish content, have brought along their knitting needles and plenty of wool – coloured, natural and bleached.

Only the oldest of the women, a wiry lightweight, whose nearly seventy-five years of toil and trouble are discernible only in moments of sudden gloom, has boarded ship without needles and wool. She is absolutely opposed to 'your stupid knitting', as she calls it. She can't even crochet. It would make her dizzy, she says, or soft in the head. But when it comes to washing, baking, cleaning and cooking, she is miles ahead of the other women, who refuse to be diverted from their knitting patterns, for which reason she takes over the galley. 'Look here, you females. I'll cook for you, but don't bother me with your knitting.'

Even with a stiff breeze blowing, the other four seafaring women never lose sight of their balls of wool and clicking needles. The moment the captain relieves the helmswoman and takes the wheel in both hands to confront rain squalls from the east, the helmswoman reaches for pure lamb's wool and gets to work on a solid-coloured, patterned sweater so spacious that it calls for a great hulk of a man, who, however, is never mentioned, except for dark hints that he should be put in a straitjacket.

When the captain, whom I affectionately call Damroka, relinquishes the wheel and the helmswoman, as the west wind abates, steers a two-handed course, the captain loses no time in starting to enlarge a many-coloured blanket, consisting of woollen leftovers, by one square, carefully securing differently patterned patches with chain stitches, without ever losing sight of the compass and barometer. Or else she sews together the motley squares with their spiral or ribbed patterns, marked by dropped stitches, or scaly like armour plate.

When the engineer doesn't have to squeeze into the cramped engine room to service the diesel engine, one can be certain that her knitting, a poncho-like monstrosity, is also growing; she's a workhorse and has run herself ragged all her life. They say it's always for others, never for herself.

The same with the oceanographer. Industrious out of habit, when she's not weighing or measuring auriculas in glass tubes amidships, she's knitting, knit two, purl two, baby clothes for her grandchildren, among them cute little rompers with pine-cone or hourglass patterns. The fine-spun pink or light-blue yarn glides over slender fingers, which only a moment ago were skilfully handling the velar flanges of jellyfish.

In Travemünde they have not only shopped for provisions and taken on diesel oil; they've also bought a supply of wool, intended to last as far as Stege, the principal town on the Danish island of Møn.

But Stege is far ahead. Chugging loudly – that's the air-cooled diesel engine – *The New Ilsebill* is just putting into Neustadt Bay. And at that point, even if they don't hang out the 'shark' to take in jellyfish, the women won't feel like knitting for a while.

No, She-rat. I take wool and knitting seriously; I don't laugh when the yarn snaps, when a stitch is dropped or a slack row has to be unravelled.

I've always had that clicking in my ears. From infancy to my present sweater, women have kept me lovingly warm with their knitting. Something or other with a simple or complicated pattern has always been in the works for me.

Even if my Christmas rat won't believe me, you, She-rat, should. I shall never make fun of the women the world over who knit out of need or kindness, anger or grief. I hear them clicking needles against the flow of time, against the menacing void, against the beginning of the end, against fate, or out of defiance and embittered hopelessness. God help us if this should should give way to sudden silence! Considering them from a stupidly detached male point of view, I admire the way they keep bowed over their knitting.

Now, She-rat, that forests and rivers, plains and mountains, manifestos and prayers, even banners and leaflets, not to mention heads emptied by speculation, provide indications that our yarn may be running out; now that the end is being postponed from day to day, knitting women are the last counterforce, whereas men just talk everything to pieces and finish nothing, not even mittens capable of supplying warmth to freezing humanity.

Chapter Two, *in which master forgers are named and rats become fashionable, the end is contested, Hansel and Gretel run away, the Third Programme runs something about Hamelin, someone hasn't decided whether or not to take a trip, the ship drops anchor at a scene of misfortune, dumplings are served afterward, human aggregations are burned and multitudes of rats stop the traffic worldwide.*

'WE ARE creating the future!' cries our Herr Matzerath to his top executives with the voice of a prophet who knows his audience, at a time when films with real media appeal are getting rare in the studios; but as soon as I propose material from my stock, the death of the forests as the last fairytale for instance, or the infestation of the Baltic with jellyfish filmed as created future, he shouts me down.

'Too much apocalypse. Decreeing the end of the world as if you were God almighty. You and your everlasting last tango!' On the other hand, cheered by his own words, he wants to take up the Malskat case if I can supply sufficient material about the fifties; as if future could be made out of flashbacks.

And so, to his mind, our conversation develops into a picture of the Adenauer–Malskat–Ulbricht era. 'Three master forgers,' he cries. 'If you can manage to flesh out my admittedly skeletal thesis, it will make an edifying movie.'

I try to talk our Herr Matzerath out of our pan-German triumvirate of forgers, but promise nevertheless to look into the Malskat case. In the end, I succeed in directing his curiosity to a project whose legendary inner lining is so full of hiding places that it really ought to tempt him.

He paces the floor from rubber plant to rubber plant. Standing at the slate on the end wall of his executive office, he hesitates. No sooner does the humpback little man come to rest at his desk than I say: 'This ought to interest you, my dear Oskar. They're working up a festival at Hamelin on the Weser. After seven hundred years they're honouring the memory of the Pied Piper, who in times of great confusion and feverish ecstasy – signs were seen in the heavens and the end was thought nigh – lured thousands of rats into the river, where they all drowned. According to another legend he also abducted children, who were never seen again. Lots of contradictions. Wouldn't this be a good chance to feed the media comparisons between the delusions of 1284 and present-day anxieties, between the processions of flagellants and our present-day mass demonstrations? The Year of the Pied Piper offers all sorts of possibilities. The flute, for instance. The shrill sweetness. The glittering silver dust. Trills lined up like beads. Long before your time, a musical instrument was seducing people. Oughtn't you, who have long seen the medium as the message, to strike while the iron is hot?'

Our Herr Matzerath passes silently from my field of vision. Other sounds come in. That hissing, that chattering, that piping Once-upon-a-time, as though it were all over and done with, as though we existed only in retrospect, as though we were in need of facetious and at the same time pious obituaries – that's not our humpback little man any more, it's the She-rat of my dreams . . .

Toward the end, we became fashionable. Young people who liked to move in groups and set themselves apart, by hairdo, dress, gestures and manner of speaking, from other young people, called themselves, and were called, punks. True, they were a minority, but in some areas they set the tone. Themselves frightened, they frightened other people. Iron chains and clanking tin were their ornaments. They exhibited themselves as living scrap iron, rejected, cast-off garbage.

Probably because they associated themselves with dirt, the punks bought young laboratory rats and tamed them by regular feeding. They carried them tenderly on their shoulders, on the palms of their hands, or bedded in their hairdos. Never a step without their chosen rodents; they carried them everywhere, over busy squares, past well-fed shopwindows, through parks and sprawling greens, past church portals and bank portals, as though they were one with their rats.

It wasn't only the white ones with red eyes that were popular. Soon we grey rats, bred for snake-feed, appeared in the pet shops. We were in demand and shortly before the end more popular with children than the hitherto coddled, spoiled and often overfed golden hamsters and guinea pigs. When after the punks, children of good family began to keep rats as pets and for the first time in the long history of humanity, the privileged classes opened their doors to us, old people as well took a liking to us. What began as a fad, became an acknowledged need. I've even heard of a gentleman in his middle fifties wanting a rat for Christmas.

At last we had gained recognition. In bringing us sewer rats, who had always lived in darkness, to light, in removing us from the smell of drains, in literally discovering our intelligence, in letting themselves be seen and photographed with us, in accepting us as creatures associated with the human race, they enabled us to go public. Triumph! Belatedly received into Noah's ark. Admittedly, we felt rather flattered. Hope was conceived. Maybe man was capable of insights that might save him.

At first they thought it was witty to call us public rats. But when the punk vogue spread, when office workers and even government employees began to take their rats to work with them, when young Christians took us to church services and confession, when we were admitted to town halls and lecture halls, to conference rooms and business offices, when finally recruits in every branch of the armed forces took us to prohibited areas, we heard the first protests. Parliamentary boards of inquiry were set up; after long debate a bill prohibiting the public display of rats was brought in. It was argued that the presence of rats, especially brown rats, in public places was a threat to security and public health, and an offence against good taste.

Stuff and nonsense. Anyway, there was no majority willing to pass such a law. A few parliamentarians even had the audacity to drag us into the Upper House. So-called rat hearings were organized. Questions were asked that might have been asked in Noah's times when male rat and female rat were refused admittance to the saving ark.

One of those late questions was: What has the rat to say to us today? Others: Will the rat help us in our hour of need? Is the rat closer to us than we have supposed since time immemorial?

Much as these new attentions flattered us and tempted us to underestimate man's inveterate hatred, we were nevertheless surprised at so much sudden affection. It surprised us to see how shyly, yet passionately intimate the young people became with us, especially the garbage-oriented punks. Regardless of whether they carried us on their necks, close to their jugular veins or on their scrawny chests, what terrifying gentleness was then for the first time shown in man's dealings with us, what superfluous tenderness. What devotion! They let us run up and down their spines, nestle in their armpits. How our fur tickled them. Our cool, smooth tails felt like caressing fingers to them. Oh, the barely audible whispers of their blackened lips, as though our ears were good to confess to – so much stammering rage and bitterness; such fear of profit and loss, of the death they were seeking, of the life they hungered for. Their moaning for love. Their 'Tell us, rat. What should we do, rat? Oh, help us, rat.' Lord, how they pestered us.

Everything was charged with fear, not only their sordid pads, their garishly painted happiness as well. That's why their colours were so strident. Perpetually frightened children, who painted one another with deathly pallor, painted themselves presentiently corpse-green. Even their yellow, their orange were tinged with mould and rot. Their blue was a longing for death. On a chalky foundation they daubed red screams. They painted pale worms, veering to violet. On their backs, their chests, their necks, some wore black and white bars, others welts as though from whippings. They wanted to see themselves bloody. Their carefully dressed hair took on every colour. Oh, their solemn death dances in bankrupt factory grounds, as if they'd escaped from the Middle Ages, reincarnations of flagellants.

And how much hate they had in store for everything human. Always poised for attack and always harried. They jangled chains, like galley slaves. They wanted to be brutalized. Insufficiently informed about us, they wanted to be like us. When they went in pairs, they were rats, male and female. And that's what, affectionately and imperiously, they called each other. They cut themselves hoods shaped like our heads and hid their faces behind masks with demonically ratlike expressions. Hanging long, naked tails on their behinds, they poured from all sides, motorized and on foot, all heading for one particular place, as though all roads led there, as though their salvation were there and only there.

That's right. In hordes. No missing the ill-famed town. A magnet drew them there. In short, they were determined to meet and to overcrowd the town involved in our legend, to treat themselves to a festival there. The noise they made and how they showed us off! Doing their best to frighten the townspeople by acting like animals.

They didn't succeed. They'd have been drummed out of town, in any case. The police were all over to the end. The poor kids, they wanted to be rats, but they were never anything but poor forsaken punks, forsaken even by us. They were fond of us, as no human had ever been. Lost children from the start, said the She-rat of my dreams, loved by no one but us. If we had known of a place to escape to, we'd have taken them with us in the end . . .

What do you mean by end, She-rat? We're not finished yet. No hole plugged, no riddle solved. Never before have there been so many loose ends. With smirking incompetents in the saddle. All the newspapers shout it from the rooftops, all the talk conceals it. We're not even halfway through, fallen behind would be more like it.

So you can't say finished, *basta*, enough. That would be desertion, running away. In mid-sentence, what's more. Leaving the indispensable, and this, that and the other, to be done. Secure pensions, for instance, and garbage removal. Because if we don't do something about the steel crisis and certain other things – the butter mountain, all the cables that need to be laid, finally getting a census taken, clearing up the immigration question . . . And then hold on until there's a drop in interest rates and the recovery we've all been, and without which nothing, no light at the end of the tunnel, and gone is the yolk from the egg.

No, She-rat, no, we're not done for. Especially now that the great powers are finally sitting down to make decisions, the right kind, because everybody realizes by now that only even-handed measures taken simultaneously by both sides can enable us in the foreseeable future, if only at the last minute.

And you, She-rat, say cut, fade out, close the books, end of the line, curtains and amen, Doomsday so to speak. But we've got our mission and it's our duty, if not to ourselves then to our children, lest one day we stand ashamed and without any, great aims I mean, the education of the human race for instance, and getting rid of the garbage mountain, at least getting it out of sight until at last supporting measures can be taken and a few fish reappear in the Rhine and Elbe. And, oh yes! there's got to be disarmament before it's too late.

But you say we're washed up. As if we'd run out of juice long ago. As if this that and the other didn't remain to be done. And soon, no, right away. Because by now it's become clear to everyone that apart from peace, a little more justice, the forests, not only the German forests, but forests as such and in general should at least – if it's too late to save them – be filmed. In colour every mood and season, to be preserved for all time, and never lost to our memory and our children's. Because without forests, She-rat, we'd be in a bad way. For which reason, and because we owe it to ourselves, we pause to ask what forests and not just German forests, but I've already said that, mean, no, have to tell us, so that later, at least at the movies with our children, while there's still a little time.

And this before you, She-rat, say finis, cut, end of the line. It's still up to us to decide when the end will be. It's our finger on the trigger. We're in charge of the push button. We're responsible to our grandchildren for all that, for the garbage and immigration questions, and for at least the most blatant hunger, not to mention the butter mountain.

> Because men
> are killing the forests
> the fairy tales are running away,
> the spindle doesn't know
> whom to prick,
> the little girl's hands
> that her father has chopped off,
> haven't a single tree to catch hold of,
> the third wish remains unspoken.
> King Thrushbeard no longer owns one thing.
> Children can no longer get lost.
> The number seven means no more than exactly seven.
> Because men have killed the forests,
> the fairy tales are trotting off to the cities
> And end badly.

I know this stretch of road. From Lauterbach, where a stocking once got lost in a song, the 'German Fairy-Tale Road' once led through a dense mixed forest.

Other roads as well might lead along breaks to the Pfälzer Wald, up into the Black Forest, down into the Bavarian Forest, into the Fichtel Mountains, the Solling and the Spessart, wooded regions which here only at second glance, there patently, have suffered the harm that has everywhere been demonstrated and everywhere been denied. Brown needles, panic shoots, thin crowns, wet seeds are reported, dead branches are falling, dead tree trunks are losing their bark. The first question is therefore: How long can the road from Lauterbach continue to be called so heartwarmingly 'The German Fairy-Tale Road'?

That is why I send the Chancellor's motorcade with him and his ministers and experts, not to the Black Forest or the Fichtel Mountains, but by way of an example here. Behind blue light, flanked by police protection. Black limousines with curtained windows make their way through a dying forest. We recognize the Chancellor's car by the pennant. We assume that inside it the Chancellor, while riding through the dying forest, is reading expertises and counter-expertises, statistics on pollution, on the mortality of the silver fir; it's his duty as Chancellor to work hard and keep generally well informed. Or else, he's trying to relax in preparation for a major speech, doing crossword puzzles, trotting out the name of Hölderlin, and taking pleasure, down and across, in his supply of general information.

Wrong again. The inside of the Chancellor's limousine is saturated with family atmosphere. For the sake of his public image and of my scenario, the Chancellor is accompanied by his wife, son and daughter.

What should he be like? Readily interchangeable, but definitely of a type familiar to us, stuffy and glum. At the moment, he is eating, no, shoving a wedge of Black Forest Cherry Torte into his mouth, to the displeasure of his wife.

Because the Chancellor's daughter has pushed the window curtain aside, we see in passing a carved wooden road sign, on which, between two elves, we read in raised Gothic letters 'The German Fairy-Tale Road'. Here, in the event that the dying forest becomes a film with the help of our Herr Matzerath's production company, the motorcade should slow to a walk.

In a parking lot framed by dead trees, the Chancellor and his

Günter Grass

party are expected. The finishing touches to the preparations are being hurried, for the police outriders have walkie-talkied ahead.

With the help of tubular scaffolding, woodsmen in regulation hard hats, supervised by a forester, are putting up tree-high backdrops with healthy trees painted on them, possibly in the style of Mortiz von Schwind: gnarled oaks, dark firs, light beeches, merging with dense virgin forest. Plenty of ferns and underbrush.

At the top of a tall ladder projected by a ladder truck, a painter is adding songbirds – chaffinches, a robin, a song thrush or two, some nightingales – at high wages, as though for piecework. The forester cries out: 'Finish up, men. The Chancellor's coming!' And then, more to himself: 'It's enough to break your heart.'

Quick as a flash, the woodsmen make themselves scarce. Behind the backdrop, a sound engineer puts on a tape. A rich mixture of bird songs is heard, among them the freshly painted chaffinch, robins and song thrushes, as well as an oriole and several wood pigeons. As the ladder truck drives away, the ladder and painter are lowered with the result that the last bird in the painted forest, which should have been the indefatigable cuckoo, remains fragmentary. The forester's face now puts on a welcoming look.

For behind blue lights, the Chancellor's motorcade advances. The window curtains of the limousines are thrust aside. Amazement at the sight of so much nature. The Chancellor, with wife, daughter and son, alights, as do ministers and experts. Press and TV are on the spot. As though to convey a message, the media catch the Chancellor – and his retinue – taking several deep breaths.

No sooner in the public view than the Chancellor's son, aged thirteen, and his daughter, aged sixteen, plug Walkmen into their ears. Their gaze turned inward, the children seem absent, which upsets the Chancellor's spouse. But her words of reproach – 'If you do that, you won't hear the birds singing in the woods' – are disregarded as is the tape behind the backdrop. (The Chancellor's children, as we conceive them, are on the plump side, but they could just as well be slender to skinny, if that's what our Herr Matzerath wants. A costume suggested by a forester's coat unifies the family: loden, knee breeches, laced boots, horn buttons.)

While off to one side a male chorus and costumed players take their places in front of the forest backdrop, the ministers and experts group themselves casually around the Chancellor; one of them is Jakob Grimm, the minister for forests, rivers, lakes and fresh air; beside him stands Wilhelm, his brother and under-secretary.

We have chosen to make this historical loan for the sake of its popular appeal and of our scenario, and to have Jakob Grimm, in modern dress, say to his brother: 'Once again Painter Schwind has done a good job.' We then see Wilhelm Grimm smiling sadly. Both brothers manage to prolong the utterance of their timelessly courageous 'And yet' – as if they were pleased with their repeated failure. Two upright men, prepared to resign if need be, but at the same time two story-telling daddies, who know how to turn a blind eye; they have always been aware of what it really looks like behind the scenes, but because of their constant worry about limiting the damage, they don't speak up.

To one side, policemen are frisking the male chorus for weapons. Declared 'clean', they gather on a platform. Soft or loud pedalled by the conductor's gestures, they sing the song: 'Oh, forest fair, who hath raised thee so high above us . . .' The Chancellor is tempted to join in.

After processing by the security service, all the costume wearers, at a sign from the Brothers Grimm, hereinafter referred to as the Grimm Brothers, step forward as fairy-tale characters in the best old German taste: a demure Snow White; the Seven Dwarfs; Sleeping Beauty with spindle; the prince who wakes her with a kiss. And under the long-haired wig, who can it be but Rapunzel? Hansel and Gretel bow, curtsy, and present the Chancellor and his spouse with significant gifts: a seedling fir, a basket of plump acorns and beechnuts, a gleaming old hunting horn. With open mouth and pursed lips the male chorus sings: 'Hansel and Gretel were lost in the woods . . .' Even the policemen enjoyed the singers whom they had previously pronounced clean.

Number follows number. Next, turned more to the media than to his ministers, the Chancellor speaks, reading adroitly from his notes. In images he invokes a healthy world menaced by evil. 'Thus once again,' he cries, 'fate is putting us to the test!' as though the German people were favoured with a life subscription to tests of fate.

As we are aiming at a silent film with only occasional use of subtitles, the forest evoked in the Chancellor's speech can be seen rustling healthily. In fade-ins the forest cathedral opens. Grazing deer. The stag pricks up his ears. From every treetop quotations fall. With perfect timing a little boy empties the Boy's Magic Horn over a princess bedded on the grass: flowers, dragonflies and butterflies.

The Chancellor's closing words – 'And so, live on, O German forest' – provide a splendidly succinct subtitle for a silent picture. Then, as the tension produced by his speech can be heightened no further, the Chancellor's son and daughter leap into the picture.

Plump or skinny, they throw the donated acorns and beechnuts at their father. The daughter kicks a dent in the gleaming old hunting horn. The son smashes the fir seedling, pulls the Walkman out of his ear, jumps up on the platform, and, addressing the horrified ministers and experts, the frightened fairy-tale players and choral singers, the once-more worried policemen and security guards, the note-taking journalists and imperturbably filming cameramen, not to mention the Grimm Brothers, makes a counter-speech.

'You're talking the same old shit,' he assails his Chancellor father, and proceeds to evoke reality: parking lots and traffic jams, belching factory chimneys, voracious concrete mixers appear. Forests are cleared, ground is levelled and covered with concrete. Acid rain falls. While developers and industrialists hold forth at long tables and have plenty of thousand-mark bills handy at conferences, the forests are dying. Dying visibly, openly. Raised high above us, still standing corpses. With logical consistency, the Boy empties the other magic horn – garbage, toxic waste, scrap-iron – over the princess, who is still asleep, but in a dead forest. As though to symbolize exhaust fumes, he farts in the princess's face, which – thanks to the lead content of the boy's wind – wrinkles instantly.

After the son's concluding sentence and subtitle – 'That's your German forest!' – the Chancellor's daughter takes action; with a knife stolen from the forester in a little side show, she cuts the ropes holding the forest backdrop in place. In slow motion the scenery collapses. None of the painted little birds seeks safety in flight. No deer hare hedgehog runs away. Not just the tubular scaffolding, but the dead forest as well, is left standing; one can't fail to see it.

The Chancellor's daughter turns off the recorded birdsong. Silence. Parched branches crackle, snap. The hoax exposed, crows fly into the air. Fear stalks naked: death.

Of the horrified fairy-tale players, Sleeping Beauty and the prince who wakens her with a kiss take refuge in laughter. Speaking to Jakob Grimm, Wilhelm says words good for a subtitle: 'Good God! The truth has come to light.' While I take advantage of the long moment of horror to present the Brothers Grimm, whose works have continued to be written down to the late twentieth century, as intelligent, sensitive men, only occasionally pusillanimous but secretly suffering from a lack of radicalism, in short, as liberal Grimm brothers. And now, as they wring their hands, our silent picture girds itself for a new action. The Chancellor's son and daughter rip the cap and bonnet off the costumed Hansel and Gretel, throw their Walkmen away, make faces at father, mother and television camera, and making a mockery of the Grimms' version of the tale, run off into the forest in the roles of Hansel and Gretel.

The Chancellor's wife cries out: 'Hans! Margarethe! Kindly come back here this minute!'

The media are having a field day. Journalists dictate their catchy hard-boiled phrases into tape recorders. Press photographers shoot volleys of running-away pictures from the hip. Mercilessly, the TV camera records. The flight of the Chancellor's children is beginning to make history. The Chancellor, however, stops the police from photographing the pursuit of the fugitives as they have learned to do. He cries out: 'Two more dropouts. Ingrates. But never mind. We'll get over it.' He takes refuge in a stance that he regards as dignified but can't prevent his face from being overrun by a grin, which could do with analysis.

While the two ungrateful dropouts can be assumed to be far away among the dead trees, Wilhelm Grimm might say softly to Jakob: 'You see, dear brother, the old fairy tales never die.'

To dispel the persistently disastrous mood, the male chorus assembles in haste and, egged on by the conductor, sings a merry song which though toneless might be entitled: 'Timber in the Greenwood, timber in the Greenwood, is being auctioned off.' To cap the climax, acid rain begins to fall. The Chancellor feels a need for comforting sweets. The runaway children are seen no more.

My Christmas rat and I hear on the Third Programme that this year is marked on the Chinese calendar as the Year of the Rat, of Hard Work, Savings and Increased Production. But that's not all. In addition, a town on the Weser calls attention in a cultural broadcast, laced with flute selections, to the anniversary of its legend. The programme is to include a speech by a Czech poet, the first performance of a puppet play, scholarly lectures on the legend, the sale of special Pied Piper stamps with special postmarks, and processions in which present-day burghers are expected to watch children in medieval costume chasing after a suitably pied Piper. Pictures of relevant subjects are to be on sale, and pieces of an enormous Pied Piper cake are to be sold outside the Guild Hall. The local tourist bureau is exultant: a rush of tourists is expected, even from overseas. The Texan 'Pied Piper Club' and the Japanese 'Children of Hamelin' have given notice of their arrival. True, the town's political bigwigs fear undesirable visitors – appropriate measures will be taken if so-called punks from the big cities turn up with their pets – but because of the historically documented anniversary, which the Church, too, has agreed to celebrate fittingly, the notables are rubbing their hands.

The Third Programme's cultural survey offers all this to me and my Christmas rat. The speaker's pleasing voice, matured by numerous broadcasts, is never free from ironic overtones and critical parentheses, yet has the information down pat and knows more than we do about Hamelin, its background and dark underside; it comes to us from the box placed on my tool rack to the right of my Christmas rat's house, while I, though sitting to the left of my rat, am already, with rectilinear purpose, on my way to Hamelin.

That's where we're going. To punch a few holes in the old figment of lies. We owe it to ourselves. For this much is certain: seven hundred years ago and for several centuries thereafter, there was no record of any rats or Pied Piper, but only of a piper who 'on St John's and St Paul's Day' led some hundred and thirty children out of the town and into a mountain or over the hills, and not one of those children was ever seen again.

Did they march out of the East Gate? Has the taking of hostages after the battle of Sedemünde some bearing on the legend? Was it based on St Vitus dancers, who danced their way to God knows where? No document reports the incident. Even a hundred years later the church chronicle, which records everything that ever happened in Hamelin town, every fire, every flooding of the Weser, every coming and going of the Black Death, had nothing to say about the exodus of any children. A dubious story, hushed up by the authorities and probably having more to do with the expulsion of some flagellants who were then making a nuisance of themselves or with some young citizens of Hamelin who had been lured away to new settlements in the east, than with the magical tricks of any piper; especially as it was not until five hundred years after that St John's and St Paul's Day that rats and piper were amalgamated with the questionable legend. Whereupon poets, Goethe in the lead, began casting about for rhymes.

Later on, the Grimm Brothers discovered various legends about the exodus of the children of Hamelin intermingled with the usual Pied Piper tales. And because the two collectors of folk tales wrote down everything that was told by the hearth, around the spinning wheel, or outside the door on balmy August evenings, we read that a strangely dressed young man rid Hamelin town of rats for a promised fee, by luring them with magical music into the Weser, where they drowned. We also learn that because the burgomaster and his councillors denied the young man his fee, he piped the children, enumerated in other legends, out of town and all hundred and thirty of them vanished for ever into Calvary Mountain.

A moral tale, in which not only rats are punished but promise-breaking burghers and gullible children as well. And not just children. All those who act without thinking, follow like sheep, the credulous, the guilelessly trusting, who put their faith in every promise, are regarded as victims of the Pied Piper, for which reason he was seen at an early date as a political symbol. In pamphlets and leaflets, he was represented as inciting the peasants, making the poor covetous, stirring up unrest among the middle classes, raising questions to which only the Devil knew the answer. Anyone who listened to him was playing with fire, rumbling in the lower regions, plotting insurrection, at once a revolutionary and a heretic. Thus pied pipers, some dressed conventionally, others in motley, each calling himself by a different name, have led desperate peasant bands and rebellious journeymen, heretics and deviationists, as often as not mere radical minorities, but sometimes whole peoples, to perdition. And not so long ago the trusting German people – when the always identical Pied Piper did not cry out, 'The rats are our misfortune' (which would hardly have gone down) – put the blame for all the country's misfortune on the Jews, until just about every German thought he knew where all misfortune came from, who had imported and disseminated it, and who had therefore to be piped out of town and exterminated like rats.

It's that simple, that easy to derive a moral from legends – one need only smudge them up thoroughly – and in the end they'll bear fruit; namely, full-grown crimes.

This is also the opinion of our Herr Matzerath, who like the harried rodents has sought a refuge all his life, even when it occurred to him to pose as a piper. He says: 'Whenever there has been talk of exterminating rats, others, who were not rats, have been exterminated.'

He has an address, writes letters and receives mail. Ever since a gallstone was removed two years ago, he claims to be in good health but complains of difficulty in passing water, of painful retention of urine after fatiguing meetings and during embattled press conferences; it seems likely that stress irritates his prostate, but he dreads the urologist's scalpel.

He has lately been collecting gold coins, wearing silk ties, sporting ruby tie pins, using toilet water after shaving. He likes to smell of old lavender in the evening, no doubt because it reminds him of his poor mama, who always had that clinging fragrance about her. Except for the carefully waved wreath of shimmering silvery-grey hair that hangs down over his collar, he is bald. How smoothly shines his bald spot, tanned at all seasons. One is tempted to stroke it; it seems there are women who succumb to this temptation – tenacious rumours which he never contradicts.

One rarely sees him in company, but when he does give a reception the humpback little man positions himself among conspicuously tall ladies and gentlemen, as though his still diminutive proportions needed to be emphasized. For that reason his employees, in management as well as production, are all over five foot nine. This quirk is well known in the motion picture industry, but is no longer smiled at, for one thing because the ratings show who's bigger than who. He plans his calendar with foresight; furious spells of hard work, devoted exclusively to the video department, alternate with periods of rest in secluded spots. If he visits watering places – Marienbad, Baden-Baden, Lucca and Bad Schinznach in Switzerland – it's not just for his prostate. His favourite dictum is often quoted: 'The future belongs to the rats – and of course to our video cassettes.'

While curing and resting from curing, he mulls over everything that enters his head; many-layered theses and their contrary.

Sometimes he wants to film events yet to come, fabricated future, so to speak, for once they happen they will already be available in film; and then again he has an urge to film everything that happened before the cinema existed, such as the boarding of Noah's ark. In compliance with a rigorously drawn-up check list, pairs of everything that creeps and flies should come into the picture: wart hog and wart sow, goose and gander, stallion and mare, and time and again the one, particular pair that is not admitted to the ark and persists in trying to smuggle itself in among the admitted rodents.

During breathing spells that he seldom allows himself, his childhood becomes important to him; ageing, he wants to relive it: the fall down the cellar stairs, visits to the doctor, too many nurses . . . But he no longer reminisces in writing about his beginnings, much less by word of mouth, fervently as the ladies of his choice implore him to. 'Old stuff,' he says. 'Now we are living in the present, each day for the last time.'

Already he is looking forward to next September, but he doesn't know yet how to celebrate his sixtieth birthday. Does he wish to sit quietly at home – surrounded only by photographs – or among long-legged guests?

But first Anna Koljaiczek, his grandmother, should be honoured with choice presents and a surprise he has thought up in Bad Schinznach and put into production the moment he got back from his cure.

The one object on his over-spacious desk top, which must at all times be kept clear, is an invitation written in her stead by the vicar of Matarnia, formerly Matern: '. . . I have the honour to invite my grandson, Herr Oskar Matzerath, to the celebration of my 107th birthday.'

He reads the words over and over, but doesn't know whether or not to travel. On the one hand, he's afraid of going back; on the other, he keeps thinking up presents and telling everybody about the impending celebration. As it pleases him to hear people call him 'our Herr Matzerath', he does not turn a deaf ear when they whisper among themselves: 'Imagine, our Herr Matzerath may be going to Poland. Did you know that our Herr Matzerath is planning a trip to Poland?'

He's still hesitating. Someone who deliberately stopped growing, then grew a few centimetres after all, is up to his old game. Should I or shouldn't I?

Another consideration is that for once Bruno, his chauffeur, who is ordinarily prepared to drive him without a murmur wherever he wants to go, has misgivings, and would like to postpone if not prevent this particular trip. He speaks of doctors who have advised against it. He characterizes the political situation in Poland as unstable. He warns of arbitrary military despotism. Though adducing no substantial reasons, he intimates that our Herr Matzerath would at present be *persona non grata* in Poland.

A visa has not yet been applied for. Nevertheless, Oskar buys silk ties and dons large-checked sports clothes. He refuses to fly, much less take the train. 'If I go at all, I shall return home in the Mercedes.'

As a precaution, he adds to his coin collection, although or because the price of gold is declining and the dollar rising. As though circumstances might oblige him to leave us for some time, he has advice on tap for everyone. I am advised to give my full attention to the Malskat case. When I ask him at last to take other projects under consideration, he replies impatiently: 'We'll talk about the forests and Hamelin later,' and leaves me standing there with my too many stories, which are trying all at once to go beyond their beginnings.

Before the motorized barge, *The New Ilsebill*, leaves the low-lying island of Fehmarn behind it and steers a course toward the sheer chalk cliffs of Møn, the women on board, in pursuit of a prearranged plan, take sample measurements in Lübeck Bay. As sufficient data on Kiel Bay are available, the vertical movements of plankton are investigated here. With the help of six nets the shark is put into play. With a hauling time of five minutes and water depth ranging from eighteen to twenty-three metres in the stretch to be measured, it is possible to haul from five depths at once, in addition to the vertical haul.

While the helmswoman pulls up the shark and the graduated jellyfish counter, the oceanographer and the engineer handle specimens measuring over four centimetres in diameter. They are measured at the level of the velar flanges. Small jellyfish are called ephyrae, large ones medusas. To determine their volume, the medusas must be drained briefly, then several of them are dropped into upright cylinders filled with formaline. The resulting shrinkage must of course be taken into account. In jellyfish of all sizes, the diameter after two days of fixation decreases by roughly four per cent. The oceanographer learned all this and more – e.g., the comparative weighing of herring larvae and medusas – in adult education courses. She is teaching the engineer, who actually works for a haulage company, and the helmswoman who directs a law office, how to count, measure and weigh medusas and ephyrae. Patiently she demonstrates applied oceanography. Never have medusas been discussed more matter-of-factly.

At first, the women fished with their specialized equipment two miles off the beach at Timmendorf, then off Scharbeutz and Haffkrug; now they are taking samples in Neustadt Bay as far as Pelzerhaken in the Baltic. Farther north, the jellyfish concentration diminishes. But off the coast of eastern Holstein oceanography and its applications suddenly take on a new dimension when the helmswoman says to the captain: 'This is where we caught the Flounder in the early seventies. By accident. With a pair of nail scissors. Man, was he a talker! Promised the moon and the stars. Came to nothing. Nothing but jellyfish that shrink the moment you look at them.'

As though really summoning him, the helmswoman calls out over the smooth sea: 'Hey, Flounder. You screwed us. Nothing has changed. Men still hold the key positions. Things are going to the dogs faster and faster, but the men still have all the say. In those days we thought: the women are winning out, an intelligent gynocracy is around the corner. False alarm. Or have you still got something clever to say? Okay, Flounder, okay, bigmouth. Say something.'

The sea offers no comment, but the helmswoman's outburst, her long-unheard cry for the talking flatfish, brings the oceanographer and the engineer from the erstwhile hold of the motorized barge, where they have been measuring the latest jellyfish catch. No sooner on deck than the engineer cries out: 'Leave us alone with that prehistoric crap.'

The oceanographer says: 'And stop bellyaching. There won't be any men on board this ship. Isn't that good enough for you?' And from the galley, the Old Woman cries: 'Flounder or no Flounder, there's always been something doing around here. Let's drop anchor.'

While the captain throttles, then shuts off the engine, then drops both anchors as obediently as if the Old Woman had assumed command, the oceanographer takes off her disposable transparent gloves, throws them overboard, and points successively in the direction of Pelzerhaken, Neustadt and Scharbeutz. 'That's where the three ships were. I wore braids with big bows, I was just twelve when the *Thielbeck*, the *Cap Arcona* and the *Deutschland* dropped anchor here. We'd been evacuated from Berlin. We'd been bombed out twice. That was in April 1945, not long before the end. Every morning when I went to school, they were there. They looked like a picture. I sat at the kitchen table and drew pictures of them. With coloured pencils, all three of them. The grown-ups said there were concentration camp inmates on board. On the third of May, when my mother sent me to town because there was sugar to be had for coupons, I saw from the shore that something was wrong with the ships. They were smoking. They were being attacked. Today we know more. The prisoners came from Neuengamme and a few hundred from Stutthof. And they were being attacked with rockets by British Typhoons. It looked terrific from the beach, like an exercise. Anyway, the *Cap Arcona* was on fire; it capsized later. The *Deutschland*, that didn't have any prisoners on it, was sunk. The *Thielbeck*, on which prisoners had hoisted bedsheets by way of white flags, capsized in flames and went to the bottom. Naturally you couldn't see from the beach what was going on in the ships. It's hard to imagine. Though I went on for some time drawing burning ships with coloured pencils, oh God. Anyway, before the raid, there were about nine thousand prisoners aboard the *Arcona* and the *Thielbeck*. About three hundred died of starvation every day. And about five thousand seven hundred from the concentration camps – Poles, Ukrainians, Germans, and of course Jews – burned, drowned, or, if they managed to swim ashore, were shot dead on the beach. By SS-men and navy commandos. I saw that when I was twelve. Stood there with my pigtails and watched. A lot of grown-ups from Neustadt were standing there, too, looking on as the prisoners climbed out of the water, dripping, and were shot dead. Those people still claim they didn't see or hear a thing. The same in England, it's never mentioned. An unfortunate accident and that's that. Two years later, corpses were still being washed up on the beach, bad for the sea bathing. Because the war was almost over. The hulks could be seen for a long time. Until they were towed away and scrapped.'

While the oceanographer recalls the names of the gauleiter of Hamburg and the captains of the ships, the women look out over the sea, which communicates nothing. No wind. A slight drizzle as so often in this rainy summer. The Old Woman in the galley says: 'Naturally. There's no place in history for that kind of thing. A dumb mistake. Upsets people. So they forget it. Let bygones be bygones, as they used to say. – So let's eat. Meatballs with fried onions, mashed potatoes and cucumber salad.'

As there's nothing more to say, the captain heaves both anchors and announces the course: open sea. Nice that the engine starts right up. Standing beside the helmswoman, Damroka clutches her coffee pot. 'Let's just get out of here,' she says. Not another word. But she has the real aim of the voyage well in mind; and I too wish the women would forget about the past and concentrate on jellyfish.

For lunch the table amidships is cleared of charts and data sheets. All praise the meatballs and the cook. Chitchat about the weather and the rainy summer. Luckily, no one has brought it up again. With their meatballs and mashed potatoes the women drink beer out of bottles. When they've finished eating, the captain relieves the helmswoman at the wheel.

Later, as the low-lying island of Fehmarn drops out of sight, all gather on deck with their knitting. The short-winded sea throws up ripples. Light breeze. In the distance the rain is falling in veils. Now and then the sun shines through. As the low-lying coast of the Danish island of Lolland heaves into sight, the *Ilsebill* moves into jellyfish fields of varying density. Here no data are gathered. The shark can rest. The barge is doing eight and a half knots.

But suddenly – merely because a white-bodied ferry is approaching from the southwest – no more chitchat about this and that. I can't prevent the oceanographer from putting aside her knitting and resuming her talk about the concentration camp ships. Because the engineer wants more details – 'Why did they put the prisoners onto ships? And the English – why didn't they?' The Old Woman is in the galley, washing dishes. I make her say: 'Sure, of course. Humans starving, burning, drowning, swimming and then shot dead. Humans letting other humans starve, burn and drown, and looking on as the few humans who reach the shore are shot dead by other humans. Always humans, and the things that humans do to humans. What about rats? Who says anything about burned or drowned rats? I bet you there were plenty of rats on board, several thousand at least . . .'

Here the She-rat of my dreams spoke up, though she didn't enter into the picture or displace the ships. 'Correction. Slight correction.

It's true that rats have always been close to people. But we've steered clear of their sinkings. We knew what was coming. We didn't stick to ill-famed ships. Much as we loved the human race, we had no desire to burn or drown with them.'

That was no wheelchair that I'm dreaming of. It was a space capsule and I was strapped into it, imprisoned in my orbit. I, knowing nothing of the cosmic space jazz, unburdened by the specialized, high-tech knowledge that reaches for the stars and knows all the galaxies by name; I, ignorant of a nomenclature that has become familiar not only to garrulous astronauts, but even to schoolchildren; I, old-fashioned fool, to whom even the telephone is still an incomprehensible miracle, sat strapped into a space capsule. Earth, I cried, answer!

But all my monitor showed me was the She-rat. She alone answered me, waxed loquacious. In despair, I cried: We're still here. We still exist. We haven't evaporated. Unimpressed, she talked about times gone by; sadly and patiently, as though to mother me.

Friend, said the She-rat. Listen to me. You've called Earth. Earth speaking. You wanted Earth to answer. This is the Earth answering. We dug ourselves in. Because we had a hunch. Seeing that humans, as though incapable of anything else, had gone off their rocker again, but this time for good, that they were hell-bent on outdoing themselves, we dug ourselves in. Don't talk to me about instinct; our ancestral knowledge, our memory, prepared for such events since Noah's day, recommended underground passages, survival in air bubbles thanks to a system of stoppers. The often thoughtlessly parroted human saying – 'The rats abandon the sinking ship' – was no accident. Since the injunction that barred us from Noah's pinewood tub – three hundred cubits in length, fifty cubits in breadth, and thirty cubits in height – we've taken a very dim view of ships. Every time we heard that some cowardly rats – cowardly from the human point of view – had abandoned the ship, sure enough, that ship went down.

Absolutely, said the She-rat. That saying consolidated our reputation. But when Earth became the ship there was no other planet to move to. So we looked underneath the human bunker system. Sought safety under buildings and fortifications. And we stored up provisions, something only the Bengali rice rat had done in the human era.

Though I in my space capsule tried time and again to get the monitor to show cheerful images, the She-rat led me through systems of trenches, corridors and transverse passages, through narrow tunnels serving as entrances to nesting chambers and to spacious silo-like bins full of cereals and seeds. A labyrinthine underground world opened up to me.

I wanted to get out into the light and dream about something pleasant: Damroka!

She said: There was no other way out.

I cursed our Herr Matzerath. He should say yes and produce my picture about the dying forests. She took my sound away and piped: The general mood of the human race, their exaggerated, totally groundless hope of peace, their hope that lived on hope, their bustling hope factory, while the human mechanism was running down – all that hopeless hoping alarmed us.

They hamstrung one another with appeals to realism. As if they had all the time in the world, they adjourned themselves. Their statesmen seemed to think it was funny; in any case they grinned to the end. Oh, their stupid talk! Whereas previously humans had been capable of far-reaching, if sometimes weird ideas, just before the Big Bang, they were merely parroting obsolete ideas, archaic aberrations, such as: space ships built and manned on Noah's ark-and-selection principle. Obviously, man had abdicated. He whose head had thought up all that; whose thought had hitherto taken body; he, who had hitherto prided himself on his intelligence and its triumphs over darkness and superstition, obscurantism and witch-hunting; he, whose mind had given weight to innumerable books – resolved to forgo the use of his head and rely exclusively on his feeling from then on, although man's feeling is even more underdeveloped than his instinct.

In short, said the She-rat of my dreams, more and more humans put their money on a life without reason. Writers began talking like seers and high priests. Every unsolved problem became a myth. In the end, the peace demonstrations, which had been usual for years and at first had made intelligent use of words and proofs, became religious processions. Sad to say, our punks, whom we had learned to love and who had learned to love us, joined in. We rats remembered medieval processions of flagellants; driven by fear, they afflicted the Christian Occident, touching off whipping orgies and pogroms, stopping at nothing, because at that time the Plague, termed the scourge of mankind, was running rampant. Whereupon guilty parties were sought and found; we and the Jews were accused of bringing in the Plague. From Venice and Genoa. And spreading it. Old stuff, I agree; but forever new . . .

In any case, we saw a revival of flagellantism toward the end of human history, though not directed against the Jews and us. Rather, parades and processions were followed first by individual, then by collective self-immolations, first in Amsterdam, then in Stuttgart, then simultaneously in Dresden, Stockholm and Zürich, and toward the end daily in every big and little city of Europe, in football stadiums and mess halls, at church meetings and on camp grounds. After a while, this fad, as one might call it, took on in other continents, in Atlanta and Washington, in Tokyo and Kyoto, and, I don't have to tell you, in Hiroshima. In the end, when self-immolations were reported even from underdeveloped countries, not even the Soviet Union was immune; the calamitous fire that shed no light leapt from Kiev to Moscow and Leningrad. Wherever reason broke down – let's not forget Rome or Czestochowa – the procedure was identical; young people grouped into a solid mass. And in the middle of this singing, praying mass, who injected peace into every prayer, into every line of every song – there seem to have been five hundred of them in front of Cologne cathedral – in the middle of this human mass, a sudden silence would be followed by a warning flash fed by open cans of petrol passed through the crowd. Petrol was plentiful to the end.

Ah, mankind. Oh, the human race! Even in a state of hopeless confusion, they had it so well organized. Orderlies disciplined the self-immolating crowds. Ambulances stood ready, as many as the size of the crowd seemed to warrant. A surprising lot of mothers were there among the victims with their babies. Teachers with their pupils, priests and pastors with their congregations. In Neckarsulm and Wolfsburg, whole industries lost their trainees and instructors. In some garrison towns recruits kindled the warning flash while taking the soldier's oath. Later on, quite sensibly, the newspapers, radio and television stopped publishing the casualty figures.

And then I saw what the She-rat had described. I saw warning flashes against suddenly illuminated city backdrops, saw babes and mothers, pupils and teachers, Young Christians and their chaplains, apprentices gathered round their masters, and oath-taking recruits all going up in smoke. I screamed but I was still imprisoned in my space capsule. Stop! I screamed, Wake up, I pleaded, I whimpered, I addressed her affectionately as dear little rat, dear Christmas rat. Absurd suggestions occurred to me. Couldn't we, mightn't we . . . but she went on with her sober record of the past.

Of course we could have, of course it would have been better . . . and at first attempts were made to check the spreading madness, break up the human masses by force. But in Brussels, Nuremberg and Prague, after a sprinkling of policemen, then whole companies, changed sides, wishing, as they said, to share in warning self-sacrifice, the forces of order were restrained from interfering. They looked on inactive as the warning flashes multiplied. In densely populated urban areas these self-immolations became a feature of daily life, just as death by starvation was an everyday occurrence in outlying regions. Against this background of smoke, stench and – as a well-known publicist wrote – increasing death wish, statesmen found it easy to give their aimless activity the appearance of reason, with the result that concerned members of the older generation turned for a time to a 'Re-arm the Peace' counter-movement that gained a certain popularity. Naturally, when the two groups clashed, the warning flashes made correspondingly more victims.

I had the impression that the She-rat was smiling in her network of trenches. Or maybe she wasn't smiling, and it was only to me in my space capsule that it all seemed insanely funny, side-splittingly funny. And sure enough, I shouted: She-rat, stop making jokes. Stop making fun of us. It's easy for you people to laugh in your rat holes.

True enough, son, said the She-rat. All the same, you should know what made us go underground. Toward the end of human history, the human race had developed a soothing, appeasing language, which spared people's feelings by never calling anything by its name, which sounded rational even when it represented nonsense as wisdom. Marvellous how their politicians succeeded in making words supple, in bending them to their purposes. They said: The more terror the more security. Or: Progress has its price. Or: Technological development cannot be halted. Or: You can't set the clock back. And this language of deception was accepted. People learned to live with terror, they went about their business or pleasures, deplored the victims of the warning flashes, called them weak sisters, unable to cope with the conflicts of the times, shook their heads once or twice, and turned back to the order of business, which kept their hands full. They didn't say 'After us the deluge' in so many words, but made themselves as comfortable as possible with the certainty that humanity and its attempt, many times repeated since Noah's day, to make man behave less murderously, had failed. The last philosophy to find supporters was 'end of time' consciousness. People would say casually to their friends and acquaintances, Won't you drop in before it's too late. A frequent greeting: Nice to see you one last time. People stopped saying *Auf Wiedersehen*, *Au Revoir*, See you again. And parents would say tenderly, but seriously enough, to their children: It would really have been better if our little darling hadn't been born. People began to take stock. Eschatological quotations were trotted out at family gatherings and on official occasions, even at dedications of bridges. No wonder we rats dug in.

I stopped arguing. I grew more and more content with my space capsule. Why should I keep bellowing: Earth! Answer, Earth. I tinkered with to me incomprehensible buttons, switches and other instruments. I even got diverting images, which capriciously effaced one another. I took pleasure in the absurdity of these fade-ins, thought I was having a pleasant dream and yet, already convinced, listened to the She-rat.

Still on our final phase, she said: Devoted to humans from time immemorial, we rats tried to warn them before digging in. By the hundreds of thousands we left their farflung underground traffic systems and our favourite homes, the sewers. We evacuated garbage dumps and junk heaps, slaughterhouses and waterfronts, the service chutes of highrise buildings, and our other dwelling places. In broad daylight, going against our nature, we scurried down the main arteries of the European cities: armies of fleeing rats, an unstemmable flood of rats. After a while we stepped up our programme. Not just once, several times a day, down Gorki Street to Red Square. In Washington we thrice circumscurried the White House, in London we debouched on Trafalgar Square from all directions. Two streams of rats moving in opposite directions blocked the Champs-Elysées. This was how we demonstrated our concern for the human race. Since humans believed in images, we came up with terrifying images. Up and down boulevards. Tails outstretched. We were determined to show humankind: Look how terrified we are. We, too, know that this world is headed for twilight. We know the relevant Bible passages as well as you do.

Our demonstration, prompted by apocalyptic fears, said: Stop, O man, stop thinking yourselves into the grave. Make an end to making an end. The wisdom of the Proverbs is being confirmed a thousandfold . . .

I affected surprise. What then? Was there a panic? One great outcry – or what? As though wanting to make up for mankind's omissions. Imagine the scene. With the afternoon business traffic. And the women with their shopping bags . . .

The She-rat's answer sounded tired, and, I can still remember, disappointed. Oh yes, we heard the screams of horrified passersby, who may even have interpreted our demonstration of mass flight correctly; yes, the traffic was disrupted in the business sections; the windows on all the main thoroughfares were full of people gaping. But otherwise nothing happened, except that the television crews gave us miles of footage as we fled picturesquely across the Seine bridges, over and over again past Buckingham Palace, around the tall fountain of Geneva. Tourists began to take snapshots. Since our swift-footed demonstrations often went on for hours, we offered plenty of subjects.

But didn't they? I cried. Counter-measures, I mean. Water cannon at least. Or helicopters. Or simply . . .

Sure, sure, said the She-rat. Naturally, their first thought was poison. But it was only in a few big cities that they tried to oppose our mass action with offensive weapons, in Rome they even used flame throwers; the result was rapidly spreading fires on the Via Veneto. As many humans were killed as rats. How stupidly they relied on violence to the end. Only in Peking, Hong Kong and Singapore, where the Chinese variant of humanity was predominant, and in New Delhi and Calcutta, where we had always been respected if not worshipped, were our walking danger signs understood. But the central computers were elsewhere.

I couldn't think of anything better to say than Too bad, too bad. You went to a lot of trouble, a hell of a lot of trouble. You shunned no risk.

It was only then, she said, after all that vain effort, that we rats began to dig in.

That was a mistake, I cried. Or at least premature. You certainly should have tried again and . . .

We did. For days on end . . .

No! I cried. You abandoned us humans. A lot too soon . . .

Once again, as though she had wanted to impress the idea of vain effort on my mind and her own, the monitor of my space capsule showed me in quick sequence: punks fondling rats; hundreds of punks on the way to Hamelin with their rats, warning flashes kindled in massed formations of humans; circular and bidirectional streams of rats. And then I saw them digging in. Like wedges they threw up earth. Thousands of holes spewed sand, gravel, marl. At first their tails stuck out, then the earth seemed to swallow them up. Everywhere at once. So many ultimate images. In the end a potpourri of images, into which the She-rat kept intruding, but subliminally, without sound. Then I saw our Herr Matzerath, getting ready to speak, I saw the Chancellor's children in the roles of Hansel and Gretel running through the dead forest, then the She-rat again, my Christmas rat, rolled up, asleep, affecting innocence, then painter Malskat mixing paint for strange Gothic pictures, then suddenly Damroka knitting with other women on the jellyfish-saturated sea, and the She-rat digging deeper and deeper, and the children in the rigid, corpse-like woods . . .

A relief when our Herr Matzerath finally produced his application, neatly filled out in block letters. To Poland, that's where he wants to go, to Poland.

High time, I said to myself in waking, because Kashubians between Ramkau and Matern are getting ready for the celebration. Flowers are being twined into the number one hundred and seven.

In the end, when there was nothing left to laugh about, the politicians took refuge in unanimous grins.

Unmotivated because there was nothing funny in sight, they began to smirk worldwide.

Breakdowns of controlled facial features.

Not embarrassed smiles.

Eschatological grimaces, no more.

Even so, they were interpreted as merriment; the grinning and smirking of unanimous politicians were photographed.

Photos of the last summit meeting bore witness to infectious good humour.

They must have their reasons, people said to themselves, for throwing seriousness overboard.

As conferences were held to the end, humour survived to the end.

Chapter Three, *in which miracles happen, Hansel and Gretel head for the city, our Herr Matzerath doubts of reason, five hammocks are occupied, the Third Programme is reduced to silence, there are bargain sales in Stege and shortages in Poland, a movie actress is canonized, and turkeys make history.*

MY CHRISTMAS rat doesn't like me to run after Malskat, the painter. She sniffs the air in alarm whenever I spread out press reports beside her cage, or such headlines as 'An East Prussian Eulenspiegel'. It upsets her when I compare press photos of Malskat with my conception of Malskat. He looks as if his wit had been sharpened by the passing of centuries, as if he ought to be wearing shoes turned up at the toes, slit trousers, puffed sleeves, and a cap and bells instead of his matted woollen head covering.

Meanwhile What's Doing in the Media is on the air. We hear news of the video market, which our Herr Matzerath and others regard as promising. Passing by my Christmas rat's cage, I find the button which in mid-sentence takes the Third Programme out of the room; my search for Malskat behind printed paper brooks no competing sound. My little rat ought to understand that, much as she likes to hear about the latest in science or the water levels of the Elbe and Saale.

No merry tricks or practical jokes. Not a jester. I note that Malskat's nose – its asymmetrical curvature makes his eyebrows look as if he were always seeing miracles – recurs like a signature in Malskat's murals. It is especially becoming to angelic boys and saintly old men in the Schleswig Cathedral and in Lübeck's Church of Saint Mary. They all, with their painfully distended eyes, see more than was visible in Biblical times. Not only do they see blessings to come, they also scent impending horror, thanks to the nose which was noted as early as the early fifties in a doctoral dissertation that fell for Malskatian Gothic: 'Noteworthy are the long noses of the figures in the nave and choir. They bring out the visionary gaze of the saints. They express a certain Nordic boldness, which may be sought in vain in other High Gothic murals, excepting those of Schleswig Cathedral, where the nose formation of the Salvator Mundi and of the figures on certain of the buttresses, suggest that the studio of the Lübeck nave and choir master must here too have been at work.'

I have a hunch why my Christmas rat sniffs the air uneasily and even ignores sunflower seeds whenever I bend over those yellowed papers of the fifties. She wants me to be without memory, born yesterday, forever wondering what horrible calamity may happen any minute.

All right, Ratkin, I say, we'll go bankrupt yet. But before I balance the books, I want to find out why Malskat's gift for being authentically Gothic despite the bad pay was timely at the time, falling in with a basic need, a general forgery-mindedness; like the crows in the dead forest the swindle is bound to be flushed someday, high as its stock may be at the moment. Ah, lies were not lame, they strode sturdily in those days.

The years following the Second World War in Germany behaved as if a bad dream, something unreal, happened to their pre-decessors, something that had to be suppressed for fear it would bring on nightmares. Sweet dreams were in demand. I remember a faith healer, who was going about the country at the time, selling pellets of silver foil, good for every sort of disease. People flocked to him as if they had been rehearsed. Foam-rubber sweet-dream-inducing cushions could be bought on the instalment plan. In the illustrated magazines princes were always marrying princesses and the sunset over the Bay of Naples never ceased to be red.

In paintings later adapted for wallpaper, the horror that people had just lived through proved to have been non-objective. Yet politics, which everyone was good and sick of, remained, as though by divine decree, entrusted to old men, for whom the divided country was cut up more at random than into proper halves.

And behold, the old men succeeded in purifying the defeated Germans, transforming them into Germans amenable to the victors, Germans who, having miraculously survived the war thanks to their native industriousness, immediately made themselves useful to both victor camps. Before you knew it, the Germans were again respectable and rearmed. Thus the German people were grateful to both benefactors, even though they detested the Goatee, as Ulbricht was called, and though, even if they elected the old fox Adenauer, they didn't love him from the bottom of their hearts as the united nation had loved Hitler in years gone by.

Malskat was just right for those times. His murals, which passed for authentic, were termed 'the Lübeck miracle', because when a nation considers itself relentlessly harried by misfortune, and – incidentally, as it were – has brought misfortune to other nations, yet is favoured with so many Gothic saints, it can reasonably hope to benefit by God's grace in the secular realm as well. Thereupon further miracles happened, among others the economic one, whose fallout made itself felt by the early fifties. The government with its (purportedly temporary) seat in Bonn counted out one hundred and eighty thousand marks in new currency to the elders of the Lübeck church to the end that more and more saints should be made manifest and – no work without pay – that painter Malskat should be able to count on ninety-five pfennigs an hour.

But this and other miracles are of no interest to my Christmas rat. Wealth based on the miracles of those days means nothing to her. Forget it! she might cry. It won't even leave a trace. But she only scurries restlessly around in her litter of wood shavings, and pays no attention to flashbacks. Whatever her polished black eyes may take in, they do not reflect Malskat.

Not until later, when I made Hansel and Gretel run through the dead forest and the Chancellor's runaway children wouldn't stick to my scenario, but, because there was no action in the forest deserted to the punks where there was no action either, my Christmas rat, here doubling as the She-rat, said: Those two are great. Not a crumb of the past. Just look at what they're carrying, whom they're caressing, into whose ears they're whispering, whose naked tails make them ticklish, and whom they both love in the hope of being loved body and soul, and whom only Hansel and Gretel are friendly to . . .

And I saw that the Chancellor's and his wife's runaway children were hugging two rats. They may at one time have been white-haired laboratory rats. But now the one was dyed zinc-green, the

Günter Grass

other violet, just as Hansel's Iroquois hairdo shone zinc-green and Gretel's numerous dreadlocks violet. The two children seemed to be one with their animals.

I tried to send them back to the dead forest and without animal companions into the continuation of my scenario, but they didn't give a damn about its message. All they wanted with their garish rats was to be garish punks among punks. More and more punks crowded into the picture till it was full to bursting. The punks had all festooned themselves idiosyncratically but uniformly with scrap iron; Hansel and Gretel did likewise and were hardly distinguishable from the others. Padlocks and extra-large safety pins held their scrap together. I counted the group and in my dream the She-rat helped me to count. We counted a hundred and thirty punks and exactly that many rats.

I must, I cried, tell our Herr Matzerath this, tell him that Hansel and Gretel, who look amazingly like the Chancellor's and his wife's children, have become authentic punks, who live in Berlin-Kreuzberg and make faces at the world to frighten it with its caricature. A fine lot they are. They won't listen to reason. They and their rats have all crept into one of the last squats. It's a house with boarded-up windows on a back court. Look, She-rat, I cried, Isn't it typical? That Gretel has the say in the group and gets her Hansel and the rest of them to do what she wants. He says: If they come with their battering ram, we've had it. But she says: If they move us out, we'll beat it to Hamelin and crawl into the mountain, like they did once upon a time when things were as bad as now. And Hansel cries out: Take a look at those squares. They don't know which way is up. They're just dead.

Whereupon the She-rat of my dreams said: The children screamed but no one wanted to hear them. So we rat nations said: We'll have to dig in. Too bad about humans. Especially the punks who are good to us.

Suddenly our Herr Matzerath takes an interest. Disparaging only yesterday, today he is devoted to Hansel and Gretel. Standing at the wide blackboard between the rubber plants, he says: 'Quite aside from the forests, their story appeals to me. It needs to be pointed up. If we decide to do it, the picture could begin something like this: While everywhere the rats come out of their holes and go public in broad daylight, the rats of the divided city, living separately on either side of the wall, scurry simultaneously down the main streets; while on the other side Frankfurterallee strikes them as suitable, on our side they judge Kurfürstendamm from the Gedächtniskirche to Halensee to be long enough.

So the rats come into the picture. In both halves of the city the traffic is disrupted at exactly the same time. Mass pile-ups result. In their wedged-in vehicles of various makes, terrified motorists see innumerable rats scurrying in either direction over immobilized cars, Wartburgs and Opels, Tatras and Fords. No one, no pedestrian or motorist grasps the deeper meaning of the unannounced demonstration. What in the eastern part of the city is passed over in silence because it is regarded as detrimental to socialism and therefore shameful, is viewed in the West as a shortlived sensation. On both sides people whisper: They come from over there.

But when the telex carries news of rat processions the world over – in Washington as well as Moscow – and time comparison shows that the rat nations worldwide have put on their show on the dot of 4:30 p.m. for three successive days, no one dares to shoot his mouth off about accident and even leading politicians find no words capable of appeasing their trembling, nauseated subjects, and say nothing, grin and say nothing; and it's only then, only when the flood has subsided, that articles appear which come somewhere near explaining the worldwide rat processions; though they, too, fail to see that the rats were trying to warn mankind.

Zoologists speak of the rodents' highly developed warning system. Psychologists are beginning to speak of a panic syndrome. Theologians call upon Christendom to take God's warning sign, revealed by the humblest of creatures, seriously and to put their trust in faith from now on. Some speak of an inexplicable phenomenon. Feature articles quote the Book of Revelation, Nostradamus, Kafka and the Vedas. As usual, some of the West Berlin newspapers come straight to the point. They put the blame on the Kreuzberg punks with their rat cult. Ever since punks were seen running around with rats, rats, they say, have been all the rage; people have ceased to feel the normal amount of disgust. Drastic measures, drastic measures are in order.

Only a few of the letters to the press, those written by children, tell the truth: I think the rats are afraid because people aren't afraid enough any more. – In my opinion the rats are trying to say goodbye to people before everything comes to an end. – My little sister, who has seen the rat processions on TV, says: First God abandoned us, and now even the rats are clearing out.

But then something else took centre stage: the spasmodic rise of the dollar, disorders in Bangladesh, an earthquake in Turkey, Soviet wheat purchases; the flood of rats, it seemed, had been just a bad dream.

Anyway, that's how our Herr Matzerath sees it. He jumps up and stands undersized at the enormous blackboard between his rubber plants. He casts about him with figures and adduces proof. In a series of quick cuts and fade-ins, he hops from Tokyo to Stockholm, from Sydney to Montreal, from East to West Berlin, and fills his video cassettes with horrified passers-by, nightstick-wielding police, water cannon and flame throwers, fire and chaos, panic in Soho, looting in Rio, in short, with everything that happened during the flood of rats.

'And,' he says, 'in a series of appalling scenes, we see the two children with their violet and zinc-green pets; running, teaming up with other children, occupying an empty building, being brutally evacuated and forced to flee again, tracked and harried by police-men and bloodhounds, taking refuge with the rats, and after the great rat demonstration vanishing with them – to safety, it is hoped.'

After some reflection, as though wondering whether or not his cassette will be saleable, he says: 'Look at it this way: an endless flow, panoramic but clear in every detail; try to visualize the gravity, the superhuman grandeur of this last demonstration for peace.'

After arguing for an hour or so about the possibilities of visual education – I favour cinema films; he thinks only video and home movies have a future – our Herr Matzerath says suddenly: 'Maybe we should do all this in the manner of the grand master of cinematic education, the great Walt Disney. People are fed up with documentaries. Too much reality is fatiguing. Anyway, nobody believes in facts any more. The only convincing facts are dreams from the magic box. Let's not kid ourselves. The truth is Donald Duck, and Mickey Mouse is his prophet. – Yes, I agree, it was a good idea turning Hansel and Gretel into punks; but what we really need is to invent a super-rat, a ringleader, cleverly drawn in fantastic fits and starts, that's it, a female rat, your She-rat, so to speak, at the head of all the rat demonstrations. In Rome and

Brussels, in Moscow and Washington: she, too clever for words, in the lead. We could simply call the female rat in our animated cartoon May, no, Dorothy, no, I've got it, Ilsebill, and build her up as the idol of the media . . .'

Our Herr Matzerath repeats all this to his staff at their weekly programme conference. The big tall ladies and gentlemen nod. He dictates media-oriented directives to the blackboard. The production people want to know where they are at.

No, said the She-rat of my dreams; it's too late for educational animated cartoons, or anything else.

> As I say: nothing.
> Words stumble into their hole.
> Mere afterthoughts.

> A long talk about education,
> which broke off
> inconclusively.

> According to the latest reports.
> As announced toward the end
> and immediately retracted.

> As a last effort, a few specimens
> of genus homo tried
> to start from scratch.

> Somewhere, toward the end of the season,
> there seems to have been an attractively priced
> ground for hope.

> In conclusion there was talk
> of good and evil and
> their nonexistence.

> But when,
> or God for that matter
> with his everlasting stupid excuses.

> Word has come down to us
> of a decision to adjourn
> for the present.

> We thought it was a joke,

then suddenly,
we lost our power to laugh.

After that, however,
no one was hungry
worldwide.

But in the end, a lot of people would
have been glad to hear
Mozart one last time.

They are tiny islands, whose names became known the world over when involuted smoke mushrooms were sent up into the sky above them – as an experiment, so it was said. On those islands we put ourselves to the test. Our behaviour can therefore be characterized as the Bikini reflex. Since then we've known. Since then our misgivings related not only to ships with an aura of impending doom, visible only to us; we also had presentiments of other disasters: ravaging fires, tidal waves, earthquakes, drought. Thus we were able to change our habitat before it was too late. No steppe fire from which we would not have wisely run away. Furthermore, we always knew what species, however powerful, however thriving it might think itself, would soon become extinct. Admittedly, in the case of those ungainly dinosaurs, we helped a little to speed up the process; but as for humans we'd gladly have kept them company a while longer, much as their hatred for everything ratty distressed us. It wasn't only the Jews that they likened to rats; the Japanese, as well, the Japs as they called them.

After those crushing blows against Hiroshima and Nagasaki, which took us by surprise, we included the new peril in our prescience. Consequently, the American, French and British experiments with nuclear and thermonuclear bombs, which were exploded on several of the South Sea Islands, did not catch us unprepared. True enough, our people couldn't get away as they had come, by boat, but the interior of the earth offered itself as a refuge. As soon as the human population evacuated the islands, we built deep and widely ramified escape structures, air bubbles which, in application of our anti-Noah principle, we were able to seal off with the help of self-sacrificing elderly rats. Already we started laying in provisions – coconut meats and peanuts. Even so, very few rats survived.

It seemed to me that she paused to reflect. Or was the She-rat only observing a moment of silence in memory of rat victims on Bikini atoll and other experimental islands?

After a certain time – in so far as the yardstick of time is applicable to a dream – she said with marked lack of feeling: Years later, when the radioactivity on the affected islands was measured, it was judged too high to allow the homesick natives to return. No one, it was held, could live there, though we were noticeably back again, in large numbers and in good health.

But the fact of our survival didn't mean much to humans. Apart from miscellaneous news items, published more for their curiosity value than as information, there was no reaction. No deep-seated horror. At the most, an astonished smile over the morning paper at breakfast. Hey, look at this. Rugged little beasts. They can live through anything.

That's the way humans were. Of both sexes. How they bellowed, talked big or, sure of their power, kept silent. They talked about immortality, and yet they suspected that if anybody had it in him to be immortal, it was us rugged beasts.

When we dug in the world over – and not just on islands – we spared no pains. The hardest ground gave way. If something barred our path, we gnawed our way through. Nothing resists our teeth. They are the expression of our patience. We undermined their concrete. In certain regions mine shafts had been left open. We extended the Roman catacombs. And in that city which is of special interest to you, my friend, safe in your space capsule, we used the casemates in Mount Hagel, which side by side with Bishop's Mountain has dominated your city from time immemorial. These are terminal moraines which in petering out took the shape of hills. Jagel, a Prussian prince or god, was said to have made his home on Mount Hagel. The Swedes dug mines in that mountain. But the actual casemates date from the Napoleonic era: solid masonry shelters and stables, which served as munitions dumps during the interim war. As we'd always lived there, it was easy for us to build deeper escape passages and nesting chambers. But only a few of our tribes resident in Gdańsk and environs took refuge in Mount Hagel; most dug themselves with tooth and claw into the Kashubian hinterland. For the present we had no place in the upper world.

I have no desire to go down there. As a child, I played in the casemates and found bones, even a skull, I don't know whose. Let her! Let her dig herself into the bowels of the earth, let all the rat nations of the world vanish off the face of the earth with her. I take out a fresh sheet of paper and want the world to go on. I want to grow rings, put on wrinkles, grow old, doddering, toothless and tell my Damroka wicked fairy tales: once upon a time, long long ago . . .

If this silent film, which cannot save the forests, is nevertheless to be titled *The Forests*, and if I manage to get our Herr Matzerath, who has always had a weakness for disasters and always taken a dark view, to produce it, then I shall have to acquaint him with the further developments, with all the other things that happen in the dead forest, and give him detailed descriptions of the characters; for though Oskar dislikes to reveal particulars concerning himself, he loves details. What, he might ask, would the Chancellor and his wife look like? Where did their children, before becoming Hansel and Gretel, go wrong? Are they the usual victims of prosperity? Should they continue to be punks?

As our Herr Matzerath expects an answer before his trip to Poland, I have to make up my mind. Under no circumstances must the film Chancellor's looks be cut to the pattern of the present Chancellor. But when I screw up my eyes and try to imagine a silent-film Chancellor, I have an unfortunate tendency to put together a composite Chancellor from spare parts; to avoid an undesirable resemblance, we must make him sensitive.

I therefore suggest a Chancellor who is unsure of himself, doesn't know what to do with his hands, is afraid to deviate from his prepared text, but for reasons attributable at best to inertia, remains in office. Try as they may, they can't manage without him.

And his wife? She's always looking for something in her handbag. Oh, if only they could be cozily at home again. How contentedly they could live if only he hadn't got to be Chancellor, if only she didn't have to be the Chancellor's wife from morning to night.

And the poor children. How bored they are. Put here, put there, when they'd rather stand, run, loaf, get lost somewhere else. As we see, they hate it. They're so fed up they could puke. Obviously, they'd rather be punks and go around with dyed rats. But they can't do that, because our Herr Matzerath says: 'They can't get lost in the jungle of cities, because they've got to run off into the dead forest.'

To win him over once and for all – it's him that's producing the picture – I'll fit the Chancellor's children out with qualities that remind our Oskar of the cast of his childhood. When you come right down to it, doesn't the Chancellor's daughter show a certain resemblance to the skinny little girl whose name was Ursula Pokriefke, whom everyone called Tulla, and who lived on Elsenstrasse in an apartment house that belonged to master carpenter Liebenau?

And doesn't the Chancellor's son, who is always staring darkly at something that's not there, remind one of a boy known as Störtebeker, leader of a teenage gang which made the city of Danzig and its waterfront unsafe? That was during the final phase of the last war. Störtebeker and his Dusters were notorious far beyond the borders of the Reichsgau of West Prussia. And didn't little Oskar, on leaving the church of the Sacred Heart in Langfuhr full of dark thoughts, meet up with ringleader Störtebeker and his gang?

These two are at least conceivable as the Chancellor's children. She, spiteful and malicious, he sternly aloof, she fearless, he prepared for great deeds, she thirteen and a half, he fifteen, she and he, then wartime children, now the unripe fruits of lasting peace. Both have Walkmen and very different music in their ears.

Questioned about these two, our Herr Matzerath remembers the teenagers of his childhood. 'Right,' he says, 'the little Pokriefke girl, a very special kind of bitch, they called her Tulla, but she was known by the *nom de guerre* Lucie Rennwand. I wouldn't have wanted her for a sister. She smelled of carpenter's glue and toward the end of the war she was a bus conductor. That's it! On the No. 5 route. Went from Heeresanger to Weidengasse and back. They say she left Danzig on the *Gustloff* and went down with her. Tulla Pokriefke, a nightmare that's with me to this day.'

He falls silent, the picture of an elderly gentleman who can afford to let his mind wander. But when I press him, trying to cut off all escape routes, he cries out: 'Why, of course, of course. The head of the Dusters gang. Of course I remember. Who in those days hadn't heard of Störtebeker and his exploits? Poor fellow. Always full of wild ideas. They made short shrift in those days. I wonder if he survived the débâcle? I wonder what became of him. He had a gift for teaching. Probably ended up as one more teacher.'

But when I ask our Herr Matzerath to approve my suggestions, he seems distraught and a little tired; looking back at his childhood has exhausted him. He rubs his all-embracing forehead as though to massage sharply pointed thoughts away. Then suddenly he pulls himself together, he's boss again, a man of decision. 'Definitely,' he says. 'They're right for Hansel and Gretel. Better still, they are Hansel and Gretel. I can see this Störtebeker making a shambles of the Chancellor's forest party. I can see Tulla, the little bitch, cutting the ropes that hold up the forest backdrop. Green light. Get moving. We'll go into production as soon as I get back from Poland. – Strange my burping up those two again. I see them as Hansel and Gretel. Running hand in hand. Deeper and deeper into the dead forest . . .'

In the forecastle of the motorized barge *The New Ilsebill* hammocks respond to the movements of the ship, which is taking its course amid diesel chuggings. When occupied, they hang on hooks, tautened at the head and foot ends. Now, during the day, as the barge is making for the isle of Møn over a light sea, they dangle limply, leaving room for wishes: new sleepers, a change of hammocks.

Mightn't different women have come aboard in Travemünde? For instance, all those who declined, preferring to sleep in beds?

I picked five. Or I was left with five. I took my choice though I had none; I wanted to people or was free to people the hammocks just this way and no differently; but the women often change their positions. Every change of the watch upsets plans. They always lie as I don't want them. Where the engineer lay down yesterday in her oilskins, the oceanographer wakes up today in her pyjamas; not the helmswoman, naked except for her woollen socks, but Damroka in her long nightgown lies in the extreme starboard hammock; the Old Woman in her flowered nightgown has crept away to the port side, she wants to stay there and not, as she says, change places with 'any of these women'; I'll consent to that, though I'd rather have her in the middle hammock.

They lie close together, for the barge's width has from birth measured four metres seventy. Only Damroka lies with her head toward the bow. Stretched to full length, not quite flat on her belly, the helmswoman sleeps soundly. It touches me to see that the oceanographer and the Old Woman sleep curled up on their sides, like embryos; one of the two is sucking her thumb. The engineer is tossing and turning restlessly in her sweaty rags. The captain's sleep is relaxed. Now and then she snores; so does the helmswoman, identically loud, but interspersed with whistling notes. The oceanographer whimpers softly; no doubt she's dreaming of herself as a child. The sleeping engineer groans as under a heavy burden. Suddenly words. Muttering, cursing. That's the Old Woman.

Close as they've all been to me, that's all I know about their dreams. How fortunate that only five women came aboard and not twelve as announced. They would have made for serious crowding in my head and elsewhere.

As a matter of fact, three women would have been enough to run the ship, and for me as well. But who, apart from Damroka and the oceanographer, would have been the third? Probably the Old Woman, who was always around, standing to one side, moping in the background, and putting up with everything.

I couldn't make up my mind. That's why it's cramped. How fortunate that seven cancellations came. The ship is too small. So am I.

But why couldn't I have gone to sea with just Damroka – as her bosun, her cabin boy – aye aye, sir! – She'd have had to teach me to tie knots, heave an anchor, read navigational signals, run the diesel engine, and measure all the jellyfish, more properly called medusas, with the . . .

While the motorized barge nears Møn: private thoughts. All the things there's room for in unburdened hammocks. It's early morning on deck, but even those who aren't on watch don't want to lie down, much as I urge the helmswoman and even more the oceanographer. They've all brought their sleeping bags up on deck to air – and their knitting, it goes without saying. I test the hammocks from port to starboard. Three of them sag. I pull them up, tighten the knots, close to the hooks. Two are made of colourless string and were probably bought in shops dealing in sailing accessories. The others are coloured, one red and white, one faded blue and yellow, the third of knotted red string. The coloured hammocks are edged with patterned trimming, fringes and tassels. They come from Latin America.

Now I'd like to know what I'm doing here. I'm shy, inhibited, afraid of being caught. My greying fear that all untrue stories will be exposed and that only boring truth will prevail.

Their steps on deck. This is wash day. They hang white and coloured washing on a long line to dry. Merrily may it flutter in the light breeze between foremast and pilot house. They sing the songs people sing while hanging out washing. Where, oh where can Damroka have put her coffee pot? Let's hope it doesn't rain.

Below decks just me. I rummage through their belongings, under the hammocks or in seabags and suitcases, in the forecastle locker. Shamelessly fingering everything. Looking for letters from earlier, still earlier times – confessions and protestations – without finding any scrap of paper that identifies me. Quickly, I glance through photographs from which I'm missing. Mementoes, ornaments, necklaces of plaited silver, but including no present given by me. All alien. Nothing of mine has stuck. They've written me off. Not seaworthy enough. My substance has been left on shore.

Only that yellowed map, torn at the edges, which I find triply folded in her seabag, looks familiar. It shows the coast and offshore islands of Pomerania. Two masked men holding a heraldic griffon, and below them, partly in Gothic, partly antique lettering: 'MARE BALTICUM, vulgo, De Oost See'. On the hand-coloured engraving, half land map, half sea chart, a red crayon has drawn, near Usedom, east of the Peene estuary, a circle. The name within it is that of the submerged city. Certain at last where the barge is headed, I fold the map and put it back in the seabag.

They've often hoisted their washing. Up top, the women are knitting for all they're worth. Later the hammocks lurch more, because the wind has shifted to the northeast and the *Ilsebill* has taken a new course, around the southern tip of Falster island.

I don't know when Damroka conceived the plan. Undoubtedly some months ago, while still on land, because an application for permission to navigate the coastal waters of the German Democratic Republic was submitted at an early date. The stated purpose: jellyfish measurements. But there won't be any stamped papers until they get to Gotland; they're with the Visby harbourmaster. Nevertheless the other women, especially the helmswoman, soon suspect that jellyfish are not the sole purpose of the trip. Looking out of the pilot house, she and the Old Woman have seen Damroka sitting in the bow for a good hour, talking to the sea. That was east of Fehmarn, after the last jellyfish measurement with the shark. One of them said: 'She's been talking with the Flounder.'

'And yesterday evening again,' said the engineer. That was when the Grømsund opened up on the port side. Møn lay straight ahead, the washing hung dry. Toward evening the wind shifted from northeast to east, then died down.

'No, I didn't see the Flounder, but they were arguing. In Plattdeutsch.' The engineer said: 'I don't get it,' and as an after-thought: 'Unfortunately.' But she insisted that she had clearly heard the call: Flounder, time and again: Flounder. And in broad Plattdeutsch they had spoken of a deep named Vineta after the submerged city.

Now the women know where else the barge is headed. Even if the oceanographer keeps saying: 'I don't believe it. You're crazy. We're heading for Møn's Klint and Stege. I'd never have come along – certainly not with you people – if there'd been any such foolishness on the programme.'

Nor does the helmswoman want to go there. 'Nothing was ever said about that. It would be contrary to our agreement.' Yet both went along, though under protest. The name Vineta doesn't come up.

'That's exactly where you'll want to go in the end,' says the Old Woman. 'There's no place else to go.'

The helmswoman is tired, and she's not the only one. The endless struggles for the women's cause, the everlasting conflict, not only with the washed-up sex, but also with their sistren, exhausted their will, in the midst of a deaf society, to build a women's rule opposed to male power. This plan was abandoned long ago, although they all, and especially the helmswoman, go right on saying: 'We ought to, we should, from the start we should have . . .'

That is why, while they are fishing in Bogøwasser and later off Møn for medusas and herring larvae, their thoughts fly away to a city under the waves. It had been promised them. According to the Flounder, it would be open to all women. Speaking with Damroka, the captain, he seems to have said: 'Well, women, so you're going down under.'

Let the women in their five vari-coloured hammocks dream of Vineta. Close together as they are lying, their women's rule can become attainable, if only they want it to. The motor barge rises and falls gently. It is tied fast in the port of Stege. At the sugar factory dock, shortly before the bridge leading into town. In the background pale-green silos and a mound of coke. The shallow water smells putrid. Too many algae. Heaps of jellyfish.

All five are asleep. 'On Møn,' Damroka has said, 'we won't need a watch.' They are lying the way I want them. The Old Woman, who mutters and curses in her sleep, curled up in the middle; on the starboard side the helmswoman with her mouth open; on the port side Damroka, her back unmoving; between her and the Old Woman the oceanographer, curled up on her side; while between the Old Woman and the helmswoman the electrician tosses fitfully.

The women are planning to do the town next day. There's a sale in Stege. Provisions are needed. They're running out of wool and other things. The Old Woman doesn't know if she'll go along.

Utopia Atlantis Vineta. This last seems to have been a Wendish settlement. According to some authorities, sunk off Usedom; but Polish archaeologists have lately been digging on Wollin and finding broken crockery, fragments of walls, and Arabic coins. Originally Vineta had a different name. The women there are believed to have had the say for a long time, until one day the men wanted to share in it. The old story. In the end, the men had the floor. There was feasting, and gold presents were given to the children. And then Vineta sank with all its wealth, in order that the submerged city might one day be saved – by women of course, five in number, one of whom, Damroka by name, is of Wendish descent.

Sleepy by day, she rolls up in a ball, turning her back on my stories. But she likes listening to the Third Programme with me. It offers: In the morning, lectures, Educational Radio for All, festive baroque music, news at intervals, Report on the Media; then later, Echo of the Day, more baroque music, this time religious.

Amazing the interest she takes in water levels. She finds it worth while to hear that the level of the Elbe at Dessau remains unchanged at one eighty and at Magdeburg has risen to one sixty one. Day after day she pays attention to the level of the Saale at Halle-Trotha, then from Geesthacht to Fliegenburg. But, when current events are reported, my Christmas rat takes no interest at all. Everywhere unsolved problems are running rampant. No growth except for crises; and my young rat, no longer than an index finger if you discount the tail, grows like crises which, being so crowded, coalesce to constitute a so-called rat's nest.

In the Report on the Media for instance, recent worries over cable TV are crowded out by still greater worries limping in after satellite

TV. Our Herr Matzerath, who amuses himself mapping out an all-embracing media consortium on his wide blackboard, says: 'Believe me, soon, thanks to the media, we shall create a reality that rids the future of all vagueness and arbitrariness; whatever the future may bring, we shall be able to produce it in advance.'

And how, ratkin, do things stand with our media consortium? By night in my dreams you are full grown, with a fat tail. And my daydreams as well are by no means free from rats. You seem to be intent on leaving scent marks, staking out your territory wherever I might have planned for an exit.

The Third Programme is reduced to silence. No Educational Radio for All, no nuclear fission made easy. Instead, now that the motor barge *The New Ilsebill* is tied up at Stege, I am drawing up a long list of the things our Herr Matzerath might take to Poland with him, for he has at last applied for visas for himself and his chauffeur.

In addition to birthday presents for his grandmother, his luggage should include a little bag of blue-and-white plastic dwarfs. This multitude of smurfs, it is hoped, will give pleasure to the latest batch of Kashubian children.

I know the preparations that are being made for Anna Koljaiczek's hundred and seventh birthday. Whole sacks of sugar and flour, because numerous crumb- and poppy-seed cakes are to be baked. At the present moment pigs' heads are being simmered until they promise to jell of their own accord. Preserving jars full of last autumn's mushrooms are being counted, among them slightly sandy greenies. Someone is bringing enough caraway seed for the coleslaw. In response to a request from far away, goose fat is being rendered. Eggs are pouring in from Kaschemken, Kokoschken and elsewhere. Will enough peonies be ready to cut? With help from the church, a hundred and seven candles will be available. There's still no bottled potato schnapps.

As for painter Malskat, all I can say is this: As soon as the She-rat lets me, I'll get around to him. When and where he was born. To whom apprenticed. Where his years of travel took him. What made him dream so Gothically on high scaffoldings. Why he was put on trial in Lübeck, a city famed for more things than marzipan.

Perhaps, while Hansel and Gretel are still running through the dead forest, I should follow the women to town. Only four of them have gone ashore. The Old Woman says she has to precook red cabbage.

Günter Grass

As Stege on the island of Møn is mostly a shopping centre and 'Udsalg' (sale) is posted all year long up and down the main street, the women do a big shopping. In a self-service store named Irma, they fill three carts with cans and jars, foil-wrapped fruit and vegetables, meat sealed and deep frozen, various brands of crisp bread, cottage cheese, rémoulade, popcorn for the oceanographer, odds and ends, detergent, toilet paper, plenty of bottled beer and two bottles of aquavit for the Old Woman. Fresh parsley and chives are available. They leave the store heavily laden. At the baker's they get coffee rings, at the fish market fresh herring, at the tobacco store newspapers and what this one and that one smoke.

On the second trip ashore the Old Woman comes along. While the engineer buys motor oil and kerosene for the lamps, the oceanographer runs to the post office, and as all the stores are having sales, the helmswoman goes looking for sweaters, while Damroka takes in a fresh supply of yarn in a wool shop across the street from the Bank of Møn. The Old Woman buys a bag of licorice.

Now, little rat, that everything is stowed away in the galley, the forecastle and amidships, we can listen to the Third Programme. Lute music followed by the usual news.

Let's hear who's denying what . . .

I dreamed I had retired and
my hollyhocks were growing high outside my windows.

Friends passed and said from across the fence:
How nice that you've finally retired.

And I, too, in my gourd-vine arbour, said to myself:
I've finally retired.

Thus calmly contemplated,
the world, my property, is large.

What bothers me oughtn't to,
because I've retired.

Everything has its place, becomes memory,
gathers dust, stays put.

If I were to take stock,
I'd call my retirement well-earned.

The Rat

Ah, I dreamed, if nothing interfered,
I'd be sitting pretty, without needs.

If only she – I beg you, my Rat –
could retire too.

With her an appetite awakens
that starts me running hornily between desk and bed.

And then, to make her leave me alone,
I jumped mischievously over the fence.

Now we're both on the make
and our friends are worried.

Oxtemosch shemmeck dosh taram! she cried. Which was
supposed to mean: Fear makes long legs. Then she corrected
herself: There had been no need to hurry. There had been plenty of
time, because the human end-game programmes had been staged
with elegiac deliberation; plenty of theatrical pomp, as if to say: If
you had to die, you might as well do it gracefully.

Calmly the She-rat reported: Before we dug in, we moved our
offspring; in other words, we evacuated first-strike targets, such as
the Rhine–Main region, the Saxon industrial zone, the Swabian
bases. And at the same time, thinking in continental terms, we
shifted excess population from Milan and Paris to the interior of
Switzerland. Austrian valleys were available. This new spatial
concept had long been overdue. And since there was famine again
in Poland and help was needed, not only humans but we rats as well
sent food from the glutted West – they by mail with food packages,
we via the so-called rat relay – with the result that the need of Polish
humans and rats was soon in some measure relieved. And along
with foodstuffs we also managed to shift threatened populations.
Rat clans were moved from the Ruhr, a region, incidentally, on
which immigrants from Poland had once set their stamp.

The She-rat of my dreams said all this to her latest litter, which
she proudly introduced to me as the first brood without mutative
defects. Then she had to provide answers to questions from her
nestlings: What are Poles? What exactly are Germans? How
differently did they look? What has become of them all? Were there
German and Polish rats before the Bang? How come that the
humans are gone and we rats are still here?

Patiently, while my dream lasted, the She-rat answered the questions of her nine-tailed litter. From the standpoint of the daily life of the rat community, she discussed the planned economy that leads to shortages. Look at it this way: no clan is allowed to supply its needs by simple methods that everyone can understand; instead, at some far distant centre, to which every clan is subordinate, all food is collected and redistributed. The consequences are losses in transit, inefficiency and envy. Which accounts for the permanent shortages in Poland. Though there'd been plenty of everything in the warehouses: coarse-grained bread, butter, fat, canned pork, tasty Polish sausage. A pity, this human incompetence.

Still excited in retrospect, the She-rat cried out: Even today, for fear of offending delicate sensibilities, it can only be whispered that the disorganization, which to the German mind is typically Polish, remains characteristic of the Polish rat. And that is why, though there was no perceptible difference in the appearance of the Germans and Poles, conflicts and even hostility were inevitable between them; and likewise between German and Polish rats. So much hatred, so much spurned love

But that, says the She-rat, is human history and lies far behind us. She told her nestlings about Teutonic Knights and what riches had been won on the battlefield of Tannenberg. She talked about the partitions of Poland, how chunks were seized not only by the Russians and Austrians, but by the Prussians as well, until Napoleon, then first and foremost Bismarck, but subsequently became free and independent again with double eagle, until a certain Hitler and a certain Stalin gobbled up the whole country, after which Poland still refused to give up, but once more, as it says in the song . . .

Here she broke off – This isn't getting us anywhere! – and said to her nine-tailed litter: It wasn't just Poles and Germans. In human times, relations were just as murderous between Serbs and Croats, English and Irish, Turks and Kurds, blacks and blacks, Christians and Jews, Jews and Arabs, Christians and Christians, Indians and Eskimos. They cut each other's throats and mowed each other down, starved and exterminated each other. And all this germinated in their heads. And because man thought up his end, then carried it out as planned, humans ceased to be. Maybe the human race just wanted to prove that its capacity for last things wasn't limited to thought. Admittedly: they proved it. But it may also be that human beings allowed that other faculty, which has always been ingrained in us rats, namely, the will to live, to wither away. In short, they lost their taste for life. They gave up; despite all their hatreds and conflicts, they were united when it came to putting an end to themselves. Do Minsher nifteren ultemosh, she cried.

After so definitive a speech I found nothing to say. And her litter asked no more questions, but just lived — by carrying out the biblical commandment: Multiply. A merry scramble, constant rearrangement of tails. How quickly nestling rats became adult rats, which in turn engendered nestling rats. But because they were so singlemindedly intent on reproduction, my dream was free to look for other images. For just a little way, it chased after the running children in the dead forest; then it ploughed through the jellyfish-saturated sea, stirred up exercise-yard fears and tribulations of the flesh, until at last it seized upon painter Malskat, who, however, was not perched high on a scaffold painting Gothic frescoes with deft brush, but sitting with our Herr Matzerath in Lübeck's Café Niederecker, eating mouthful after mouthful of marzipan tarts. In my dream, they understood each other well. They laughed, exchanged memories, and chatted their time away during the fifties.

> There was once a land, its name was Deutsch.
> It was beautiful, hilly and flat
> and didn't know what to do with itself.
> So it made a war, because it wanted to be
> worldwide, and that made it small.
> It thought up an idea that put on boots.
> Booted as war, it went out to see the world,
> came home as war, played innocent, said nothing,
> as though it had put on carpet slippers,
> as though it had seen no evil in the outside world.
> But read in retrospect, the booted idea
> could be recognized as crime: so many dead.
> The land named Deutsch was divided.
> Now it was twice named and, though still
> beautifully hilly and flat,
> it still didn't know what to do with itself.
> After brief reflection, it offered, on both sides,
> its services for a third war.
> Since then not a murmuring word. Peace on earth.

There was once a painter, who was to become famous as a forger. Yet scarcely begun, the story has got it wrong, for he never forged anything; with both hands he painted genuine Gothic. If you don't believe it, no amount of expertises will help you.

Our painter was born in 1913 in the East Prussian city of Königsberg on the river Pregel. The son of an antique dealer, he grew up among deepened oil paintings and madonnas gleaming with old gold, surrounded by authentic and inauthentic pieces, under layers of varnish so to speak, never far from the woodworm, in the midst of dusty junk. He watched his father who knew how to age votive tablets and paintings by the lesser Dutch masters. On leaving elementary school, the youngster was apprenticed to a house painter, learned what there was to learn of the trade, and in his free time copied fourteenth-century North-German panels. At an early age the apprentice developed a taste for Gothic suffering and Gothic sweetness.

The Malskat family – for that was our painter's father's name – lived on Flinsenwinkel in Königsberg.

The river Pregel flowed into Frische Haff, which emptied into the Baltic near Pillau. Today Königsberg is called Kaliningrad and the river has a different name too. Flinsenwinkel exists no longer. Nothing is left but crumbling memories and books written in vain by the philosopher Immanuel Kant, who lived in Königsberg all his life, and tasty dishes named after the city – such as meatballs in sweet-and-sour caper sauce, and East Prussian names such as Kurbjuhn, Adromeit, Margull, Tolkmit and Malskat. These names are of Old Prussian origin. They were taken over intact from the Old Prussians, who were exterminated in order that Prussia might come into being, for which reason, before we speak of forgeries and specifically of the forged paintings trial, it should be pointed out that the name Malskat is authentic.

After a short stay at a school of applied art, where he learned nothing new about Gothic, Lothar Malskat went travelling with a hide-covered knapsack. He wore knickerbockers and sandals and seems to have got as far as Italy, where he learned that there are mountains behind the mountain and that opportunities are rare. He was one of the many itinerant artisans and mountebanks, who in the mid-thirties polished doorknobs, repaired barns, beat carpets, and lived from hand to hungry mouth without permanent address, while first in Berlin, then throughout Germany, history, which meant little to Malskat, was being made.

Nevertheless, his hour struck in the capital. While looking for work, he made the acquaintance, in Berlin-Lichterfelde, of Ernst Fey, an art professor reputed as a restorer. In exchange for hot soup and pocket money, he painted the professor's garden fence, an activity allowing for flights of fancy: a divinely pretty little face, now sad, now mischievous, was pictured and could be discerned after working hours and before the second coat of paint was laid on. In those days, Malskat often went to the movies, where he saw the popular actress Hansi Knoteck, first in *Schloss Hubertus*, then over and over again, until she so impressed herself on his style that her subsequent influence on certain Gothic murals in North German brick churches should not come as a surprise. Be that as it may, the restorer soon recognized the fence painter's special gift. Malskat's Eulenspiegel-like nose, the visionary curve of his eyebrows, and his humble, not to say inspired devotion to every single pale of the fence may also have influenced the professor.

In the spring of 1936, he was given the chance to accompany Fey's son, whose name was Dietrich and who, with his long eyelashes and long narrow face, fascinated women wherever he went, in a yellow DKW sports car to Schleswig on the Schlee. That is a city after which half the territory between the North and Baltic Seas is named. Work was awaiting them in its cathedral.

From the handsome Dietrich, who gained credibility all over the cathedral town, but most conspicuously in the music room of the rectory, for which reason he had soon surrounded himself with a circle of pastors' daughters, Malskat, who continued to find films in which Hansi Knoteck played leading and supporting roles more entertaining, learned only one trick: to mix the particular reddish-brown paint suited to contour painting in the cloister of the cathedral. Entirely on his own initiative and quite effortlessly, he learned to paint old things newly and to age his new paintings with the help of a potsherd and a wire brush. The rest was done with a dust bag full of ground lime mortar.

Malskat had to paint quickly, for as soon as the red-brown contours on the cloister walls dried, they had to demonstrate their Gothic origin. Encouraged by recognizable traces of the originals, he succeeded in producing well-rounded, vigorous yet controlled contour paintings, bold in overall design and startling in detail, on nine of the ten fields; the last field on the west side remained vacant.

He painted the Three Kings and the Adoration, John the Baptist, the Massacre of the Innocents, the Flight into Egypt, the Betrayal, the Flagellation, and whatever else it takes to make a cloister complete. At the bottom of each ogival field, he painted an animal frieze; under the Flagellation, for example, alternating cocks and stags in medallions; under the Betrayal, eagles and lions. But the frieze bordering the fourth field from the west made history by sparking off a controversy; it will therefore be given special mention.

And, while pretty-boy Fey was paying his respects to pastors' daughters with sensitively arranged baskets of flowers and inviting matrons and young ladies to boat rides on the Schlee, Malskat was also doing good work in the choir of Schleswig Cathedral. On the window jambs surrounding the main altar and on the rows of buttresses, he quickly painted twenty-six heads, which he framed in medallions. One of these shows him with long nose and boldly arching eyebrows; a cigarette behind his ear, though half concealed, tells us that in those years Malskat favoured 'Juno' cigarettes – 'For reasons eminently sound Juno cigarettes are round'.

In addition, all the while smoking, he painted the companions of his childhood years by the river Pregel, on the light-catching window jambs and buttresses of the high-arching chancel. The sketchbooks of his Königsberg apprenticeship were helpful; always industrious, he had sketched the older journeymen, and time and again the master, the other apprentices, as well as the customers of his father's antique shop, such as Lawyer Maximilian Lichtenstein and Dr Jessner, who now, long present in his mind, took form, hatched, on vacant fields.

Malskat then applied his tested methods to these piously intended heads. Potsherd and wire brush did the work of roughly seven hundred years. The dust bag supplied the finishing touches. And he kept at it until twenty-six saints, though slightly the worse for wear and nibbled around the edges, looked down at the cathedral's chancel and nave with expressions of early Gothic piety. He completed the last head on 3 May 1938. While outside history was being made blow by blow, to the end that Germany might get bigger and bigger, Lothar Malskat celebrated his twenty-fifth birthday high on the scaffolding. Not until evening was he, along with Fey, a guest at the rectory, surrounded by pastors' daughters named Heike, Dörte and Swantje, if not Gudrun or Freia.

Woodruff punch was served. We see him embarrassed, out of

place. When Malskat wasn't at the cinema, he spent his free time in the fishermen's quarter, down by the Schlee. At that time, Knoteck was on the playbill in *The Girl from Moorhof*.

The *Salvator Mundi* on the romanesque vault of the central nave of the three-nave cathedral, which has given many a rapt viewer a stiff neck, is also by his hand, and impressive to this day: a multi-faceted composition, which included the rainbow of the sixth day of the Creation. Despite its contradictory styles, it forms a coherent whole, and for that very reason confronted art historians with puzzling problems. In the end, they concurred in calling Malskat's *Salvator Mundi* 'an epoch-making work of art'.

Numerous monographs, though without mentioning – even in parentheses – either his first or last name, expressed esteem for the painter's overall contribution, and went so far as to praise it as 'true to type'. This praise was addressed in particular to the Nordic-looking heads in the window jambs and on the buttresses and to certain runic inscriptions which Malskat, at the request of Fey, who was eager to propitiate the Zeitgeist of the late thirties, had scratched into the plaster of the vacant fields and of the field surrounding his *Salvator Mundi*: alliterative nonsense such as 'the deathless deeds of dead heroes'.

In the forefront of the experts, an art historian by the name of Hamkens, writing in specialized journals, celebrated the strong-willed gaze of the heroic saints, their long noses and distinctly Nordic chins. No sooner had these briskly aged paintings, which, it seems worth mentioning, brought Malskat an appreciable increase in his hourly wage, come into being than Hamkens had their Aryan heads photographed, and by order of the Reichsführer SS the whole set of photos, whose authenticity no one contested, was purchased by the German Heritage Foundation and shown in travelling exhibitions.

Malskat's work attracted attention, and the animal frieze, which he had been inspired to paint in the cloister as a border fillet to his *Massacre of the Innocents*, was to have well-nigh irreversible consequences; in four out of seven medallions Malskat had painted not stags and cocks, not griffons and mountain goats, as he had below the touching motif of Hansi Knoteck as Virgin with Child, but easily recognizable turkeys. In the remaining three medallions, thanks to potsherd, wire brush and dust bag, only traces of poultry were discernible.

But the four intact turkeys were enough. They clinched it. At last, what had hitherto been no more than a dubious presumption, often ridiculed as a nationalistic fantasy, was established. Thanks to Malskat, historical truth came to light. For this early Gothic painting proved that not the wop Columbus, but the Vikings, Germanic Norsemen with long noses and jutting chins, had brought that undeniably American bird to Europe. From that time on, Malskat's turkeys, those simple red-brown contours captured with a sure eye, provided, according to numerous learned papers, a basis for a long-overdue rewriting of history. From spring 1939, through the outbreak of war in the following autumn and as long as the victories lasted, but undeterred by the battle of Stalingrad, the smashing of the cities or the consequences of the Allied invasion – the experts pursued their so-called turkey controversy. I'm willing to bet that it's still going on covertly.

Yet from the very start Malskat signed his early-to-high Gothic creations with the Franco-Latin abbreviation t.f.L.M. – *tout fecit Lothar Malskat*, even if it was concealed in arabesques and lightly painted over. He was not a forger. Those who later on, in the days of the grandiose, state-preserving forgeries, prosecuted and punished him, they, in the mid-fifties, were the true deceivers. They still hold respected, if not official positions. They wink at each other and pin decorations on each other. Their wines and corpses are well cellared.

There was once a land, its name was Deutsch . . .

Chapter Four, in which leave is taken, a contract is ready for signature, Hansel and Gretel arrive, rat droppings are found, a Sunday mood prevails, it's Doomsday, a few gold pieces are superfluous, Malskat is called to the colours, it is hard to leave the women, the ship anchors under chalk cliffs.

I DREAMT I had to take leave
of all the things that have surrounded me
and cast their shadows: all those possessive
pronouns. Leave of the inventory, that list
of found objects. Leave
of cloying scents
and smells that keep me awake, of the sweet,
the bitter, the intrinsically sour,
and the hot pungency of peppercorns.
Leave of time's tick tock, of Monday's irritation,
of Wednesday's shabby gains, of Sunday's
bitchiness, once boredom sits down to table.
Leave of all deadliness, of everything
due to come due.

I dreamt I had to take leave of all
ideas, whether born quick or still, of the meaning
that looks for the meaning behind the meaning,
and of hope, that long-distance runner. Leave of the compound
    interest
of pent-up rage, of the proceeds of accumulated dreams,
of everything that's written on paper and recalls metaphor,
when horse and rider become a monument. Leave

of all the images that man has made for himself.
Leave of songs, of rhymed misery,
of interwoven voices, of six-choired jubilation,
of instrumental enthusiasm,
of God and Bach.

I dreamt I had to take leave
of bare branches,
of the words bud, blossom and fruit,
of seasons that are sick
of their moods and insist on leavetaking.
Morning mist. Indian summer. Winter coat. To cry out:
April April! One last time to say autumn crocus, mayflower.
Drought frost thaw.
To run away from tracks in the snow. Maybe
the cherries are ripe for leavetaking. Maybe
the cuckoo is playing crazy and calling. One last time
to make peas spring green from pods. Or
the dandelion. Now for the first time I know what it wants.

I dreamt I had to take leave of table, door and bed
and in taking leave test, open wide, lie down on
table, door and bed.
My last school day: I spell the names
of friends and say their phone numbers: debts
to be repaid; finally, I write a word
to my enemies: Let bygones by bygones – or
was it worth quarrelling about?
Suddenly I have time.
My eyes, as though trained to take leave,
search the horizons all about, look for
the hills behind the hills, the city
on either side of the river,
as though the obvious required to be remembered spared
    rescued;
relinquished, to be sure, but still
palpable, wide awake.

I dreamt I had to take leave
of you, you and you, of my incapacity,
of the residual I, the decimal remainder

that has languished for years.
Leave of what is alien and over-familiar,
of politely self-righteous habits,
of our registered and documented hate. Nothing
was closer to me than your coldness. So much love
remembered exactly wrong. In the end
everything was taken care of; heaps of safety pins.
It remains to take leave of your stories,
which are always looking toward the wharf, the steamer
that's coming, laden with fugitives,
from Stralsund, the burning city,
and leave of my eyeglasses, which have always
had shards in mind, only shards, shards
of themselves. No,
no more standing on my head.

And no more pain. Nothing
that expectation runs to meet. This end
is on the school programme, known. This leavetaking
was practised in classrooms. Just see
how cheaply naked secrets are. Betrayal no longer pays off.
At bargain prices the enemy's decoded dreams.
At last the profit is cancelled out, the final
reckoning makes us equal,
for the last time reason wins
and nothing
that breathes, that creeps
or flies, that's still
unthought, that may ultimately
come into being and die
makes any difference.

Yet when I dreamt that I would have to
take leave this minute of every creature
lest of all the beasts
for whom Noah built the ark, any
aftertaste should remain, I dreamt,
after the fish, the sheep and the chicken,
who all passed away with human beings,
one solitary rat, which threw nine young
and had a future.

Not us! She whispered, denied, contested. Never infatuated with ourselves. No need of mirrors. We never found profundity in hot air; no goal outside ourselves tempted us, magnified us, exalted us. There has never been a super-rat.

And no multi-storied edifice of thought, in which we transcended, sky-high, to the raving delusion of immortality. Free from such human shenanigans, we were numerous but never counted ourselves. We lacked consciousness of our own being, a shortage that didn't starve us.

We may have provided exemplary material for the metaphors that man forced into being when it became necessary to call plagues, the biblical ones, for instance, by name; but for us there were no examples, nobody, certainly no other animal, could set us an example, not even man, to whom we have been devoted from time immemorial, who amazed us, yes, but did not, as long as he actually existed and cast a shadow, become a god to us.

Once he was gone, we began to miss him. Not only did we miss the provisions and garbage, raw as well as cooked, in his kitchens; we also sorely missed his ideas, which we had all literally gobbled up; we would gladly, figuratively speaking, have held the basin for his overflow, we the foot soldiers of his deliriums, we the model of his terrors. That's why man made word pictures of us. He feared ratbite fever, he cursed rats' nests and rat races. We, evil incarnate, were present in the bottommost horror chamber of his mind, we who disposed of whatever he secreted, in mucus or in pieces, his faeces, his fermenting remains, whatever he vomited up in his misery, we cleaned it up without fuss or bother, removing it from his squeamish sight, we, who delighted in his vomit, were to him objects of disgust. Even more than spiders we disgusted him. No jellyfish, no worm, no woodlouse disgusted him more. If we came up in conversation, he would gag. If he saw us, he would retch. Because our tails were naked and unreasonably long, they were especially repugnant to him; we were the embodiment of disgust. Even in books which celebrated self-revulsion as specific to human existence, we would be read between the lines; for when man felt disgust for man, as he had seen fit to do from time immemorial, it was we once again who helped him to find names for it; whenever he had his enemy, his many enemies, in his sights, he would cry: You rat! You rats! And because so much was possible for man, he, in his hatred of his fellow man, sought us in himself, found us with little hesitation, identified us and destroyed us. Whenever he exterminated his heretics and deviants, those he regarded as inferior and counted as scum, today the mob, yesterday the nobility, there would be talk of rats in need of being exterminated.

Or maybe it was like this: because the human race couldn't get us down with strychnine or arsenic, because, despite the invention of newer and better exterminators – toward the end there was talk of using ultra sound waves – he was never able to get rid of our offspring. We, like man, became more and more numerous, he eliminated his fellow men in our stead, and, as one might have expected, successfully.

Only recently, said the She-rat of my dreams, have we begun to form images of him, to look for the man concealed in us rats, and find him. He is becoming more and more beautiful and wants to be reflected: his elegant proportions, his upright gait, which we practise and practise. We are now aware of our inadequacy, our incapacity for feelings, for moods. Ah, if only we could blush for shame as he did, usually for absurd reasons. Ah, if only we had the gift of headbirth, if only one of his ideas could get us with child.

No, we rats do not take leave of him, as he took leave of his grandeur. No, said the She-rat, before fading out of the picture, we are not giving man up.

A working lunch for two. He ordered saddle of venison with chanterelles and cranberries. Across from me, seated on two cushions, our Herr Matzerath would like to know how, in the silent film about the dying forests, which on the one hand should accuse, so as to save the forests at the last moment, but on the other hand aim to take leave, because it's too late, much too late, I see the historical Brothers Grimm in present-day roles.

'Until this question is settled,' he says, 'I'm reluctant to go to Poland, especially as there too all sorts of things are losing themselves in traditional Catholic clouds.'

My explanations take us up to the desert: raspberry jelly with vanilla sauce. While Jakob is Minister of the Environment, Wilhelm, his undersecretary, is competent for the increasing damage being done to the forests. In any event, they both see the forests as their responsibility. They know all about toxicity and intromissions. With government funds they promote ozone research. Years ago, in theses that were laughed off at the time, they both cast doubts on the stability of the ecosystem in the event of uninhibited economic growth. While much quoted, their criticism of government energy policy has remained ineffectual. Their catalogue of indispensable measures meets with little opposition, but never gets majority support in parliament. They have often offered to resign, but are still in office.

The Grimm Brothers are said to be too liberal. In tolerant silence, they let every other minister say his piece, while they themselves are rudely interrupted, addled by catcalls, ridiculed by the rest of the cabinet as unrealistic dreamers, or at best respected as eccentrics – it takes all kinds to make a world. They are an affordable luxury. The Chancellor shows them off to state visitors.

And yet, for all their modernity, the Brothers Grimm, now Grimm Brothers, have remained true to themselves. Side by side with their respected though ineffectual government activity, they collect data on the social and cultural condition of foreign workers; and they also collect neologisms, just as they formerly collected legends and words from A to Z, until Jakob, while approaching the letter F, became buried in index cards.

Furthermore, they publish. While Wilhelm Grimm gains the approval even of the feminists with an article on *The Role of Turkish Women in the Everyday Life of the Federal Republic*, a book by the present-day Jakob Grimm entitled *Smurf Language* has gained wide attention, because the author, by pointing out the numerous 'smurfs', or comic-strip phrases, in the language of synthetic fabrics, has been able to throw light on the general deterioration of the German language ('once-flourishing word fields are clogged with weeds') and the decline of literary German. Some years ago the Grimm Brothers were much applauded all over the country when, along with other scholars, they protested against a change in the constitution – with their usual eloquence, though they went unheard; the change, it was argued, was grounded in the shared tradition of the divided country.

But because in my film, which will deal with the dying forests, the Grimm Brothers are involved in a linear fairy-tale plot, their secondary activities and scruples are hardly worth noting. For example: their two adjoining offices, the door between which is always open, bear witness to their collectors' zeal. Wilhelm's office is the smaller. Between bookshelves crammed with sociology hangs a wall covering, knotted from thirty or more motley-coloured head scarves, originally belonging to Turkish 'guest worker' women; in Jakob's ministerial office one is struck, side by side with a portrait of the Prussian scholar Savigny, by a cabinet with shelves chockful of amusing smurfs, arranged in groups. The Grimm Brothers take an ironic view of their scholarship.

And another thing our Herr Matzerath is curious about, while I stir up a last remnant of raspberry jelly with a last remnant of vanilla sauce: yes, they're both musical; they favour better instruction in the arts and believe that the film industry should be encouraged to produce quality pictures. They are not opposed in principle to new media, but warn against uncontrolled monopoly of the media.

We raise our glasses, drink each other's health. No, no, the Grimm Brothers are not armchair scholars. They are divorced, with a taste for variety in ladies. We see them in sports clothes, photogenic, and not only when together. They are wearing bow ties with patterns that go with their tweed jackets. They even spend their vacations together in the Spessart, in the Vosges, wherever there are forests. The film might simply be called *The Forest*, or more ambitiously *The Grimms' Forests*; only it should be shot while there are still forests to be seen.

'But why,' asks our Herr Matzerath over coffee, 'why does it absolutely have to be a silent film?'

Because everything has been said. Because there's nothing left but to take leave. First of firs, pines, spruces, then of smooth beeches, a few oak forests, the mountain maple, the ash, the birch, the alder, the elm that was ailing anyway, the light fringes of the forests, with their underbrush rich in mushrooms. What's to become of ferns if their leafy covering is gone? Where shall we escape to, where shall we get lost?

Leave of crossroads, deep in the forest. Of the anthill which taught wonderment, we take leave without knowing of what. Of the many enclosures, which promised profit and Christmas trees, of the hollow tree that had room for every terror, leave of the flowing resin, which imprisoned the beetle for ever. Leave of the twisted roots one stumbled over and at last found a four-leaf clover for luck. Leave of the fly agaric, which gives one a special sort of dreams, of the honey agaric, which lives on tree stumps, of the tasty craterellus, which opens its funnels late while the stinkhorn sounds from afar. Fire break, deforestation, copse, leave of all the words that come from the forest.

In conclusion, we take our leave of conflicting signposts and of the Wild Man Hostelry, of rising sap and vernal green, of falling leaves and of all letters beginning with such talk. Erased is everything that is written about the forest and the forests behind the forests. No vows carved in bark. No burden of snow, falling from fir trees. Never again will the cuckoo teach us to count. We shall be without fairy tales.

Therefore a silent film. Because the camera will see the forest as though for the last time. What need then of talk? Dying, the forests speak for themselves. Only the plot – which wants to get ahead, which is in a hurry and would like to leap, which needs cries, complaints and directions – requires subtitles, and they must be short. Luckily nobody knows it. Mirror, mirror on the wall. Yet behind the Seven Mountains. What big ears you have! Let down your hair for me. My child, my fawn. Princess, youngest princess. There's blood in the shoe. The wind, the wind, the heavenly child . . .

For though Hansel and Gretel are still running silently through the dead forest, someday, no, soon, the forest will come to life and help the children with pointers, and when they get there, they'll be welcomed with a subtitle: 'Hello, there you are at last!'

By now our Herr Matzerath, who likes to talk and admits that he has always been a chatterbox, realizes that it has to be a silent film and that he – who else! – should produce it. Arching his little finger, he stirs his demi-tasse and says nothing.

Should I put pressure that will finally make him agree to be the producer? He ought to know that his projected trip will be delayed until he says the word.

To put me off the track, he shows me his visa.

I point to the production contract. 'Here, right here, it needs your signature.'

He regrets that the market for video cassettes is glutted.

But I don't want a cassette. 'I want a silent film with subtitles.'

He says: 'As soon as I'm safely back from Poland, I might . . .'

I say: 'It just might occur to me to let your visa lapse . . .'

'Blackmail,' he calls it. 'Author's arrogance . . . Oh, all right . . . For one thing, it's only in a movie that the forests can be saved.'

Quickly I say: 'Would tomorrow be too soon to see you off?'

While paying for saddle of venison and trimmings for two,

leaving the waiter a handsome tip, then writing the title *Grimms' Forests* in the appropriate space, and finally, in Sütterlin script, signing himself as Oskar Matzerath–Bronski, he says after a lengthy digression about his trip and the political situation in Poland: 'I'd rather have done something with Malskat the painter. His Gothic appeals to me.'

Hand in hand through corpselike petrifaction. In the dead forest, they run past garbage dumps, toxic waste disposal sites, and off-limits military areas. (In the meantime, their father and mother, the Chancellor and his spouse, tell the press how inconsolable they are.) On billboards and on television screens, all over the countryside, it is made known that the runaway Chancellor's children, whose names are Johannes and Margarete, are 'wanted'.

No longer hand in hand, Hansel and Gretel run as if they could do no otherwise. Barely tired and not the least bit desperate. Sometimes Hansel and sometimes Gretel in the lead. While they run, the dead forest, which looks like the Erz Mountains in modern photos, first hesitantly, then resolutely, then fiercely green, more and more densely picture-book green, then finally a jungle-green fairy-tale forest.

A jay, an owl take flight. Creaking trees make faces. Mushrooms sprout visibly from beds of moss. Blinking elves lie hidden under roots, as though fastened to the tubers and taproots. From a busy anthill a long-fingered hand beckons to the children and points the way. The unicorn bursts out of the underbrush, it has one fiery, one sad eye, and trots off through the beech trees, as though required to be unique of its kind somewhere else.

They are not terribly afraid. 'There are no real monsters here,' says Gretel. They both see the forest as though struck with their first wonderment. They aren't running any more, but peering about and feeling their way. Amid tree trunks so big that the two of them together can hardly girdle them, they lose and find each other. The leafy roof closes over them, pierced by few sunholes. They are swimming in chest-high ferns.

At last a wood pigeon, pulling a golden thread behind it, leads Hansel and Gretel through the forest to a clearing. There, beside a dark pond with seven swans gliding over it, stands a wooden house with an upper story and a shingle roof. As the children come closer, a painted sign saying Gingerbread House identifies it as a forest hostelry. To one side of it there are stables. In a nearby enclosure, a deer looks up. For a moment the caged wolf stops pacing back and forth.

A lady in a long dress is sleeping beside a well. Hesitantly, Hansel and Gretel approach. A frog is sitting on the lady's forehead, breathing as though pumping air. The look that Hansel and Gretel exchange suggests that they are pretty well acquainted with this story. (Accordingly, while the frog breathes on the lady's forehead, no explanatory subtitle is needed.)

White curtains blow from open windows. There's an old-fashioned vending machine in front of the house; the ornamental painting on it represents gingerbread and other goodies. Hansel looks through his trouser pocket for change, but finds neither coins nor a slot to put them into. Instead, he sees an ornate inscription in Gothic print, saying: 'Dear children, help yourselves.'

First Gretel pulls out a drawer; there's a bag of hazelnuts in it. Hansel pulls out another drawer and is surprised to find a piece of honeycomb. Hungry from running first through the dead, then through the green forest, they empty both bags.

While they are still nibbling and finding beechnuts in a third drawer, a woman behind flowering dogrose bushes rises from a deckchair, in which she seems to have fallen asleep over the newspaper. The name of the newspaper is *The Forest Messenger*; it was founded early in the past century, shortly before the battles of Jena and Auerstedt. The woman, who is neither young nor old, is at once ugly and beautiful. She is wearing hair curlers and a necklace with air-dried ears on it. As she buttons her large-flowered housecoat over her bra, Hansel sees her enormous tits, bigger than the ones he sometimes dreams of. But Gretel recognizes the witch out of their fairy tale.

(In case our Herr Matzerath wants to know how beautifully ugly the witch is, I'd better describe her, because our silent film is to be in colour; she is not a redhead, but she squints slightly out of amber-coloured eyes.) Not in the least surprised, she says her line for the subtitle: 'Well, children, here you are at last.'

As she comes nearer and pinches the lobe of Hansel's ear, he finds himself close not only to her tits, but also to the numerous air-dried ears on her necklace. Suddenly, as though not wishing to encourage any improper ideas, the witch starts shaking, faster and faster, a wooden rattle, of the kind that was formerly used to scare ghosts away. (Our silent film admits of such sound effects, as well as of bird song and other natural sounds.)

The rasping of the rattle has consequences. One after another, all the boarders step out of the gingerbread house; a more skinny than svelte Snow White is held up by the wicked stepmother, an imposing figure in travel dress. Sleeping Beauty rubs her sleepy eyes and has to be kissed by the prince, who is a kind of male nurse and keeps having to awaken her with a kiss; Little Red Riding Hood, recognizable by her bright-red beret (her boots are of the same colour), leads her grandmother, who is hard of hearing; Rübezahl in a playsuit is identified as the hired man by the pliers and ruler in his breast pocket; from a window on the upper floor Rapunzel, to help people to guess her name, lets her hair blow loose between the blowing curtains; clad in black velvet, the saddest of all hand-holding pairs, Jorinde and Joringel.

All the boarders have aged in beauty. They are glad Hansel and Gretel have finally got there. Nobody asks where they've come from. The wicked stepmother says, 'We want you to feel at home here.' Only Little Red Riding Hood is rude. 'I always thought of Hansel and Gretel as proletarian children, not as dropouts corrupted by affluence.' Again the witch shakes the rattle.

Then comes the girl with bloody scabs on her arm stumps; she is carrying her chopped-off hands tied with string and slung over her shoulder. (If our Herr Matzerath should raise objections to this scene – 'No audience will put up with such cruelty!' – I shall counter them by crying out 'Censorship!' and reminding him of his childhood, that calvary of choice bestialities. Besides, *The Girl Without Hands* is typical of the Grimm collection, whereas Rübezahl, who at Herr Matzerath's suggestion is to be the hired man in this film, is only a character in a crazy artificial product by a certain Musäus.)

Now that all are assembled, Rumpelstiltskin steps out of the house, dressed as a waiter and carrying a tray. Slightly but unmistakably limping, he offers the Gingerbread House boarders assorted drinks: 'A hawthorn flip. Or would you care for a glass of dogrose wine? Or a wild honey cocktail!' And his subtitle, made to order for Hansel and Gretel, is: 'And for you, children, excellent wild strawberry juice, freshly squeezed.'

While all drink, sip, chat, whisper or, like Jorinde and Joringel, read black-velvet sorrow in each other's eyes, while the prince conscientiously and repeatedly wakens his Sleeping Beauty with a kiss, while Little Red Riding Hood shouts insults into her grandmother's ear, such as 'Now don't get drunk again!', the witch, now wearing spectacles, runs her fingers over Hansel more than Gretel, Rumpelstiltskin gallantly presses a glass of elderberry juice to the lips of the girl without hands, the wicked stepmother arbitrates the immemorial quarrel between Snow White and Rapunzel, and off to one side Rübezahl, as though the spirit of the Riesengebirge were intent on displaying tree-uprooting power, piles wood for the hostelry kitchen; while all this is happening, clouds come up and a shower of rain comes down, which sets off a gauge consisting of glass tubes and located beside the well; whereupon the alarm bell rings, because here as throughout the country there is acid rain, and the fairy-tale characters are afraid of it.

The frog jumps off the sleeping lady's forehead and into the well; a moment later the frog king emerges, wearing a tight-fitting diver's suit, but crowned. The ladylike princess wakes up and, as though suffering from a headache, rubs her forehead, on which the frog was sitting before. As the frog king helps her up and offers her his arm, all run into the house, last of all Hansel and Gretel and, after she has read the alarming figures, the witch. 'This,' she says, 'is more than even our fairy-tale forest can stand.'

Inside, the Gingerbread House is furnished like a museum. Glass cases crammed full. Every exhibit is explained by a written label. Snow White shows Hansel and Gretel her miniature glass coffin, in which she is lying adorably doll-sized; beside it, encapsulated in artificial resin, the life-size poison apple with a bite out of it.

The wicked stepmother drags Hansel and Gretel away from Snow White's coffin and leads them to her magic mirror, which covers the front of a wooden chest and is placed conspicuously in the middle of the room on a bureau, the drawers of which might contain books, such as herbals or first editions of collected fairy tales.

All want to show Hansel and Gretel their exhibits. Rübezahl demonstrates his gnarled wooden club. The limping waiter Rumpelstiltskin shows, preserved in alcohol, a leg which, as some versions of the tale named after him maintain, he tore off in a rage because his name had been guessed. The frog king calls a ball golden – 'genuine ducat-gold' – which once upon a time, when his lady was still a youngest princess, had rolled into the well. The girl without hands points both arm stumps at her father's axe. The witch's bone collection is displayed in a glass case, the contents of which are neatly labelled and dated with precision – 'That was in the merry month of May, 1789.' – 'That happened in the autumn of the year 1806.' Seven dwarfs' caps are hanging on seven hooks, as though their owners were likely to turn up at any moment.

There are also colour prints portraying the Brothers Grimm. On every wall one sees fine-line drawings by Ludwig Richter and Moritz von Schwind. Plus silhouettes representing the Musicians of Bremen, the Wolf and the Seven Young Kids. And other fairy-tale subjects. (Maybe I should smuggle into this collection a photo showing our Herr Matzerath as a little boy in his sailor suit, with his instrument slung round his neck, though I would rather have shown him bald-headed as a film producer.)

But all the objects here are not static museum pieces. Broom and flail are standing in their corners. At a sign from the Witch, they begin to dance across the room and around the magic mirror, chasing after the limping waiter Rumpelstiltskin, who joins in the game and moans resignedly under the gentle blows, as though he deserved a thrashing. The fairy-tale characters are rather bored with this too-often repeated performance. The girl without hands prefers not to watch. Jorinde and Joringel remain motionless and starry-eyed. Only Hansel and Gretel are impressed.

After the witch has ordered broom and flail back into their corner, she asks the wicked stepmother to demonstrate her magic art. With an ironic smile that bares several gold teeth, but respectfully, as though introducing a sporting competition, she points at the magic mirror.

The wicked stepmother doesn't have to be asked twice. In the side pocket of her suit jacket there is a small lacquer box with a keyboard which she manipulates with her little finger. Instantly, the magic mirror comes to life and after a moment of flickering fades in the story of Hansel and Gretel.

As though watching television at home, the Chancellor's children see the beginning of their story in a black-and-white silent film. Several times, faithful to the Grimm version, the poor parents, basket weavers or woodcutters, try to lose their hungry children in the forest. The Gingerbread House is made of crispy gingerbread. The film ends with Hansel and Gretel (who look like the runaway Chancellor's children and should also remind our Herr Matzerath of Störtebeker and Tulla Pokriefke) pushing the witch into the oven.

The She-rat of my dreams laughed as though a rat were capable of laughing scornfully or heartily, uproariously or good-naturedly. Sure, sure, she said, laughing, that's how all your stories ended and not just your fairy tales. Into the oven, finish. All your speculations tended toward that solution. The stories we made light of as mere lies were to you bitter earnest. It shouldn't surprise, let alone disappoint us that the human soap opera came to so corny an end. So let's laugh and heave – as they said in human times – a sigh of relief.

It was only then that, suspicious as usual, I realized that what she was laughing at was our end, which laughing she pretended to regret: Obviously we are horrified at your discontinuation. Your total extinction perplexes us. We still fail to understand the all-too-human scenario of your demise. Open oven, push witch in, slam door, witch dead! Curtain, show's over. Out of the question, we say to ourselves. Only the day before yesterday there was hopeful talk about educating the human race: new kinds of lessons, fairer marking, man to be improved in every way, and today, or more accurately yesterday, the school shuts down. Horrible! we cry. Inconceivable. All those uncompleted tasks. The class goal unachieved. A damn shame. That clever educational system, forever setting new goals, but in the end leading to nothing. A shame about the teachers too. But to claim that we were responsible for your end, that we closed your school, wiped out your study plans and teaching jobs – it's not funny; unless you think of it as the very last human joke.

The She-rat soft-pedalled her scorn. Exchanged bitter laughter for fairness: of course we realize that in both camps – that's how it always was with humans – the question of guilt was raised as soon as first and second strikes were exchanged – to begin with, only in the European medium-range zone. A misunderstanding fraught with consequences. Since both sides were convinced that the misunderstanding had been intended by the other side, since moreover both security systems precluded unintentional misunderstandings, it was publicly – where there was still a public – repeated for half a day: The other side started it. Trimmings aside, the accusations of both Protector Powers were identical. So close together and so much alike were the two camps just before the end. But by then the joke that had made us laugh caught on.

Listen to this, sonny, cried the She-rat. Once it became impossible to take back any first or second strike, once no border or enemy was discernible and no sign of life could be heard, not even in code, when good old venerable Europe was pacified once and for all, baffling, inconceivable, unheard-of foreign bodies were found in the Western Protector Power's enormous central computer which, having been programmed for the global end game, was built like an amphitheatre. At first just a few, then more and more fingernail-sized pellets, which were identified as shit, excrement, faeces, then with no attempt at proof, as rat droppings, that's right, rat droppings.

The She-rat giggled. The word made her giggly. She repeated it in various tones of voice, spoke in ratgibber of kaporesh rottamosh and playing games with the language thought up silly variations on the fatal substance: doroping, pingador, poroding and so on. Finally, repeatedly interrupted by laughing fits, she reminded me of biblical times, when, to Noah's consternation, rat droppings . . . On the palm of God's hand! she cried and didn't calm down until I expressed doubts about this discovery of rat droppings and spoke of old wives' tales. That, I said, is an old wives' tale.

Getting back to my story, said the She-rat. While the exchange of strikes continued and spread to all Europe, a call was put through to the Eastern Protector Power's strategic central computer; good connection, incidentally, because both powers thought it in their interest to be able to converse by Red Telephone to the end. It developed that there, too, animal turds had been found in Security Section One, probably rat droppings. In any case, animal action had triggered off the 'Peace among Nations' programme. The highest authorities had countermanded the order, but to no avail, and everything was proceeding according to plan.

Even so, the She-rat went on, they talked to each other a while over the Red Telephone and, incidentally, as peaceably as can be. With unprecedented openness, the Protector Powers exchanged data concerning the foreign bodies. They compared findings and to the amazement of both parties came to the same conclusion. Put into direct contact, the High Muckamucks, as we called the chiefs of state, two old gentlemen, who up until then had had little to say to each other, and in their Sunday speeches only the worst, made an attempt to talk. After a bit of throat clearing, they did all right. Both old geezers were sorry they hadn't found a chance to converse before: tight schedules and all that. They began to chat, asked about each other's ailments, and had taken quite a liking to each other before mentioning the escalating second and third strikes of their peace systems, as though reporting bad news, the cause of which both declared to be first inexplicable, and then indubitable. On both sides the proofs were only too positive.

The She-rat hesitated. When she went on with her report, a note of regret had been injected into her voice. We rats, she said, are grieved to note that once the question of guilt came up the two Protector Powers found no difficulty in coming to an agreement. As soon as the alarm message – Rats in the Computer – came through, both sides agreed that they were confronted with a diabolical third power; both Peace Powers, they had to admit, were at the mercy of an international plot. Though it was too soon to say who was pulling the strings, it seemed obvious that a worldwide rat conspiracy was out to destroy the human race. A plan with a historical past: what the rats had attempted more than six hundred years ago by deliberately introducing the Plague, unsuccessfully despite the thousands on thousands of human victims, was now to be achieved by nuclear means. All this, the two High Muckamucks agreed, had its logic which, unfortunately, was not unlike human logic. Evidently this rat plan, perfected in every detail, was now being carried out. Why, those shameless rats had even given advance notice of their final solution. Too late, men were beginning to remember the demonstrations the rats had visited on all the world's big cities not so long ago and to fathom their meaning. Now, the High Muckamucks further agreed, we can understand the sudden disappearance of that prolific and widespread species. Ah, if we had only known how to interpret those omens before it was too late. Ah, if people had only taken alarm worldwide.

That's it, said the She-rat, if only. The Protector Powers, she assured me, had insisted to the end that neither one nor the other had pressed the button and that the 'Makepeace' and 'Peace among Nations' programme had been set in motion by rat instructions and, as is now known, simultaneously despite the time difference. And set in motion irrevocably, because the ultimate command power had been transferred to the central computers. The next phase of the peace-securing programme – the release of inter-continental missiles – was therefore a certainty. They were reciprocally on their way. May God or somebody else, the chiefs of state had called out to each other, protect our country and yours.

A pious but belated wish, said the She-rat. But no sooner had the two Protector Powers agreed on the guilt question than they began to curse the Third Power: Damn rats! Damn vermin! Ungrateful scum that we've fed for thousands of years and nursed back to health after periods of human famine. A third of the human production of corn, rye, wheat, rice and millet had gone for rat food; cotton harvests had been halved. And this is the thanks we get.

Still, said the She-rat, the powers confessed to a share of the guilt. Both chiefs of state admitted that precautions had been neglected in setting up the computer-aided security systems. The millions of chips and clips should have been poisoned. It would also have been advisable to equip the central computers with long-lasting ultra sound waves, that would have thrown the rats' hearing off. Nothing of the kind had been done. Who can think of such things, cried the High Muckamuck of the East, while the Old Man of the West, known for his homespun wit, had chosen to crack jokes. Have you heard this one, Mr Secretary General. A Russian, a German and an American arrive in heaven . . .

But then they joined in the same recriminations. Obviously the rats were to blame, though the possibility cannot be excluded that certain circles, or perhaps one should say, certain persons of a certain origin, or to come right out with it, persons of the Mosaic faith, but fanatical Zionists as well, in a word, Jews, an international conspiracy of Jews, may have had an interest in developing this diabolical plan, in breeding and training a hyper-intelligent strain of rats which, as has been known for thousands of years, have the same sort of slyness as Jews . . .

Again the She-rat laughed in her own way, but no longer loudly, more on the inside. Her body shook with laughter. She blurted out a few scraps of ratgibber – Futze Ivri! and Goremesh Ippush! but then stored-up bitterness restored her gravity. The rats and the Jews, the Jews and the rats are to blame. As once upon a time with the help of the Plague, so now with the help of nuclear fission. After all, it was mostly their invention. Their way of taking revenge. This is what they've always been after, their only aim. Diabolical, crafty, inhuman. So now Zion's wish is coming true. Obviously that inseparable pair, the Jews and the rats, are to blame.

That's how your High Muckamucks were going on, said the She-rat. And when they weren't accusing, the two old men were sympathizing with each other. Isn't it rough to be a chief of state? Stupid thing to happen! When negotiations were still in progress and they'd been coming closer and closer together, learning to trust each other.

But, I heard myself cry out in my dream, that's absurd.

Yes, said the She-rat, that's what it was all right: absurd.

How, I doubted, could rats?

But, she cried, who says it was us or the Jews?

Then it wasn't the rats after all?

We'd have been perfectly capable.

So then it was us humans who, contrary to all our declared intentions, ended it all?

It went off according to plan.

And no one wanted to stop ending it all?

Don't make me laugh, said the She-rat. She rolled up in a ball, as though getting ready to sleep.

Hey, She-rat! I cried out. Say something. Do something. That can't be your last word.

Then the She-rat said: All right. An anecdote to top it off. When the elderly chiefs of state in their end-game theatres were compelled to look on as their thousands upon thousands of intercontinental ballistic missiles, baptized 'Peacemaker', 'Peace Among Nations' and so on, approached their targets, namely the security centres, the High Muckamucks, through interpreters, begged each other's forgiveness. A thoroughly human gesture.

> My anger, a criminal with premeditation,
> must not erupt.
> Insight, that fence, which only foresight
> can penetrate, restrains it.

> And so from a distance, sated by stored-up anger,
> which has curdled and ripened as cheese ripens, I see
> how, quite rationally,
> attentive to detail, they are preparing the end.

> Unwavering archangels have qualified.

The Rat

They have shattered our petty fear, which wants to live,
to live at any price, as though life
as such were worth something.

What can I do with anger that can't erupt?
Waste it on letters, whose only result
is more letters, acknowledging
and deeply deploring the situation?

Or tame it,
direct it against fragile objects?
Or convert it into stone
that will remain after the end?

Fenced by no insight
my anger would at last be free,
my anger which must not erupt
would bear stony witness.

A space observer squeezed into a space capsule. What stops me
from getting out: if not over Sweden, then over the Bay of Bengal?
Why are dreams, which everything contradicts, compelling nevertheless? And whose logic governs dreams?

I am miscast. They haven't given me a cosmonaut's handbook.
Buckled in, naked under my night shirt. Unversed in cosmic space,
I've managed to make out the silly old moon, the Milky Way, the
Big Dipper, and by a stroke of luck a show-off planet named
Venus. Where, damn it all, is menacing Saturn? True, I know a few
astrological saws, I know how self-righteous Sagittarius is and how
hard Scorpio on the ascendant is on Libra. But I haven't the faintest
idea what lies beyond the fixed stars or what planets are. A washout
in cosmic matters, I was nevertheless obliged to be a witness.

Things were looking bad, even a little worse than in the movies
which, shortly before the end, found their apocalypse-minded
audiences and broke box-office records worldwide. I remembered
the excitement at the countdown and the solemnly opening silos.
They were masterfully made films, every degree of horror was
given naturalistic treatment. The new quota, so and so many
megadead, was met. So everything I saw from my space capsule
looked familiar to me.

So there's nothing to report. No need to describe the horror of it.

Nothing inconceivable happens. The worst prognoses are confirmed. It's enough if I say: Seen through the earth-oriented oval window of my space capsule, things everywhere, especially in Europe, looked bad, very very bad.

Nevertheless, still the fool that I couldn't help being, I cried out: Earth! Earth, come in! Answer, earth! Without fear of repetition I cried out for my blue planet, now burned to a crisp.

At first I heard scrambled words, but they gave me a familiar feeling, because I had heard a similar word mix in those technically perfect end-game films – abbreviations, curses, code numbers, etc. Then I was left alone with my voice, which echoed eerily. I tried to talk company into being – What do you say, Oskar? You looking forward to Poland and your grandmother? – or I did what I could to save the forests with a silent film, and off and on I tried to call my Damroka, get her to start the engine of the research ship – but only the She-rat, the She-rat, the She-rat stayed in the picture, now insistent, furious, her hair standing on end, every whisker alert.

She ignored my objections – What's the point of this, She-rat? I'm not fit for space travel. What at the start of this dream, assuming that this dream could have a beginning and an end, had struck her as funny, rat turds the size of little fingernails lying beside central computers, now supercharged her rage. Typical! We know the story. How convenient: Blaming us for human failure! We've always been the scapegoat, always. Were they beset by plague, typhus, cholera? By famine, high prices? The answer was always: The rats are our misfortune, and sometimes, or often in the same breath: The Jews are our misfortune. Such massive misfortune was more than they thought they could bear. So they sought relief in extermination. Before all other nations the Germans thought themselves chosen to liberate mankind, to determine who was a rat, and to exterminate, if not us, then the Jews. We were there, under and between the barracks in Sobibor, Treblinka, Auschwitz. Not that we camp rats were included in the count, but after that we knew how completely man is able to transform his fellow men into numbers that can be crossed out, simply crossed out. Cancellation, they called it. Just a matter of bookkeeping. How could they have spared us who, along with the Jews, were their cheapest subterfuge? Ever since Noah: it's their nature. And that's why to the bitter end: they're rats. They've destroyed. They've undermined. Obviously rats, Goddammit. And in all their computer systems, the Russian, the Yank. – Until their dying day, they childishly put the blame on us.

I'd never seen the She-rat of my dreams jump so frantically from image to image: here on the alert, there erect with bared teeth, here demonic, a whirling dervish. Why had she stopped laughing? Why wasn't she sharpening her wit on me, her whetstone? Nothing could have struck her as more ridiculous than me in my space capsule. She-rat, I cried. Laugh at me!

Still bitter. She kept explaining herself, she wanted to be innocent, to be acquitted. Now, after the fact, she demanded exact proof. As if I could have caused or prevented anything, she appealed to me as the ultimate authority: Tell me, why were they in such a hurry to call the droppings found in the central computers rat turds? Why did no one order an analysis of this faecal matter? Why couldn't some other rodents have triggered off the end-game programmes? Your cunning little golden hamsters, for instance? Or, as seems only too likely, couldn't it have been mouse shit that was found?

I affected indignation, spoke of block-transcending sloppiness. A scandal, I said, that no Yank, no Russian should have put the shit under a lens. But deep down, I thought: Obviously, it had to be the rats. Who but rats could have so deliberately . . .

Then, in an undertone, as though her rage had spent itself, she said: Over and over, the consequence of our supposed subversive activities was trumpeted to the world, as long as it had ears to hear with. 'Peacemaker' and 'Peace among Nations' programmes irremediably set in motion by subversives under foreign guidance. End of communiqué.

No longer jumping around the screen, quietly contemplative, her whiskers out of action, the She-rat said: We happen to know it was mice. Not on their own initiative. Too stupid for that. They acted according to a human plan. The idea was to paralyse the command computers of the Protector Powers with the help of trained mice. That way one power would be able to reduce the other to zero. Very clever.

They were laboratory mice, white with red eyes. We found that out from our laboratory rats, who weren't very bright either, but at least they were reliable. After years of tests, men learned to breed litters that could be trained to do programmed work as well as if they'd been fed on silicon. Of course the geneticists did their bit.

Anyway, the security organs of each Protector Power managed, as though responding to one and the same impulse, to smuggle these specialized mice into the enemy computer at the same time.

As the results showed, excellent work was done. Or perhaps my praise should be qualified: all it amounted to, after all, was putting programmed mice into critical positions. Thoughtfully, the She-rat added: as a matter of fact, they were poorly programmed, because the computer systems were not paralysed. Instead, the mice – what can you expect of mice? – triggered off the countdown in both computers. The result was the Big Bang.

But She-rat, I cried, that really is funny. In a way, she said, if you confine your thoughts to those stupid mice.

In my opinion, I said, it's much more plausible and sounds a lot nicer to speak of 'mice in the computer' than to voice the malicious imputation: Rats!

Yes, she agreed, cheerful again, though thoughtful, subdued. Basically this irony should amuse us. Despite the tragedy of it, isn't it apt that mice, cunning little laboratory mice, should have brought about the end of the proud, the glorious human race with all its multifarious abilities? Of course it sounds frivolous. No self-respecting person wants to be led off the stage in such an uninteresting way.

I had the impression that she was mulling something over.

Spit it out, I cried.

A certain something is missing.

Yes, I cried, perspective.

The whole thing, she said, looks like a thoughtless oversight, like the usual human bungling.

I agreed: a pathetic breakdown.

That, said the She-rat, is why I tend to think the original suspicion, based on rat droppings and resulting logically in the outcry: Rats in the computer, was not so wrong; because actually we, and not those stupid mice, should have gone into action. We'd have had reason enough at any time.

To economize on harbour fees in Stege and Klintholm, *The New Ilsebill* dropped anchor one Sunday off Møns Klint and started for Gotland on Monday. After giving me final instructions about the Malskat case, our Herr Matzerath decides to attend a coin auction on Wednesday, to set out on Thursday, to dash across Poland on

Friday, and to be in Kashubia on Saturday, before Anna
Koljaiczek's birthday. Because that's the way I want it, his
departure will be put off until Friday; but he seems to have left on
Sunday.

Sundays, says the She-rat of my dreams, Sundays have always
been catastrophic. This seventh day of a bungled creation was from
the first chosen to cancel it out. As long as men have existed, it was
always on Sunday – call it the Sabbath or whatever you like – that
the previous week was declared null and void.

In short! she cried, as usual when my misgivings – my whining! –
interfered with her flow of speech. In short: despite the tight
security attending their control systems, the mood in both central
bunkers was definitely Sundayish. All the monitors and the wide
intercontinental screens showed an unusual radiance. A certain
global pre-vacation mood prevailed. Though there wasn't a single
fly in those immense rooms, they buzzed as only Sunday boredom
can buzz. Anyone who took an interest in man's doings would have
been reminded of the seventh day of creation: Good job, though
room of course for improvement.

Of course there were spoilsports and pessimists outside the
central bunkers, who looked for hair in the soup even on Sundays.
Still, we had reason to be pleased with ourselves. True, Power was
up in arms against Power, but Power had secured itself against
Power by means of carefully graduated terror and supervised
supervision, by shifting all responsibility to chips and clips and
leaving no room in the decision-making process for human
bungling, for man's propensity, observed since Noah, for going
against the rules. That traditional factor of uncertainty, man – so
lovable, so spontaneous, by definition prone to error – continued to
perform certain secondary functions, but had been stripped of all
responsibility.

We saw him as unburdened, released, free in the higher sense.
That entitled him to venture a joke from monitor to monitor. Not
explicitly of course, but as a tacit concession, he was allowed, on
Sunday in the one Protector Power, to feed silly words into the
computer or to comment on the baseball scores, and in the other to
list and make witty comments on soccer scores, as long as nothing
was running on the master screens – and just then nothing was
running.

Oh, beautiful concord. Both sides had attained the highest degree of consciousness and took a childlike pleasure in so wide a range of knowledge. Global time and local time made possible comparisons to the effect that a radiant Sunday was coming up on one side and drawing to a close on the other. Routine inquiries made for still greater security. Besides, everyone knew that responsibility was at home somewhere else. Everyone's duties were secondary, and no mistakes were possible.

Global and local time passed. Dynamo Kiev and the Los Angeles Dodgers had won. Slight, by no means sensational shifts in the standings. Other harmless news. No earthquakes or tidal waves. No hijackings, not even a Putsch. Nothing unforeseen, except those strange, unprogrammed sounds in the central computers. After some turds were found more or less by accident, a minimal crackling was diagnosed – too late – as emanating from an independent energy source.

We have no Sunday, said the She-rat. But we knew that in the territories of both Protector Powers the human race indulged in Sunday, on which day people tended worldwide to be sleepy and subliminally irritable. It had always seemed to us that humans were capable of everything imaginable, and its opposite. That was how we knew them: lacking in concentration because deep in thought, lost in wishes or regrets, longing for love, thirsting for revenge, on the fence between good and evil.

We noted that man, inherently divided, was especially fragmented on Sundays. Not really present. Lost in the crush of his states of being. For all his willingness and zeal, he crumbled. In addition, human society seemed to be flooded by a shoreless melancholy, to delight in casting farewell glances at things it had learned to love; even at things that were impalpable and therefore clothed in concepts, such as God, freedom, or what it regarded as progress or reason. Even in the security centres this melancholy mood hovered over every device and instrument.

That's why the day of the Lord struck us as the best time. That's why it happened on a Sunday in early summer. In June, at the height of the sports season. As usual, we took advantage of the sewage system, made our way through the supply channels in the foundations of the central bunkers and entered the central computers from below. We had no trouble with the light metal, we knew our way around, we knew at a glance what went where with which, manipulated tiny little gadgets and fed in our code at the crucial place. Instantly it infected all the adjoining security systems, though in appearance it left the usual control programmes in force. Once our code word 'Noah' released all impulses, we began the countdown in both control stations, allowing of course for the time difference.

We, said the She-rat, merely set off what man had thought up: enough of it, in the words of their vengeful God, to destroy all flesh wherein is the breath of life. Many times over, in fact. That is how determined human beings were to destroy themselves and all other creatures. Shulas por erresh! she cried. Closing time on Earth!

As we replaced the ongoing programme almost soundlessly and people were not very alert on Sunday, no one recognized us, so we had to give hints. We left the building and placed our visiting cards outside. A risky undertaking, which owed its success to chance. Only then did the foreign bodies, which were soon found, permit of conjectures, then certainty. The end of all Sundays.

Since then we rats have spoken of the Big Bang. No, cried the She-rat, not at all. We regret nothing. It had to be. Too often we warned them in vain. Our processions in broad daylight were plain enough. Yet nothing that might have appeased our concern was done. Absurd, or hardly worth mentioning, were the hysterical reports that were going around shortly before the last of all Sundays. For instance, of loose cloud formations over the western Baltic that seemed to form a picture, no, not isolated clouds drifting from northwest to southeast, but an endless procession of small clouds, hundreds of thousands of them, covering southern Sweden, then Gotland: running rat-clouds, cloudily running rat nations, no, not little lamb-clouds, definitely clouds in the shape of grey rats, outstretched, in a hurry, their long tails extending like hyphens between rat and rat. All this, this terrifying sign from heaven, had reportedly been seen from Danish islands, from ships and from the shores of the Baltic Sea, seen and photographed and interpreted as a warning from God. Even atheists had cried out: A typical apocalypse!

Don't you believe it, young friend. There were lots of things we could do, lastly to destroy the Day of Rest by setting off the human 'Peacemaker' and 'Peace Among Nations' programmes. But to produce cloud pictures, magnify ourselves into signs from heaven, no, that is beyond our powers.

Objection, She-rat! You still exist in your white enamelled cage, on sawdust litter, which I shall replenish tomorrow for the sake, my growing Christmas rat, of your future wellbeing. And I, too, exist, sitting beside you with file cards. Our plans harry the calendar. The ship should dock punctually in Visby. The punks' trip to Hamelin has been scheduled. When our Herr Matzerath, provided with a valid visa, starts for Poland, we shall wish him a pleasant journey, but previously ask him to suggest some additional presents for his grandmother, which can be stowed in the luggage compartment of his Mercedes.

We see him take leave of his coin collection, which, before he starts out, will move to his safe at the bank. We see him weighing General Mansfield's double ducats, the half louis d'or, the Prussian wilhelmdor, the gold ruble from the days of Nicholas II, a handful of Saxon and Nassau talers, and are moved to see how hard it is for him to take leave of his gold, for he beds some of the pieces on velvet in the drawers of a casket, the Bavarian maxdor, for instance, the priceless Danzig Siegesmund August ducat minted in 1555, a few decadrachms from Thrace, and the freshly minted twenty-four-carat Chinese coin, showing a panda in all its delicious drollness – and yet we have the impression that he is not taking leave of his gold for good, that he knows even now, in advance of his return, how much more his treasures will be worth, though the price of gold is falling daily.

And as he now puts further yields of his numismatic excursions into a casket, which is to accompany him on his trip to Poland, a one-ounce Krugerrand, figuring the likeness of the African spring-bok, Swiss vreneli of various weights, a Hohenlohe memorial taler that glistens as though fresh off the mint, and two commemorative coins minted in the Soviet Union and having as their subjects the dancer Ulanova and the singer Chalyapine, we cannot help wondering on the one hand what this departure and on the other hand what this selection means. Is he unable to part with his gold? Is it his intention to gratify Poland with gold? Now he's putting in Mexican coins and now at last adding the world-dominating US dollar gold piece.

Whatever our Herr Matzerath is planning, he is thinking of the future and is struggling from deadline to deadline; just as I, too, have planned even my excuses in detail; or the ship that has changed course en route; or the painter Malskat, whom, no sooner had he finished decorating the Schleswig Cathedral according to his taste, further High Gothic commissions awaited. From spring to September 1939 he helped the Holy Ghost Hospital in Lübeck to gain prestige. This the people of the Hanseatic marzipan-and- Malskat-trial city are still unwilling to accept. Authentic Gothic, cry the art experts to this day. Authentic Malskat! says the now embittered painter, sure of his own handwriting, who has retired to an island in the Deepen Moor, to which one can only accede by ferry.

In the Holy Ghost Hospital, he says when questioned, I painted authentically enough to fool anybody, until I was called to the army. For, a few months before Malskat was drafted, the Second World War had begun on all Poland's borders.

Malskat had to take leave of reddish-brown contour paint, of wire brush and dustbag, of serene solitude in the high scaffoldings of German religious edifices, of draughts and summer colds, but Private Malskat never stopped hoping that one church or another would be opened to him when the war was over, and allow him to gladden its choirs, buttresses, and window jambs – always high up, beyond the reach of dating procedures – with his Gothic hands.

What about us? We hope no less. My Christmas rat and I are still setting our hopes in our well-regulated life, the pauses in which are filled by the Third Programme. Hey, we're still here. We exist, commented in every detail. We hear what's on, what's taking place, what's been postponed. To us even water level announcements are a message. We have not given either ourselves or the forests up. We are future-fans, even though I, admittedly, am attuned to loss deep down; because when I dreamed I had to take leave of all things, I also dreamed I had to take leave of all flesh wherein is living breath . . .

With new bleached or dyed wool on board, which they had bought in Stege, not in any of the bargain sale shops with their *udsalg* signs, but in a wool shop with stable prices, the ship has dropped anchor an exact sea mile off Møns Klint, facing the steep chalky coast, which rises so high that from its wooded hills the hills of Hiddensee Island off Rügen can be seen in good weather. They have dropped their double anchor at a significant spot.

Damroka calls them all on deck. She reels off all the Danish names from Dronningeskamlen to Dronningestolen to Hytjedals Klint to Lilleklint. In the morning sun the chalk cliffs emanate a radiance that makes the green sea at its feet cloudy-milky; shaded at sunset, the coast becomes menacing. Crevasses that were sharply delineated a short while before have lost their chiaroscuro. The pale mountain looks forbiddingly at the sea, whose grey has taken on the camouflage colouring of east-western warships.

'This is the exact spot,' says the helmswoman, 'where the women are supposed to have let the Flounder go in the hope of something or other.' But she doesn't call him. She doesn't try to encourage him: 'Say something, Flounder!' or to revile him: 'You crook, you liar, you shit.'

Sitting in the lee of the pilot house, looking at the smooth sea or the crevassed chalk cliffs, four of the five women are knitting and talking about themselves, as though having to get rid of remnants – *udsalg*, clearance sale of long-drawn-out grievances, that they'd been sitting on.

The Old Woman isn't knitting but she too talks about herself while peeling potatoes, scrubbing carrots, gutting herrings; she puts the milt and roe back into the gutted fish. They are tasty Baltic herrings which are smaller than the North Sea variety and are seen on the market more and more rarely.

The women's talk changes, but always tells the same story, always revolves around cast-off, worn-out, hard, tired, aggressive, unsuccessful men, lovable for a time, now dull, in short, men of the past. And around various men's children all of whom claim – so rich in years are the women on board *The New Ilsebill*, and not only the Old Woman, who has stopped counting hers – to be children no more, but grown men.

The helmswoman mentions three daughters by name, each begotten by a different father. 'Well,' she says, 'they're independent now, they won't let themselves, the way I always did because I believed much too long and listened to the rot about two people being able to live together. Nothing ever came of it. And afterwards nothing was left. Only the girls, for whom I did everything, but everything, in the hope of stopping them from walking into the trap like stupid me.'

Then she, who contrary to all her talk is knitting a three-man sweater, says good and bad things about the fathers of her daughters: 'The first drank, the second whored around, the third was out for a career. I can't complain. I didn't lose much by it. All three were touching in their way, but kind of broken down. It just went on too long. And every time I was the victim. Well, now at last I'm through with the whole business.'

The engineer on the other hand still can't make up her mind between two men, both of whom, the one an Israeli, the other a Palestinian, live in Jerusalem, and are not prepared to be one and the same man. She keeps saying: 'Fantastic. If only the two of them could have been baked into one man, he would have been tops. They weren't nearly as different as they thought when they looked at each other through their sunglasses. They could have been good friends, even business partners, they both had a thing about cars. Why not a workshop together? Used cars or something. But they always had to tear each other apart. And me in between like a silly goose. I didn't know what was right any more, not even politically. And how well they talked, always so logical. Neither would give in. And me back and forth. They'd get so mad. You keep out of it. They used me. They'd say behind my back: Let's see who can win her over, this German woman with her complexes. They were right about that. Two suitcases full, brought with me from home. I always wanted to make everything right. Reconcile the two, possibly turn them into brothers, well, mould them into one guy. But they saw only themselves. Then one fine day I cleared out with the baby that one or the other of them had squirted into me. I even left a note on the table: Drop me a line if you ever get together. But even if they do, I don't want them any more. I'm fed up.' And the engineer goes on knitting men's socks.

Then she talks about the boy. 'He's just refused to do military service,' she says, wanting them all to know whom the socks are for. And the oceanographer knits baby clothes, because, as she says, she became a grandmother 'much too soon,' always pink and baby-blue baby clothes.

Everything that ever happened to her, most of which went wrong or wasn't quite right, happened too soon or too late, so she always ends or introduces her stories with a time reference: 'I should have known that before, or suspected it at least. By then of course it was too late. If I'd gone to London alone at the right time, before going to Brussels years too late. But I didn't realize until too late, when it was all over. Because if I'd taken up oceanography in the first place instead of later at Interpreters' School, and taken a degree and then another degree, I'd still be a housewife, but a housewife with a degree. Oh, no. A baby and another and another

Günter Grass

and every one of them too soon. And divorce too late. And the new guy much too soon. And now that I'm getting to be myself, just myself, I'm becoming a grandmother much too soon. Isn't it funny?'

'Man!' cries the Old Woman, who isn't knitting for anyone, just scrubbing carrots. 'Man! Are you females nuts! As if all the shit that's lying around were men's shit. I had only one and he's dead. He was what he was, and I wanted him. I don't know if it was too soon or too late. He was there and he stayed on. Then, bingo, he died on me. But he didn't make room for other guys. No, he's still there. Not half and half. He's just the way he was. No, not simple, more on the cussed side. And he did bad things. What things, oh my God! I had a lot to put up with. Sometimes. Or sometimes I'd just look the other way. I thought: he'll come back to me. And he always did. But once he came around with a girl from Wiesbaden. A clothes horse. He wanted me to be friends with her. She was young and tops in every way, her name was Inge. It's her or me, I said. He didn't puzzle his head for long. And after that butter wouldn't melt in his mouth. The times were hard enough as it was. Either it was prewar or postwar, with war in between. Like today, when it can break out any minute.' The Old Woman gestures disparagement. 'Real love,' she cries out. 'That's the only kind that counts.'

Damroka says nothing, just knits at her wool-remnant blanket, which would be big enough to keep all five women warm. Before the helmswoman can take over, she says: 'I've always been good at love, because I'm so slow. If you don't know when it's beginning and when it's ending, you avoid the worst suffering. Even when there was nothing there, I loved all the same. After all, you can't keep it to yourself. And men, oh well! The one I've got now makes an effort and he's there more or less, when he's not travelling . . .'

Now she falls silent, because she's so slow and has to catch up with herself. But when she sees all the fish filled with milt and roe that the Old Woman has lined up head to tail on the chopping board, she counts the herrings, counts to eleven, and can't help laughing because as she counts, her servitude on the organ bench repeats on her.

'You know the story,' says Damroka. 'In seventeen years eleven pastors. And I've got all eleven behind me. About the first there's nothing more to be said. You know about the second, too. The third passed away in the nick of time. The fourth was a born-again Swabian. Didn't know a thing about liturgy but even on the toilet seat the Lord Jesus spoke to him . . .'

One by one, she listed her blackskirts: 'The fifth was from Uelzen he had a thing about liqueurs . . .' She omits none. 'The sixth tried it both ways . . .' – 'The seventh's wife ran away with the sexton . . . The eighth and the ninth . . .'

In between, the other knitting women talk as though in fear of losing the thread, and not until late afternoon, when the chalk cliffs lie deep in shadow, does the suspicion dawn that they might soon run out, not of wool, but of men, that there's nothing more to be got out of them. In silence they eat potatoes cooked with carrots and seasoned with butter and parsley, and eleven fried herrings. Pale-grey, the chalk cliffs of Møn come closer. Because everything has been said, no one wants to say any more. Such stories only make you sleepy.

The engineer in the lead, the women go to the forecastle. Though the boat is almost motionless, their hammocks are swinging side by side. The Old Woman clatters awhile with the dish-washing, then she too climbs down the companionway. Only the starboard hammock jiggles unoccupied. Damroka has stayed on deck with her coffee pot. 'Just listening to the weather report,' she calls out. 'I'll be right down – later.'

Because the summer night comes on so slowly in the north, now that the black cloudbank in the northwest is breaking up, little fleecy cloudlets are drifting across a still-light sky. Crowded tatters. Cloud animals on the run, running and running. No wind on the water, but up there it's blowing. My Damroka, however, is not trying to read the heavens. She wants advice from somewhere else.

Behind the pilot house she calls the Flounder. Three times. The Flounder, who in former times spoke only to men, who, for better or worse, busied himself exclusively with the male cause, whose advice was expensive, until his long story came to a a bad end, whereupon he repented and resolved to answer women alone from then on; he, the thrice-called Flounder, answered Damroka from behind the stern, where she is squatting with her hair tumbling over her knees.

What the two of them are saying rushes past me. Slowly her questions form; he answers succinctly. I do not see the Flounder, who presumably lies almost within reach, just below the surface of the water. But I do see the other women, climbing up the companionway from the forecastle. The helmswoman in the lead. Grouped around an oil lamp, they keep their distance. The Old Woman holds the lamp. If I were below deck now, I could lie down in their hammocks. But I mustn't. I'm outside. I too have been dismissed.

Damroka has finished her conversation with the Flounder. She is still squatting there, her hair is still tumbling over her knees. She's not surprised to see the other women gathered around the lamp in the forecastle. Coming closer step by step in the lamplight, the four of them form an image. The Old Woman with the lamp in the lead. 'Well?' she says. 'What does he know?'

Damroka speaks calmly, allowing herself pauses, but leaving no room for backtalk. She gives no orders, she merely states the case: 'It's urgent. We're weighing anchor right away. Heading straight for Gotland. To pick up our stamped papers. That leaves only half a day for going ashore at Visby. We won't bother with the jellyfish any more. He says the end is near. He says: At the latest by Saturday before sunset we've got to be off to Usedom, over Vineta Deep.'

The piles of grey and black stones
fallen from the chalk, which are lying
off the coast of Møn, are said to be
older than we can imagine.

Summer after summer we are tourists,
We crane our necks
and look up at the tops of the chalk cliffs,
which are known as *klinter* and have Danish names.
And then we see what lies heaped up at our feet
below the *klinter*: flints rounded like bodies,
some with a sharp cleft.

More and more rarely,
only when luck grazes us like the wings of a gull,
do we find animals turned to stone,
a hedgehog for instance.

Leave of Møn and the view across the water.
Leave of the island of summer and children
on which we might have grown older and more Danish.

The Rat

Leave of beech forests surrounded by radar installations which
are supposed to screen us.

If only we could bed ourselves in chalk and survive ourselves
until, in exactly seventy-five million years,
new-style tourists arrive and, touched by good luck,
find parts of us petrified: my ear,
your pointing finger.

Chapter Five, *in which a space capsule orbits, our Herr Matzerath takes a dark view, the She-rat deplores insufficient fear, the city of Gdańsk remains outwardly intact, the women quarrel over jellyfish, Hansel and Gretel call for action, the education of the human race is continued, and a prize oration is delivered.*

WHILE I tried to dream vacation prospectuses, she said: When at length the central bunkers of both Protector Powers took each other as targets and after a predetermined time were wiped out, so that nothing capable of saying boo was left – because our specialized rats carried out their mission to the end; when everything shut down worldwide, over the waters and in cosmic space, except for the circular storms that distributed the accumulated dust and soot, so that all was darkness, in a word Doomsday, one and only one harmless observation satellite remained true to its orbit. Actually, it turned out to be manned, for its inmate, a little man unversed in technology, familiar neither with the language of astronauts nor with the data communicated by his still functioning instruments, and whose aptitude for cosmic missions seemed questionable, kept shouting Earth, Answer Earth. As we couldn't help feeling sorry for him, we told him how God-forsakenly he was describing his orbit, told him why humans had stopped transmitting, and that there was no one left on earth but us. As soon as we emerged from our flight corridors, which was not without danger, we cried out: Don't be afraid, friend. We won't leave you in the lurch. Whenever you shout 'Earth! Answer Earth!' we'll be answering from now on.

No! I yelled. How am I going to talk about my Damroka if the She-rat keeps interrupting? How can her hair luxuriate on my paper if smooth fur is forced on me in every dream? How can I say: From Møn's steep chalky coast the women steered a course toward Gotland in the eastern Baltic, if this journey, as well as that of our Herr Matzerath, who is bent on going to Poland, has been over and done with since yesterday – or tell me, She-rat, when was Doomsday – over and done with for ever? Ah, if there were hope somewhere, a spark of life, some furtive human sign to tell me: We're still here. We're alive and kicking. A few survivors are starting all over again with pick and shovel. In the future we shall . . .

Yes, of course, said the She-rat. That's what you always liked to think after disasters in movies or in life. Final scene: a few damaged but surviving heroes, plus an ultramodern version of Noah's rescue ship, and the eternal good news that your history goes on. But, we regret to say, your history is finished.

Again her voice oozed compassion. O man! Surviving him, we shall miss him. Too long in his shadow, we ask ourselves: Is the rat even conceivable without man? Though capable of enduring man's grandiose legacy, we might nevertheless languish. What if corrosive yearning for mankind should eat away our marrow? Ah, we said to ourselves right after the Big Bang, if only we could keep them with us, just a few specimens at least. And even before the end, we cried out: Dosh minsher hissoreth! What are we without his stories, in which we have certified our place? What would be left of us without his dread that there might be a rat somewhere, possibly baring his teeth in the toilet bowl? While the human era was still in force, though perceptibly drawing to a close, we foresaw that man's demise would mean sorrow and wanted to preserve him in reasonable numbers. Unfortunately, only one exemption proved possible. Ah, if it weren't for you orbiting in your space capsule, you, full of stories and curly-headed lies, you, our friend, faithfully preserving the image of man for us, we rats would be reduced to despair.

Thus the She-rat lamented. But while she yearned for us, our demise was being enacted indisputably. And yet I disputed, cited present facts. As if there were a chance of shaking off my dream, I shouted my No No No! I conjured up the Third Programme: We shall shortly hear the Review of the Press. Shortly, something else will be real. I said: There will soon be lead-free petrol. I contended: Famine will cure itself. I told her about the next economic summit,

which would undoubtedly take place, about efforts being made by
the peace movement in Stockholm and elsewhere, even about the
Pope and his next scheduled journey. With all due allowance for
scepticism, I cried, we can hope again. I rejected reality. Listen to
me, She-rat, I concluded, this very day I am going to plant a tree.

She spoke to me as one might speak to a child: Splendid, my boy.
Keep it up. Dream anything you can think of. Women, as many as
are good for you, Malskatian Gothic, your Herr Matzerath's gold
ducats. Your subterfuges appeal to us. Don't let our knowledge
bother you. Act as if the human race were still there. Go on
believing you still exist, numerous and industrious. You have
plans. You want to save the forests. Let them revive, let the research
ship sail, let those women you're so fond of count all the jellyfish
and herring larvae in the Baltic Sea, let the painter go on painting
Gothic madonnas and turkeys on lime mortar, and let your hump
back little man finally start for Poland. If he doesn't, his visa may
lapse.

And another thing, said the She-rat, before fading out. Keep on
listening to your Third Programme, as if there were still news.

I ought to advise him against it. He should send a wire: 'Sorry
illness cannot come.' His prostate could be inflamed. His grandmother would understand. Good old Anna Koljaiczek has always
understood everything.

He really shouldn't be expected to take this trip; it's a journey
back. Too much of the past might come to life and move him and
frighten him. Suddenly removed from his executive office, his
outsized desk, his rubber plants, he'd have a background again, a
source; there'd be the Kashubian stable smell.

He should be treated gently, because when asked about his
childhood our Herr Matzerath always escapes into comfortable
irrelevances. He mentions the fall from the cellar steps only
casually, calls his growth during the period in question 'inhibited'
or 'hesitant', as though the early phase of his life were still a source
of pain to him. True, he does not contradict the stories that have
come down to us about his progress and adventures in the Danzig
suburb of Langfuhr, his excursions into the Old City and out to the
Kashubian hinterland, but he refuses to confirm any episode, such
as his contribution to the defence of the Polish Post Office or his
glass-oriented exploits on top of the Stockturm. As for his

grandstand number and brief guest performance on the Atlantic Wall, he leaves the question open and says at the most: 'My childhood and youth were not devoid of unusual happenings.' Or he says: 'You of all people shouldn't believe everything that's written there, though it's true that my early childhood unrolled more imaginitavely than certain scribblers suppose.'

Most often our Herr Matzerath says nothing and smiles only with the tips of his lips. Persistent questions get a harsh rebuff: 'Let's leave my childhood under wraps and think about tomorrow's weather. The forecast is rain. Disgusting.'

That's why I say he shouldn't take this trip. There's no going back. It could be a one-way trip. You can't fool with a prostate, it's sensitive, irritable. There's no point in saying that he needs his background. A successful businessman can live without a background. Düsseldorf offers examples enough. When I called on him yesterday in Upper Kassel to say goodbye, I felt that in spite of all the lifeless rooms his villa was right for him. 'Oskar,' I said, 'you'd better not go.'

He wouldn't listen, told me about Maria and her daily worries over young Kurt – 'The little rascal is running up debts, debts all over the place!' – called the obese quadragenarian a misbehaved brat, then led me first into the basement museum and later into the drawing room, all the while supplying explanations, as though finding it necessary to show me his treasures from the fifties, such as the collected shards of valuable glasses as well as his recent acquisitions. His words 'I've always had a special relationship to glass' offended me. Not until we were looking at the framed photos of Bebra, the once popular musical clown, did he recognize me as contemporary and say: 'You know that Bebra's success as a concert manager was based on my talent for public relations. Oh, what box-office triumphs!' And the transition: 'That was during my career as a solo entertainer' – took him back to his favourite themes, the early fifties, himself, Maria and little Kurt, but also the painter Malskat, whom he likes to contemplate in the company of the leading statesmen of the day.

When he asked me to supply particulars – 'I'm a stickler for detail' – I again promised to make up for lost time, but deplored the fact that very little material was available about Malskat's military career from spring 1940 to May 1945, expressed cautious misgivings about lumping two such antithetical statesmen with the belated Gothic painter and going so far as to call them a triumvirate. Then changing the subject, I came right out with it and asked our Herr Matzerath what presents he had bought for his grandmother's hundred and seventh birthday.

He spoke of visits to numismaticians and showed me an enamelled casket suitable for keeping coins in. 'In addition,' he said 'a *baumkuchen* of impressive height has been ordered and delivered. My gifts also include a special video programme; I'm curious to know how my Kashubians with their belief in miracles will react to it.'

Our Herr Matzerath went on to talk whimsically about a bag full of smurfs, which he plans to distribute among the newest generation of Kashubian children. He lifted the canvas bag, held it as though hefting a treasure, and cried out: 'A hundred and thirty of them! Look!' Reaching into the bag, he took out a handful at random. 'All hard-working little fellows. Look. One of these smurfs is a mason, another a mechanic. Here are two smurfs playing tennis, these two are drinking beer. Some are tillers of the soil, wielding the pick or the scythe. And here's the village band: one plays the trumpet, another the flute, this one plucks the double bass and this one – look, will you! – is beating a red-and-white drum.'

Once that hitherto shunned word had dropped, our Herr Matzerath fell silent for a time, and after that he spoke only of business matters. He paced the floor with short steps, his hands clasped below his hump. He spoke of increasing competition in the video market, of theft, highway robbery, video pirates. It would be difficult, he said, to finance anything as old-fashioned as a wide-screen film; but conceivably the dying forest was a subject capable of prying loose a government subsidy; of course, there'd have to be a subplot or two. 'For instance,' he suggested, 'Rumpelstiltskin might fall in love. That's it. With the girl with the chopped-off hands. There'd be room for some heart-rending scenes.' Next he wanted to know whether in a silent *Grimm's Forest* film a happy ending would be conceivable or at least feasible. 'All fairy tales don't have to end badly.'

At length, Oskar stood before an athlete-size mirror, plucked at his tie, stood this way, stood that way in full figure, took a brush and freshened the silvery wreath of hair around his glinting tanned scalp. While the electricity was still crackling in his hair, he asked:

'By the way, how's your Christmas rat? And are you still having such catastrophic dreams?'

When leaving I wished him a pleasant trip and asked him casually whether by any chance the *baumkuchen* erected for Anna Koljaiczek measured ninety-four centimetres in height, our Herr Matzerath managed a smile of sorts, but his eyes went round with fear. Now that the time has been set for his departure – he's finally going tomorrow – he thinks he can hear the darkness growing.

He ought to send a telegram. He ought to take my advice. A man who fears the worst at every step shouldn't go to Poland. Our Herr Matzerath is terrified.

How often we've wondered: Why? But since the Big Bang we've known what was wrong with you people. You were short on fear, said the She-rat. Dosh minsher kiyummes balemosh, she repeated in ratgibber, then went on talking about us in a more conversational tone. True, she said, man was anxious about all sorts of things and took out insurance against everything, even bad weather and adultery; more and more he dreamed of insurance against every possible risk, but while petty fears flourished and turned a quick buck, the great fear had crumbled, so to speak. At the altar of the great god Security, you cried out to one another: We want no more fear. We refuse to be frightened. Deterrence is the thing. And deterrence, above all, must be credible. The Russians know that. The Americans know it. The more we deter each other, the more secure we shall be.

You took heart, said the She-rat. By means of mutual deterrence you gradually banished fear. Fear was outlawed, forbidden to show its face. No one wanted to be seen with it. In the end, humans were too cowardly to be afraid; and anyone who continued to show fear, or like the punks displayed it in the form of rats, was shoved aside. You wanted to be free of fear, just as you wanted to be free from worry, from sin, from debts, just as you have always wanted to be free from responsibility, inhibitions, scruples, rats and Jews. But humans who are liberated from fear are especially dangerous.

After hissing awhile in angry ratgibber, the She-rat said: We saw that lack of fear made you first blind, then stupid. One of the heroic slogans on your posters was 'No sacrifice is too great for freedom'. But you had long sacrificed your freedom to the idol Security. You were the opposite of free, you were the prisoners of an all-embracing technology, which kept everything, even your last accumulated doubts, under lock and key, so in the end you were made free from responsibility. You fools! Feeding your last vestiges of reason like crumbs of cheese to voracious computers, handing the responsibility over to them. Yet buried within you there was fear thrice denied, tied, packaged, forbidden to come out, to show itself, to scream: Mamma!

Look, said the She-rat. We were afraid and showed it, you could have come to us and said: Teach us, dear rats, to cohabit with you. We humans have been stupid enough to think we were self-sufficient. Everything we did, though, squeezed into rhyme, fashioned into pictures, many-voiced music, hubristic towers, was aimed at immortality. But lately we have been plagued by the thought that in the future you alone would exist, and we wouldn't. Teach us, we implore you, to be immortal alongside of you. Never again shall we harm you in word or deed. Please, teach us.

Nonsense, we'd have cried, said the She-rat. We'd have been aghast at the thought. We too are mortal. Even rats are temporal, we have always known ourselves to be limited in time. But if we'd been able to teach you anything, the first lesson would have been this: From now on human educators will stop talking about immortality. Man lives as long as he lives. After death he is nothing. And only garbage will remain of him. Therefore, ye men, be afraid, fear and be mortal like us. Then perhaps you will live a little longer.

But they didn't come to us, said the She-rat. They were drunk on their endgame. No warning helped. Free of charge, we displayed our fear-driven nature. Only when our last attempt to inculcate the fear that is essential to life in these people who were free from fear – we produced grey-black clouds in the shape of fleeing rats – resulted in nothing better than Bible quotations and stupid remarks about phantasms, was our patience at an end. We gave up on humans, and finished them off before they could take us by surprise and press the button . . .

I said nothing. Keep talking, She-rat, keep talking.

She spoke for some time in didactic generalities. But then she noticed me in my space capsule and said: You, little friend, hear us and understand – but too late. Dosh minsher nibbelet ultemosh, as we used to say. And yet we have good news for you. In your region, where you grew up, things still look pretty much as they did before; there's quite a lot of Gothic. That may surprise you, but that's how it was planned, on the basis of man's last caring insight.

Take a look! she said, but apart from herself brought nothing into the picture. She merely explained that four or five conservation bombs exploded over Gdańsk had destroyed all life in the city and the environing Vistula estuary including Kashubia, but that because the blast had been minimal and the multiple warhead had exploded at an altitude of nine hundred metres, the city's historical buildings had all been spared, as had the nearby housing developments and port installations. All that was now intact. Only the wooden Crane Gate had burned and the window panes, even in the churches, were all gone.

In other places, she said, it looks bad. The industrial city of Gdynia and the neighbouring cities of Weijnerovo and Sopot were razed, but in your home town life would still be possible. Though during the period of bitter cold and crushing darkness storms spread soot, dust and ashes over everything that was still standing, the cityscape is unimpaired; its beauty lives on, you ought to be pleased.

The She-rat's ensuing lecture was so technically long-winded that it bored me even in my dream. To give the gist: These specialized weapons were a development on the neutron bombs first produced for the short-range Lance rocket, which met with opposition early in the final phase and might have been banned, because the fact that they spare only solid, inanimate bodies was thought to be inhuman. It cannot be our task to refute this notion from the rat's point of view, but this much at least can be said in favour of the system which was later perfected: the production of neutron bombs effective over broad areas made it possible to protect cultural monuments. And both Protector Powers possessed this potential for preserving cultural treasures. To the best of our knowledge, quite a few groups of architectural monuments have remained intact worldwide. Jerusalem, unfortunately, despite multilateral efforts, was lost, but the cluster of pyramids near Gizeh have survived in the form with which we too are familiar. In the nick of time, an agreement between the two Protector Powers provided for an evenhanded number of no-bomb zones, and the central computers were reprogrammed accordingly before it was too late.

At the end of her lecture, the She-rat, who up until then had been as it were unlocalized in my dream, was sitting in a cunningly wrought fifteenth-century copper pitcher of Flemish origin. Impelled by the force of the lecture, the pitcher kept rolling and the She-rat was obliged to run as on a treadmill.

Isn't it lovely? she cried. Isn't it beautiful and worth preserving?

That pitcher and similar pieces, I said, are known to me from the museum on Fleischergasse. Even as a schoolboy I was wild about art, and often visited the museum. With a sketching pad and a head full of fleas. Sometimes I even went during intermission, because the school was right next door . . .

And this museum piece from Fleischergasse, said the She-rat in her rolling pitcher, has survived along with other art objects, thanks to the bomb which in the last years of the human era was called 'the friend of the arts', though it was known how strictly limited this friendship was . . .

With a quick leap she left the Flemish copper pitcher, which continued for a long while to clank while in the foreground the She-rat went on with her report: Similar images everywhere. In the preserved cultural centres of the West, humans shrank, because before death set in all moisture was removed from them. Months after the Big Bang, when the cold and darkness abated and we emerged into the still-dingy light and started cleaning up, we saw leathery little men, mostly on all fours, crawling but apparently trying in vain to hoist themselves, as though their last impulse were to regain their capacity to stand erect. What a gesture! What tragic body language! We were reminded of early Gothic ecstasy. No, never had man found more powerful expression than in his final dehydrated state.

I saw the past conjured up by the She-rat of my dreams, saw bodies shrunken to dwarflike proportions lying on streets and squares, trying, entwined, to hoist themselves, saw them outside soot-blackened Renaissance palaces and on the porches of gabled Gothic buildings, at the portals of brick churches, all sublimely beautiful under the soot, arches both round and pointed intact, not a pillar cracked, all saints present, not a tower fallen, not a keystone, not a finial, not a roof turret missing; man, on the other hand, was no more than a shell, a mummy of himself, good, as I could see, for rat food, nothing more.

Nobody listens to me. It was bound to happen. True, *The New Ilsebill* is heading full speed (eight knots) for Gotland over a calm sea, but on shipboard opinions are brutally at variance.

The women are quarrelling. How soft and shrill, how harsh and barbed, how wounding they can be. Tragedies about queens getting in each other's way have remained playable down through the ages. Immortal roles. Voices hurling curse and anathema. Profiles more sharply etched. Imploring hands raised heavenward. Distended index fingers, entreaties. Hair roiled like the inner psyche. One gesture throws away, another gathers in. The way they stride back and forth, take the open deck as a stage, stand firm or elastic and never let the tension die down, is indicative of long practice. Only persons sure of being more beautiful when quarrelling can quarrel like this.

But what are they quarrelling about? Whose property is to be held, won back, shared? What crown, O Queens, is contested?

It's about the ship's course: Should, as planned, the skerries of southern Sweden be searched for medusas, or must the *Ilsebill*, just because the Flounder has spoken, make straight for Visby on Gotland and thence, as though driven by the flatfish, hurry to the flat coast of Usedom?

'The jellyfish must have precedence,' said the helmswoman. 'Won't you ever get it through your heads that the Baltic Sea is going to die one of these days? Not only in depths under thirty metres. No. The whole sea is going to be stinking dead.'

'But in eighty-one Kiel Bay was as good as dead. The following year – here are the readings, see for yourself – it came back to life. A change of climate helped, sufficient wind, a shift in the currents.' This is the oceanographer, who, because she's sick of it all and not just of oceanography, has decided she wants to go to Vineta with Damroka.

From out of wind-blown hair the helmswoman screams: 'Climate. Wind. That's a lot of shit. Such fluctuations are beyond human influence. The sea is dying and that's that. It's the trend.' The engineer joins in. 'But what about the jellyfish? Our beautiful medusas that shimmy and shake? Our damned *Aurelia aurita* that we're supposed to be studying?'

Because Damroka has several times calmly forbidden any hauling with the 'shark' and silently kept on course, the oceanographer talks in her stead: 'Basically, the jellyfish are proof that the

Baltic is alive, because where there's life there's plankton. And where there's plankton there are plenty of herring larvae. And where there's a lot of herring larvae and plankton, in Kiel Bay for instance, there's a conspicuous lot of jellyfish. Get me?'

'Sure,' screams the helmswoman, 'and in the end the whole sea will be jellyfish. One enormous *Aurelia aurita*.'

The engineer sticks to her guns. 'Our job is . . .'

Damroka says nothing. The Old Woman shakes her head and listens. When there's a pause she says from the galley, 'You're off your rockers' or 'Bicker bicker!' or 'Leave me alone with your dam' jellyfish or I'll cook you some with leeks and dill.'

True, the women are arguing about the course, but under the surface they are carrying on a private quarrel that never grows old, a quarrel that seems to be imbricated and multistoried. Sharp-edged words may have been spoken, which the women remember but which I, as though unconcerned, have forgotten. Close as the five are to one another and readily as they call one another sister in fair weather, they clash and get on one another's nerves when something goes wrong. Too many queens. There's always a possibility of murder, whether planned or on the spur of the moment. Poisoned hairpins, little powders. Which of the women is thinking of stirring arsenic or strychnine into Damroka's coffee pot? Hatred bares its fangs, wants to eliminate. They are incompatible, so to speak. And yet my head wants them to be harmonious.

The Flounder doesn't come into it, because only Damroka talks to him. So if they fight, it has to be about jellyfish. Though deep down it's about me, or actually about Vineta, their new destination. Their spoken words are: When will it die? Should the jellyfish in the Baltic Sea be regarded as menace or do they prove that it's alive? Why are we squabbling about jellyfish in the first place?

They belong to the family of the Schyphozoa. They're not the stinging variety, they're harmless and rather boring in their milky bluish whiteness, yet seem beautiful to anyone whom a transparent creature inspires with wonderment or religious awe, as if he'd come face to face with an angel.

Aurelia aurita, the common jellyfish, is met with in almost all coastal waters between seventy degrees north and seventy degrees south latitude. It owes its wide distribution to drift. Has been sighted off Hong Kong and off the Falkland Islands. Common in the Black Sea and in the coastal waters of Japan and Peru. Jellyfish clog the cold water intake of power plants. Not only grasshoppers, bark beetles and rats, but jellyfish as well are termed collectively a plague.

All medusas are either male or female, and that disgruntles the helmswoman. 'A freak of nature,' she says, but is appeased when the oceanographer explains that the sperm is taken in not directly but with the food. The fertilization of the eggs in the ovary takes place more or less at random. The mature eggs move through the gastric zone into the brood pouch, and so on and so on.

In the workroom of the *Ilsebill*, which is also the dining and living room, charts are hung between portholes, showing the development cycle of the jellyfish, the influence of local wind conditions on the jellyfish population and the frequency of *Aurelia aurita*. A diagram indicates the density of *Aurelia aurita* in Kiel Harbour, another in Lübeck Bay, a third off the chalk cliffs of Møn, a fourth in the Swedish skerries, a fifth between Gotland and Öland, and a sixth to the east of Rügen, in Tramper Cove and off Usedom Island. All these diagrams, which the oceanographer has hung up and labelled in rounded, easily legible letters, are based on data collected during the late seventies and early eighties.

'Old stuff!' says the engineer, who attaches a lot more importance to direct observation than to scientific theory. 'The day before yesterday, as we were leaving Møns Klint our engine told us all about the jellyfish concentration in that area. We should build a jellyfish counter into the propeller. Anyway, while we were running through the jellyfish fields, the dial showed that our speed had been cut down by one knot. That's what your medusas can do.'

As grey cloud banks break up into scudding tatters, *The New Ilsebill* leaves Bornholm behind and makes its way through unvarying calm water toward Visby on Gotland. In the open sea the jellyfish concentration diminishes, but the readings remain distinctly above average. The helmswoman insists on slowing down and letting out the shark every half hour. As the engineer supports the helmswoman, as the oceanographer gives in – 'We do have this stupid research mission after all' – and the Old Woman leans now to one side, now on the other, Damroka has to put up with the reduced speed; with a gesture that makes a virtue of resignation, she gives the helmswoman the wheel.

The Old Woman says to her: 'Cheer up.'

More to herself than to anyone else, Damroka says: 'We're wasting time.'

The oceanographer says: 'These measurements are absurd. The concentration is minimal. Nothing compared to eighty-one.'

And Damroka who has suddenly – I don't know why – cheered up, says: 'There have always been jellyfish years. In the migrations, for instance, when the lots were drawn and the first batch of Goths wanted to leave Gotland. These old Goths had a rough time of it, rowing away. It seems to have taken them half a day to get out of the jellyfish field so they could board ship and make history. And in 1636 – on the twenty-sixth of June, to be exact – when Gustavus Adolphus was approaching Usedom before landing in Peenemünde with fifteen thousand young Swedish and Finnish peasants, he had a hell of a fight on his hands, not with Tilly or Wallenstein but with jellyfish, which were incorrigibly Catholic and clung to the king's landing craft like glue. Nevertheless, the Goths got to Rome where they perished. Nevertheless, the Swedes enjoyed themselves in Germany for quite a while. You see, friends, there's nothing to get excited about. It's all happened before. The sea is older than our worries.'

That hair, that superabundance, that weatherproof confidence. She's lighthouse and reef at once. Her perseverance, which unravels every quarrel like a sweater too hurriedly knitted. She is good for metaphors. I take refuge in Damroka's hair. Her ship is now going full speed ahead. The helmswoman has stopped grumbling. The oceanographer is entering the latest data. Somewhere the engineer is whistling out of tune. In the galley the Old Woman is cooking Königsberg Meat Balls with sour caper sauce. All the women are looking forward to my favourite dish. A pleasant dream with a calm sea and an offshore breeze. No She-rat to bother me. Only briefly, our Herr Matzerath on his car telephone. He's in his Mercedes between Düsseldorf and Dortmund. He wants me to make good use of his absence. The Malskat case, he says, is a ray of light in the dismal fifties. He doesn't want to have to worry about anything in Poland. Of course he's coming back. Referring to himself, he assures me that you can't keep a good man down. He warns me against false hopes. End of telephonic instructions.

Ah, Damroka. Just see how innocently the sea forms ripples. Why talk about the end of the World? Plenty of plans left in my dream. Tomorrow I'll get back to saving the forests.

The Rat

Children, we play at getting lost
and find one another much too quickly.

Now we know what lies
behind the Seven Mountains: The 'Behind the Seven Mountains
    Hotel',
at whose newsstand cute souvenirs are on sale,
dating back to the days of ignorance
when the Rumpelstiltskin syndrome
was still Greek to us.

All fairy tales interpreted. Good and bad
fairies knitting in the seminar.
The dwarf's cooperative.
The witch and her social milieu,
Hansel and Gretel in late capitalism, or
The holdings of Thrushbeard & Co.
A case study
is devoted to Sleeping Beauty's condition.

In the opinion of the Brothers Grimm, however,
the children would be saved
if they could get lost.

The black and white film is over. The magic mirror has gone
dull. The story of Hansel and Gretel is ended. All laugh when the
film is over, even the witch, who bears the oven into which she was
shoved no grudge. The frog king in a black diving suit hugs the
Chancellor's children, whose past history strikes them as funny and
somehow unreal. Hansel says to Gretel: 'Man, wouldn't that story
be rough without the happy ending?'

Now all those who have foregathered at the Gingerbread House
Hotel are talking about the good old days when straw was spun into
gold and three feathers left room for three wishes, when fairy tales
still foretold the future. While trying to conjure up the past, they
grow sadder and sadder. Melancholy is contagious.

As it has stopped raining, the frog king has to go back into the
well. The ladylike princess lies down to enable the king in the guise
of a frog to jump on her forehead. That relieves her headache.

On the stairs leading to the front door sits the girl with the
chopped-off hands, which are hanging limply on their string. She is
staring at the blood-encrusted arm stumps.

At a window in the upper storey of the Gingerbread House Rapunzel is combing her hair; hovering golden threads appear in the picture.

In front of the house Jorinde and Joringel impart their grief and its sad-sad story in the fingerplay that looks like deaf-and-dumb language.

Over and over again the prince has to awaken Sleeping Beauty with a kiss; he does his work conscientiously but without enthusiasm; time and again, Sleeping Beauty opens her eyes in wonderment, only to be recaptured by sleep. (If I have understood our Herr Matzerath aright, more is to be said elsewhere about this kissing compulsion.)

Still indoors, Rumpelstiltskin stands gazing meditatively at the large apothecary jar, in which the leg he once ripped off – at the knee – is keeping fresh in alcohol.

With a bleary look, as though no longer wishing to take part, Little Red Riding Hood's grandmother sees the child going over to the wolf, getting into the cage, opening the zipper on the wolf's belly, crawling in and closing the zipper from the inside.

For a moment the wicked stepmother switches on her magic mirror, sees herself talking to the mirror in the black-and-white version of the tale, sees Snow White's pretty little face in the mirror, switches off the picture. Her angry eyes look for Snow White, who is stroking a glass museum piece, her coffin in miniature.

While toying with her necklace of dried ears, even the witch seems worried. Rübezahl the hired man stares at her enormous tits; he can't take his eyes off them.

In vain Hansel and Gretel try to console the fairy-tale characters by making faces and horsing around. Cries such as 'Come on, Rumpelstiltskin, let that old leg of yours sleep!' or 'Isn't there something I can do for you, witch?' are no help. Gloom lies over them all like a magic spell. Old sorrow consumes them; but greater sorrow lies ahead.

In pinstripe flannel suits and carrying sample cases, the seven dwarfs are back from a long trip. Grumpily, they grab their seven caps off seven hooks. They bring bad news and display distressing evidence: dead branches showing joint anomalies – the lametta syndrome – diseased bark, fir branches shedding brown needles, parched roots, photographic plates showing, in segments, the waterlogged heartwood of diseased trees.

The bad news brings the fairy-tale characters back to present reality. Even Little Red Riding Hood crawls out of the wolf's belly. With the subtitle, 'The shoots are deceptive. The trees are in a state of panic', the seven dwarfs display panic shoots and the pseudo-blossoms on dead branches.

A button is pressed and the magic mirror confirms facts. After the wicked stepmother's subtitle: 'Mirror, mirror on the wall, which are the sickest forests of all?' shots are shown of the Fichtelgebirge, the Bavarian Forest, the Black Forest, the Spessart, the Solling and the Thuringian Forest. Windbreaks, bare west slopes, falling trees, tree corpses, bark beetles.

No longer fixated on the witch, Rübezahl wants to see the Riesengebirge: 'That's where I come from.' Whereupon the screen shows dead trees far and wide.

It's as if the end had already overtaken them. All realize that if the forest is dying they too will die soon. Snow White and the seven dwarfs are crying. The witch lets Rübezahl, the hired man, thrust his face between her tits. Little Red Riding Hood wants to crawl back inside the wolf; but Hansel holds the would-be deserters back with the cry: 'This is no time to cop out!'

And now comes good advice. With the help of a longish subtitle, Hansel and Gretel, speaking by turns, say: 'Don't be sad. We know a way. The Grimm Brothers, whose oldtime pictures are hanging on your walls, are today minister and undersecretary. The dying forests are in their jurisdiction. They're still pretty nice. The Grimm Brothers will help you. It's not yet too late. Don't let this happen to you. Hear that, witch? Without forests you're done for. Without forests you won't exist. Listen to me. Defend yourselves!'

The seven dwarfs are the first to chime in: 'Defend yourselves! Defend yourselves!' Others join in the cry. The mood in the Gingerbread House is one of excitement. A little later, the camera registers, outside the house, preparations for departure.

Rübezahl and the seven dwarfs push an old Ford out of the barn. As the tank has long been dry, the witch has to provide a substitute for petrol; luckily, she remembers an old recipe.

Amidst cheers and laughter, the witch is lifted up and put down on the boot of the old Ford. She squats down on a funnel, picks up her skirts, takes aim and pisses straight into the funnel. A splashing is heard from inside the tank. Even the girl with the chopped-off hands allows her hands to clap. All are happy, only the grandmother grumbles and orders Little Red Riding Hood to look the other way. Surprisingly enough, Jorinde and Joringel are smiling. Squinting all the while out of her amber-coloured eyes, the witch pisses and pisses. The dwarfs cry out: 'More! More!' At length, the car is fuelled with witch's best.

Rumpelstiltskin picks the delegation. As the wicked stepmother, under the witch's influence, refuses to participate – 'I can keep a good watch on developments here' – Sleeping Beauty and the prince who wakes her with a kiss take their places in the back seat of the car. One of the seven dwarfs is chosen by a throw of the dice. He sits beside the driver. Rumpelstiltskin at the wheel. At the last minute Rapunzel wants to go along. 'I want to go to town too and do something wild' – 'So do I!' cries Little Red Riding Hood and pushes Snow White, who is shouting: 'Me too!' No one else is allowed to go, not even the girl whose chopped-off hands are signalling 'pretty please'.

Rübezahl turns the crank. The witch's best petrol does its duty. The spark plugs spark, the engine starts, the old Ford starts moving. Slowly, between forest lake and deer pen, it drives out of the clearing.

As Gretel (who in our Herr Matzerath's opinion has fallen in love with the frog king) has poured a pail of water into the well, the frog jumps off the lady's forehead and into the well, whence a moment later he rises in the shape of the frog king.

He, the ladylike princess, Hansel and Gretel, all wave and shout as the old Ford drives off. Even the chopped-off hands flutter and wave on their string. The remaining six dwarfs proclaim the car's destination: 'On to Bonn!' is the subtitle, as though salvation were localized in Bonn.

Too late, she scoffed and occupied my dream. Hopping from branch to branch in a dead tree, the She-rat called out: You should have got started sooner. You should have learned from your mistakes. You should have this, you should have that. The dying forests, all very well! Need I mention the stinking rivers, the oceans that can barely breathe, the poisons seeping into the ground water? The millions of particles that weigh down the air, the new plagues, and the old plagues that are coming back, ipputch and cholera. Need I enumerate the encroaching deserts, the dried-out bogs, need I shout from atop the garbage mountains: You robbers, you exploiters, you poisoners!

The Rat

Already she was proclaiming her scorn from atop a garbage mountain. Pitiful, your bottom line. Everywhere ravening hunger. Endlesss petty wars, serving, you humans thought, to avert a big war; millions of unemployed, liberated from toil in your parlance. And other euphemisms. Your expensive congresses. Ten thousand knights of the expense account, travelling to no purpose. Money supply productive of nothing but indebtedness. Rehashes of worn-out ideas. Your inability to derive a little late knowledge if not from new words, then at least from the wishful old ones, such as liberty, equality, fraternity. The human race, while drawing to a close, was strong in self-deception, at one and the same time omniscient and stupid. In the end, you wearied of the most precious wisdom, from the Proverbs of Solomon to Ernst Bloch's most recent work.

No longer from the garbage mountain, the top of the rat world, but from within reaching distance, she spoke: Yet you could have learned from us. You'd only have to emulate our ego, our ego saturated and continually enriched by experience, our ego which has bitten its way through, always bitten its way through. We rats, said the She-rat, who had furnished my dream like a schoolroom with blackboard, chalk and pointer, possibly taking the blackboard in our Herr Matzerath's executive office as a model, we rats didn't have to have everything explained to us over and over again as in your schools. Unlike humans, we learned from our mistakes. You humans, recidivists from the start, have always fallen into ingenious traps, it seemed to amuse you. You'd only have had to read, in the Book of Genesis, for instance – and the Lord God said: Behold, Adam is become as one of us, to know good and evil – to realize what bitter fruit your tree of knowledge bore. Ah, you godlike fools!

And then she wrote. In my dream the She-rat took chalk and wrote on the blackboard. Wonderfully well read, she drew up a long list of all the mistakes from which we humans, if we had been as wise as the rats, might have learned to stop being individual I's and become a collective We. And while the She-rat wrote with chalk – in the old-fashioned Sütterlin script I detested – her talk, that nasal piping, grumbling, muttering, went on and on.

Because, she pontificated, we were always two steps ahead of their experiments, men thought us rats remarkably quick to learn. From a strictly scientific point of view, what they accomplished with our help in their laboratories, that is, what they got sterile breeds, the relatively stupid laboratory rats, to do, was far from negligible – without rats there could have been no human medicine – but would, with free rats, which from the laboratory point of view are arrogantly termed sewer rats, have brought entirely different results that would have changed man's whole nature; an epoch-making idea, that still arouses our enthusiasm and is praiseworthy even by human standards.

On she went. In the grip of an obsession, she sat on a lectern which, along with the blackboard, belonged to the furnishings of my dream. She spoke as though addressing a large audience. For instance: We transmit knowledge by inheritance. Every human had to study his multiplication table for himself, not so we rats. No sooner born, we know what is worth knowing and pass on our knowledge from litter to litter. That is why we smiled, insofar as rats can smile, when humans, proud of their experiments with so-called laboratory rats, called us intelligent animals. Such arrogance, such condescension. If only they'd allowed us to test their forced repetition, their massive repressions, their inborn aggressiveness, their cruelty, hardness, love of evil, to apply our methods of evaluation to the traits that gave rise to all man's conflicts. Ah, if only man had adopted our welfare system and seen how the commandment to love thy neighbour, which they merely parroted and we never uttered, was fulfilled among rats. If only, we say: then perhaps man, that inherently admirable creature, would still be with us.

I didn't like that dream. Without proof I reproached the She-rat with blindly rabid rat wars, with the destruction of the black house rat, with spreading the Plague, with parasitism, with nibbled babies, all items gathered from my reading. And while she patiently refuted my imputations – the rat could only survive by adapting to you humans – I yearned to escape, to get out of that dream. But where to? To the fairy-tale forest? To Painter Malskat's Gothic drapery? To a ship manned with wishes and women? Or without a visa to our Herr Matzerath's car, now on its way to Poland?

The classroom remained locked. Compulsory education governed my dream. Her teaching methods allowed of no excuses, no childlike snapping of fingers: Teacher, please, I need to. In my dream, to be sure, the chalk didn't squeak, there was no smell of floor wax polish, but the writing was in Sütterlin script, the bane of my childhood with its points and its loops.

The Rat

The She-rat accused. Man had been ungrateful. He had never honoured anyone but himself. All he felt for us was contempt, horror and disgust.

But She-rat, I heard myself protesting, I praise you in line after line of verse and in my drawings. There's always been room for you in my escutcheon. Early in my career, during *The Flood*, I made two rats, Point and Pearl, converse wittily about humans. And recently, with old age staring me in the face, I even asked for a rat for Christmas. I found your infant image and likeness under the Christmas Tree. How she grows, believe me, how my little rat grows! Well cared for, she lives in an open cage on a dresser full of blank paper, and she doesn't want to leave, she wants to be entertained by me.

To the left of my Christmas rat is my desk, on which too many stories have bogged down. To the right, on a tool rack, sits our radio. Together we listen to the Third Programme and learn that the education of the human race is far from concluded.

Admittedly, the situation looks critical. Everywhere, at government expense, commencement exercises are being held. Even artists participate. With fireworks and laser beams, geniuses project expensive constellations, which sumptuously anticipate the end of the world and garner applause. With genuine animal blood – three thousand litres of it – Golgotha was recently celebrated in Austria before invited guests. Everything, even spreading hunger, is termed myth. It's true, She-rat, we humans are going to quite a lot of trouble preparing our exit. It has to be possible thirty-six times over, either successively or simultaneously, to be on the safe side. Some people call it madness. There's been talk of resistance. I've been present in Mutlangen, Heilbronn and elsewhere. And in time we may succeed, I mean, possibly we humans will realize at last, so soon before Doomsday, that we must learn from our mistakes, become more modest, less arrogant. Then perhaps the education of the human race – remember, She-rat? – will be on the programme again, but from now on, She-rat, with your help.

> Our intention was that men should learn
> little by little
> to handle not only knife and fork
> but one another as well, and reason too,
> that omnipotent can opener.

Günter Grass

That once educated, the human race should freely,
yes, freely, determine its destiny and free from its shackles
learn to guide nature cautiously,
as cautiously as possible,
away from chaos.

That in the course of its education the human race
would cultivate the virtue of eating with a spoon
and diligently practise the use of the subjunctive and tolerance,
difficult as this may be
among brothers.

A special lesson enjoined us
to watch over the sleep of reason
to domesticate all dream animals until
grown docile they eat out of the hand
of the Enlightenment.

Halfway enlightened, the human race
ceased to play crazily, aimlessly in the primordial muck
and began to wash systematically.
Acquired hygiene spoke plainly:
Woe to the dirty.

Once our education claimed to be advanced,
knowledge was declared to be power and
no longer confined to paper.
The Enlightened cried:
Woe to the ignorant!

When finally violence, all reason to the contrary,
could not be banished from the world,
the human race taught itself mutual deterrence.
Thus it learned to keep the peace until some unenlightened
accident happened.

Then at last the education of the human race
was virtually complete. A great light
illumined every corner. Too bad that afterward
it grew so dark that no one
could find his school.

Letters should be written to Stockholm. Thousands of people, doctors and scientists in the lead, should write long letters to Stockholm, listing all the rats' achievements. Then at last those gentlemen up there may realize how impoverished human medicine and biochemistry, basic research and just about everything else would be without rats. You'd stand a pretty good chance, She-rat.

Of course, from what I know of the gentlemen on the committee, they would think at first of the white-haired, red-eyed laboratory rat, but the world would understand that all rats were being honoured. I'm told there are five and a half billion of them at present. Won't they be pleased! And I, with quiet satisfaction, shall put a new ribbon into my typewriter, pass your cage and turn the knob, because my Christmas rat and I will want to hear that on the Third Programme. News of the Scientific World will be announced, and then suddenly, not some space-and-satellite rubbish, but a long message about you because you – yes, you have every right to be happy! – have at last won the Nobel Prize for achievements in the field of genetic research. At some length the speaker recalls the work of your forerunners, Professors Watson and Crick, who long ago – it is more than twenty years since they were invited to Stockholm and honoured for their discovery of the helical structure of DNA. But then, She-rat, we would hear me – who else? – on the Third Programme delivering an encomium on the rat family.

Honoured Academy! – Thus might I begin on Swedish soil. In my next sentence I might greet first you, the rat as such, even though you don't seem to be present, and only then the King of Sweden. I would go straight to the point: At last, your Majesty! It was high time that recognition was accorded to certain achievements and contributions to human medicine, which would have been inconceivable without rats – I am referring especially to genetic research and the manipulation of genes with its enduring consequences.

No, ladies and gentlemen. Let us not make things easy for ourselves by confining this honour to the laboratory rat. That would be incorrect and it would be disingenuous. Our praise and thanks should be addressed to the rat as such, that being so close to man, addressed to rats in general. The rat, misunderstood, hitherto classed among animal pests; the rat, for centuries blamed for every evil and plague; the rat, invoked in execration whenever foaming hatred demanded expression; the rat, greeted with fear and disgust and at all times associated with carrion, stench, garbage; who at the very most won the love and trust of confused young men and women who had placed themselves with screams and loud colours on the fringe of society. Let us here praise rats for the benefits they have conferred on the human race.

But, you may ask, mightn't the same be said of laboratory mice, guinea pigs, rhesus monkeys, dogs, cats, etc? Yes, indeed, these animals, too, deserve to be honoured. Their services to mankind cannot be contested. Along with rats, monkeys and dogs were the first mammals to be sent into cosmic space. The name of the Soviet dog, we recall, was Leika. The experimental guinea pig has become proverbial. And I am certain that in casting about for prizeworthy candidates, the Swedish Academy carefully weighed the question: Should the rhesus monkey or the dog, or else the mouse or the guinea pig be honoured? And undoubtedly it was a hard decision for the gentlemen to make.

But they did well to select the rat. From time immemorial, the rat has been with us. Long before us, rats were on earth, suckling their young, as though in fulfilment of their mission to make other animals and then man possible. And that is why, when God sent the flood over the earth and commanded his servant Noah to build an ark for the salvation of everything that creeps and flies, the rat, as the Book of Genesis attests, was not excluded.

Since then, all literature has been aware of the rat's existence. Rattiness has become a category. Take Camus's novel *The Plague* or Hauptmann's play, named after our laureate – though in the plural. Further examples of the rat's role in the development of world literature might be cited from Goethe to the often-mentioned Orwell; when not identified in so many words or directly invoked in a title commemorating the bravest of rats, it can be read, long-tailed, between the lines. True, our writers have seen fit to consolidate our laureate's negative reputation, though in unforgettable images and with myth-making power; gruesome the torture scene in Orwell's famous novel; questionable the overemphasis on the exception, the hungry rat nibbling at the baby; fortunate, however, that thanks to the Grimms' collection of tales and Robert Browning's narrative poem, the Pied Piper of Hamelin became known; and incidentally, I feel sure the citizens of that town will be delighted with the prize committee's selection for this year.

The Rat

Let us bear this in mind: for the most part subservient to human misery, poverty, hunger, horror and to man's need for disgust, the rat, thus far, has acceded only to questionable literary honours. Plagues have been foisted on it, gnawing misery has forced it into the picture, its abode has been termed sewer, slum, dungeon, concentration camp. It has stood for calamity, hard times, sinking ships.

Yes, we need only consult the annals of history; it has always been with us. Since the present prize is being conferred in Sweden, let us start with Swedish history. The great migration set out from the overpopulated island of Gotland, ship rats secreted under the floor boards accompanied the Goths southward across the Baltic Sea until land was sighted, the Vistula estuary, whereupon history took its course with the rats in its train. And when the great King of Sweden carried his peasant army across the Baltic on a mighty fleet, to take part in the war of religion that was then afflicting Germany, rats had made their nests on all his ships. And it goes without saying that when the royal corpse was carried back to Sweden, rats were present above the keel.

When, however, early in our century, the Russian Baltic fleet lay at anchor in the roadstead of Libau, a small town on the Baltic, and when all the ships got under steam and anchors were weighed in preparation for the long ocean voyage to Japan, thousands upon thousands of rats left the ships of the line, the armoured cruisers, the supply ships and torpedo boats, because it was in the cards that this fleet would be destroyed in the Yellow Sea. The rats saved themselves by swimming ashore. But no one understood their warning flight. Curses were shouted after them, and that was all.

The rats are our contemporaries. The vicissitudes of human history are unthinkable without rats. And now at last, late, but, it is hoped, not too late, they are being honoured. Human gratitude is being expressed. Yes, we have learned from the rat. Patiently and selflessly, rats have helped us to new departures in medicine. What, one is entitled to ask, would the pharmaceutical industry be without rats? And if the average life expectancy of modern man has exceeded the biblical three-score and ten, this advance must also be attributed to the rats and their sacrifices.

They have had to suffer for us. It has not been easy for scientists to withstand the protests of the societies for the prevention of cruelty to animals; but their experimentation has not been an end in itself, it has brought results; the rats have not suffered in vain. After years of collaboration with world-famous geneticists, they have finally succeeded in being associated with man, not only in an ideal, symbolic or poetic sense, but by becoming part and parcel of mankind. The rat in man and the man in the rat are beginning to take effect. For after the atomic nucleus the nucleus of the cell has been split. The genetic code has been broken. And behold: the cell's memory, which was preserved in its nucleus, enabled it to become inheritable elsewhere. From now on, all sorts of manipulations will be possible on the basis of the genetic formulas. Just as peasant shrewdness once derived the useful mule from horse and ass, it has now become possible to derive from micro-organisms unpro-grammed bacteria, which in response to genetic orders are eating up oil sludge all over the world. Ah yes, the Faustian element in human nature has made all that and still more possible; for our rats are sacrificing themselves to future progress.

I know that progress has numerous enemies, who have tried at all times to disparage great ideas and to stifle great deeds in pusillan-imity. To them be it said: What was neglected in the Creation is now coming to pass. Where God – with all due respect – thought he had done a good job, long overdue corrections are now possible. We know that the crooked tree which, in the words of the philosopher Kant, will forever image man, can at last be made straight. The most excellent characteristics of both species, the priceless heritage of man and the well-known qualities of the rat, can now be combined in selected genes; for if everything were to remain as it is and has been, man would be free to go on behaving as he has since the days of Adam; the deficiencies in his make-up would ensure his doom. His genes, which have now been decoded, reveal terrible traits. Wretchedly endowed, he would inevitably destroy himself. Arrived at the end of his possibilities, he would have no choice but to destroy his incorrigible fellow man.

This must not be. Measures must be taken to prevent it. Reason and ethics command us to make it clear that only a choice additive can open the future to an improved version of man. Only when the human substance is enriched, complemented and corrected by an infusion of rattiness, which will cushion it on the one hand and strengthen it on the other, give a bit, take a bit, liberate man from the I, open him to the we, and by improving us make us viable again – only then can we hope for a future. *Homo sapiens* will be healed by

The Rat

Rattus norvegicus. Creation will become reality. The future belongs to the rat-man.

Today, your Majesty, we can have only an intimation of his coming. His contours – honoured Academy – are not yet firmly set. At the most, we can see him clearly in dreams. But even today the most recent manipulations enable us to perceive the first indications of his existence. Whether in American research centres or in Soviet laboratories, whether in the institutes of Japan or of India, everywhere, and, it goes without saying, in Sweden's venerable University of Uppsala, he is taking form, coming into being; everywhere rat and man are resolved to create a new being.

Accordingly he too – the rat-man – should be honoured. While congratulating our prizeworthy rat on his Nobel Prize, we also wish to congratulate him who is not yet here, whom we long for. May he come, to relieve us of our burdens and transcend us, to improve us and make us possible again, to relieve us and redeem us. May he come soon, I cry, soon, before it is too late. May he come into being: the glorious rat-man!

Chapter Six, *in which the rat-man becomes thinkable and is dreamed while someone is mounting guard, the She-rat turns out to know her way around, the Kashubian plant proliferates, false names cling to the women, post-human history begins immediately after the clean-up, I am recognized as a source of error, big money has the power and Wilhelm Grimm an idea.*

'WHY NOT?' cries our Herr Matzerath over the phone as his chauffeur drives him eastward on the Autobahn. 'Why not a rat-man?' he says, and because I contradict him, prepares to launch into a long speech: 'In this particular case,' he says, 'a mere idea already has trousers, shoes and socks on . . .'

'Not everything man thinks up should materialize!'

'God the Father should have said that when he set to work with both hands baking Adam out of clay.'

Our Herr Matzerath gets his chauffeur Bruno, to whom Oskar's phantasms were reality back in mental hospital days, to back up his opinions. The monstrosity appeals to him, all the more so as the rat-man leads directly to Malskat and his paintings: 'If the painter, after painting a Gothic turkey frieze in Schleswig's Cathedral and at last bringing movement into the frozen face of history, had transferred still other fabulous creatures to lime mortar, man's immemorial dream of becoming man and beast at once would again have achieved symbolic force and become credible to all art critics.'

Our Herr Matzerath lists: four-hoofed centaurs, the smiling sphinx, Picasso's delightfully bull-headed men, the Indian Ganesha's whimsically trunked elephant head, water nymphs and nereids, bird-, dog- and snake-headed gods. Hieronymus Bosch's garden of delights invites our Herr Matzerath to stroll from motif

[138]

to motif. Positively ecstatic, as though longing for claws and an animal's head, he shouts into the phone: 'The Gothic cathedrals of France are larded with grotesque, demonic, diabolical waterspouts, every one of which, if you come right down to it, amalgamates the human species with other animal varieties. I've seen jackal- and lynx-headed monsters. Goat-faced women and men with horns. We've always longed to see ourselves transformed into animals, stag, eagle, fish for that matter, with scales or wings, even if only over half our bodies. What beautiful woman hasn't yearned to be pleasured by a monster? And think of the angels with their mighty wings. And the he-goat in the devil and the stinking devil in the he-goat! Puss in Boots is credible to adults as well as children. We see ourselves as bugs: lying helpless on our backs. How often against our will and because there is such power in fairy tales, we have turned ourselves into a deer, a frog, into seven swans, when in reality we were only humans under a curse. Ask the frog king, who lives in the well right next to the Gingerbread House and is evidently to be nothing more than an extra in your film . . .'

Here our Herr Matzerath has to stop. The crash, the screeching of brakes, and the chauffeur's curse were clearly audible over the auto telephone. Shortly before Helmstedt – 'Typical!' says Bruno – a BMW driver has caused an accident in his hurry to pass. Luckily there's no need for the police, who appear on the scene instantly, to radio for an ambulance. The adverse party is described to me as a 'quarrelsome couple, mid-thirties'.

'Not a good omen!' I predict.

'We will not be put off.'

'My advice is to turn back on the double.'

'Come off it!' cries our Herr Matzerath. 'The usual body damage. An hour lost. We'll arrive in Poland with a dent and a few scratches, which, I agree, are unbecoming in a Mercedes. These infantile speed demons are annoying. – But, getting back to our subject. Why shouldn't there be rat-men in the future? Painter Malskat would have had no objections.'

For the present he was unable to paint Gothic cathedrals, cloisters, transepts or buttresses, because war was prevailing far and wide. After washing off a damaged nineteenth-century casein binder painting, which was held to be authentic Gothic, replacing it with his own quickly aging Gothic, and completing other assignments

Günter Grass

for the Fey company in already occupied Upper Silesia, Malskat was called to the colours.

Most of the time he was with the army of occupation in northern Norway, where he mounted guard and was made a corporal. As far as I know, he never fired a shot. No record of indiscipline or stockade. No medal was ever pinned on him, no mention of any act of heroism, few anecdotes.

Some former comrades, who at the behest of Dr Flottrong, the defence counsel, testified at the Lübeck forgery trial, agreed that 'He wasn't much of a soldier, but he was an interesting man.' Even then, it seems, Malskat had joked about the art historians' turkey controversy. For anyone who asked him, though never for officers, he had sketched endless specimens of this bird. One witness expressed regret at having lost a turkey signed Malskat in the course of the retreat. Further testimony revealed that during the long winter nights Malskat had entertained his barracks companions by reading pages from a book in which a professor of art history cited the turkey frieze as proof that the Vikings had discovered America. You could die laughing!

According to other witnesses, Malskat had decorated the inside of his locker with a photo of Hansi Knoteck, the popular film star. During the war it is true, the photograph of a movie actress in a soldier's locker could mean all sorts of things, but according to Malskat la Knoteck embodied something very special and had served as a model for any number of Gothic madonnas, angels and saints; moreover, he had worshipped her and had never missed one of her pictures.

In the course of his trial in Lübeck, the painter owned that he had remained faithful to the pretty film star even after the war; he had seen her most recently in *The Jolly Petrol Station* and *Homeland Bells*, both several times, as could be seen by his murals in the choir and nave of the church of Saint Mary.

Comparisons showed not only the likeness, but also Malskat's gift of expressive heightening. From the merely sweet face he distilled sorrow and inner fire. Not only the now well-known Virgin with Child in Field 1 of the choir, but also the Mother of God in the crucifixion group in the nave, Mary Magdalen, a blank spot in whose left eye had given her a heightened, fragmentary effect, and the Mary with dove of the Annunciation are all Gothic sisters of the movie star, whose photo – a still from the operetta film

Homeland – had for four years moved from locker to locker; for Malskat's unit was constantly on the move, and wherever it went he did guard duty.

Munitions depots, barracks, paymaster's offices. The cold is indescribable. His long nose freezes. He would love to visit the painter Edvard Munch, whose scream- and silence-charged pictures are to be seen in Oslo, to learn expression from him, but no military mission takes him to Oslo.

Otherwise there's little to say of his military career. At a time when advances were turning to retreats described as a straightening of lines, when submarines were ceasing to surface, when one city after another was succumbing to saturation bombing, when the Führer's speeches were becoming less and less frequent, when people believed in miracle weapons, and admissions to still nameless extermination camps were being recorded as departures, Lothar Malskat was doing pastel landscapes with Norwegian subjects and exchanging them for cigarettes and Chococola. He had always been a heavy smoker. But all the witnesses agreed that the East Prussian, well liked both by officers and by enlisted men, never painted anything to order, but only when he felt like it.

But then it happened that in the night of Palm Sunday, 1942, while he was mounting guard in the far north, the city of Lübeck was bombed by British planes. Malskat read about it in a delayed army newspaper, headlined as a terror raid. The Inner City and the brick churches were especially hard hit. British Air Marshal Harris had wanted it that way. The church of Saint Mary was burned out. Several vaults in the choir caved in. When a temporary roof was built and the vaults were replaced, the Bishop of Lübeck, who like many Evangelical clergymen was a Nazi, arranged for the choir vault to be completed with a keystone in the shape of a swastika. Malskat must have seen this hallmark of the Lübeck German Christians in 1949 when he climbed high in the scaffolding with his paint pots and his wire brush, and found plenty of work waiting for him.

Of course the swastika was soon removed, as was being done everywhere in the early fifties; the bishop, however, if he isn't dead, has remained a Nazi at heart to this day.

But what if painter Malskat, as our Herr Matzerath has been speculating for some time, had painted not only American poultry, but under the Betrayal, second field from the door, instead of alternating eagles and lions, had painted rats, running rats, mating from medallion to medallion with twisting little humans? And if he had carried this motif, matured after the war years, further, and had succeeded in the so-called bestiary window next to the Lübeck Briefkepelle, in giving legendary form to the meeting, nay more, to the reconciliation of rat and man?

But no rats are demonstrable in Malskat's painting. He never went beyond turkeys. True, as smudged fields bear witness to this day, his twenty-one saints in the choir were ruthlessly expunged soon after the trial; there is still room for conjecture that one or another capital, on which his saints stood cheek by jowl in groups of three, rat-men may have been interwoven with leafy ornaments. After all that guard duty in the far north, one cannot put it past him.

Our Herr Matzerath has his body-damaging collison behind him and now, arriving with considerable delay at Helmstedt, where he sees before him the German Democratic Republic with its over-emphasized border, he picks up his car telephone for the last time to express agreement with me, also in the name of his chauffeur. 'I like the idea!' he calls out. 'Why not? Malskat's abilities have too often been underestimated. He must have looked for opportunities to express his daydreams, if only in detail. Look at the clerestory of Saint Mary's in Lübeck, and tell me if the Prophet Jonah isn't depicted in the mouth of the whale as though whale and Jonah were one being. And isn't the rat in man, just as the biblical Jonah is in the whale?'

Evidently the border formalities involve a certain amount of waiting time. The chauffeur suggests that they deviate from their timetable by spending the night in West Berlin. Our Herr Matzerath insists, however, on hotel beds in Poznan and then waxes talkative, anticipating his first visit to his grandmother and remembering copiously: 'If we spend the night in Posen, we'll get there in time. I wonder if there are still sunflowers along the fence. And whether she still wears four skirts one over another. When I was little, by the way, a figurehead exhibited in the municipal museum played a mysterious part in a number of accidents. A full-bosomed woman in painted wood grew out of a scaly fish's tail; she was called Niobe, or popularly, the Green Marjell, and her inlaid amber eyes were said to deal death. The rat-man, by contrast, may be expected to be life- giving. If Malskat didn't do it, then someone else should depict our future, whether terrible or laughable. In any case, I'm curious. Doesn't it seem likely that the superseded human, who has largely become a bore, has long been in need of bold manipulation? To the best of my knowledge, an increasing number of zealous technicians are going into this new procedure, which consists of subtracting a gene here and adding one there.'

At this point, the barrier must have been raised. Our Herr Matzerath hangs up. In a slightly damaged Mercedes he will ride through the German Democratic Republic at a speed of one hundred kilometres an hour, until in Frankfurt on the Oder, after the bridge across that river, another barrier, this one red and white, is raised and Poland, Catholically suffering its fate, lies flat before him.

How curious yet diffident he is. Is his grandmother as spacious as he has always wanted her inner life to be? I'm afraid he's afraid. But now he must go. In keeping with the good half of his questionable existence, Oskar is going home.

> Even in sleep, frozen in expectation,
> I know what's coming: a mouth odour that I know.
> Already, answers are standing at attention.
>
> All gifts may remain wrapped
> and every secret guarded.
> This role rehearsed for years.
> Sated with foretaste, I know
> the end of all history.
>
> What do I nevertheless expect?
> Stuttering and losing the thread.
> Dearest, that we are strangers to each other
> Is something I never expected,
> that you make me permeable
> to words that whine and whimper.
> No more hope medicine, spoonful after spoonful,
> no tablets or smooth round happiness pills,
> but fear of blank paper.
>
> The milky screen is still flickering,
> looking for its programme.
> The ship isn't getting there,
> the plot has escaped from the forest,

no news from Poland, and yet
the picture is filling up, and I know it's you, She-rat,
rat of my dreams.

Frozen in expectation, I sense
what's coming now: serialized,
our end.

Facing me, her whiskers pointing in all directions to make sure
that nothing of foreign origin gets into her territory, she said:
Actually it's irrelevant whether clever mice or we rats in person
occupied the two central computers, because the human programs were set up exclusively on the basis of human ideas. We
couldn't have thought up that inferno. The result was most aptly
termed 'scorched earth'.

She paused and put a few of her whiskers back in place. Now I
could imagine what has often enough been described and sometimes called the final condition, but expressions like 'lunar landscape' and 'total devastation' would have fallen short of the mark.

Even lovely Kashubia, she said, once known as Kashubian
Switzerland, with its potato fields, its blackberry hedges and mixed
forests, its lakes teeming with fish, and its little river known as the
Radaune, lost its face. Though not directly hit, this hinterland
nevertheless suffered from neutron and gamma rays, the effect of
which extended to Tczew and Kartuzy, and even more from atomic
hits having their ground zero points in the city centres of Gdynia
and of Elblag to the east of the Vistula. The flat country offered no
resistance to the blast, and the hilly forests were consumed by fire
storms which reduced everything inflammable to ashes as far as
Tuchler Heath. But the ancestral home of the Kashubians suffered
most from the darkening of the sun, the drop in the temperature,
and the radioactive dust storms which after the Big Bang changed
the weather worldwide and destroyed virtually all life; even today –
and many years have elapsed since then – we fear what these storms
bring with them.

You, my young friend, are familiar with your scientists' detailed
prognoses. In the last years of the human era, scientists vied with
one another in computing and formulating definitive forecasts.
They counted in megatons and megadeaths. They called their
forecasts scenarios. But much as these scenarios differed in detail,

taken as a whole they confirmed the ultimate achievement of the human race, to which innumerable specialized minds contributed. No region was spared, no idyll survived, the devastation caught up with the most southerly havens, though that took time. Radio-active particles penetrated everywhere; no valley was too narrow, no island was forgotten. Here death was instantaneous, there the suffering was prolonged. Not a stirring of life, no, let's look at it from the human angle, of higher life. In a word, nothing was left.

Because I did not protest or ask questions, she spared me the details, and said: We won't document the end of the human race down to the last hiding place. No, much as you've delighted in travelling, why, you've even been to India, China and Alaska, let's stick to this place. Wherever curiosity may have lured you, your home was not Calcutta, but between the Vistula estuary and the Baltic Ridge. Be that as it may, your Kashubia reverted to a treeless terminal moraine, with water holes between boulders, crusted with mud, crevassed, blasted, hospitable only to us rats, though we had lost more than two-thirds of our population. Of course we were right to dig in while there was still time, but those of us who came through owed our survival to hoarding, a form of economy that rats had never practised before, and to rigorous fitness training.

Then she tried to make me believe that toward the end of the human era certain picked families of rats had been settled in atomic power plants and nuclear waste facilities with a view to hardening and immunizing them. That's ridiculous! I protested. A typical rat story.

She further reported, somewhat too casually: Anyway, as soon as we surfaced from our escape systems, we saw that we were terribly alone. For along with the humans, all their domestic animals had perished. Not a dog, not a cat survived. Along with the forests, the game had perished: not a hedgehog, not a wild boar was left. It wasn't until much later that we noticed, with annoyance but also with relief, that we were not so completely alone as we had thought.

She couldn't get over her astonishment. Amazing, don't you think, that a few sparrows and pigeons had survived along with the cockroaches and bluebottles? And in the Kashubian waterholes, frog and fish roe survived, so we knew there would be living water in time. Soon lizards and salamanders appeared. Later, much later, new life was sighted around the waterholes: mosses and lichens, horsetail, rushes and small shrubs. By then, not only gnats but also dragonflies and those everlasting slowpokes, the land and water snails, were back again. Oh, yes, and a disgusting variety of worms, not exactly earthworms, we called them soot worms. But all that didn't amount to much. Something was missing. Ah, my friend, the She-rat lamented, how lonely you have made us!

As I played dead, unwilling to venture any objection, she started in again at Doomsday: A few days after your endgame, when the silence in our system of corridors and escape chambers became too oppressive, we sent a few young rats up to the surface. At the same time all the litters that had been born during the Big Bang and had perished instantly had to be evacuated. None of the young rats came back. That happened several times. In the end, wanting to spare the rising new generations, we sent up old rats, some of whom reported back before going into convulsions and dying of internal bleeding and tumours. Believe us, my boy, the news from the surface sounded like human exaggeration. There was nothing up there, they said. Their last words would be no-man's-land or flunkerte erresh, scorched earth, that kind of thing. And when most of us were driven out of our shelters, because especially in the larger nesting chambers our social order was threatening to disintegrate, our first impulse was to go back down, to suffer anguish underground rather than emptiness up above.

The She-rat fell silent, as though to make the void, the nothingness, palpable with her silence.

At that point I stopped playing dead: And yet you lived through it. First dug in down below, then exposed to the void up above?

What else could we do? she said. Since all escape hatches were closed to us, we had to adopt a policy that we had practised from time immemorial. Yet few of us survived that early phase of the new era. Many fell sick, others proved incapable of throwing healthy offspring. Time and again, misshapen litters had to be bitten down. It took us a long time to convert to posthuman conditions. To tell the truth, we are still suffering from the after-effects . . .

But luckily, cried the She-rat, those clans which at the end of the human era had built up resistance by settling in nuclear power plants and nuclear waste facilities, adapted to the dust storms with their radioactive fallout and managed to produce the first healthy litters. But healthy doesn't mean unchanged; since then our formerly greyish-brown fur has become green, as if we had wanted to rescue a colour which humankind had made virtually extinct. And we're not alone in having changed. Sparrows and pigeons now have white and scarlet plumage. Frogs and amphibians are a lot larger than they used to be and have become almost transparent. The fish in the waterholes look like traditional roaches, carp and pike, but they too show changes in their gills and fins, as though trying to grow limbs that would enable them before long to move about on land. And yet another thing: bluebottles bear living young, which they suckle, I ask you, yes, suckle their young the same as you or me. There are flying snails and spiders that spread their nets under water. And the soot worms – useful creatures, because they live on soot deposits, though they're inedible, even for us . . .

She-rat, I cried, you've read all that. Picked it up in some cheesy book. You and your science-fiction menagerie. Malskatian inventions, Brueghelian monsters. The usual mutation rubbish.

Calmly, as though my objections had long been overdue, she said: Listen, pops. You don't have to believe what you don't want to hear. But any time you like, we'll be glad to show you walking fish, snails that go whirring through the air, and flies that suckle their young. You'll be surprised.

Her familiar forms of address were getting on my nerves – pops, she called me, good old pops. But despite my malicious remarks about bookish fantasies, the She-rat went on serenely: Anyway, we moved back to the earth's surface. But our provisions were still stored underground. Up top, for the moment, there wasn't much to eat, and what little there was had been spoiled by pollutants. We had to develop warning systems and dig into our stocks until we were more or less immune and able to fill up on what we found. We found plenty in our region, which had once been yours. Because the buildings man had erected, housing silos and barracks, terraces and factories, churches and theatres, remained intact. Their cellars and storerooms provided all we needed to feed our families. We weren't too badly off during the transition period, and we think back fondly of the food storage facilities of the Polish militia. We had no problem with tin cans. We found pork and cabbage with caraway seed, there was knackwurst and goulash, tripe in cans and pails, goose giblets cooked with barley. We located a big supply depot, set up by the government as a measure of self-defence, on

Hochstriess, in the suburb of Langfuhr, where a regiment of the Crown Prince's body hussars had its barracks long ago, and the militia its headquarters toward the end. In Danzig we found any number of food warehouses and the supply rooms of the Lenin Shipyard canteen, which was well stocked with canned goods. On the other hand, the pantries and deep freezes of the humanless city struck us as poorly supplied. We had to search and search, and we became citified in the process.

You see, said the She-rat, our situation was bearable. Since the conservation bombs, true to their nature and purpose, had merely destroyed all life, not only was every building in the centre and in the waterfront area substantially preserved, but vehicles and machines were also intact. Not a tower and not a gable was lacking in the Old City, repeatedly destroyed by human hands and afterward expensively rebuilt. Saint Mary's clucked as it had always done. Gilded under soot, the graceful Rathaus tower still bore some king or other heavenwards. Rows of houses on Long Street, Lady Street, Hound, Breeches Maker, and Baker Streets vied with one another in ornamentation. Open and beautifully arched were the Old City gates, magnificent though soot-covered was Green Gate. On all sides, stairways and porches hewn in stone. With grace and musculature, the bronze, trident-brandishing Neptune in front of the Artushof, where he still stands implacable, recalled the one-time human race.

Damn it all! I was beginning to find her credible. She knew her way around. She knew that Weaver Street leads to the Arsenal and past the Big Mill to the Orbis-Hotel Hevelius. She was even familiar with Warehouse Island to the left and right of Milk Pitcher Street, and she knew the Lower City; up Long Garden Street to Kneipab. But this part of the city, she said regretfully, was hopelessly clogged with mud, and indeed mud slides from all sides had blocked the city up to Oliva Gate and the gable of Trinity Church. She knew just where the suburbs of Ohra and Schidlitz are located. And when she spoke of an express train standing at Platform 3, ready to leave for Warsaw, she put the Central Station exactly where it belongs. And the Workers' Monument outside the gate of the Lenin Shipyard was as well known to her as the shipyard grounds. I was tempted to believe her when she claimed to have seen ships of diverse origin and tonnage under construction or repair on the slipway, in dry dock or moored by steel cable to the wharfs. All, of course, devoid of humans. The mopeds and bicycles of the dehydrated longshoremen and shipyard workers, she said, seemed to be in good condition.

Wait a minute, I cried. What did you do with those dehydrated people? They must have been lying around all over the place, shrunk, as you say.

Watch it, said the She-rat reproachfully. A little more sympathy, if you please. You're speaking of human beings, of your fellow men.

Yes, we found them everywhere. In houses, on the streets, in churches, in the Haymarket, in the Coal Market, on the Long Bridge, in streetcars, suburban trains, in the express that was all set to leave for Warsaw. Desiccated corpses, leathery and soot-black since the dark days of the dust storms. Lying, sitting, crouching. Some of them knotted together as though, at the end, they had taken our sometimes agglutinated, matted litters, our so-called rat's nests, as their models. In the ships' cabins, on every deck, on the docks, in the canteen of the Lenin Shipyard, everywhere the blood, the snot, the water, every last bit of juice had been removed from human beings. Reduced to dwarflike dimensions, they didn't seem heavy as we carried them away. Many – tourists, I should think – clung to their cameras. And yet – believe us! – man was beautiful in his remains. His limbs twisted in frantic gestures, grimacing and beautiful. Without the redness of his lips, the light of his eyes, the bashful smile, the commanding voice, without the nimble finger-play and the upright gait, man was still beautiful. Nor could the sticky black coating that we cautiously, patiently removed from everything later on, detract from his beauty. For a long time we were unwilling to part with those eloquent vestiges of former splendour. But it was not only hunger that compelled us to remove the dehydratees; we were determined that the post-human era should belong entirely to us, the surviving nation of rats.

The She-rat of my dreams seemed to have taken me by the hand. Far from my space capsule, she led me through deserted streets, through the unmanned city. I cast no shadow, but I heard my footfalls. All the walls were covered with soot, and yet the old inscriptions had been preserved. In round Latin letters, in German and in Polish, they spoke of Danzig and Gdańsk. What I could not decipher, the She-rat spelled out. On Long Street Gate there was still the motto of the once wealthy, hyperactively commercial centre, which for centuries was cited in the preface to the city charter and had now been taken over by the rats: *Nec temere, nec timide*. Yes, said the She-rat, that's what we aim to be: neither too bold nor too timid. Ah, my young friend, how splendid your city is and for us so comfortable.

What I saw corroborated her contention that every façade, though blackened and unglassed, had remained intact to the last curlicue. A sombre picture, to be sure, but recognizable. Evenly coated, sills, gable ornaments, porches, and the figures in the built-in reliefs were more sharply delineated than before. How breathtaking, still, was the view from Long Street down Bagmaker Street to the towering steeple of Saint Mary's. I wondered whether the interior would still be so Protestantly whitewashed, crying out for Malskatian murals. I wanted to go in, but the She-rat permitted no church visits. Later, she said, maybe later.

Across the Long Bridge, through all the arches as far as the Mottlau, rats were active. Either eating or mating. I didn't want to see what they were gobbling. God only knows what those tough leather bundles may have been. The She-rat spared my feelings, suspended her incessant chatter, and confined herself to Bible quotations relating to the ratty activity that is adequately subsumed in the word: multiply. As though blindly, males mounted females, who let themselves be mounted without choice or preference. Then they went back to eating – something or other.

That's the way we are, said the She-rat. The quest for food to help us multiply keeps us moving. Do you know of anything better, my boy?

Love, I said, great, all-embracing, selective love, that celestial but at the same time profoundly human feeling which, when I think of my Damroka, makes me . . .

Forget it! cried the She-rat. When you humans were nearing your end, you'd forgotten who was male and who female. Confused by your headbirths, you wanted to be both at once, male and female, determined to take your pleasure with your own cocks in your own twats.

We both laughed. OK, She-rat. Dreaming is good for you. I'll tell that to the seafaring women, who have written me off, put me ashore, slight difference and all.

Then we left the Old City, which, the length of Wall Street and on all its borders, was enclosed in mud and boulders. Tongues of the muddy sludge, which however appeared to be dry and passable, reached as far as High Seigen, Key Dyke, Jacob's Gate and the entrance to the shipyard, which in metallic letters was still named Lenin Shipyard. There, composed of three tall iron crosses, on which, as though anchors could be crucified, hung three forged-iron anchors, towered a monument to the workers who had been shot by the militia in December 1970.

I said: Frankly, She-rat, frankly, what do you rats think of Solidarność? In practice, she said, their idea has always been ours. And would you, in the future, if Power oppressed you . . . Never again, she says, will the rat nation crawl into holes. But if, just supposing, a super-rat . . . Ridiculous! she cried. Only human brains think up such things. No. We recognize no superiors.

In the port area stood and lay what had been standing or lying since the human era: cranes, containers, fork-lift trucks, weapons of various calibres. Moored to bollards: three minesweepers ready to put to sea. But no hands, no crew, no gulls. Only rats, everywhere rats, here too deferring to the biblical commandment. On every ship's deck, piled up around containers in which they had gnawed holes, up and down the wharves. Their zinc-green fur on and against blackened scrap iron. They alone brought colour into the picture.

Again the She-rat laughed. Incidentally, young friend, do you know the Polish for rat?

I didn't want to know anything. I wanted to move back into my space capsule, to be wafted far away, to dream pictures that would be stirring in a different way. As long as I got away from there.

Szczur, said the She-rat, before vanishing. That's the Polish for rat. *Szczur*, she called after me. Please repeat: *Szczur*.

It should not be supposed that Kashubia is a mere hinterland, a province forgotten by great events, a hilly, backward, self-sufficient region behind the Seven Mountains: Anna Koljaiczek's Kashubian plant has put out shoots all over the world. As one more war was drawing to a close, branches of the Woyke line, harking back to Zukovo, which was a monastery before becoming a demesne, emigrated to Australia: leaving their mother Stine behind; two illegitimate Woyke brothers had boarded ship, accompanied by fiancées from Kokoszki and Firoga.

After one and another war various members of the Stomma

branch and one Kuczorra went to America, where in Chicago and
Buffalo they fell in with descendants of Josef Koljaiczek, who as we
know had disappeared under some rafts at the beginning of the
century and had never been seen again by his Anna; since then, quite
a few Colchics have prospered in the retail and wholesale trades.

Already under the Empire a Bronski from Anna's paternal line
found his way from his native Matarnia to Japan, where he learned
to eat with chopsticks. One of his grandchildren made good and
raised a family in Hong Kong.

After 1945, in addition to Anna's grandson Oskar, who took up
residence in the Rhineland, several grandchildren of her late sisters
Amanda, Hulda and Lisbeth struck root in Swabia and the Ruhr,
because, as people said in those days, and not only around
Kashubian tables, it's nicer in the East, but better in the West.

From Anna's maternal line, the Kurbiellas, as can be seen by the
church registers of Kartuzy, Matarnia and Weijherowo, time and
again forged lifelong ties with the the Woykes, Stommas,
Kuczorras and, collaterally, the Lemkes and Stobbes. One such
Kurbiella went to work in the merchant marine but jumped ship in
the mid-fifties and stayed in Sweden, whence he emigrated to
Africa. His postcards, featuring exotic fruit and palm-girt beaches,
were mailed in Mombasa, where he is active in the hotel business.

Emphatically as all emigrated Kashubians identify themselves as
United States citizens or members of the Commonwealth, and
overemphatically as West Germans, there is a certain Kashubian
something, a smell of buttermilk and sugar-beet syrup that clings to
them, and under a layer of cologne our Herr Matzerath, who likes
to think of himself as a well-travelled man of the world, exudes a
homey smell of cowbarn.

When Anna Koljaiczek proclaimed her hundred and seventh
birthday in postcards of invitation, the call was heard on all five
continents, in Montevideo, for instance, where a great-grandson of
the vanished Josef Koljaiczek dealt, like all the Colchics, in lumber
and precious woods. Certain Colchics are thought to have played a
part in deforesting the Brazilian jungles and others to have owned a
box factory in Iceland.

Thus as our Herr Matzerath draws near via Poznan and
Bydgoszcz, which used to be called Bromberg, he's not the only
one; while a Woyke, who now sports the adventurous name of
Viking and has something to do with the railroad, arrives by sea

from Australia with wife, and a Colchic, accompanied by a wife née Stomma, flies in from Lake Michigan.

From Hong Kong Mr Bruns, formerly Bronski, who exports cheap toys from the British crown colony, has flown to Warsaw via Frankfurt and is now wondering anxiously how the unmistakably Chinese Mrs Bruns will get on with the Kashubians.

Unfortunately, the precious woods dealer from Montevideo has had to call off his visit at the last moment, but the former seaman, who found his way to Africa via Sweden, is expected. He is a hotel manager and still calls himself Kurbiella.

Although the grandchildren of Anna's late sisters Amanda, Hulda and Lisbeth live relatively close to Kashubia, only Herr Stomma and his wife, née Pipka, have promised to come and bring their two teenage children. From Gelsenkirchen, where their bicycle business with repair shop and branch in Wanne-Eickel supports a business manager, the Stommas arrive by rail.

Our Herr Matzerath has tried in vain to persuade his presumptive son Kurt and Kurt's mother, née, as we know, Truczinski, to come with him in his Mercedes; Maria considers herself indispensable. Since her husband's death towards the end of the war, which, as Oskar believes today, could have been avoided, she has remained unmarried and concentrated on business.

'Nothing doing!' she reportedly cried out. 'I'm not going back there.' And then there was a quarrel, in the course of which doubt was cast on paternities, but to expatiate on this tiresome theme would lead us too far. Maria Matzerath stood by her refusal; she couldn't very well leave her chain of stores to shift for themselves.

When, shortly before his departure, I asked him casually: 'Tell me, Oskar, all these Kashubians scattered about the globe – with how many of them are you personally acquainted?' And he replied: 'Up until now a certain diffidence has prevented me from pursuing my past in travels. There has been some correspondence, but apart from photos – the Colchics especially are inexhaustible photographers – there has been nothing concrete. But now I'm hoping for a glimpse, if not of my Uncle Jan, whose intimacy with my poor mama took so tragic a turn, then at least with his son Stephan, who is only two months older than I am.'

After a pause that he made use of to twist the rings on his fingers, he said: 'Oh, well. What we find to say to one another probably won't dig very deep. You know about these family reunions. Lots

of crowding and not much intimacy. I'm mostly interested in my
grandmother. She alone has remained real for me. If I'm going to
Poland, it's to see her and no one else. It's true that Anna Koljaiczek
doesn't live in Bissau-Abbau any more, but more in the vicinity of
Matern, which is now called Matarnia. She was moved out to make
room for the new airport. That's why the potato fields my
grandmother had planted and tilled all her life vanished under
concrete like many another myth.'

While he is on the road in his damaged Mercedes and approaching Posen from Bromberg after a dreamless night, other questions
must be put, if not to him then rhetorically: Why resuscitate Oskar?
Couldn't he have gone on being thirty years of age and in his mental
hospital? And if he was going to resurface, grown older and
media-crazed, why did we have to wait until this hundred and
seventh birthday? Why couldn't it have been years ago, when there
was a round number to celebrate? And why did Anna Koljaiczek
refuse to have a fuss – or, as she called it, 'a kerfuffle' – made about
previous birthdays, and then suddenly have invitations sent all over
the world?

Because she was taken with unrest, which sat down with her on
the bench in front of her house. Because words she had murmured
fervently for so many years: 'It can't be much longer now' no
longer referred only to one very old woman, but had taken on force
and universality: 'It'll soon be over, and there won't be anything
left.'

And that is why all those near or far who were close to her
received cards, which the priest in Matarnia had to write for her;
because Anna Koljaiczek had said to His Reverence: 'I don't mind
celebrating, but somebody else will have to do the writing.'

And one such postcard summoned our Herr Matzerath, who, to
be sure, had punctually honoured his grandmother's birthdays year
after year, but had never returned home since the end of the last war
when gravely ill he had journeyed westward in a freight car. Now
he is driving in a northeasterly direction, staring anxiously, as
though in quest of stability, at the back of his chauffeur's neck. For,
like Anna Koljaiczek, he takes a rather dark view.

Throw a cloth over it and that's that. My Christmas rat's cage
remains covered because I don't want the She-rat to start in again. I
want to hear nothing, see nothing. No Third Programme, in which

between bursts of baroque music the world breaks up into commentaries. Because no one has to tell me that things are going downhill, faster and faster, in fact. And in my notes things are no more cheerful. Everywhere the forests are dying. Malskat? That was long ago. (Who is interested nowadays in knowing the name of the Lübeck bishop who had a swastika-shaped keystone put into the choir vault?) There is still the ship. Maybe that's why. I'd better stick to the women . . .

They've sighted Gotland. *The New Ilsebill* is doing nine knots. The research barge is loud with the clatter of the diesel engine. Damroka wants to make up for all the time lost in arguing and in counting jellyfish for reasons of principle.

The women have stopped quarrelling. The oceanographer assures the others that plenty of material has been gathered.

The helmswoman says: 'If we make a few quick measurements between Öland and Gotland, we'll be through, and for all I care we can . . .'

Damroka says nothing. She doesn't want to keep repeating what the Flounder said to her.

The Old Woman, washing dishes in the galley, cries out: 'We won't be late. Your Vineta won't run away.'

And at the helmswoman's suggestion that the shark should be let out a few times between Rügen and Usedom – to make the East Germans believe in our passion for research – the engineer says: 'Martha is right. They won't open their waters to anyone who's just looking for Vineta.'

That was the prim, old-fashioned name of the helmswoman, who, however, if I were addressing her familiarly by name, would be called not Martha but something entirely different. And if the engineer is here suddenly called Helga and the oceanographer Vera, they both have entirely different names in the places where they exercise – quite successfully, by the way – their real professions. And similarly Damroka: only here is she called Damroka; where she is close to me she manages with fewer syllables. Only the Old Woman might always and everywhere be called Erna.

I have to say all this because under the names they bear elsewhere these five women could never man a ship together; it is my will and my will alone that has placed them on deck, amidships, in hammocks, and on the desired course. It hasn't been easy. Typical! they said. Only a man could get such an idea. Harmony is what he's after. A peace trip. That's what he wants it to be.

Günter Grass

I had to think up tricks and white lies and promise just before they started out that there would never be a storm and that there was no reason to fear engine trouble on the high seas.

But conditions are imposed on me: I was forbidden to count dimples, to discover birth marks, to interpret the slightest wrinkle, be it vertical or horizontal. None of the women wants to be identified by resemblance. They refuse to see themselves as I would like to see them. Accordingly, I mustn't draw profiles, make one forehead round, another low, or cut out eye patterns. When I make them talk or keep silent, the speaking or silent mouth must be disregarded. There must be no description of how eloquent or sealed lips open, meet, press, moisten each other. Wide cheekbones, a sensitive or firmly jutting chin, webbed or detached earlobes, must not be typical. No smell – for no two smell alike – is permitted to look for adjectives. And never must there be colour. That is why none of the women on board is blue-, grey-, or doe-eyed. No mention of dark-brown, ash-blonde, deep-black or wheat-coloured hair is permissible. Only Damroka's flowing tresses – that may stand. And it can also be said the the hair of all five is more or less shot through with grey. They have grown older and older since I've known them, from the mid-forties to far over seventy, although the Old Woman in particular makes a show of girlishness.

So many years have been lived through. If I may say so, they have become more beautiful with time. Since – so I'm told – they were good looking from the start, they have managed in aging to throw a veil over their beauty, which had been worn too openly before.

That's how it is: five veiled beauties bound for Vineta. Even their stories, all of which are about past men, are veiled stories; for I shall never be permitted to say how I became estranged from them, how they lost me, how I was never real to them, how I came their way when I was hungry or by chance. Nor can the question of who hurt, who used, who misses whom, or of who left whom standing in the rain, serve as a ballast for a ship that will soon be searching – because already *The New Ilsebill* is putting into the port of Visby on Gotland – for the submerged city of Vineta.

'Man!' cries Helga the engineer, swinging her arms and legs, 'do I feel like shore leave!'

Vera the oceanographer says: 'I'm putting in a new film. I've heard about interesting ruins in Visby. All genuinely medieval.'

The Old Woman, who is called Erna either way, lists necessary purchases: 'And we absolutely need something to drink. A few bottles of aquavit. How do we know what they'll have in your underseas queendom?'

The helmswoman, whose name is Martha, absolutely wants an adventure when they go ashore. 'I'm going to pick up a man on the double,' she says. 'For luck.'

The moment they dock, Damroka, whom I've always called Damroka in secret, insists on going to the harbour master to pick up the stamped papers. She says: 'When we pass Mönchgut to starboard and the East German coastguard come alongside, we'll show them our A-1 papers. After that, practically nothing can happen to us.'

I keep out of it. I don't tell them what I know. I don't tell them that it may be too late. Oh, if only Vineta were open to the women!

The She-rat dates us according to her own chronology. Of everything that happened before she appeared in Europe and was dated rather accurately according to our time reckoning, she disposes with the formula: That was in the era of the black house rat. Its origin remains obscure. More mythogenically than illuminatingly, she says: For years we lived by the shores of the Caspian Sea, until one day we decided to swim across the Volga and to migrate, which earned us the name of migratory rat, though in some languages we are known simply as brown rats.

As their arrival in Europe during the seventeen-fifties was reported concordantly from the seaports of the continent and of the British Isles, the plague-disseminating migration took place, according to the She-rat, in the era of the black house rat.

Similarly, all the rats which during the Thirty Years War fetched a price in Magdeburg, Stralsund, Breisach and elsewhere and had food value roasted or boiled, were black house rats.

Nevertheless, the She-rat, as a member of the migratory species that made its way here from Asia and has absurdly been called the Norway rat, identifies herself with the species *Rattus rattus*, whose presence since then has seldom been demonstrated, and with the long history of the black house rat, which is said to have been somewhat smaller, with a more pointed nose and a proportionately even longer tail.

We, she says, do not make these distinctions. A rat's a rat. And as rats, we have been present in all migrations, in the progress of the Plague, in the shadow of every crusade and procession of flagellants, at the burning of Joan, before Macbeth's castle, with all the emperors of Rome and on the battlefields of the Thirty Years War. If rats were reported present on Gustavus Adophus's ships when he crossed the Baltic Sea to Pomerania, then it was us in our black form. And when in Hamelin house rats, though known to be excellent swimmers, were said to have been drowned by the thousands in the Weser, then again it was us that they tried to drown.

But the migratory rats did not become conspicuously active until the start of the French Revolution, which according to the She-rat ended with the defeat of the uprising known as the Paris Commune; for which reason she attached special importance to the year 1871, when once again rats raw and roasted fetched their price. When preparing for a long disquisition, she always says: In the days of the Paris Commune or: That was just before the uprising known as the Paris Commune . . .

According to the She-rat's calculations, it was shortly before the Paris Commune that the dismal and, as she puts it, degrading history of the white-haired and red-eyed laboratory rat began. In the eighteen-fifties, it became fashionable in England and France to shut up a hundred or two of these rats with an especially vicious dog, usually a terrier, and make bets on the time it would take the dog to do away with the rats – an entertainment not confined to the lower classes. But when there were albinos among the captive rats, these were singled out and exhibited as curiosities in showrooms and menageries. This went on for about ten years until a law prohibiting rat-baiting was promulgated first in France and somewhat later in England. But since the demand for red-and-white rats increased in the meantime, it became customary to keep pairs of albinos suitable for display, and this became a source of numerous red-and-white litters.

A doctor in Geneva, the She-rat tells me, was the first to perform laboratory experiments with red-and-white rats. He started by using them to test foodstuffs. Later, he mixed medicines with their feed, and finally he infected his laboratory rats with common human diseases – diphtheria, scarlet fever, whooping cough. But it was not until thirty-five years after the Paris Commune, when the Wistar Institute in Philadelphia began large-scale production of the laboratory rats which continued to be termed useful until shortly before Doomsday, that the red-and-white variety asserted itself worldwide as experimental animals.

The She-rat said: About a hundred and fifty years after we landed in Europe – we came by boat – the entry of the laboratory rat into human history ushered in the development that was to lead to the Big Bang.

At this point in her history course she said: Incidentally, did you know that in the last year of human history the breeding laboratories in Wilmington, Delaware, had produced eighteen million laboratory rats for the domestic and foreign market and reckoned their profits at thirty million dollars?

I can't talk her out of a time-lapse history of the twentieth century. She treats the First and Second World Wars and the third unleashed by her fellow rats as a single conflict which, in her view, had its logical conclusion in the Big Bang. Accordingly, when getting ready to tell a story, she speaks of the period before or after the Big Bang. Recently she has been using terms like human and post-human era.

In a recent dream, she said: That was still during the human era, but a good hundred and fifty years after the house-rat era. Then, at the start of the laboratory-rat era, when the Russian Baltic fleet under Admiral Rodjestvenski put to sea from Libau, we left his ships. And not so long after the naval battle of Tsushima, in which we participated aboard Japanese ships, began the Great War, that three-stage conflict which, despite breaks inventively utilized for the development of new means of extermination, set itself the aim of obliterating mankind and ushering in the post-human era.

Not so long ago the She-rat, taking our time reckoning into account, said: According to human dating, it was in 1630 that we landed on the Pomeranian island of Usedom with the fleet of the Swedish King Gustavus Adolphus, and off the coast of Usedom discovered a submerged city which, founded in the era of the house rat, was at first called Jumne and later something else.

When in her next sentence the She-rat gave the name of the submerged city, I lamented: Oh, God! If the women knew that the She-rat knows where Vineta is, they would despair. I must warn them. The moment I wake up, I'll tell Damroka about the She-rat, about the house rats and brown rats, about *rotta, radau, rät, radda* and *rotto*, which were not called *ratz, ratze,* Italian *ratto,* French and

English *rat*, and German *Ratte* and *Rättin* until after the sound shift.

I interrupted angrily when she launched into a lengthy disquisition: It was after the Big Bang that . . .

Not true! I shouted. It's all a pack of lies. There hasn't been any Big Bang. And if there is one, which doesn't seem entirely unlikely, you rats, which includes you, She-rat, will not survive that X-Day.

Untroubled, she once again explained the stopper system that had proved its worth since the days of Noah. Even before the Big Bang, she said, whenever the exterminators tried to fumigate our corridors and nesting chambers, we stopped up the passages with elderly rats, who sealed off our refuges hermetically with their fat rumps.

When I again shouted Lies! and No!, she singled me out for special attention. Your stupidity, my boy, demands a good deal of patience. I'm afraid I'll have to keep you in after school. For your edification – because you don't know anything, no, not a thing! – I am going to diagram our security system on the blackboard with school chalk.

So once again – as though my schooling were never to end – a blackboard was moved into my dream: and incidentally, I heard, we never had to compel our senior rats to protect us. Often there were so many volunteers that we used three corks for every access and made every one of our nesting chambers absolutely secure against all human attempts at gassing. Just as we can stretch and slenderize until we are able to squeeze through the narrowest conduits, we are capable of pumping ourselves up into stoppers not only against poison gas, but against water as well. This, it seems to me, should make it clear, even to your stupidity, how we survived the Flood but also how we hope to survive your stupidity.

Whereupon she sketched passages, chambers and stoppers on the blackboard: a labyrinth. Her lesson went on and on. When we were walking through the old city of Danzig a while ago, you, our friend, showed unconcealed pleasure over the soot-blackened but substantially well-preserved condition of numerous historical monuments. Amazing, you may have thought, how comfortably everyday rat life has gone on since the Big Bang. But that impression is deceptive. We are still plagued by sudden dust storms. The only protection against their demoralizing effect is flight into our system of passages and trusty old stoppers. At the beginning of the post-human era we had a hard time keeping our population up. Any number of litters had to be bitten down because of missing limbs, open heads, knotty tails. For that reason, we still secure our nesting chambers with senior rats. Their festering rumps still show what a necessary service they are performing. Take a look, my young friend, take a good look.

The She-rat turned around and showed me her rump, which had been doing stopper duty against radioactive fallout. What I saw was one great festering wound. Bones uncovered. The tail reduced to lumps of cartilage. No fur at all. Oozing tumours. Her vagina a throbbing, foaming crater, disgorging trickles of fluid.

She-rat, I cried. You're dying on me.

So what? – Slowly, too slowly, she turned away her gaping wound, her rump.

Without you, I'll be alone in my space capsule, dreadfully alone.

Don't exaggerate.

Be well again, She-rat, I implore you.

I heard her laugh softly, her whiskers were back in the picture. Silly old pops. Hasn't it dawned on you that we'll always be with you, ever new generations of us, that your human self with its mortality is unknown to us, that our self transcends death because it is made up of uncounted rat lives? Don't be afraid. You won't lose us. You'll never be without us. We are attached to you, because you made yourself useful when we needed a source of error with which to spark off the Big Bang and usher in the post-human era.

> Something must be wrong
> I don't know what, the direction maybe.
> Some mistake, but what, has been made
> but when and where wrong
> especially as everything's been running like clockwork,
> though in a direction
> which signs demonstrate to be wrong.
>
> Now we are looking for the source of error.
> Frantically looking for it outside ourselves,
> until someone says we,
> we could all of us, just for the sake of argument, be
> the source of error, yes,
> it could be you or you or you.
> We don't mean it personally.

Each gives the next man precedence.
While everything is running like clockwork
in the wrong direction,
which even if it's wrong is said to be
the only one, men greet
each other with the cry:
I am the source of error, you too?

Seldom had there been such consensus.
No one asks any longer where what and when
a mistake was made.
Nor does anyone ask about
guilt or guilty parties.

For after all we know that each of us,
contentedly as never before we all run
in the wrong direction, follow the signs,
hoping that they're wrong
and that we're saved again.

Buckled into my cosmic armchair, I froze with horror. Cut it out, She-rat. Stop making jokes. I should, I have, I alone am.

Play dumb, deaf and dead, I shouted to myself, and played dumb, deaf and dead.

Then at last I realized: this suits her to a T. She sticks me in a space capsule and makes me the source of error. She's worked that out very cleverly, because it's true that I fill the bill: a technological idiot, who's out of place in this module, a bad risk. Incapable of working a simple pocket calculator and without the slightest idea of what this that and the other microprocessor knows and can do, I am simply the ideal source of error. So she claims that I fiddled stupidly, irresponsibly with knobs and buttons. That I, a bungling ignoramus let loose in cosmic space, suddenly took it into my head, because I was bored or because Sunday was going on and on, to toy with those cute little silicon chips; and worse, by way of video transfer, to feed footage from science fiction movies, specifically from end-of-the world thrillers, into the real output and disregard the warning signal, with the result that my catastrophe programme – unidentified objects approaching target – went straight to the earth terminal first of the Western, then of the Eastern Protector Power; after which, as you can well imagine, neither of them let the grass grow under his feet.

Which, said the She-rat, goes to show that the Big Bang could be set off without the help of any rats. Hadn't I, she went on, succeeded, with dreamlike, playful certainty and sharpness of image, in feeding those singleminded foreign objects into the machine and in resynchronizing the time code, which had been off kilter at first?

So I'm the source of error. I of all people am supposed to have playfully ended it all. No! I yelled. You can't foist that on me. You, She-rat, ought to know that I can barely change a light bulb, that I can't even drive a car. I've always been like this, even as a Hitler Cub and later as an air-force auxiliary with the rank of gunner sixth grade, was never able to make the mechanical pointer of our 88 millimetre gun catch up with the electrical pointer. To this day I dream about that and other incapacities. And now you want me to be an orbit observer. A space gymnast. When I haven't the faintest idea what chips and clips are. When all I know of the cosmonaut lingo is what I've heard at the movies. I, who only a moment ago was trying desperately to stop what was going on by shouting Stop! False alarm!

In vain, of course. I can't do that kind of thing. I'm too stupid. Earth! I shouted. Answer, Earth. But all I got was a squeaking. Then silence. My own sound.

I said to myself in my dream: I'm going to wake up now. I don't want to be dreamed as a source of error. The moment I wake up, I'll reach, even before drinking tea, for the newspaper. We'll see what they have to report. There won't be one word about a source of error. On the contrary: everything will be functioning as usual. Of course there are dangers, but when haven't there been? Never has the desire for peace been so great.

Still, they should be warned, those old men whose fingers are trembling so close to the pushbutton. Listen, I shouted, you powerful old men. I hear you want to talk to each other and not be quite so angry at each other any more. Good for you. Talk, please talk, about anything you like, so long as you talk. And yet we can't help wondering: What good do these recent peace talks do the world if first teeny weeny errors and then pretty big ones creep, no, gnaw their way into our security system, as certain rodents gnaw their way through wood, concrete, even metal, until they – let's just suppose for the hell of it – get into both central computers and foment mischief or worse, muddle our chips and clips, our so carefully engineered security, no, worse, not muddle, no, spark off something that's already there just waiting for an opportunity, something definitive and irrevocable. Rodents can do that. Mice, for instance. They go in and out where they please, no hole is too small, no crack too narrow.

Therefore, old men, it's time to sound the alarm! Do you hear, the alarm! Promptly, no, immediately, the computerized command centres of both Protector Powers must be secured against the incursion of mice. And not just mice. There is also a possibility that other, especially tenacious and intelligent rodents, which moreover are immune to poison, rats, for example, ignoring man's thirst for peace, will circumvent all those security measures that are effective against mice.

Why? For what motives?

Well, because they want to get rid of us, of all mankind, because they're sick of us, because they dream of a post-human era in which they'll have fun all by themselves; or at the most with such company as woodlice, stinging bluebottles and flying snails.

Just listen, you bigshots, condemned to bear such overwhelming responsibility, to what I've dreamed. We've gone out of existence. I was in Gdańsk, where I lived as a child, as a Hitler Youth and airforce auxiliary, and all I saw was rats. And then another dream: I'm sitting in a space capsule. But I'm not investigating astronomical phenomena, I'm trying to feed what's happening on earth into my computer, so people down below will finally get it through their heads that this can't go on. I mean, all the many problems which, seen from above, are lying around unsolved. Such as where to put the garbage? Or: How can so and so many jellyfish be counted? Or: Who will make the dying forests well again once we, like the prince in the fairy tale, have finally hit on the source of error?

Shortly before waking, I managed in my space capsule to bring the monitor to life. After the usual scrambled images that occur in dreams I – again an incompetent gunner sixth grade – saw several fairy-tale figures going somewhere in a car . . .

With Rumpelstiltskin at the wheel, the selected dwarf beside him, Sleeping Beauty and the prince who wakes her with a kiss in the back seat, they are heading for Bonn, which is said to be the capital of the German Federal Republic.

The dwarf is sitting on two cushions; a map of Bonn is resting on his lap and he is exploring it with one index finger. Unfamiliar with the city, Rumpelstiltskin follows the dwarf's instructions. 'Take the left lane.' 'Third on the right.'

Time and again, the prince wakes his Sleeping Beauty with a kiss and points out the sights: the Rhine seen from the Rhine Bridge, Beethoven Hall, then after some meandering through the lobbyists' quarters, a highrise building heightened by three capital letters and a low, modern structure, which, however, is supposed to suggest a shack.* Sleeping Beauty's long-lashed eyes are shut tight; she has to open them wide, but immediately falls asleep again. Rumpelstiltskin almost overlooks a stop light. 'Red!' screams the dwarf.

In midtown, the old Ford, which is still going strong thanks to witch petrol, encounters several demonstrations carrying banners with strident, often mutually antagonistic slogans. The prince and the dwarf read: 'When is the year of the baby coming?' – 'Turks, go home!' – 'Dump the missiles!' – 'Arm the peace!' – 'No to experiments with animals!' – 'Down with rats and bluebottles!' – 'Forests or no forests, life goes on.' – 'The forests are dying and the Grimm Brothers sleep!'

Some of the demonstrators are hooded, others armed with staves, many are disguised as corpses or zinc-green rats. Someone is standing on a street corner, reading a newspaper with the screaming headline: 'Russians holding Chancellor's children.' Because the traffic has come to a halt and the newspaper reader is not far off, the dwarf reads the headline aloud. He giggles and claps his little hands.

At last a sign: 'To the Chancellery'. A little further on they stop at the entrance. Rumpelstiltskin identifies himself to the duty officer as chairman of the 'Save the Fairy Tales' Committee. Once again the prince has to wake his Sleeping Beauty with a kiss. 'Dearest, we have arrived.'

When the duty officer hesitates, the dwarf reels off a longish subtitle: 'We are looking for the Special Ministry for Medium-Term Forest Damage. We have an appointment with the minister and the undersecretary, Jakob and Wilhelm Grimm. Our password is Fairy Tale Road. It's urgent.'

On instructions from the duty officer a clerk types the password

---

* The Social Democrat Party Building in Bonn is known affectionately as *Die Baracke*, The Shack.

into the computer. The monitor reads: 'Password Fairy Tale Road.' And then the answer: 'Admit Fairy Tale Road.' The barrier goes up. The duty officer salutes. The prince hands out a tip through the open window. The young, rather overworked officer is astonished to see a gold coin in the palm of his hand. (Our Herr Matzerath might advise us on this point. Should it be a maxdor or a gold ruble?)

In the Gingerbread House the fairy-tale characters see what is happening in Bonn. They applaud as the delegation alights from the old Ford and is welcomed by Jakob and Wilhelm Grimm in the doorway of the ministry. The girl's chopped-off hands clap too. Hansel and Gretel explain to Rapunzel who Jakob is and who Wilhelm is. The witch nibbles excitedly on bones from her collection. The grandmother, who is hard of hearing, says to Little Red Riding Hood: 'I do hope they bring me the dictionary. It needn't be all the volumes. The dwarf promised.'

On the walls of the Grimm Brothers' offices large maps show forests and degrees of damage indicated in different colours. Jakob invites the fairy-tale characters to be seated around a table. Wilhelm produces an early edition of *Grimms' Fairy Tales* and asks for autographs. Sleeping Beauty signs first, then the prince. The dwarf signs as the 'Third Dwarf'. Rumpelstiltskin winds up for a big signature, hesitates, then makes three crosses. It takes Sleeping Beauty's assurance – 'But the gentlemen know . . .' to make him add in parentheses: 'Rumpelstiltskin'.

After admiring the amusing arrangement of smurfs in Jakob Grimm's cabinet, the third dwarf (following out one of our Herr Matzerath's suggestions) imparts Little Red Riding Hood's grandmother's wish for a copy of the Grimms' Dictionary. 'She's so hard of hearing and so fond of reading.' Flattered, Jakob Grimm holds out a signed copy. 'At last it has appeared. The first volume, from A to Bumblebee. We shall gladly furnish further volumes as they appear.'

Now, at last, the fairy-tale characters present their grievances. Rumpelstiltskin jumps up, demands, stamps his foot, shakes his fists. The prince steps forward, as elegant and ingratiating as a diplomat. The third dwarf agitates with anarchistic undertones. Sleeping Beauty, who has just been awakened with a kiss, laments tearfully.

The plaints of the fairy-tale characters should be underlined by eloquent gestures – bended knee, wringing of hands. Few subtitles are needed: 'Without forests we are lost.' – 'If the forests die, so shall we.' – 'How bereft people will be without forests and fairy tales.' – 'We shall avenge ourselves.'

Jakob Grimm points at photos of gigantic factories and car dumps. 'Unfortunately,' he says, 'there is nothing we can do. Democracy is a mere petitioner. The power is with the big money.'

Wilhelm Grimm is close to tears: 'Not only the powerful, all of us will share the guilt if the forests die.'

Sleeping Beauty starts blubbering and the prince is unable to comfort her. The third dwarf curses: 'But after the forests the population will die.'

In a rage, Rumpelstiltskin pulls off his leg, which had been specially prepared for this scene, and bangs it down on the desk of the Minister for Medium-Term Forest Damage.

In the magic mirror the fairy-tale characters who have stayed at home see the hopeless situation in Bonn. All are downcast. Rapunzel wraps herself in her hair, wants to see nothing and hear nothing. Snow White makes a move to eat the poison apple encapsulated in artificial resin. One of the six remaining dwarfs cries out: 'Must capitalism triumph for ever?' Little Red Riding Hood stamps her little red boots in despair: 'Shit!' she cries out. 'I'm going to let the wolf eat me!' And she runs out of the house.

The grandmother doesn't understand, she shakes her head, picks up the wicked stepmother's little enamelled box, switches Bonn off and the black and white film *Little Red Riding Hood and the Wolf* on. After a moment of scrambled images suggesting various fairy-tale motifs, she finally sees the fiery-eyed wolf gobbling up Little Riding Hood.

Angrily the wicked stepmother shuts off the magic mirror and cries out: 'What is this nonsense, grandmother!'

While Hansel tries to comfort the despairing fairy-tale characters, Gretel runs to the well and pours in a pail of water, which makes the frog king come popping out. Smiling sadly, the ladylike princess acquiesces in an incipient triangular relationship. (Our Herr Matzerath has requested this complication.)

But now the witch laments loudly: 'Alas! Without forests, children will never be able to get lost again.' Hansel comforts her, but manages to break loose before she can enfold him in her tits. 'Enough lamenting,' he cries. 'There must be a solution. Where there's a will there's a way. Man just can't live without forests. Can't you get that through your heads?'

Suddenly in Bonn Wilhelm Grimm has an idea. He searches the forest maps on the wall and says: 'We must finally get the Chancellor to visit the dying forest with us and other experts.'

Jakob Grimm agrees. 'Maybe a miracle will happen.' The third dwarf wants details: 'Exactly where will this be done?'

Jakob Grimm points out the spot on the big forest map. Wilhelm Grimm circles it with a red pencil. Sleeping Beauty in tears has fallen asleep. The prince wakes her with a kiss and points a long, aristocratic finger at the scene of future events, while Rumpelstiltskin buckles his leg back on again.

In the Gingerbread House the happy turn of events is captured in the magic mirror. Hansel makes a note of the spot. The dwarfs produce a rudimentary map. Hansel's note is compared with the map. They find the place, mark it and work out a plan with Hansel.

The other fairy-tale characters are watching television. The magic mirror shows the departure of the delegation. In leavetaking Sleeping Beauty has given Wilhelm a kiss. The Grimm Brothers wave as the old Ford drives off. The girl without hands is spellbound, her chopped-off hands start waving as well. Angrily, the grandmother switches off the magic mirror and cries out: 'But where's Red Riding Hood, the silly little minx!' She hobbles out of the house. The others follow.

In his cage, the sleeping wolf is turned over on his side. Rübezahl opens the zipper. No sooner has Little Red Riding Hood crawled out of the wolf than her grandmother slaps her face.

With the help of the map, the dwarfs explain the plan to the other fairy-tale characters. Hansel, Gretel and the girl without hands bring tools, shovels, rakes, picks.

The old Ford with the delegation approaches from the forest. The two parties greet one another with jubilation. The witch flatters Rumpelstiltskin. Noise and backslapping among the dwarfs, whose number is again complete, now that the third is back.

The grandmother gets her present: Volume I of Grimms' Dictionary and (in accordance with the change of scenario requested by our Herr Matzerath) reads words which appear as subtitles: 'agony, anguish, anxiety, anxious . . .'

All these anxiety-ridden nouns fail to trouble the others. Amid loud cheers the witch fills the tank again. Hansel and the dwarfs cry: 'Forward!' and 'Äktschen pliess!' Rübezahl cranks the old Ford up.

At the witch's bidding, one of the dwarfs fetches Sleeping Beauty's spindle. Another dwarf puts picks into the hands of Jorinde and Joringel. The wicked stepmother hauls the magic mirror out of the Gingerbread House. Rapunzel feels enterprising and puts her hair up. The girl with the chopped-off hands orders her hands to pick up a shovel.

All are eager to get started, only the grandmother with the dictionary wants to stay at home. She reads aloud: 'Abandon, abeam, aberrant, aberration, abeyance, alienate . . .'

The fairy-tale characters answer with goodbye kisses. Rübezahl gives the grandmother her last kiss over the Dictionary.

Only now does the girl with the chopped-off hands dispatch her hands with the shovel. They fly away, followed by the seven ravens. Overloaded with fairy-tale characters, the old Ford vanishes into the forest. Only the grandmother and the wolf stay behind. She reads the dictionary to him: 'Anal, analysis, animadvert, annul . . .'

Those beautiful words
Nevermore shall solace be spoken.
No tongue is moved to speak with melancholy.
Never more will voices proclaim beatitude.
So much sorrow speechless.
Leave of the words which tell us that the man in the land of Uz
came naked out of his mother's womb.

If we could go on saying beer curds
or granary, or honeypot, or jug.
Let us then regret the oldwife.
Who knows that the woodpecker was once called bee-wolf?
Who wishes he were called Nepomuk, Balthazar, Eulenspiegel,
    Puck.
Adieu to words that ask for
viaticum, repast.

Who, as we go, will cry farewell,
who whisper: the bed is made?
Nothing will come upon and overshadow and dwell with
and know us, as the Angel

promised the Virgin.

Struck with deafness in leavetaking
we are running out of words.

Chapter Seven, in which someone addresses the Bundestag, the seven dwarfs are individuals, five women go ashore in quest of experience, jellyfish sing loud and low, our Herr Matzerath arrives, Malskat does Gothic gymnastics in the choir loft, She-rat complains of loneliness, Sleeping Beauty pricks her finger on the spindle and the ship drops anchor over Vineta.

WHEN I dreamed of the She-rat along with the city of Danzig, through which I, lone pedestrian, was walking, when the ship hesitated, tarried on its way to Vineta and didn't want to dock in Visby – just as Oskar tarried on the roads of Poland – I, after insisting several times in other dreams: No! there *must* be a way out, there *must* be some wee little hope, dreamed I'd been given leave to face the Bundestag and read or extemporize a speech. And when I saw the members sitting before me and knew the President of the Bundestag was sitting raised behind me and the Chancellor with his cabinet to the right of me, I spoke as follows:

Mr President, ladies and gentlemen. I seem to see you all in your well-considered seating order as in a dream. And because I stand behind this lectern in a dream, it may be that certain details of my remarks will be blurred at the fringes, while others will be painfully sharp-edged. Dreams, as we all know, have their special perspective; they insist on disproportion. Science has established that on a higher plane, they tell the truth, but off the record they are not so punctilious. For even now, after my first glance at this fully occupied hall, the dividing lines between party and party begin to blur; no longer do I recognize parties, I see only interests.

I am aware of troubling incidentals. No sooner do I begin my speech than a swarm of paymasters force themselves on my attention; moistening their thumbs, counting out banknotes, handing them to certain deputies, and to members of the cabinet as well. I also have the impression that while I'm speaking the Chancellor at my right is pushing wedge after wedge of Black Forest cherry torte into his mouth.

Of course I know that deputies and ministers are not publicly paid off. Never would the Chancellor surrender so visibly to his weakness for sweets. It's only my dream that makes this possible. It lays bare the reality and even allows me to ask the paymasters, who are still rushing about, to take a well-deserved breakfast break; there's no need to bribe and subvert around the clock. Moreover, Mr Chancellor, I must ask you to save a piece of cake for the speaker after me, for then I shall be able, undeterred by amusing distractions, to put forward a suggestion having no other purpose than the furtherance of culture.

It concerns the neutron bomb which, you will recall, ladies and gentlemen, has been an object of controversy. There was talk of banning it. Indignation was expressed. I too was opposed to it at the time. Inhuman, I called it. And so it is. It is still inhuman. For where the neutron bomb strikes, man perishes, and with him every living thing.

I have been told that the accelerated neutron and gamma rays first paralyse the human nervous system, then demolish the gastro-intestinal tract, at the same time provoking internal bleeding, violent perspiration and diarrhoea, and finally inducing death by removing the last drop of water from the body, dehydrating it, as the doctors say.

This is horrible, the mind boggles. The many protests were understandable. But apart from the dehydrated humans and other living creatures, neutron bombs destroy next to nothing. Buildings, implements, vehicles remain unscathed, as do banks, churches, and multi-level garages with everything in them. Still, it was rightly said at the time: that is not enough. What can undamaged factories, efficient war machines and intact barracks mean to us if all human beings are to perish?

But now, ladies and gentlemen, I must ask you: what would the picture be if the neutron bomb had a culture-saving task to perform? What would we say to an art-loving bomb with a mission of conservation? Would we be able to live with it if, as planned, it left not only tanks and cannon, but also Gothic cathedrals and baroque façades intact? In other words, I hold that you and I, all of us who only yesterday were incensed, should develop a new and more relaxed attitude towards the neutron bomb and learn to recognize its true and, why mince words, its art-loving character.

Let us look back: the violent discussions of those days impeded progress from mere tactical projectiles to strategically effective neutron bombs. But there is no lack of talents or resources, and we can make up for lost time. Those of us who would like to see our highest cultural treasures preserved for all eternity – and I am sure that such is the heartfelt desire of every one of you deputies – are bound to favour the production of conservation bombs.

Of course this imperative is valid for both Protector Powers. A balance of terror calls for a corresponding balance of conservation. What we therefore need is a special pact, which will strictly confine the neutron or conservation bomb to the defence of culture. We have only to wish it and a committee, constituted by both Protector Powers, will become active, first in Europe and later on in all the other continents. It will draw up a list of the most important cultural centres. The next step will be to specify conservation zones of equal scope on both sides, to be designed as important target zones. For this the present potential will not be sufficient and both Protector Powers will have to enlarge their striking forces. Why? Because we are determined to preserve as much cultural substance as possible from atomic destruction.

If, ladies and gentlemen, I interpret your heckling correctly, you are beginning to be interested. You wish I would come to the point. Your passionate cries are telling me that art is a matter of taste.

How right you are! But our taste in artistic matters will define itself once we, here at home, on German-German territory, give names to what is worth preserving: I propose Bamberg and Dresden as cities to be neutronized. Here you may find it helpful to recall Semper's, since rebuilt, Opera House in Dresden, and the Bamberg Horseman. Our next choice, though I prefer not to be too explicit, might be on this side Rothenburg on the Tauber, and on the other side Stralsund, then Lübeck and Bautzen . . .

I beg you, ladies and gentlemen – many thanks Mr President – to refrain from such recommendations as: What about Celle? or: Why not Bayreuth? Because the all-German aspect of the projected conservation programme deserves priority.

[*173*]

Since it must be assumed that most cities – for there are vestiges of culture everywhere – will apply for the privilege of art-fostering neutronization, the deliberative commission, which remains to be set up, will incur great responsibility. It will have to demonstrate its appreciation of art. But it will also have to learn to say no when it proves necessary to preserve the traditional targeting of one or another city, be it Leipzig or Stuttgart, Magdeburg or Frankfurt-on-Main.

Yes, indeed. I, too, regret this deeply. It grieves me to say that many of the big cities in Europe cannot lay claim to neutron protection. But if timely action is taken, it will be possible to transfer a significant part of the art treasure threatened by nuclear destruction to cities assured of protective neutronization.

For instance: the treasures of the Vatican could be moved to Avignon, the art works of the Louvre to Strasbourg, those of Warsaw to Cracow, and the splendours of Museum Island in East Berlin to the conservation-warranting cultural sphere of Weimar. I do not exclude the possibility that certain cherished cathedral portals, certain baroque façades that have become dear to us, baptismal fonts that have served their purpose for generations, wayside saints familiar to us from childhood, should be voluntarily relegated to conservation zones; an all-European process, I might add, certain to create jobs. Why, for example, should it not, with our technical know-how, be possible to move the Cologne Cathedral to Dinkelsbühl or the Tower of London to Stratford-upon-Avon?

In short, ladies and gentlemen, is there anything we wouldn't do to save the monuments of European culture? Europe would be enabled for the last time to demonstrate greatness, to set an example of conservation for other continents to emulate. I therefore beg you to allow me – with Mr President's permission – a personal remark, which seems appropriate at this time. If my native city of Danzig, which has been called Gdańsk since the end of the provisionally last war, should be fortunate enough to be included among the neutronized cities, if in other words its towers and turrets, its gabled houses and porches, its Neptune Fountain and all its brick Gothic severity, were to survive the Third World War, I should accept any and every sacrifice with a light heart.

Of course some of you may exclaim: This is inhuman cynicism. And at first I too said to myself: What good does all this conservation do us if in the neutronized cities every living creature, in whose flesh as it says in the Bible there is breath, is dehydrated until death ensues? Who would be left to behold what has been preserved and to cry out in amazement: What imperishable beauty!?

But let us not be misled. We have no choice. Art like freedom exacts its price. Therefore, ladies and gentlemen, you must be firm, you must be resolute.

But as I gaze upon this assembly hall and see how drastically your ranks have thinned, nay more, see that I am alone in this high house – for the Chancellor and his cabinet have also vanished – I am assailed by doubt. I begin to wonder: Will the absent deputies be prepared, in their love of art, to act with the same unflinching consistency as they did on another occasion when called to defend our freedom, and a majority said Yes to that medium-range thingamajig – what *was* it called?

But they're gone. Beyond reach of any words. Yet I'd have liked to make further proposals, of a nature to complete our neutronization programme. I am thinking of the grime that follows.

After the Big Bang, as I have been informed by a post-human source and as all experts assure me even now, clouds of ash will darken the sky. Storms will carry this concentrated expression of man's ultimate potentiality around the globe, and before long cathedrals, richly ornamented palaces, smiling baroque façades will be black with soot. Everything will be covered with soot. Thick, greasy soot. The damage would be inestimable. A shame. A cultural disgrace. Will no one listen? Hey, Chancellor!

He's gone. Nothing left of him but crumbs. When counter-measures are needed. Now, at once. Research grants should be funded, the German inventive spirit mobilized, our chemical concerns encouraged to develop a removable protective coating to prevent the soot from being for ever . . .

Yes, I know, the question remains: Who in God's name is to remove this protective coating? If you, ladies and gentlemen of the opposition, were still present, you could embarrass me by shouting: But everybody has been radiated, dehydrated, bumped off. However, I know a way. All labour and sorrow, as the Bible says, need not be confined to the human race. I wish to remind you of the common brown, or Norway, rat's capacity for survival. It will live on when we are gone. It will find the cultural monuments that we have caringly preserved. The rat, the survivor, has been devoted to man from time immemorial. Curious as rats are, he will peel off the soot-blackened protective coatings centimetre by centimetre, and gaze in wonderment at the intact splendour . . .

Then I ceased to dream that I was addressing the Bundestag. Wide awake, I heard myself pronouncing my concluding sentence: I thank you, ladies and gentlemen, for your eloquent absence.

How fortunate that nothing is decided as yet: our Herr Matzerath is on the road, the ship is putting into the port of Visby, my Christmas rat is asleep, dreaming perhaps of the Third Programme, but in the Grimms' forest resistance is building up; the fairy-tale characters are all ferociously resolute.

How are we to conceive of the seven dwarfs individually? What more can be said of Jorinde and Joringel than that they are the saddest of sad couples? Is the kissing compulsion worth looking into more closely?

Our Herr Matzerath will want to know this and still more as soon as he gets back from Poland. He's pleased that I've made all seven of them anarchists, but he wants to see each one fleshed out as an individual. The second, like a bookkeeper, might enter each of the prince's kisses on a tally sheet, the fourth might ape the kissing prince; later on, we shall see the first, sixth and seventh dwarfs eye the insatiable kissing mouth with suspicion.

It's obvious that all seven exploit their Snow White; not only must the sickly little thing wash and iron their clothes, sew on their buttons and shine seven pairs of shoes to a high polish; we also see one or another of them disappear into an attic room with their always obliging little housekeeper. Every time the customer comes whistling down the stairs after a relatively short visit and Snow White staggers out of her bedchamber exhausted, the wicked stepmother takes in old coins, such as Prussian talers, gold pieces.

They are rough, noisy fellows, crazy about their dice games. Group sports keep them physically fit: finger wrestling, tripping one another up. The only one of the boarders they're polite to is the witch, who is respected by all, even the wicked stepmother; the two women often plunge into conversations, in the course of which questions relating to women's lib do not go unanswered.

The mistress of the Gingerbread House invariably behaves like a house mother, at once strict and caring; only occasionally, when she toys with Hansel's fingers, does her true nature shine through.

The Rat

It seems likely that she is having an affair with Rübezahl the hired man, or with Rumpelstiltskin, or both, for she has only to lift her long index finger for the hulking giant and the limping waiter to comply in a fright. She doesn't like to see Rübezahl letting Rapunzel comb his beard. She detests seeing Rumpelstiltskin unbuckle his leg to compare his stump with the girl's arm stumps.

The witch often asks for the frog king; more often than the scenario calls for, she and Gretel pour water into the well to bring him out. They both like to chat with the crowned diver, whose underwater stories are rich in punch lines. The lady disregards the chatter, and once the frog jumps off her forehead and into the well, she loses interest in everything but her headache. Admiration for the suffering beauty is apparent when the witch gives her lenitive pills made of dried frog spawn moistened with a frog-green liquid.

The witch would like to lie beside the well; but when with the lady's permission she takes the lady's place, the frog refuses to jump from the well rim to the witch's forehead. As though wanting the proverb 'Follow love and it will flee thee' for a subtitle, the lady lies down with a smile, and is immediately rewarded with cooling wetness. Gretel, who has seen it all, grins suggestively as though she, a mere child, might know how to lead the royal frog into temptation.

Not all our Herr Matzerath's suggestions make sense – for one thing, if only to annoy me, he wants giant snails to drag in the Grimms' Dictionary volume by volume, until the grandmother is in possession of all thirty-two tomes; moreover, before setting out for Poland, he decrees that Little Red Riding Hood should open the zipper and crawl into the wolf's belly whenever her grandmother refuses to let the silly little thing crawl under her skirts. I shall make no comment on this meddling with my scenario, though I fail to understand our Herr Matzerath: Little Red Riding Hood's grandmother is not Anna Koljaiczek; but we see eye to eye when Oskar wants to have the prince's kissing compulsion developed a little more.

The absurdity of kissing, the kisser as recidivist, waking with a kiss as a mechanical reflex, kissing as stupid disregard for hygiene – all this calls for an actor who has a talent for kissing, with unvarying indifference, anyone who looks like Sleeping Beauty; because, as the story proceeds, the prince is deprived of his specific kissing object, after which he not only dispenses kisses to Rapunzel and

[177]

Snow White, but practically rapes a doll made by the seventh dwarf from straw, moss and rags.

I would never go so far as our Herr Matzerath, who calls kissing a sickness that gives a foretaste of death; but the film should show the dangers involved in the prince's kissing mania. Handsome and vacuous as he is, he will lose his mind without Sleeping Beauty.

And what of Jorinde and Joringel? How is one to portray a sorrow that calls for unchanging mimicry? And Rapunzel? Her impossibly long hair? So superabundant, beyond the powers of any comb?

No, in my scenario there will not be a wig, torn off by anarchistic dwarfs who play ball with it until nothing is left of Rapunzel but ridicule. The hair that blows from the upper story of the Gingerbread House should be dreamily long, spun from red gold, yet a natural growth, the hair of wishes, the hair of dreams, the only flag I am prepared to follow. This is why I speak of my lovely-locked Damroka. With her hair she gives me more than the She-rat – there she is again! – can take away with her chatter. And because I am literally suspended by Damroka's hair, Rapunzel – No, Herr Matzerath! – will not be given a wig.

After mooring their ship in the port of Visby on Gotland, the five women have in a sense arrived, though they are farther from Vineta than ever before. Their ship has travelled a good three hundred and fifty miles in an easterly direction. After the island of Møn, they have seen the island of Bornholm sink below the horizon. They have been close to the Swedish mainland near Ystad and then, while quarrelling in Hanö Bay, within sight of it: a flat coastline, marked by factory buildings. Finally, the long island of Öland passed them by on the port side. According to my calculations, they had consumed more than seven hundred litres of diesel oil after running for sixty-two hours, and their auxiliary tank was just about empty when they put into Visby. All their supplies were low. They were running out of drinking water. Not a shred of wool left. No more stories to tell or retell. The quarrel in Hanö Bay, when the last jellyfish were hauled, had used up a lot of words. So they merely shouted in half-sentences what the ship demanded of them.

As too much time has elapsed, they have only a few hours left for their shore leave. Damroka goes to the habour master's office for the stamped G.D.R. papers. The engineer and the helmswoman fill the tank and the reserve jerricans as well with diesel oil. The Old Woman and the oceanographer find a supermarket, where they raid the freezers for their kitchen needs. As there's only watery beer and no aquavit on the shelves, the Old Woman curses Sweden and Swedish puritanism. In the end, with the help of a drunken Finn, she scares up two litre bottles of rotgut at an exorbitant price.

Now at least the women are free to go ashore. Quickly they change their clothes and roll up their oilskins. Actually Damroka wants to stay on board, but because the Old Woman and the oceanographer appeal to her – 'It wouldn't be any fun without you' – and because the engineer and the helmswoman protest: 'Then we'll stay on board too' – she changes her mind. Slightly bemused, as though having to call back her thoughts from far away, she finds the keys and locks the pilot house, but unfortunately not all the companionways.

Since Visby, a town which according to the prospectuses offers more than can be seen in a short time, is a pretty lively place, the oceanographer gets little opportunity to photograph the ubiquitous ruins and the helmswoman's wish to pick up a man remains unfulfilled. The Old Woman is unable to find more liquor. Damroka has no wishes. And when the engineer, who simply wanted to go ashore, sees the hustling-bustling town, she says: 'Let's join one of these crowds. Maybe something will happen.'

At this time of day, in Visby as in many other towns, people are protesting against one thing and another. Four or five demonstrations are marching in different directions, coming out loudly, in chants and on placards and banners, against experimentation with animals and for freedom in Nicaragua as well as Poland. Damroka, who remembers a few scraps of Swedish, has to translate the banners and chants.

After brief consultation, the women decide. They are sick of demonstrating against the armaments race. 'I've never,' says the Old Woman, 'messed with drugs.' 'You can't,' says the engineer, 'lump Poland with Nicaragua.' So they join the preventers of cruelty to animals. 'Let's see,' says the oceanographer, 'if they're against counting jellyfish.'

They march past ruined churches, then along the partly ruined, partly rebuilt city wall which, as it says in the tourist guide, bears witness to Visby's history. At the edge of the town, the procession stops outside a low, austerely scientific-looking building, which has evidently fallen into disrepute, for all thirty or forty children, women and men, among whom the five women on shore leave can be numbered, shout many times in Swedish that they are opposed to experimentation with animals. In German the Old Woman, first alone, then supported by the oceanographer, shouts: 'Jellyfish counting is ridiculous. It should be stopped.'

As often in this rainy summer, rain is falling. Otherwise nothing happens until a stone is thrown and glass is shattered, whereupon many stones are thrown. Soon all the front windows of the Institute for Fundamental Research are smashed.

I am sure the engineer threw the first stone and the helmswoman the second. It's only after the third stone, thrown either by the Old Woman or the oceanographer – because Damroka isn't throwing – that I see Swedes throwing stones. In any case it's the engineer – to make something happen – who throws first. Pebbles the size of pigeon's eggs, left over from some construction job, are piled ready to hand by the roadside.

In the low building nothing stirs. No one stops the Swedish mob from pouring in through the unglassed door. With the cry: 'Come on!' the helmswoman wants to follow. Already the engineer has picked up a board. The oceanographer snaps, as she puts it, 'two or three souvenir shots'. The Old Woman shouts: 'Let's go. Maybe we'll find a couple of bottles lying around.' But Damroka decides: 'We've got to get out of here. That'll do. Shore leave is over. In one hour we cast off.'

So the women don't see what I see: which experimental animals are liberated by the Swedes, who are all wearing yellow or red plastic capes to shield them from the weather. In addition to guinea pigs, laboratory rats and laboratory mice, ten rabbits, five dogs, and four rhesus monkeys. As more and more protest marches block the way, as the police finally come out with howling sirens, set up road blocks and send out search parties with bloodhounds, the women have to zigzag their way to the harbour and are worn to a frazzle when they get there.

The engineer's conjecture: 'I bet they let a lot of animals go' is received in silence, as is the Old Woman's complaint: 'The poor critters, running around loose. We should have taken one. There was a sweet little dog.'

Damroka needs no instructions. As the cables are pulled in, she opens up the pilothouse and grows thoughtful at the sight of the last companionway, for the forecastle is open.

The engineer starts the engine. The oceanographer asks: 'Does anyone know where my pocket calculator has got to?' Before the Old Woman can uncork her Finnish rotgut and pour herself a drink, *The New Ilsebill* casts off.

It's early afternoon. Not raining at the moment. None of the women feels like talking. There's nothing more to be got out of the stone throwing. Has their shore leave been a disappointment? The women seem to be bound by an oath of silence and – if nothing unforeseen happens – won't be released from it until they're over the submerged city.

But when in the bright northern evening they pass Hoburg Banks, a shallows south of Gotland, and enter a large field of jellyfish that cuts down their speed and seems to follow them even when they try to avoid it by veering to starboard, the silent women, and I, too, who am keeping them silent, seem to hear a rising and falling sound over the waters, a wordless singing without beginning or end, as though millions of medusas – who else? – had suddenly found their voice in the shallows or been miraculously set to singing by a higher will.

Already the oceanographer is dragging the shark onto the deck. With the helmswoman's help, she throws out the special net, pulls it in again while the engine slows down – for Damroka, too, wants this extra haul – empties the catch out on the table amidships, spreads twelve or more medium-sized jellyfish out on the work surface and hears what the helmswoman and engineer also hear, namely, a sound. No, a music emitted by the aurelias; it is lower pitched than the singing over the water, but it swells to a choral song which can even be heard on deck above the noise of the engine, for the Old Woman leaves her spaghetti in the galley, breaks the oath of silence imposed by me and cries out: 'Man, they're really singing!' After that all five women, last of all the oceanographer, believe what they hear in high and low register.

Aurelia aurita, she of the graceful design, she whose flabby middle part is stigmatized by a bluish-violet four-leaf clover, can sing. These astral, transparent medusas, which breathe with the sea, which drift in swarms and are cursed as pests, which ordinarily, no sooner spread out on the table, shrivel without a murmur and lose their radiance in contact with the formalin that is supposed to stop them from shrivelling, are singing despite their flabby velar flanges: a swelling sound, trembling on the high notes, resounding

Günter Grass

organlike on the low ones, makes the workroom of the former freight barge narrow. Never before, unless perhaps in the biblical fiery furnace, has there been such fervid singing.

Even those willing to believe want proof. Damroka authorizes a second, a third haul with the shark. She gives the helmswoman the wheel and at the oceanographer's suggestion tapes the song of the medusas with the help of a device that has hitherto served for Bach cantatas and organ preludes, as though high tech offered the only hope of confirming the incredible or – the women hope and secretly fear – confuting it by playing back not so much as a peep.

So they play the tape back and, since it reproduces the song of the medusas perfectly, the oceanographer takes the tape recorder out on deck. The recording harmonizes beautifully with the higher-pitched singsong over the water, as though technology and nature were for once inclined to make common cause.

Not until much later, when the jellyfish fields are past, does the original sound fade. But even then the women do not take to their hammocks. Over and over again, they run the tape and listen to what was recorded first in the workroom, then with a microphone suspended from a long fishing pole close to the water. While listening, the women speak little. The oceanographer says: 'No one in the Institute will believe me when I tell them what we've recorded live.'

Nevertheless, they smile when the Old Woman speaks of an inexplicable phenomenon. Speculation runs wild. The engineer, for instance, wonders whether the density of the jellyfish population can be inferred from the pitch of their song. 'If so,' she says, 'we'd have no need of the shark and suchlike contraptions.'

Damroka calls the singing jellyfish fields polychoral and mentions choral works by Gesualdo. The oceanographer has data at her fingertips. 'Yes, the swarm over Hoburg Banks was unusually large, but not as dense as the swarms in Kiel Bay. There, between March and October, as many as seven billion individuals have been recorded; given the average weight of a medusa, this amounts to a total weight of one point six million tons. Imagine this biomass singing. Why, with our microphone we could . . .'

Long after midnight the women are still trying to imagine the singing of that many medusas. Damroka draws comparisons with church music. 'Gregorian chant,' she says, and 'pre-Palestrina.'

The Old Woman says: 'All a lot of nonsense. Why do you want

[182]

to explain everything?' And toasts the inexplicable phenomenon
with rotgut.

Who spoke of 'cosmic influences'? The engineer? The helmswoman?

All talk at once. That's the way I like them: excited, fluttery,
bewitched, resembling good or wicked fairies. Their gestures,
violent or sweeping. Their smile, which no longer means to be
disabused. Enchanted, they sing medusa style while the tape plays,
reconciled at last – in song. I would never have been able to
intertwine their voices so harmoniously . . .

When they nevertheless manage to find their way to their
hammocks for a few hours, Damroka, who takes the helm with
freshly brewed coffee, says: 'Man, at first I thought: That's the
"Suscepit Israel" from the *Magnificat*, but now I could bet that
jellyfish are twelve-toners.'

The rest of the night belongs to the diesel.

But when at sunrise the medusas' singsong hovers again over the
sea, the women, who have had little sleep, abandon the hauls that
would delay their progress. Instead, they run tape after tape,
recording the softer song of the thinned jellyfish swarms and at the
same time erasing older recordings, not only of Bach cantatas and
organ preludes, but also of Joan Baez, Bob Dylan, and whatever
else they had listened to while growing older.

The oceanographer reads numbers off the counter and enters
them in her sea chart. They now have the shallows of the middle
banks behind them; northeast of Bornholm, they are in water about
a hundred metres deep. Nevertheless, a thinly woven fabric of
voices hovers over the sea, helping, until late in the afternoon, to
give them a smooth passage.

Only toward evening, when northwest of the Oder Banks they
are again traversing shallow water, when first through binoculars,
then with the naked eye, they recognize Rügen, Cape Arcona,
Stubbenkammer and the chalk cliffs, does the song swell and make
them slow down. While passing Greifswald Bay they are stopped
by a GDR border patrol boat.

Polychoral medusa song overlays the chugging of the throttled
engines. Three men in uniform come aboard. Damroka submits the
stamped papers. The members of the border patrol are polite and
thorough. Evidently prepared for the arrival of the research ship in
German Democratic waters, they search it conscientiously. With-

out comment, hammocks are counted, approving glances are cast at charts and statistical tables. But when questioned over-enthusiastically about the song of the medusas, the members of the border patrol are seized with ever-ready suspicion. The answer is a harsh No; they hear no singing. The jellyfish concentration is perfectly normal. What's more, everyone knows, at least in the German Democratic Republic, that jellyfish do not sing.

By means of a noticeable poke, the engineer manages to deter the oceanographer from switching on the tape recorder to prove the contrary. Damroka appeases official suspicion. 'You must know, gentlemen, that we women sometimes hear the grass grow.'

The boarding party reward the captain with a laugh. They even risk a macho sort of joke. 'Incidentally, can you ladies swim?' But they decline the rotgut which the Old Woman offers them in half-full glasses with an all-German turn of phrase: 'Duty is duty, schnaps is schnaps.' They wish the ladies 'calm water and a pleasant weekend'.

As the patrol boat casts off, one of the men shouts: 'We'll issue a news bulletin: GDR jellyfish can sing.' As though in confirmation, the song of the jellyfish swells while the boats move apart.

I now contend that this singing, which the border patrol could not hear, was strictly in honour of the women and their destination; for when, proceeding at half speed, they take a southerly course toward the offshore island of Usedom, the choral song of the medusas gains not only in volume but also in expressiveness, as though to introduce a Hosanna. Choruses of jubilation welcome *The New Ilsebill* and guide its course, for whenever the bow veers westward toward Greifswald Bay or too far eastward in the direction of the Polish coast and the island of Wollin, the singing abates, but jubilates once more when the ship heads due south.

Damroka has taken the yellowed map with Vineta Deep marked on it from her sea bag and spread it out. The name of the submerged city is written above the mark to the east of the island of Ruden, north of Peenemünde. Damroka hears only the song of the medusas, which shows the way, steers accordingly and finds the charts confirmed. Late that evening they anchor over the indicated spot. But as the darkened sea bars them from looking into the depths, the women, much as they would like to move straight into their city, are obliged to wait until the next morning.

Even under the starless night sky, the song of the medusas refuses to die down. There's still a sound sustained by a soft breath. Damroka hears a Kyrie, then an Agnus Dei. The oceanographer hears electronic sounds, the Old Woman a Wurlitzer organ. Neither the helmswoman nor the engineer says anything about the music of the spheres. Until late they sit huddled behind the pilot house, hearing what they want to hear, until at length they take Damroka's advice: 'We'd better get some sleep. Big day tomorrow.' They get into their hammocks but no sleep comes.

Tomorrow is Sunday. I don't know if the Flounder will be called again later on. And if I knew, I wouldn't hear what it had to say.

No no, She-rat. Someone else is nearing his destination. I won't listen, not to you. The other journey must come to its end.

The She-rat of my dreams said: That's all right, son. Even if all that is past and washed up, stay with your present and say: They toss and turn in their hammocks, he in his big fat Mercedes is driving up Grunewaldska toward Oliva Gate, tomorrow at the crack of dawn the women will, before this day is out, no, right away he will . . .

On Saturday afternoon our Herr Matzerath and his chauffeur arrive in Gdańsk and go straight to the rooms that have been reserved in the Hotel Monopol, across from the Central Station. After a short stroll in town, surrounded by too many tourists comparing what they see with picture postcard views, after finding his way from the Stockturm through Long Street Gate to Long Street, where after side glances into side streets he has seen but not recognized his Danzig, he decides, though the Neptune Fountain and the brackish water of the Mottlau make him feel at home, to drive to Kashubia this same day, the eve of the birthday party, and allow himself only a short detour through the streets of his childhood in the suburb of Langfuhr; but an obstinate restlessness drives him so imperiously grandmotherward – or is it her gravitational field that pulls him, sucks him, tugs him? – that after a quick look-around on Labesweg and outside the elongated brick Pestalozzi School, he puts all he has seen behind him. Losing all desire to enter the Church of the Sacred Heart and possibly stand before its lady altar, he urges his chauffeur to take the direct route, via Hochstriess and Brentau to Matern, where Anna Koljaiczek has been living in a cottage since her expulsion from Bissau-Abbau.

The cottage has a garden with apple trees in it and sunflowers along the fence. A pre-birthday gathering was already in progress under the chestnut tree in front of the house. The low-ceilinged parlour, in which Oskar's grandmother will be a hundred and seven years old tomorrow, is too small to hold all the people who have come from near and far.

Bruno has stayed with the Mercedes, which attracts the Kashubian children. And there stands our humpback little man surrounded by Woykes and Bronskis, Stommas and Kurbiellas, and by Vikings, Bruns and Colchics from across the seas. In a tailor-made suit, he executes semi-bows and mingles under the chestnut tree with the guests, who marvel at seeing him in the flesh, though our Herr Matzerath's legend is known to all and seems to have gone ahead of his Mercedes. He is greeted with smiles that express something more than family feeling and seem to say: We know all about you.

Nevertheless, he introduces himself to a random choice of guests and finds an interpreter in Siegesmund Stomma, the portly bicycle dealer, who has come from Gelsenkirchen with his wife and two teenage children, and who translates the Kashubian civilities of his relatives into the German spoken in the Ruhr Valley. With Herr and Frau Bruns, who have come to Kashubia from Hong Kong and who lend an exotic note to the festivities, our Herr Matzerath converses fluently enough in English, as he does with the Australian Vikings and the Colchics from Lake Michigan, who, like Kasimir Kurbiella from Mombasa on the Indian Ocean, will embrace him in the overcrowded parlour and greet him rather noisily.

But now he's still standing under the chestnut tree, where he refers to Missis Bruns as a lady, with the result that all the others are soon speaking of 'Lady Bruns' as though she were Chinese nobility.

He eats poppy-seed cake and does not say No to a glass of potato schnapps. On a long table outside the cottage is served what, even in lean years, the Kashubians have to offer: pickled mushrooms and hard-boiled eggs greened over with chives, coleslaw with caraway seed and platters full of head cheese, radishes, dill and mustard pickles, crumb, poppyseed and cheese cake, finger-thick slices of sausage, vanilla-flavoured semolina pudding. Further, crackling, applesauce and piroshki, which are offered to our Herr Matzerath by the priest from Matarnia, who wrote the many invitation cards and sent them all over the world.

The blackskirt introduces him to other relatives, among them two young men with timely moustaches, who work at the Lenin shipyard and are so strikingly blue-eyed that Oskar is not surprised to learn that he is speaking to Stephan Bronski's sons. 'Unmistakably,' he says, 'your dear grandfather, my Uncle Jan, who was so close to my Mama, is trying to look at me as he often did, as though wishing to keep a secret and at the same time come out with it.'

The Bronski sons have to bend down to let Oskar embrace them. On the other hand, his meeting with the two shipyard workers' father seems a bit stiff, though there's no need for the priest to interpret. No doubt more closely related than they would care to admit, they are about the same age. 'So we meet again,' says our Herr Matzerath to Stephan Bronski and keeps his distance.

So many relatives. In addition to affectionate greetings, medical histories are exchanged. Then the priest, with a directing gesture and the words: 'But now let us venture into the parlour,' leads Oskar into the house, where behind crowded guests, who drink hastily, laugh, and keep greeting one another, his grandmother sits hidden in an armchair by the window.

For the last few hours she has been wearing a red-and-white decoration which two gentlemen from Warsaw have conferred on her in the name of the People's Republic of Poland, and forthwith pinned on her black Sunday dress. Once portly, she has been shrunk to daintiness by old age. Her face suggests a winter apple. The rosary which, all the while beaming at the onsurge of guests, she fingers bead by bead as though prayers were still in oversupply, seems welded to her hands.

Ah, I think to myself, how frightened our humpback little man must be! How joyfully or fearfully he must follow the priest through the dense cluster of guests! Is it not because everyone wants to see our Herr Matzerath approach his grandmother that the drinking, laughter and back slapping have stopped?

The armchair is decorated with flowers. Sunflowers look in through the window; after the cool and rainy spring, they are not particularly tall; still, they are bright, and remind one of the sunflowers which many years ago grew much taller along grandmother's fence.

Don't be afraid, I call out to our Herr Matzerath. The two government officials are standing on the left, while a prelate from Oliva sent by the bishop stands to the right of the flower-decorated armchair. Between church and state sits Anna Koljaiczek, undoubtedly wearing her black Sunday dress over additional skirts. Don't be afraid! Already the priest from Matarnia pushes the humpback little man into the dreaded though long-dreamed-of spot. In an attempt to give him moral support, I advise him to kneel.

But our Herr Matzerath maintains his dignity. He bends over the bead-fingering hands, kisses one, then the other, says into the silence of the serried guests: 'Revered grandmother,' and introduces himself as her grandson. 'I'm sure you remember, I'm Oskar, yes, little Oskar, now grown to be almost sixty . . .'

Since Anna Koljaiczek can only speak as she has always spoken, she first, though without releasing her rosary, fondles the little man's hand, then repeats over and over: 'I knowed you'd come, Oskarkins, I knowed you'd . . .'

After that they talk about olden times. About all that used to be and isn't any more. How things kept getting worse and once in a while got a little better. About everything that should have happened and always turned out entirely differently. About who's dead and who is still alive, here and there. And who has been lying since when in what graveyard.

I'm sure they both burst into tears whenever the conversation turns to Anna Koljaiczek's daughter and Herr Matzerath's mother Agnes, to Jan and Agnes and Alfred and Agnes and Jan, Agnes and Alfred. But as the serried guests are busy again with one another and disinclined to suspend their noisy greetings, I can record only a few sentences of this conversation. There's a good deal of: 'Do you remember, Oskarkins?' and 'I won't forget that if I live to be . . .'

Finally, after a casual inquiry about Maria and little Kurt, I hear the question: 'Hev you gone to the post office to see the place where it happened?'

Whereupon our Herr Matzerath promises his grandmother to visit the now historic building on the Rähm, the Polish Post Office, and say a prayer for his Uncle Jan.

Then he leaves her, saying he'll be back bright and early for the Great Day. 'May I, my dear and revered grandmother, call you Babka, dear Babka, as I did long ago, remember, when we said goodbye at the freight station?'

With his hump under his large-checked jacket, that's how I see our Herr Matzerath disappear into the crowd. Now he is recognizable again among the Bronskis and Woykes. There's a sour smell about, as though the parlour had been washed in whey. Another greeting is exchanged with the American Colchics. In his very first sentence, Kasimir Kurbiella invites him to Mombasa. The Chinese woman looks ever so delicate among all these Kashubians. Finally, after two water-clear potato schnapses and a last piroĵôk, he finds his way to the Mercedes, where Bruno is sitting motionless in his chauffeur's cap, guarding the star atop the radiator from grasping hands.

His size four shoes are saffron yellow at the toes and heels – white in between. My Christmas rat has to listen while I outfit our Herr Matzerath: he is wearing gold-rimmed glasses and too many rings on short fingers. The ruby tie pin is part of his décor. While in the cooler seasons he wears a soft velours, he sports straw hats all summer. In his Mercedes he has a table that can be opened whenever he feels bored on long trips; on it he plays open-card skat with various people; how happy Oskar will be on his way back to the Hotel Monopol later on, when he wins a heart hand against Jan Bronski and his poor mama.

Even here, while visiting his grandmother in the heart of Kashubia, he can't help poking around in the fifties, as though precious treasures lay buried there. The prelate from Oliva, an unctuously friendly gentleman with a rather modest command of the German language, is obliged to listen patiently to the story of painter Malskat and his deceptively genuine Gothic; he's there to listen, just as my Christmas rat is there to listen to me.

After our Herr Matzerath manages under the chestnut tree to keep out of an argument – about the banned trade union Solidarność – that almost ends in a fist fight, the prelate accompanies the humpback little man with the ruby tie pin and the two-tone shoes to his noticeably body-damaged Mercedes. With the evening sun shining on his bald head, holding his straw hat over his chest, Oskar speaks as though addressing a big meeting. I hear the prelate sigh and don't know whether he is sighing because of the Matzerathian theories or whether it is the word Solidarność that's worrying the church after worrying the state. His Catholic patience puts me in mind of my Christmas rat who, I'm sure, rather than listen to my attempts to get Oskar moving again, would prefer to tune in on the Third Programme – Educational Radio for All:

something about fixed stars, the speed of light, and galaxies five thousand light years away . . .

In unchanging attitudes, she with her ears flat against her head, her whiskers never resting, her eyes as shiny as black beads, he in his black skirt and thick glasses, anointed within and without, the Christmas rat and the prelate from Oliva listen to me and to Herr Matzerath, as we talk about painter Malskat. Of course the prelate knows that the Mercedes will soon drive off with the talkative little man and the church will have the last word; just as my Christmas rat knows that I'll have to listen to her as soon as I dream of her.

But it's still my turn. The She-rat will have to wait. If an end there must be, the farce is still running ahead of it.

Starting in the winter of 1950, he did gymnastics alone and inventively at a height of thirty metres, first over the nave, then over the choir of Lübeck's Church of Saint Mary, as his dapper employer, always busy drumming up trade, seldom climbed so high. Dietrich Fey kept busy amid the debris down below. He had to shield Malskat. No unauthorized eye must see how the miracle of Lübeck became flesh. He put up warning signs on all sides: 'Beware of falling stone.' 'Caution!' 'Unauthorized persons keep out!'

Even carpenters and masons were unauthorized as far as Malskat's upper realm was concerned. When knowledgeable visitors turned up, including German and foreign art historians, who beginning in 1951 arrived singly and in groups, Fey and his assistants alerted Malskat by pulling ropes that activated sound signals. As a rule, Fey managed to fob the experts off with copies, which had been turned out for documentation purposes and for a travelling exhibition; all duplicates made by Malskat.

The travelling show was a nationwide success, all the more so as the President of the Federal Republic and the King of Sweden nodded appreciatively in front of certain exhibits. Newspapers and lecturers made repeated use of the neologism: 'Lubic style'. The city was honoured as the 'cradle of Gothic'. There was talk of a workshop directed by an inspired canon, which beginning in the late thirteenth century had created a style. The Lübeck miracle found believers.

Small wonder that Dr Hirschfeld, curator of the local museum, who first expressed doubt, was unable to sustain his cavillings. In the end he began to doubt his own doubts and wrote in his book on

Saint Mary's of Lübeck: 'At the sight of the master's works in the choir and in the clerestory of the nave one instantly senses the powerful authority which only an original can have.'

June 1951 brought another danger sign. A congress of West-German curators of monuments was held in Lübeck precisely by reason of the miracle. Certain of its members appeared at Saint Mary's and did not let Fey deter them from climbing high in the scaffolding. Fey explained, demonstrated, spoke with the tongues of angels, yet could not prevent professors Scheper and Deckert from expressing misgivings, a residue of which, in spite of all Fey's eloquence, persisted on their descent from the scaffolding.

And yet, when all the curators assembled in Lübeck met the next day, one more miracle happened: no complaint was uttered; on the contrary, the participants in the congress petitioned the government in Bonn to start a further hundred and fifty thousand marks flowing into the coffers of the Lübeck church administration. Ecclesiastical councillor Göbel was pleased, and so was Malskat, whose hourly wage was now secure.

Further incidents were hardly worth taking seriously. When a woman student, wishing to check the findings of her doctoral thesis 'The Murals of the Lübeck Church of Saint Mary' on the spot, climbed secretly into the scaffolding, Fey caught her in the act and gently but firmly called her attention to the dangerous character of her acrobatics. Though she was wearing light climbing shoes and assured him that she was immune to dizziness, she was never allowed back to Malskat. After her short stay aloft, this student asked critical questions. On the strength of photographs and copies, she found Romanesque elements in the drapery. Her admiration of the luminous colours over the choir was tinged with doubt. She pointed out that in the night before Palm Sunday, 1942, when Lübeck's Church of Saint Mary burned from the inside out, the copper blue of the clerestory, and of the choir as well, should have oxidized and turned black.

When Fey caught her a second time trying to climb up to Malskat and take samples of the copper blue, he threatened to have her expelled from the church. Thus was the inventive painter isolated on his thirty-metre perch.

A little later Fräulein Kolbe – that was the student's name – got the better of her suspicions and waxed enthusiastic over the Lübeck miracle, though in her thesis she repeatedly referred to the incredible uniqueness of the choir mural. For try as she might, she could find no similarity to the 'creased style' habitual in the North German area. Amazed at the Romanesque elements, especially in the third vault, she had come to the conclusion that the influence of Chartres and Le Mans was discernible throughout the choir. Thus the master of the Lübeck choir must have travelled and studied in France.

One might indeed speculate freely about Malskat's previous life and his travels towards the end of the thirteenth century; one thing is certain, that high in his scaffolding he was removed from the present and gained a freedom which allowed him when painting contours to harbour Gothic emotions and little by little gave the twenty-one saints in the choir and the fifty-six saints in the clerestory of the nave compelling expressions. Time had no weight. Seven hundred years could be spanned in a leap and a moment of fervid recollection.

Rightly, the disappointed, but sharp-sighted art historians observed that the murals in the Schleswig Cathedral could be viewed as preliminary studies for the paintings in Lübeck's Church of Saint Mary. Despite his years as a soldier, Malskat had remained Malskat, though perhaps more mature and more consistent in his retrospection. For when I say that the Middle Ages were his time, I see him in the flesh, high in the scaffolding seven hundred years ago, his matted woollen cap pulled down over both ears.

In the troubled, lawless years that followed the downfall of the Hohenstaufen Empire, he seems to have worked until advanced old age – shortly before the advent of the Plague – in numerous churches and Holy Ghost hospitals; his workshop left traces everywhere. Thus it seems reasonable to assume that the fifty-six saints in the clerestory of the nave of Saint Mary's are also by him. Though decades elapsed between the early secco painting of the choir and the later work in blue, green, ochre-yellow and black in the nave, all the saints, with their gaze looking beyond human misery, show in their drapery the brush stroke of the choir master.

And all 'alla prima', painted with a free hand. Only a few iconographical pointers may have been provided by manuals of painting. If, later on at the trial, a certain Bernath's book *Painting in the Middle Ages* was pronounced Malskat's source, this only confirms the early Romanesque, Byzantine and, on the right-hand end wall of the polygonal choir, even Coptic influences. What the master of the choir and nave painted seven hundred years ago, Malskat achieved anew, thus bridging centuries, cancelling out the destructive fury of the last war and triumphing over time.

Yes, yes, I know the arguments of Professors Scheper and Grundmann: in one case Malskat's inspiration was provided by the Christ of the Hagia Sophia in Constantinople, in the other by the Virgin Enthroned in Trieste Cathedral. Certain pigments were subjected to heat tests, samples of mortar were analysed, chemical and microscopic examinations were undertaken. And then Malskat's confession: The wire brush! The potsherds with which he scratched contours and painted surfaces. The ingenious aging process. The dust bag!

Here it must be said that Fey, his employer, demanded that the passage and ravages of time be made credible. Nothing new was wanted, only the old, even if slightly damaged. Malskat's talent made this possible. Then, in the years preceding the currency reform, the subsequent painter of the choir, but probably of the nave as well, painted Chagalls and Picassos, which Fey, who became his employer immediately after 1945, put on the art market. In that way they kept themselves above water.

But with the new currency, which replaced the worthless Reichsmark overnight, a new era dawned; its beginnings demanded more palpable falsification. And since forgery and falsification were becoming a universal way of life, which soon spread to the government and civil service – whereupon the old conditions, as though no horror had resulted from them, were represented as new conditions, and two German states – 'phony fifties' as our Herr Matzerath calls all products of that remote decade – came into being, were put on the market, remained in circulation, and gradually came to be regarded as authentic.

What Malskat did was in keeping with the times. If he had kept his mouth shut, he would never have been put on trial. He should have covered up the fraud, as the politicians did; their dual falsification had a future. They soon convinced the whole world that either state belonged to one or the other victor camp. Thus they transformed a lost war into a profitable double victory; two phony fifties, but coin of the realm.

Of course, the forgery was obvious to all, but the forgers accepted each other at face value without batting an eyelid, and the reinforcements were welcome to the victors, who in the meantime had become enemies. Those who recognized the imposture welcomed the pleasing illusion; for the originals were pathetic and too badly damaged: two rubble heaps with no desire to be one.

That is why our Herr Matzerath keeps saying: 'Malskat was right; he should have placed his own likeness on capitals between Adenauer and Ulbricht, acknowledged Byzantine and Coptic influence, and represented himself as the middle member of this trinity; on the right end of the south wall, for instance, where the three hermits, termed monks, had their rendezvous.'

This is easy hindsight, for when Lothar Malskat stood in the cold draught on a scaffolding thirty metres high, freely peopling the seven fields of the choir with assorted saints, and in the middle vault with the Virgin and Child, all the while smoking Juno, his favourite brand of cigarettes, when money flowed steadily from Bonn to Lübeck, his hourly wage came to ninety-two pfennigs of the reformed currency; how could he have envisaged himself between such high-priced statesmen?

No, Herr Matzerath; in far-off Kashubia, and as long as the prelate listens to you, you may be right about the estimated value of the then chancellor and the then chairman of the council of state; the 'Old Man' and 'Goatee' were genuine forgers and may for ever more be called 'phony fifties'. Malskat, on the other hand, signed his Gothic, though discreetly.

> Dual power by reason of discord.
> The one lie served up twice.
> On this side and that side
> new wallpaper pasted on old newsprint.
> The common burden reduced to a numbers game
> is mere statistics;
> totals expressed in round numbers.
>
> Housecleaning in the double house.
> A little shame for special occasions
> and street signs quickly exchanged.
> What protrudes into the memory planed off.
> Handily packed the guilt
> and bequeathed to the children as a legacy.
> Only what is should be, the past is out.
>
> Thus double innocence is entered

in the commercial register, for even the difference
is good for business. Forgery
is reflected across the border: deceptively hushed up,
more genuine than genuine and surpluses galore.
As far as we were concerned, says the She-rat,
Germany was never split in two,
it was one good feed.

True, it's been good living since then. The post-human era agrees with us: we're gaining in every respect. Free at last from humans, the earth is reviving, filling again with creatures that creep and fly. The seas are breathing again. The air seems rejuvenated. And everywhere time is on hand, an inexhaustible supply of time.

And yet we'd have liked to see humankind end more gradually, not all of a sudden. Man, after all, left open the possibility of several delayed, medium- to long-termed dooms. The human mind was always pursuing a number of aims at once. Man, for instance, was gradually poisoning the elements, but he hadn't thought the idea through to its conclusion; a gradual increase, culminating in Doomadosh (as we called Doomsday), in contamination, was even affecting us rats, though in the long run we always found a way of converting any poison into something digestible. All the same, we sniffed with alarm at what man was putting into the rivers and oceans, what he didn't seem to mind mixing with the air; we were horrified to see him deplore but take no action as his forests were going to pot. To us rats living and surviving were one, and we could only conclude that man no longer savoured life. He was fed up. He'd had enough. He'd thrown in the towel and only went on acting as if. About the future, that once so luxuriously furnished suite of rooms, he made jokes; yet he took no pleasure in staring at the void. All action – and he remained active as usual – smelled of absurdity, a smell, I might say, that nauseated us rats.

And you, too, young friend, said the She-rat, were busily taking leave. One could read about it, and we read a lot. There was so much that rhymed with doom. How euphoniously certain you poets were that the end of all days had come. With a last great burst of energy, the grand finale was treated as a competition. Funnier still, a good many artists, fascinated by the end, expended themselves as thoroughly as if laurels were still as evergreen as they had always been and immortality a certainty.

It seemed to me that the She-rat remembered us with affection
and sadness. But then she got back to her obsession. Listen to me:
The human race invented still another means of suicide: over-
population. The poorer they were, the more they insisted on
increasing their numbers; they thought they could compensate for
poverty with the boon of children; in fact, their last pope was an
itinerant preacher of this method. Death by starvation became
pleasing to God and was extrapolated, not only statistically. What
little food there was, people snatched from one another's mouths.

Why, cried the She-rat, couldn't they get enough to eat when
there was plenty for us rats? Because glut in one place fed on
shortages in another. Because you kept prices up by keeping the
supply down. Because a small minority of mankind lived on the
hunger of the majority. But they said: there are too many of us, and
that's why there's hunger.

What absurd reasoning. Futze chissoresh! Their stupid Mal-
thusianism. We found no difficulty in getting enough to eat,
though there were billions of us in the world, and the roughly
equivalent human population could easily have been fed properly at
the time of the Big Bang; the warehouses were full. Nay more: we
would gladly have kept up with the human growth prognoses and
increased our population to six or seven billion by the year two
thousand. Both species could have been happy and well fed.

After crowding my dream with statistical data, the She-rat went
on: Alas, it was not to be. Man's decision not to starve, not to perish
supersaturated with poison, or hungry *and* poisoned, not to die
slowly of thirst as the water supply dwindled, but to seek a sudden
end, that egotistical and childishly impatient decision confronts us
rats with problems to which we hadn't given sufficient thought.
We shall have to change. The post-human era demands a new form
of behaviour. We lack an opposite. Without the human race and its
harvests, stocks, garbage, without its sense of surfeit and its
destructiveness, we rats from now on will be reduced to our own
resources. Admittedly, it was easy, much too easy, to live in man's
shadow; we miss him.

When she went on complaining, I protested: But here and there
you have neutronized cities. With the help of conservation bombs,
we've provided you with outwardly intact refuges. Man's
next-to-last work was a cultural pact for your benefit. I ask you,
She-rat: weren't we walking through man-free streets just now?

And didn't we both take pleasure in endearingly familiar sights, in soot-blackened but still beautiful gables, towers, vaulted doorways?

Vain consolation. The She-rat of my dreams went right on complaining. I no longer saw her dug into her escape tunnels or running the streets of Danzig; I found her housed in garbage. Peering from piles of mangled scrap iron, she spoke of sudden dust storms still ruinous to the rat folk; elsewhere she lived in the shelter of sheets of plastic, which, buffeted by the wind, travelled like ever-full sails, travelled with the She-rat. Over and over again the Big Bang. Over and over again: the loneliness that followed. Over and over again: how much the rats miss man.

But *I'm* here, I cried. Me in my space capsule. Me in my orbit. In your dreams and mine: me, you and me!

You're right, young friend, she conceded. How comforting to have someone who keeps saying me, me, me; already we honour you a little. In the city shelters and housing complexes there are rat nations which positively worship you; when they practise the upright posture on squares or in churches, they're thinking of you. We rural rat nations, on the other hand, have someone else in addition to you, someone whose living remains are worthy of worship. An inert bundle, but alive. A very old woman, I should think. She stayed in her armchair when everyone else ran out and got killed. She barely keeps alive, fed by us rats. We do all we can for her. When she's thirsty, we get her something to drink. Just as city rats worship you, so we country rats worship her. And the old crone mumbles for us; tells us how it used to be. What she remembers of the past. What visitors came. What brought her sorrow, took away her bit of pleasure, and has never ceased to give pain.

But, I cried out, that's. Really, She-rat. Her birthday is yet to come. It won't be Sunday till tomorrow. She wants to celebrate and be celebrated.

Yes, of course, said the She-rat. But now she wants to die and can't. That's why she tells us sad stories, and funny ones too, about the old days. About prewar, war and between-wars times. How the Kashubians sometimes got along pretty well and sometimes wretchedly with the Poles and the Germans. And how as a young thing she would drive her horse and wagon from Kokoschken to the city market and later, when progress came, take the train. And what filled her panniers: potatoes and turnips, cucumbers and raspberries, fresh eggs, a gulden a peck. And on St Martin's Day two geese. And every autumn, basketsful of greenies and chestnuts, chanterelles and ink caps, because there were heaps of mushrooms in the forests of Kashubia.

Believe it or not, this forest is still flourishing. In our film, which is titled *The Grimms' Forests*, grow beeches, firs, oaks, ashes, birches, maples and elms, here bright and there darkening. Thickets open and close. Wild animals in the underbrush. At all times new greenery, but also the colours of late summer and early autumn. From beds of moss or pine needles sprout morels and puff balls and parasols. Under oak trees fly agaric heralds neighbouring boletus. Scaly hawk mushrooms. Armies of tree mushrooms sprout from tree trunks. Blueberries you can pick with combs. Then more ferns like the path over which the fairy-tale characters, Rübezahl and the dwarfs on foot, the rest in the old Ford with Rumpelstiltskin at the wheel, are making their way to the scene of action.

One of the dwarfs, the second, I think, who is riding on the running board while the others hurry along on foot, cries out: 'Halt!' All seven spread out a hand-coloured map of the forest on moss, between mushrooms growing in a fairy ring. They measure, compare, argue over millimetres, then finally point out the new direction: 'This is it. This way!' The girl's hands, which had flown ahead with the shovel, are here too, and now they set to work.

A new path must be laid out, and the old one effaced. Even Jorinde and Joringel, whose only trade is sadness, have to wield pick and shovel.

The witch commands several trees to uproot themselves and strike new roots at a specified place. The girl's chopped-off hands dig a hole, into which the third and fourth dwarfs ram a signpost, which up until then had been pointing in an entirely different direction.

The frog king lies down in a brook, turns into a frog and guides the brook into a new bed at right angles to the old one; then he becomes a king again and cools the forehead of his lady, who is suffering from inactivity, with spring water.

Rübezahl crawls down the old path on all fours. Wherever his beard touches the ground, moss appears, ferns and mushrooms sprout.

When Rumpelstiltskin stamps, an anthill has to move seven paces and set up housekeeping with eggs and young. (In accordance with our Herr Matzerath's instructions, Little Red Riding Hood crawls into a hollow tree. There the lazy thing sits sucking her thumb, watching the hard-working fairy-tale characters.) By now the false forest path looks good enough to be true, while the existence of the right one can hardly be suspected.

Now the wicked stepmother gives orders: Rübezahl must forcibly take Sleeping Beauty away from the prince. The giant, who was all sunshine a moment ago, frowns. He grabs Sleeping Beauty and lifts her with one hand; he is no longer a hired man, but a mountain troll from the Riesengebirge. The first, sixth and seventh dwarfs hold the weeping prince. Holding the spindle, the fourth dwarf runs swiftly after Rübezahl, who is carrying the already sleeping Sleeping Beauty off to the scene of action.

The prince refuses to be comforted by Snow White. Nor does he want any truck with Little Red Riding Hood, who jumps out of the hollow tree. The girl's chopped off hands stroke his curly locks, while sadly his mouth blows kisses into the air. He seems frantic. At last Rapunzel succeeds with her long hair in diverting the prince from his grief.

'Mirror please!' cries the wicked stepmother. The chopped-off hands take the magic mirror out of the old Ford and put it on the stump. The fairy-tale characters, with Hansel and Gretel in the middle, group themselves together in front of the miror, as if it were Tuesday and a large family were getting ready to see *Dallas*. The wicked stepmother switches on her miraculous TV. (As our Herr Matzerath said only recently: 'Every one of the media, even the most modern, has its source in fairy tales.')

First we see Rübezahl, carrying the sleeping Sleeping Beauty, stride through the dead forest. The indefatigable fourth dwarf follows him with the spindle.

Next we see Little Red Riding Hood's grandmother, still reading volume one of the Grimms' Dictionary to the wolf.

And now the motorcade, carrying the Chancellor, his ministers and experts, enters the picture. It is still on the autobahn, following the police car with blue light and flanked by motorcycle cops.

The wicked stepmother changes wavelength. The dwarf with the spindle is following Rübezahl, who is carrying the sleeping Sleeping Beauty up the stairs of the ruined tower, to the roofless tower room. Suddenly, the chopped-off hands come into the picture. They dust and sweep the tower room while Rübezahl carefully sets Sleeping Beauty down at a stone table; the dwarf lays the spindle in her lap.

Those looking at the magic mirror praise the girl without hands for her industry. The prince who has seen it all through Rapunzel's hair laments. He wants to break away and as usual wake his Sleeping Beauty with a kiss. But he struggles in vain and the dwarfs hold him fast. Again Rapunzel veils his eyes.

Once more the magic mirror shows Little Red Riding Hood's grandmother reading to the wolf; then it shows the Chancellor's motorcade turning into the flourishing forest. Blue light in the lead, it comes closer and closer. At a sign from the witch, the fairy-tale characters hide. The dwarfs push the old Ford into the bushes. Only Hansel and Gretel stay behind, as if they had been rejected and were alone and God-forsaken. They stand waiting on the new false path.

From the depths of the forest the Chancellor's motorcade appears behind the blue light. Hansel and Gretel wave and shout: 'Here, Daddy! Here we are!' And run shouting down the wrong road. The Chancellor and Daddy follows them toward the scene of action until the forest, which was flourishing only a moment ago, becomes sicker, swampier, impenetrable. Over the walkie-talkies we hear squeaking and whistling, then commands: 'Follow Chancellor's children! Fan out! Surround them!'

The black cars get stuck in the mud. All occupants have to get out. One after another, the cars sink into the gurgling morass, last of all the Chancellor and his experts and ministers, among them the Grimm Brothers, make their way in disorder through the dead forest. With submachine guns at the ready, the policemen are trying to provide security. The television crew groan under the weight of their equipment, but nevertheless shoot the confusion.

The Chancellor shouts: 'Children, where are you? Where are you, children?'

The experts argue about the direction. The policemen frighten one another. The Grimm Brothers help each other out of the morass. The Chancellor shouts. The television crew keeps on shooting. Seven ravens in dead trees. Hansel and Gretel lure the helpless pursuers deeper and deeper into the dead forest, shouting: 'This way, Daddy. This way!'

At the suggestion of our Herr Matzerath, who is always on the

The Rat

lookout for subplots, the Grimm Brothers now find a golden hair in the wilderness. A few steps further on, another hair glitters golden. And so on. Following the golden hair, the Grimm Brothers finally see who has led them astray. In the midst of the dead trees, Rapunzel. Beautiful to behold, she plays with her long hair and lures the Minister for Medium-Term Forest Damage and his undersecretary in a certain direction.

Other fairy-tale characters appear and disappear among the trees. The seven dwarfs carry Snow White in her coffin; Rumpelstiltskin hops, skips and shouts: 'Rumpelstiltskin is my name, but luckily nobody knows it'; Little Red Riding Hood is on her way to her grandmother's with her basket.

More and more fairy-tale characters come and dissolve; sadly Jorinde and Joringel, the poor girl with the chopped-off hands; a lady passes with a frog on her lovely forehead, and time and again we see the witch laugh. And everything else that happens in Grimms' Fairy Tales. As though in a dream, the Grimm Brothers follow their characters until the dead forest becomes a fairy-tale forest again. The fairy-tale forest opens into a clearing, and there in the middle of the clearing, hewn in stone, stands a monument depicting the Grimm Brothers shoulder to shoulder. (Here our Herr Matzerath wishes to see a group of professors assembled; fairy-tale experts and students of deeper meaning. He wants them to elucidate the sociological, linguistic and psychological dimensions of Grimms' Fairy Tales, and to draw the Grimm Brothers into a long drawn-out discussion. I'm against it.)

Jakob and Wilhelm should be astonished at seeing themselves hewn in stone as the Grimm Brothers. Little by little all the fairy-tale characters gather around them.

Snow White sits up smiling in her glass coffin. Rapunzel stands clothed in her hair. The girl without hands hides her arm stumps behind her back. Slightly embarrassed, the witch buttons her dress over her enormous tits. All, all appear, only Rübezahl is missing.

Off to one side he stands in tears, because, being a mountain troll, he does not appear in Grimms' Fairy Tales. (I, however, regard our Herr Matzerath's idea of having poor Rübezahl cry out for his author Musäus as too farfetched. It would make more sense to have the sensitive Wilhelm Grimm recognize Rübezahl's distress, go to the hulking giant and welcome him into the circle of Grimms' fairy-tale characters.) Wilhelm's subtitle is: 'Rübezahl shall henceforth be one of us.'

'Well well, gentlemen,' says Rumpelstiltskin. 'So we meet again.'

Wilhelm Grimm says: 'Look, dear brother, they have all gathered around us.'

Jakob Grimm says: 'Not all, dear brother. Hansel and Gretel are missing. And look: Sleeping Beauty is missing too.'

While the three guard dwarfs restrain the prince, who wants to blab, the wicked stepmother, who gives herself an air of self-importance on meeting the Grimm Brothers, puts down her magic mirror at the foot of the stone monument, and switches on the action programme.

At the scene of action: Sleeping Beauty is sitting with her spindle at the stone table in the tower room. The chopped-off hands are careful not to let the spindle fall off her lap. The Chancellor and his retinue are gathered around the tower. The dwarf who has brought the spindle wakes Sleeping Beauty with a quick kiss, in the manner of the prince. He then runs down the stairs and joins Hansel and Gretel who have been waiting, hidden behind the ruined tower. The three of them vanish, followed by the chopped-off hands and the seven ravens. Gretel calls out in running: 'Let's hope it works.'

At the foot of the tower the battle of the experts starts up again. The policemen form a protective cordon around the Chancellor and his remaining ministers. At the exhausted Chancellor's bidding, one of his advisers hands him a big piece of Black Forest cherry torte. 'Ah,' he cries out, 'how hard governing is made for me.' He takes a bite, chews, and while sadly chewing sees Sleeping Beauty sitting in the ruined tower room. Her eyelids flutter, she wants to fall back asleep. The Chancellor calls out with his mouth half full: 'Have you by any chance seen my dear children?'

Sleeping Beauty is frightened; she pricks her finger with the spindle till it bleeds.

At this all congeal: the Chancellor with the piece of cake in hand, the wrangling ministers and experts, the policemen with their submachine guns at the ready, the trigger-happy television crew, and the journalists on the look-out for head- and punchlines. And even as they wrangle with levelled fingers, as they seek the enemy with submachine guns, scribble notes, make the television camera whir, munch cake, all sink into a deep sleep along with Sleeping Beauty.

From the wasteland between the dead trees, a thorny hedge

springs up, grows higher and higher, becomes thicker and thicker, as impenetrable as barbed wire.

The congealed company at the foot of the ruined tower where Sleeping Beauty lies sleeping vanish behind it. The government with all its pomp and circumstance isn't there any more.

In the magic mirror on the pedestal of the monument the fairy-tale characters and the Grimm Brothers see the success of their action. All are delighted. Even the Grimm Brothers approve of this method of bringing down the mighty.

Hansel and Gretel, the fourth dwarf and the chopped-off hands are greeted with joy. The witch congratulates them. 'You've done a great job, children.'

All applaud, even the chopped-off hands. Only the Grimm Brothers are visibly distraught at the sight of the Chancellor's missing children, preserved as Hansel and Gretel; Wilhelm Grimm greets them nevertheless with the friendly subtitle: 'And we were afraid the Russians had kidnapped the Chancellor's children.' But Jakob Grimm is concerned: 'Oh, your poor parents! And besides, there's no more government! Disorder will prevail. Chaos threatens.'

At this point, the kissing prince unwinds himself from Rapunzel's hair and offers the Grimm Brothers his services. 'Should I wake Sleeping Beauty with a kiss again? I can do it, you know.'

He tries to break loose, but the three guard dwarfs hang on to him. Quite the mountain troll, charcoal burner and wild man, Rübezahl boxes the prince's ear. Hansel shouts: 'You will stay here!' (Before leaving for Poland, our Herr Matzerath said: Now the frog king's lady should offer the weeping prince her tortured forehead to kiss; but in my opinion this subplot would only distract attention from the main action.)

All the fairy-tale characters now want to show the Grimm Brothers their home, the Gingerbread House, where in the meantime a troop of carrier snails in single file have delivered all the volumes of the Grimms' Dictionary; the last is carrying the thirty-second volume, from Zanzibar to zwieback.

The grandmother from the fairy tale
is still reading the dictionary
to the wicked wolf from the fairy tale.

His wolf's belly, which opens and closes

with a zipper, is full of words
from olden times: woeful, windjammer, wolfbane . . .

And now the grandmother finds in the Grimms' Dictionary –
she now has all the volumes – the name
of Vineta city, where the Vinetans lived

until the sea engulfed the city. And now the wolf is howling,
he wants to hear from the grandmother's mouth
more than is written about Vineta.

When the wind is silent over the smooth sea,
says the grandmother to the wolf out of the fairy tale,
then bells are heard, a ringing of bells.

No, they can't sleep. A never-ending singsong finds its way to
the hammocks in the forecastle of the anchored ship. O gentle
aurelias, translucent and milky, O medusas marked with bluish
violet, O swarms of jellyfish which, as is widely known, live on
plankton and herring larvae; you, little studied and of ill repute,
because you may, tomorrow or the day after, transform my sea, the
Baltic, into one great jellyfish; O beauties drifting with the
currents, who, like the land-bound rats, can rely on human
loathing; you, as small as a saucer or as big as a platter, you of the
sensitively, mysteriously shimmying biomass – you immortals,
whose uncounted being was certified as soundless, can sing.

No wonder the women can't sleep. Too great is the power of this
music. They toss and turn in their hammocks. As usual, my
mollifying words are ineffectual. The Old Woman has begun to
curse the song of the medusas; it makes you quarrelsome, she says.
The helmswoman digs up old scores. She quarrels with the
oceanographer about obsolete words; then she goes to work on
Damroka: the captain, she says, has betrayed their scientific mission
and taken a senseless course. They haven't come to chase after
myths and legends, but to prove that the Baltic is threatened with
ecological disaster; Damroka has fallen down on the job for the sake
of private interests: 'Well, that's always been your way. But now
it's going to stop. Starting tomorrow,' cries the helmswoman, 'I set
the course.'

When the engineer and oceanographer also turn against
Damroka for no stated reason – they don't even mention me – it
looks like mutiny on board *The New Ilsebill*, or rather, in

democratic terms, as though the captain might be voted out of office. Even the Old Woman hesitates, taking one side, then the other. Finally at midnight – the helmswoman has just cried out: 'And your tête-à-têtes with the Flounder are getting on our nerves!' – the song of the medusas stops. It doesn't die down, it breaks off, as though the rapping of a baton had halted the choral competition for ever. The only sounds remaining are those of the ship. And if the medusas' singsong made the women quarrelsome, they now find the sudden silence deafening.

The Old Woman is first to jump up from her hammock. She wants to drink a schnaps and then another. 'I told you so,' she cries out. 'An inexplicable phenomenon.'

The oceanographer wants more information. With the engineer's help she lowers a ring net, which they drag alongside, twice to starboard and twice to port. Each time it emerges empty of jellyfish. Or anything else, not even a stickleback.

Gloom descends on the ship. The oceanographer nibbles her fingernails. The engineer, too, wants a schnaps and still another. The helmswoman weeps quietly, then loudly, says she didn't mean what she said when they were quarrelling. All five together, they squat, sit, stand behind the pilot house under an almost vanished moon and listen to Damroka, who, as though to dispel children's fears, talks about the Wendish settlement of Jumne, which later, after having been destroyed by Vikings and Danes, was rebuilt and named Vineta. The fishing village of Jumne developed into a city. Beside it, in the early days, stood Joms Castle, a Viking stronghold. Damroka knows stories about Gorm the Old and Harald Bluetooth, who defeated the Wendish Prince Burislav on the island of Usedom. 'That,' she says, 'was at least a thousand years ago. Right after the bloody battle, Bluetooth and Burislav came to terms. It seems that I'm descended from a grandson of this Burislav named Witzlav, who married a daughter of the Kashubian prince Swantopolk, whose name was Damroka.'

She told them about the turbulent Joms Vikings who sailed, pillaging and conquering, as far as Iceland and Greenland. 'They traded with Haithabu. And from the coasts of America, which they began to plunder long before Columbus, they brought back a new variety of poultry, turkeys, which were later depicted by Gothic church painters. But the people of Jumne were sedentary. They traded, sold loot, and transformed the wild turkey into noisy barnyard fowl. The turkey seems to have once been Jumne's heraldic animal.'

Because the sea remains so terribly calm and the anchored ship is no longer surrounded by medusas and songs of jubilation, Damroka tries to cheer her companions with turkey stories. But not even ludicrous Viking names – such as Thorkel, Pal and Knuddel – could make the women laugh.

Damroka says: 'They killed each other off. And Jumne grew rich, then poor again, then rich again, and so on, you know how it is with men. Later, they say, the city was so chockful of tinder that it burned for three days. But I don't believe it. I'm inclined to agree with Adam of Bremen, who explored the Baltic coast as far as the mouth of the Oder, and wrote about the Slavic Witzes and Vinetans, who occupied Vineta. After hordes of males had killed each other off, the city took the name of Vineta and grew stinking rich. Then it got flooded by a northeaster, that was in twelve hundred and something. But there are other reports, all partly true and partly false . . .'

She finds no end. Her stories arouse hunger for more. The women delight in hearing Damroka describe the gentle government resulting from a semi-matriarchy. She says there was a women's council side by side with the men's council, and women served as magistrates along with the men. Mention is even made of women executioners and women captains. 'But then strangers, a hundred and thirty women and men, came from the Weser, where a piper, who, as it turned out, was an itinerant recruiting sergeant, had signed them up with honey-sweet promises. New settlers they were called. With their arrival – that was on St Martin's Day in the year twelve hundred and eighty-four – begins the downfall of Vineta, because the men among the new settlers were strictly opposed to gynocracy. And incidentally they had thousands of rats in their retinue, for which reason the city's last coat of arms shows a rat under the turkey, the turkey's beak pointing to the right and the rat running to the left.'

Damroka fetches the old sea chart from the pilot house and, with little light, points out the spot where the ship is anchored. 'Here,' she says, 'offshore from the mouth of the Peene, the island-city extended far to the east. We're anchored over the centre. Before the storm tide the sea is thought to have been as smooth as today. It's also said to have been a jellyfish year and it seems that angelic singsong hovered over the waters.'

The Rat

The women decide to have another try at sleeping. On Sunday morning they will check to make sure that their anchorage, as the yellowed sea chart claims, is really Vineta; the oceanographer isn't alone in having her doubts.

They are all in their hammocks when Damroka says: 'It seems the storm tide came on a Sunday. That's why bells can still be heard when the wind dies down.'

Chapter Eight, in which five minutes of silence pass, the birthday party takes its course, the She-rat speaks of false doctrines, the cuckoo calls in the movie and in real life, the women primp, Oskar crawls under skirts, almost everything comes to an end, and crosses are set up on Bishop's Mountain.

EARLY IN the morning, an hour before his chauffeur takes his breakfast and even earlier than his grandmother in her armchair receives holy communion from the priest's hand, early Sunday morning our Herr Matzerath makes his way short-legged from the Hotel Monopol through the Old City with its partly new, partly restored buildings toward the wattle barrier on the Rähm, where, closed but readily visible, the red-brick Polish Post Office building, dating from times when Danzig was a Free City, is waiting for him, the witness and perpetrator, the turncoat and accessory to the crime; for a stone plaque beside the gate of the historic edifice lists in sharply incised characters the names of all the Polish postal workers who at the beginning of the Second World War, which began on this very spot, returned fire through windows and skylights, though they had been given only a smattering of military training. Except for the dead and two or three fugitives, they were soon taken prisoner and every last one of them executed near the old cemetery in Saspe.

He wipes his gold-framed glasses. He looks for and finds his uncle's name carved in stone. Taking a step backward, he stands, holding his straw hat to one side and pressing his white-and-yellow shoes close together. Bells ringing near and far are not for him. No one shoots the photo that will give the scene reality. To the early churchgoers hurrying to Saint Mary's or Saint Catherine's, he offers the picture of an undersized elderly gentleman in western dress, apparently concentrating his thoughts on the granite plaque in front of the Post Office building.

I am sure our Herr Matzerath is not thinking exclusively of his uncle Jan Bronski and his dear mama, but also recalls the Oskar of those days, that angel of innocence, who took part in everything without taking part. Now, in any case, he is here and not at the same time absent. So it appears. There he stands with bowed head, meditating at his grandmother's bidding. His bald head glints in the morning sun. Now and then a cloud puts him in the shade.

Five minutes may have passed, for now he unbends, hesitates, puts his hat where it belongs, comes quickly to a decision, turns around and starts back with quick steps but, I'm sure, with heavy thoughts. Outside the Hotel Monopol, after someone has offered to buy foreign currency at an advantageous rate, he climbs into the waiting Mercedes.

He has no need to give his chauffeur instructions; on the contrary, Bruno shows him, as he did the day before, that he knows his way around. From old old stories, in the course of which tram conductors called out stop after stop and all other means of getting there and back were remembered, his former keeper knows the layout: again they are on their way from Oliva Gate down Grunwaldska, once known as Grosse Allee and later as Hinden-burgallee, now down Langfuhr's Main Street, which also changed its name several times, now left on Hochstriess, past the barracks of the Hussars, then Schutzpolizei, then Wehrmacht and at present Militia, past Brentau, in whose sandy graveyard soil his poor Mama lies, into hilly Kashubian country. Too many memories. Oskar diverts himself with a journal devoted to coins.

Relatives have gathered once again under the chestnut tree outside his grandmother's house. They seem to have been there since yesterday. But today the figure 107 braided from cornflowers hangs over the outer door of the kitchen, whose three inner doors lead at the back to the stable, right to the bedroom, left to the parlour. All are open, for everywhere, even in the cowbarn that had been untenanted for years, guests are seated on benches, chairs and footstools, drinking sweetened rhubarb juice or – early as it is in the day – water-clear potato schnaps, the supply of which seems to increase miraculously.

Beside Anna Koljaiczek's armchair, in which she is sitting as though she would never leave it, stands a table, on the half of which that is closer to her a hundred and seven candles donated by the church are still burning, while the other half is already laden with gifts. Admired is a galloping porcelain horse with heroically lashing tail, which in all its fragility has been brought to Kashubia by Mr and Mrs Bruns. Swathed from top to toe in red-and-yellow flowered silk, Lady Bruns explains that the horse is a faithful copy of the porcelain horses of the Ming Dynasty.

The Vikings have seen fit to bring from Australia to notoriously meat-starved Poland an electric grill which, because technical perfection is interesting as such, must be tried out before all eyes. The onlookers are amazed to see the naked revolving spit accelerate when a button is pressed, purr at high speed and set off bell signals which, when meat is present, indicate its condition, whether rare or well done.

From Lake Michigan the Colchics have brought an over-life-size bronze head, whose features were derived from a photo taken in the twenties. It is supposed to be the posthumous likeness of the moustachioed Josef Koljaiczek, who in the days of Kaiser Wilhelm was hunted as a political incendiary, who found refuge with Anna Bronski (who later called herself Anna Koljaicjzek) with the result that a child named Agnes was born to her. When again obliged to flee, Josef, by then a father, submerged, only to surface years later in Chicago, where he made a fortune in the lumber business, engendered numerous Koljaiczeks, who later called themselves Colchic, and might even have become a senator, if in February 1945, when the second Soviet Army under Marshal Rokossovski descended on Kashubia, he had not succumbed to a heart attack in spite of the distance between Lake Michigan and Bissau. It seems that when Anna saw her bronze Josef brought back from America, she thought it over for a few moments and then said: 'He'd of lived longer if he'd stayed home with me.'

From Mombasa, an African city on the Indian Ocean, Kazimir Kurbiella had brought a deep-black polished ebony woman, about the height of a chair, whose fat rump, pointed breasts and long limbs made everybody uncomfortable, until the prelate from Oliva touched the sinful creature, called her art, picked her up and examined her in every detail with the eye of a connoisseur.

I don't know what presents the Stommas brought from Gelsen-kirchen. Probably that battery-operated cuckoo clock from the

Black Forest, which calls the half hours and has its place beside the print of the Sacred Heart with a hand-written dedication from the Polish Pope, which the prelate brought and hung with his own hand on the wall in the place of the fly-shit-spotted Last Supper.

What more birthday presents should I list? The Kashubians living between Kartuzy and Wejherovo are poor, but fond of giving presents. They put down crocheted doilies beside fleece-lined bedroom slippers and presentation cups. So many lovingly fashioned trifles. A secretary at the state post office brought a paper knife with an amber handle. The delegation from the Lenin Shipyard, which included Stephan Bronski's sons, brought a present which was soon hidden behind other presents – on purpose, although the representatives of the state hurried back to Warsaw yesterday.

This present provoked a quarrel which is still going on under the surface. And yet the artfully forged iron letters, which look as though written by hand and form the word Solidarność with the down stroke of the 'n' holding up a red-and-white enamelled flag, looks like the kind of bric-à-brac that might be at home to the right of the Sacred Heart; but it was not only the government officials from Warsaw who would have been displeased at this gift; the prelate, to be sure, called the wrought iron writing good work, inspired by a noble thought, but found it unsuited to an eminently unpolitical occasion. Today, he said in substance, the daily strife and turmoil should remain outside the flower-adorned door.

And in similar words Stephan Bronski argues with his sons. Not in the parlour but outside the house and in the kitchen, arguments are in progress until our Herr Matzerath and chauffeur arrive in the Mercedes. Immediately drawn into the hopeless quarrel, he, who loves to enunciate principles, succeeds, almost casually, in taking some of the edge off the quarrel about the banned trade union with the remark: 'Politics has indeed brought us Kashubians many memorial days, but few blessings.' In the end, only Kazimir Kurbiella, who in Mombasa is called Kazy, remembers that he was once a sailor and comes out for Solidarność. Under the chestnut tree, he demands that it should again be authorized, whereas Stephan Bronski, supported by Herr Stomma, insists more than once not only in traditional German but in Polish as well, that there's gotta be law and order. At length the prelate from Oliva appeases the forces both of law and order and of trade-union solidarity, by taking the position of the church and blessing both sides.

Only then does Bruno, who even in the parlour does not remove his chauffeur's cap, bring in one by one all the presents that Anna Koljaiczek's grandson thought up during protracted balneary visits to Baden-Baden and Bad Schinznach, and in the course of his numismatic travels. Bruno is reluctant to accept help in unpacking. Odd that he rolls up the string and puts it in his pocket. He never uses scissors to save time. Every knot demands patience. At last all the wrappings have fallen. Meanwhile, the Kashubian children have been allowed to blow out the burned-down candles. Room is quickly made for Oskar's presents.

Loud applause for the three-foot (as Herr Matzerath points out) *baumkuchen*, which Frau Stomma starts serving in good house-wifely style: a paper thin slice for each guest. The Kashubians let the cake, veined with finest chocolate, melt on their tongues like communion wafers.

All are amazed when Bruno demonstrates the next gift, a Polaroid camera, with which it is possible to take pictures of guests in varied groupings, not, as Herr Matzerath stresses, forgetting 'our dear birthday child', and no sooner snapped, tear them off the camera and gaze at them; blurred at first, they reveal their subject more and more clearly and glossily, until everyone recognizes everyone and, to his amazement, himself.

Next the company laughs at a bag which when emptied disgorges a hundred and thirty blue and white plastic dwarfs brought for the numerous Kashubian children. Loud cheers when Mr Bruns, smilingly backed up by Lady Bruns, discovers the words 'Made in Hong Kong' stamped into the soles of a good part of the smurfs, proof that at least half of them may have been turned out by the Brunses' very own toy factory and – as the guests all agree – that it's a small world.

After all these gifts for the Kashubians and their children a lacquered case comes to light. In eleven drawers a hundred and seven gold pieces are bedded on white velvet, all set apart as the birthday child's treasure. On request, Herr Matzerath comments on the gold pieces. He differentiates louis d'or, maxdor, friedrich-dor. These here, he explains, were minted in Switzerland, these in South Africa, these in the Kaiser's day, and that whole drawerful under the Habsburg Empire. There are ducats and crowns, gold rubles from Tsarist Russia and gold Soviet memorial coins. All marvel at Swiss vreneli and the US dollars that rule the world, at Mexican pesos, and Krugerrands. Even a Chinese collector's item featuring a panda is there to be admired. The coins are handed around and all come back.

'All gold, you say?' says Anna Koljaiczek incredulously, keeping a good hold on her rosary.

'Gold ducats,' her grandson assures her. 'For each year a gold piece, dear Babka.'

In the end she brings herself to heft a Danzig ducat from the days of King Siegesmund August.

Adopting his grandmother's rustic diction, Oskar says: 'So you shouldn't be poor no more.' Only to Joe Colchic does he remark, not without accusing overtones, on the steady drop in the price of gold, as though he had reason to hold the American Kashubians responsible for the decreasing value of his treasures.

But while the guests are enjoying themselves – the smurfs are good for plenty of laughs, and the first snapshots with the Polaroid camera are a big hit – our Herr Matzerath, who has spread out the gold pieces on his grandmother's lap, whispers in her ear. 'Ah, Babka,' he says, 'things are looking bad in the world. Everybody wants to destroy each other. They can do it, too. They can destroy every living thing. Signs and portents wherever you look. Bad times are on their way. If not today, tomorrow.'

Though this whispered prognostication of disaster to come does not diminish her pleasure in the noisy enjoyment of her relatives and guests, Anna Koljaiczek says, 'I know, Oskar, the devil's got his nose in the pie.'

Then she wants his ear, closer, still closer: 'There used to be rats here behind the house. Jesus, Mary and Joseph. Now they're all gone.'

After receiving this information her grandson re-enters the birthday turmoil. He has to explain coins and their weight. There's always somebody wanting to heft a gold piece. Especially a Mexican fifty-peso coin arouses amazement. Over and over again the Kashubians from Kartuzy and Wejherowo, Firoga, Kokoszki and Karczemki confirm the printed figures, thirty-five point five grams and the magic words 'Oro Puro'. Every time the golden weight passes from hand to hand, it provokes a slight shudder. Someone, a Kuczorra from Chmielno, refuses to touch it. But Kazy

Kurbiella, who likes to clown and in the company of women to play the spry bachelor, wedges a gold Swiss vreneli into his eye like a monocle.

The chauffeur, now a guest and no longer wearing his cap, makes himself pleasing as a photographer to variously grouped Kashubians. The American Colchics want to see themselves in a picture with the Woykes from Zukowo. The Australian Vikings stand between Stephan Bronski and wife, née Pipka, and the Bronski sons with their fiancées. The Brunses of Hong Kong insist on showing the birthday child the porcelain horse a second time for the photo. The Stommas with their teenage daughters, who always look rather peevish and have to be prodded, group themselves with the Stommas from Kartuzy around Anna's armchair, which today is surmounted by a red-and-white peony arrangement. Despite the whispered protests of the postal secretary, Kazy Kurbiella demands a snapshot immortalizing the delegation from the Lenin shipyard along with himself bearing the wrought iron Solidarność standard against a white shirt front.

Every time the miracle is awaited in silence before paper, blank a moment ago, gives birth to an image. Fearful expectancy as between offertory and consecration.

Time and again, our Herr Matzerath, fervently as he pleads to be left out of it, has to appear in the picture, as centrally as possible: between Poland's church and state, as connecting link between all too ramified families, surrounded by Kashubian children. And all the while the drinking, singing, laughing and crying go on. The sour smell continues to engulf the crowded guests. Once more, with undiminished enthusiasm, each tells each about some ailment, how long it has been going on and how treated. One also learns why Kazy Kurbiella is still a bachelor, how big Chicago is, the cost of living in Hong Kong, how much Anthony Viking earns working for the Australian railways. An argument or two, but only over trifles – the occasion conciliates – so that the men from the Lenin Shipyard, and the proponents of Polish as well as German law and order are all delighted with the blue-and-white smurfs. 'You know, Oskar,' says Stephan Bronski, 'you've given us another big surprise.'

The guests are all of the same opinion; they drink potato schnaps followed by egg cognac to his health. But in the luggage compartment of his Mercedes and in his heart, which could never be trusted, our Herr Matzerath has kept still another surprise in store.

In olden times we were better informed; but during the first phase of the post-human era, which was longer than can be expressed in counted calendar years, we heard next to nothing about the rat nations that had dug themselves in elsewhere. We were sure we existed all over, and that made us all the more avid for news. But when the first immigrants came from the East and were assigned to districts outside the city, in the Kashubian hinterland on the still swampy Island, the immigrants didn't know much, just that conditions were worse in Russia, a lot worse than here at home, and almost unbearable even for rats. This wasn't news. Nothing concrete, only complaints and rumours; we'd had enough of that.

It was different in the human era, said the She-rat of my dreams. From time immemorial we had travelled from continent to continent in ships of all sizes, as long as they didn't give off that sinking smell which sometimes pervaded particular ships or whole fleets. The Spanish Armada sank without us. We steered clear of the *Titanic*. There were no rats on board the *Wilhelm Gustloff*, a Strength-through-Joy ship, which in January 1945 was torpedoed in Gdynia, then called Gotenhafen, soon after leaving Danzig Bay; the same goes for the *Steuben*, carrying four thousand wounded, the *Goya* and other ships that ran into mines, turned turtle or sank stern first. Some admiral had sent them all to Courland to bring as many soldiers and civilians as possible to the West. We know that, because some of us had travelled West on ships that did not sink. Seven times, we sailed on the *Cap Arcona*, in fact we doubled in number before going ashore in Danish and North German ports, but we denied ourselves the former luxury liner when it was loaded with inmates of the Neuengamme concentration camp and thus marked for sinking.

Anyone who doesn't believe me, said the She-rat, who just wouldn't stop talking about avoided sinkings, should remember how, when we had a premonition of the naval battle of Tsushima, we fled from the armoured cruisers and battleships of the Russian Baltic fleet . . .

On and on she went, losing herself in her favourite topic. She listed the cruisers *Svetlana* and *Shemchug*, the flagship *Ostjaba*, the armoured cruiser *Admiral Nakhinov*, the battleships *Borodino* and

Suvorov. Forty-two black tubs in all, which in the night of 14 October 1904 were abandoned by all naked of tail.

But friend, she cried, why do we talk about sinkings when there are so many ships to be remembered that we boarded without a qualm and from which we landed safe and sound, though occasionally deep-frozen, like those New Zealand rats who were so dead set on travelling from the antipodes to Europe that they stowed away on freighters carrying a cargo of mutton. Yet they survived the cold shock. It had no lasting effect on the deep-frozen New Zealand rats, who recovered their full mobility on reaching the London docks. Refrigeration hadn't impaired their rat memory in the least. Far from inducing atrophy, freezing kept it fresh. They brought news and leaving again by the next ship carried news somewhere else.

The She-rat praised the intercontinental info-system of the rat nations, deplored the newslessness of the post-human era, and waxed positively lyrical about the technological perfection of the late human era, as she called it. She spoke of airborne rats, who travelled in passenger as well as cargo planes. Not an airline, she cried, that we didn't patronize. Always up to date, we were always better informed than humans. A pity that next to no news comes our way nowadays.

But She-rat, I said, what do you need news for, why do you need information? At peace, free from the pointless headlines that cancel one another out from day to day, free from daily reports of catastrophes, you are able at last to live ratworthy lives, to live for yourselves. Now that you've put an end to the hectic bustle of human existence, you shouldn't give a damn about news and sensations.

In a way, she conceded, you're right. You live more serenely if you don't know what's coming from behind the Seven Mountains. All the same, we're curious to know how rats in other places are dealing with a development that alarms the nations settled here, nay more, that endangers, nay more, that might ruin us . . .

I saw her scurrying nervously back and forth, then again blurred and tripartite, but unanimous. Of course, she cried, it's understandable that that old woman in the armchair, who would like to die but can't, should be worshipped by country rats; of course, in the cities numerous intact churches are available for collective use. But must the worship of an an old woman, must the gatherings of our nations in the cities degenerate in the country into idolatry, and into irrationality in the cities? It can't be denied. We're getting religion. No sooner has the human race perished than we start looking behind things, searching for meaning, fashioning images. All this would be bearable if not understandable if it were one unifying faith that was making us rats pious. But far from it, just like humans, we go in for deviations. Outward indications mark trends and creeds. Even now there are grounds for an irreconcilable conflict – as though we were doomed to walk in the footsteps of man.

Sharper in her contours and more sharply trinitary, inclusive of her whiskers, the She-rat said: By and large, we can distinguish three denominations. The origin of a rat nation may have something to do with it. We in this region are old settlers; but some of our number immigrated from the West via the so-called underground railway, and still others trickled in shortly before the Big Bang from the vast Russian land mass. These three nations are basically identical in character and even in the zinc-green coloration of our post-human hair; only in our pieties are they at odds . . .

When she said that, I couldn't tell which of them had said pieties and at odds, because, in my dream, three She-rats enlivened the screen. They kept out of each other's way or glared at each other ferociously. They scurried restlessly back and forth. One She-rat chased the second, who was chasing the third. I never knew which was speaking to me in my dream. They shouted one another down, vilipended one another. I heard absurd accusations; the first She-rat cursed the second, wishing her back where she had come from, in far distant Russia, excoriated the third for Polish disorder, and was in turn damned as a Prussian by the Russian and Polish She-rats, who, God knows, viewed each other with mutual hatred.

But essentially the three She-rats, each of whom may have been mine, were arguing about questions of faith. Their disputation had a Christian ring. When they invoked charity in their mutual recriminations, they sounded human. While one fulminated with Protestant zeal, the second remained stubbornly Catholic, and the third – but which one? – tried with Orthodox zeal to outdo the obstinacy of the others. Crouching to leap or confronting one another with bare-tooth fury and bristling whiskers. Then for a time each hissed to herself; I had difficulty in disentangling their embattled knot.

Apart from theological hairsplittings and other human claptrap, the question was largely territorial: who was entitled to assemble when in what churches? Those rats who had immigrated from Russia, and were reduced to living in the marshes of the Lower Vistula, claimed exclusive rights over the mud-slide-enclosed church of Saint Barbara. The rats who had immigrated from Germany shortly before the finale laid claim to Saint Mary's and demanded a share in other religious premises. On no account would the Polish Catholic rats cede the former Dominican church to the Protestants. And the German rats were no less quarrelsomely intent on Saint Bridget and Saint Catherine.

But, I shouted into the fray, what about Christian charity, damn it all? A little more tolerance, if you please.

After that I had all three of them against me. A pretty pass things have come to if this last human thinks he can teach rats how to behave. His space capsule isn't enough for him. He should mind his business. The gall! One thing the human race was never any good at was tolerance. Then the three of them went back to quarrelling among themselves again and seemed to enjoy it.

But when they went on with their religious controversy, there were four, then five female rats going at it hammer and tongs. As far as I could make out, the Protestants had split and among the Orthodox there were Early Christian–Communist deviations. This was just what the Polish Kashubians – but which was the Catholic? – wanted. She demanded restitution of Saint Barbara's in the Lower City and, it goes without saying, of the former Royal-Polish chapel next door to Saint Mary's, which the fourth She-rat quite absurdly claimed for Calvinist meetings, while the Communist Early Christians wanted the church of Saint James beside the former Lenin Shipyard as a meeting place.

Oh well, I said, there are plenty of churches around, damn it. But wouldn't it be nice if even pious rats could manage to preach, perhaps not tolerance in every church, but at least common charity!

Again I have them all, now five in number, against me. My situation seemed familiar. I'd had experience and to spare. I looked for comparisons, tried to drive the woman-manned ship into my dream, but I was hopelessly berated, and all I could do was shout charity, dammit, a little more charity!

The answer was scornful laughter. No need to preach charity to rats. We've practised it from time immemorial. Only humans have had to make it a commandment, which as it transpired they were incapable of keeping. Instead they devised murder and torture and perfected them more and more. It was high time this last man in his space capsule learned to keep his trap shut.

When I nevertheless protested and threatened them with dreams that would be true in a different way – our Herr Matzerath still has a surprise in store, the ship is still anchored over Vineta, the Chancellor and his retinue are still imprisoned in deep Sleeping-Beauty sleep – I heard all five She-rats laugh, but only one, probably the Catholic one cried out: 'Scram! Buzz off into your stories! What do we need you for! The old woman is still alive in her armchair. She mumbles and mumbles and she can't die . . .'

And again they quarrelled. But this time it was not over the use of unscathed churches in the preserved city. No longer as though preaching from pulpits, but in wild confusion, atop a mound of porcelain shards, toy-sized figurines and heedlessly rejected coins, they were fighting over the old woman who wanted to die but couldn't, who struck me as familiar, adamantly as I refused to name the old woman by name; only if you speak to her, I said to myself, will she really be lost.

Our Herr Matzerath speaks as though for the last time. Always the film director, he claps his little hands; too many rings on his fingers. Standing on a chair, so as to be seen as he speaks, he makes a request under the low ceiling, and instantly attentiveness grows around him.

At last Oskar starts to speak to the gathering of farflung kin and unrelated guests. All lift up their eyes to him. He speaks of himself, the world and himself. He has often made this speech to me, as though rehearsing. For a long time these sentences addressed to mankind have been taking shape in his mind, his last words so to speak.

'Look upon me, if you please,' he says, 'as someone who in the deceptively rich West heads a medium-sized firm, whose management began before it was too late to envisage all the possibilities offered by the media, and inaugurated a production so many-sided that today, now that we have thrown thousands upon thousands of cassettes on the market, I can say to our dear birthday child: Everything has been filmed. With the certainty demanded by the media, I should like to list: what fate has inscribed to our account, what memory holds against us – whether coloured by long familiarity or saturated with smells that were once new to our nose – what, like children's porridge, wedding cake, funeral suppers tasted good, repeated on us, made us hungry for more. This indefatigable once upon a time has been filmed. But our hopes as well, which call for future colours, smells, tastes and feelings that are not old and hackneyed but brand-new and saturated with media appeal, have become films, stored in cassette after cassette. I have said that everything has been filmed. Whatever new experience we think we are having has already been played before an audience elsewhere and become history before becoming reality. Consequently, my dear relatives, we who – so widely ramified is our green Kashubian plant – were dead sure we had never seen one another before are nevertheless well known to one another, familiar from other films that still flickered black and white, in which we engaged in other festivities. There have always been plenty of occasions: sad ones and others that made us happy. And soon there will be one more occasion, when your Oskar celebrates his sixtieth birthday. I cordially invite you all, first of all you, revered grandmother, dear Babka, to my birthday party in September, which is already passing before my eyes like a film: how it begins, develops, tends toward a climax and loses itself in innumerable subplots . . .'

While he is being thanked for his invitation to the distant West, our Herr Matzerath goes on: 'As you see, the world has little new to offer us; at the most we are rearranged, now this way, now that way and surprisingly differently, like those smurfs with which the entranced children are playing. Ah yes! We are special prefabricated smurfs – everything doesn't necessarily come from Hong Kong – made to adult measure. We find our rehearsed roles in thousands upon thousands of films, costumed now this way now that; involved in cheerful or downright silly stories, in sad plots that usually end tragically, in thrillers or tediously broad intrigues, which we regard as reflections of life, even if they are prefabricated, filmed life, and look forward to, watering at the mouth and determined not to miss a single scene of kissing or skull-cracking. Why am I telling you this? It's all old stuff. Cold coffee served up over and over again. Years ago our dear birthday child's only daughter, my dear mama, used to say whenever she saw friends gathered around her table playing skat for pennies: Life is like a movie.'

The Kashubians come from far and near are treated to insights on this order. The workers from the Lenin Shipyard, the representatives of Poland's church and Poland's state post office nod with wondering approbation. Isn't it true that life is like a movie you've seen before? Hasn't Poland's misery been ladled out over and over again? And haven't we always had an edgy presentiment of how straight or crooked the road ahead would be?

'You're right, Oskar,' Stephan Bronski cries out. 'It's the same as it's always been.'

In front of the flower-bedecked armchair and behind it, the new generation of Kashubian children from the prolific Woyke and Stomma strains play with the cute little smurfs our Herr Matzerath has brought from the opulent West in addition to the *baumkuchen*, the Polaroid camera and the gold ducats. The smurfs are all wearing white caps above their round tummies and deep-blue, bulbous-nosed faces. Most are grinning as though there were plenty to grin about, though some are morose, lonely, abysmally sad. Every smurf is busy, carrying an implement or burden. Some are holding sporting equipment, others are munching Black Forest cherry torte. One has a mason's trowel in his right hand and is picking up a brick with his left; the next is wielding an axe. The one with the wrench is a mechanic, the one with scythe and sheaf of grain embodies the peasantry. This one is regulating traffic with a red and white stop sign. This one has bitten into a sandwich, that one can't tear himself away from the bottle. All are doing something; all but one, who is unemployed and stands there empty-handed with downcast eyes. Thus the smurfs the Kashubian children are playing with, while Oskar praises the cinema as prefabricated life, present a mirror image of the industrious human race.

'How lovely,' says our Herr Matzerath, 'to be back in the family circle. Even our ailments have remained true to themselves. Hardly anything has changed. Well, yes, politics. But we've always had that. And the realization that we humans grow older has been taken into full account in my video films. As I've said before, everything that happens happens over and over again, including minor, modish innovations. We Kashubians, those of us who have stayed with their roots and those who have come from far away, are the best illustration of my thesis, for which reason I should like to show you all, and especially you, my dear Babka, a special video cassette, which has foretasted a little future and therefore fits in with my programme that will soon be distributed worldwide under the title: "Post Futurum".'

Without delay Bruno, assisted by a shipyard worker, carries a large-screen television set into the low-ceilinged parlour. A small table is quickly brought in and placed against the wall, in front of Anna Koljaiczek. The television set, into which a video tape recorder is plugged, covers the embroidered wall hanging, figuring an angel shielding a child from the abyss. The cuckoo beside the print of the Sacred Heart calls, because it's half past eleven.

The chauffeur feeds the promised cassette into the VTR. Laughing, drinking out of small glasses, but always on the verge of tears, the birthday guests, on the whole a contented, God-fearing lot, group themselves to the left and right of the peony-adorned armchair, which is flanked by the prelate and the postal secretary. The Kashubian children stop playing with the smurfs and squat, lie or stand in front of the adults. All look at the still vacant screen as though an epiphany of the Virgin Mary had been announced. 'Oskarkins,' cries Anna Koljaiczek, 'is it going to be a surprise?'

Then, at a sign from our Herr Matzerath, who stands modestly to one side, Bruno, the chauffeur, starts the prefabricated cassette. First the title fills the screen: The Hundred and Seventh Birthday of the Revered Anna Koljaiczek, née Bronski. But when in the first images Oskar's grandmother's humble cottage appears with its chestnut tree, its apple trees, garden fence and sunflowers, which because of the rainy summer have not attained their proper height, and when behind the fence the festive board and the first guests, among them Mr and Lady Bruns, enliven the screen, or more concretely, when they dig in, polish off piroshki and poppy-seed cake – then the crowded birthday company unites in an ah! of amazement, which fades, sighing, into silence when, after a cut showing over the door the figure 107 braided from cornflowers, first the kitchen, then the jam-packed parlour come into the picture, except for the birthday child, who is hidden at first; but the candles which were burning a while ago and were then blown out, are all burning now.

All the guests are pre-visioned in the film: the prelate from Oliva and the priest from Matarnia; both representatives of the Polish government, who unfortunately had to leave yesterday, and the still present delegation from the Lenin Shipyard. Even the tardy postal secretary gets into the picture. The presence of each guest is pre-produced: how loudly and cordially the Colchics from America greet the Woykes from Zukowo. How often the Stommas from Gelsenkirchen clink glasses with Stephan Bronski, who stands morosely to one side the whole time. What hotel manager Kazy Kurbiella translates into Polish from the Vikings' English in order to acquaint Antek Kuczorra, the railway man from Kokoschken, with the Australian railways. How proud the toy manufacturer from Hong Kong is of his Far Eastern wife and of his gift, the porcelain horse, both pre-filmed by the video camera, flying tail, page boy bob and all. Ah, how frail is Lady Bruns in the film and in reality.

And similarly, the Kashubian children, when this cassette was produced, were blowing out birthday candles and playing with smurfs from the opulent West before being really allowed to blow out candles and play with smurfs. Stephan Bronski's sons, as the film has foreseen, have been engaged for years to a strapping lass whose permanent curls Baltic blonde and a dainty little thing whose dark brown hair is not at all true to type. 'The place just isn't big enough,' explains the synchronized sound to the strains of a polka, now muffled, now inviting to the dance.

Only the music is new; everything else has already been. Outside the house and in the parlour as well. Drinks and enticing snacks, sweet things and sour have already been chewed, swallowed, digested. Head cheese and crumb cake, pickles and pudding have been pre-tasted. Some of the guests engaged in song long before they really began to sing to make merriment prevail. For the benefit of the film and in honour of Oskar, the older Kashubians have sung *Waldeslust, Waldeslust (O Forest Rapture)* in German, before striking up the *Waldeslust* song in real life later on. Even the argument of the shipyard workers with the representatives of the Polish government over the legitimacy of the trade union Solidarność has been anticipated with ample gesticulation and is now being replayed with the original sound. On one side Kazy Kurbiella of Mombasa, on the other, Herr Stomma of Gelsenkirchen and Stephan Bronski, shouting 'Law and Order!' in German and Polish, join the argument, until the prelate from Oliva smoothes down the contradictions. The shipyard workers laugh mirthlessly when his Reverence, blessing both parties, transforms the working population and the representatives of the state into peace-loving children of God.

At this point, Stephan Bronski makes himself heard over the sound track, shouting: 'How'd you ever do it, Oskar, tell us how.'

Our Herr Matzerath says casually: 'Isn't it true, your Reverence, they used to call it divine providence; today it's tiny microprocessors which store up everything that has been and spit out what will be. The rest is tricks of the trade. Child's play.'

As he goes on to explain that whatever can be conceived can also be produced, Oskar himself comes into the picture. In the film as in grandmother's parlour, where the clairvoyant film is playing, he is loudly acclaimed. For the second time, the guests are amazed at all the wonders Herr Matzerath has brought from the West. They see Anna Koljaiczek in her decorated armchair delighting in the *baumkuchen* and the ducats and even more in the humpback little man. 'Oskarkins,' she cries out, and again she delights.

Over the film soundtrack we hear her saying in reality: 'Oh, Oskarkins, this is like I alwies thunk my birthday would be,' while what she said in the film while hefting a gulden from the days of Siegesmund Augustus was: 'Is it all gold?'

How the Kashubian children cheer when the little bag of smurfs comes into the picture. And when in the film they see themselves playing with the smurfs just as they were doing a moment ago before the cuckoo clock called half past eleven, the children think the film is faithfully playing back what they pre-enacted.

How happy they are. Now their new toy appears in close-ups: the smurf regulating traffic with the stop sign. Several smurfs with mason's trowels. And the one with the scythe is now lined up sevenfold with other reapers. The smurf with the red-and-white drum gets more attention than all the other musical smurfs. 'Oskar! Oskar!' cry the Kashubian children crowded around the screen; they know the story. Those paying close attention notice that all the smurfs, even the one with the drum, have only four fingers, a thumb and three more. They'd like to know why. But even Uncle Bruns from Hong Kong, who has manufactured millions of adorable smurfs and had them stamped with the name of his industrious town, knows no answer either in the film or in reality.

Needless to say, the snapshots which barely an hour ago were taken with the Polaroid camera donated by Herr Matzerath found their subjects at the time when the film was produced, among them the one showing the representatives of Poland's state and church to the right and left of Anna Koljaiczek's armchair and the one grouping the workers' delegation from the Lenin Shipyard around Kazimir Kurbiella, who is holding the wrought-iron 'Solidarność' standard as if it were a relic. 'I always say,' cries Anna Koljaiczek happily, 'there ain't never nothing new, it's all been and happened before.'

In the video film now running, our Herr Matzerath, as though to confirm the law of eternal return, announces the promised surprise: a Post-Futurum production of his company specialized in prevision. And already the birthday guests see the capless chauffeur aided by the shipyard worker carrying the television set into the parlour and setting it down on the ready-prepared table in front of the guardian angel print; the two of them had been doing just that before the built-in battery began to feed the VTR and the tape started unrolling to a polka accompaniment.

But when in the film the film starts up again after the cuckoo has called half past eleven as it will twelve times a moment later, the birthday guests fall silent in the parlour. No more Oh's and Ah's, no more sighs and mirthless laughter. Aghast and rigid with horror, the birthday guests see themselves on the television screen, watching a video film in which birthday guests submit cheerfully and in good faith to a video film, which only a moment ago the prelate from Oliva approved with a smile as a high-tech version of divine providence, but now seeks to exorcise with the sign of the Cross, because the sequence of events in the film has quite logically . . .

And once again, as though in league with the Devil, the cuckoo clock that had found its place beside the Sacred Heart print signed by the Pope calls cuckoo cuckoo . . . twelve times. Even our Herr Matzerath takes fright in his tailor-made suit. In reality as in the film, he toys with his tie pin. And just as he is troubled in reality, he sees himself troubled in the film, as though seeing himself for the last time . . .

The women, too, on board the coastal motor barge *The New Ilsebill*, are weighted with leaden-footed thoughts. They've lain too long in their hammocks. They've overslept. Time has been lost, for when at last they appear on deck in their nightclothes, it is late Sunday morning. The sun is high over the Baltic Sea, and there's no more singing over it. Forsaken by all medusas, they take comfort in the sight, far away in the direction of Peenemünde, of the GDR border patrol boat, lying likewise at anchor as though to give the five women courage: Chin up, girls. You're not alone.

The oceanographer is wider awake than the others, whose staggering laziness can only yawn and stretch. She walks the deck on the port, on the starboard sides, bending over from time to time, shields her eyes with both hands while looking out over the smooth, barely breathing sea from the bow, then the stern, and shouts: 'Girls, it's time to wake up. We're there. I'm going mad. Vineta is right below us!'

Now they all bend over the rail, shaping their hands into light-screening tunnels. The engineer can hardly believe her eyes. 'It's unbelievable,' she cries out, 'it's marvellous. I've seen it before, I don't remember where.'

'Man!' cries the Old Woman. 'Not just seven churches. I see just as many bars if not more.'

The helmswoman isn't satisfied with just seeing the submerged city. 'That's it. Let's go.'

The oceanographer also thinks they've arrived. 'I've always known, I had a hunch that we'd get there sometime, because there's nowhere else . . .'

But even more concretely than the other women the helmswoman sees the woman's paradise as confidently as if all its rooms were ready to move into. It lies hospitably ready to shelter the wish she had cherished so long, that she had carried, too long carried, like an unborn child; for indeed the Wendish Jumne, the city of Vineta, is spread out below them, with all its towers, squares and gabled houses, their final haven, the unavowed, often disputed, yet predestined goal of their journey.

Why does Damroka say nothing, but only stare and stare?

How familiar Vineta looks with its tangle of streets. It is situated on a river that forms an island, on which tall, massive half-timbered warehouses give promise of wealth. Bridges across the river lead to vaulted gates. Still somewhat arrogantly, the ornate façades of gabled houses measure themselves with their counterparts on the other side of the street. Tiers of window ledges. Porches outside doors flanked by pillars. This gable is decorated with a swan, that one with a golden anchor, one with a tortoise, another with a boar's head. The engineer discovers a gable distinguished by Fortuna on a rolling ball. And on numerous gables, indeed, whichever way you look, encrusted in the vaulted doorways, at the top of the Rathaus steps the Old Woman sees – 'There,' she cries out, 'and there's another;' – the city's coat of arms that Damroka had spoken of – though now she says nothing – a heraldic turkey on top of a heraldic rat.

'There,' cries the helmswoman, 'right next to the Rathaus, where the women's council meets, that must be the women's house. Only the women's house could have such tall, tapering windows.'

And the building opposite, whose gable is surmounted by a female figure holding scales, that in the oceanographer's opinion must be where the magistrates' court sits. Everywhere they discover houses and squares suited to administering the women's cause, upholding the women's law, building their women's republic. How sparklingly clean the city is. Nowhere a beard of seaweed, no barnacles clinging to any roof or doorway. Makes you feel like going down, like walking the streets arm in arm.

'Let's go!' cries the engineer. 'Vineta, here we come!'

'You said it!' says the oceanographer.

'Follow me!' cries the Old Woman. She wants to be first to jump, but the helmswoman thinks *she* should have precedence. 'Get this straight. I was fighting for the women's cause when you were still running after guys. Dependent, voluntarily subservient, that's what you were. Admit it, dearie. I go first . . .'

At this point Damroka, who up until now has been peering into the depths and getting her hair wet, says to the others and no doubt to herself as well: 'We'll have to make ourselves presentable first. We can't go to Vineta in these rags.'

Once again my slow Damroka has maintained her position as captain. Quickly the helmswoman says: 'Exactly. You took the words out of my mouth. Let's dress up, make ourselves beautiful as if we were going to a party.'

So the five women go back to the forecastle. Though they've lost much too much time, I'm glad to see them rummaging in seabags and trunks. Off with the sweaty nightgowns!

This much I can say: none has grown plump, let alone fat, they're all somewhere between skinny and scrawny. And as long as they were close or strange to me, they devoted themselves to the business of dressing up, except the engineer, who favoured baggy smocks.

As if they had foreseen this situation, their sea kits offered an amazing selection. They spread out, choose, reject: ankle-length dresses with wide, pleated sleeves; gowns whose abundance of material permits draping and ruched shoulders; severe, formal evening dresses, amusing little summer frocks, carrying fruit and flowers to market; slinky evening dresses of the type said to fit like a glove; trouser skirts with an oriental flavour; veils, scarves, shawls of every conceivable length. And what quantities of jewellery were needed for this voyage: heavy silver pendants; raw amber strung into long necklaces; ivory necklaces, coral necklaces; paste brooches, mother-of-pearl buckles, ivory arm bands. Onyx, horn. Shoes, slippers, booties. Even hats are to be found in trunks and seabags. Underclothes, plain or openwork.

How fortunate that a mirror, cracked to be sure but still serviceable, hanging on the wood partition shutting off the forecastle from the bow, makes comparisons possible. Little by little the women decide what they regard as appropriate or becoming.

I should like them to swap dresses and gowns; but they're not doing one another any favours, they won't part with the least thing. Though I'd rather see Damroka than the engineer in the oriental trouser suit and though the helmswoman appeals to me less in the severe evening dress than in the amusing summer frock, they refuse to humour me. At the most I'm allowed to advise against this extra-wide belt and this necklace too many, and to bid them hurry, because time, too much time is passing.

In my admittedly petit bourgeois concern that they'll overdo the finery and come out on deck ridiculously overdressed, I'm beginning to dread their emergence. But when at last they climb the companionway, all the women collectively and each singly are beautiful. First comes the oceanographer in the tight-fitting silk gown, slit down the side in the Chinese manner, covered with a Spanish-looking veil. Last, as though this order had been discussed with me, comes Damroka in a saffron-yellow wide-sleeve gown, over which fall the amber necklace and her infinitely wavy hair. The engineer is wearing a turkey-red turban to go with her baggy trouserskirt. I'd never have thought that a broad-brimmed hat, and a white one at that, which she wears tilted forward and to one side, would become the helmswoman. And it's amazing how girlishly the Old Woman leaps up the stairs in her swinging, small-flowered, knee-length little dress and flowered buckled shoes.

Other things that I notice: heavy silver pendants on a black evening dress; a green-shimmering mother-of-pearl brooch holding the turban in place; the patent leather belt with the slit skirt; the paste brooch on the small-flowered dress; and as Damroka mounts the stairs, gathering her saffron-yellow robe, I see that she is wearing high black boots.

Earrings, ear clips, the coral necklace, the heavy armband. They are carrying handbags or tightly crocheted purses filled with the most necessary articles. All have put on white makeup or rouge, mascara'd their eyelashes or – as the helmswoman chose to do – given their eyebrows a pained expression.

They linger yet awhile. Though time presses, they stroll back and forth on deck, as though interested in pleasing no one but themselves. How irreplaceably precious! It seems to me that I've seen them like this, so unforgettably unique, somewhere – in a film? Saint Fellini! That crook of the elbow, the curve of the neck, those tired, tragic, yet challenging glances. Those gestures, sweeping or introspective. Back and forth they stride, from pilothouse to bow. The Old Woman hops. The oceanographer loses an earring that Damroka finds. The hatted helmswoman stands like a monument, around which the engineer in her baggy trousers leaps grotesquely. And what I hoped for but never thought possible: they speak to one another, smile at one another, take notice of one another like loving sisters. But now Damroka says: 'It's time.'

When once again from the port side and starboard side, shielding their eyes against the midday light, the women look down into the watery depths, Vineta is still there, but now, it seems to them the streets of the submerged city are busy. They see darting shadows. Mere light effects? No, not phantasms or reflections. Neither sticklebacks nor schools of herring. It's rats running through the streets, rats that inhabit Vineta and have set up their state there. Busily pouring through the vaulted gates leading to the Rathaus market. Rushing from the women's house into the magistrates' court. Pouring into Vineta's many churches or loitering at the doors after services. Crowding around the Neptune Fountain, across bridges to Warehouse Island, onto the porches of the guild halls, up and down stairs, up and down towers big and small: everywhere rats.

Mating with the gable ornaments, with the goose, the tortoise, the turkeys. On the roof turrets of the cathedral, at the top of the Rathaus tower, high up, scarcely below the smooth skin of the

Baltic Sea, they are palpably close with whiskers aquiver, as though wishing to tell the seafaring women: We are already here. Vineta is taken. There's no room here for any human republic, for any republic of women; unless you choose to cast your lot with us and dwell among rats for ever more. Come to us, come! . . .

But no sooner have the women understood that there is no place for them on earth, unless they suppress revulsion and abstain from crying out what they are already screaming: 'Ugh!' and 'How disgusting!', unless they stride solemnly, dressed just as they are, into ratland, to live for ever more among rats – no sooner, I say, do the women realize that there is no other refuge for them on earth, but refrain from jumping – Come, jump! – refrain from jumping, than lightnings rend the sky far and near. Such light as has never been seen. They are blinded. A blast of consuming heat. They vanish. Where I point, where I look, there is nothing left.

To the southeast and west of their anchorage and beyond the northern horizon, the often described mushroom. Three peals of thunder nearby – addressed to Stralsund, Peenemünde and more distantly Stettin – and three blinding flashes of lightning are followed by shattering blast and intense heat. Along with the women, the ship's superstructure – the pilot house, the mast, the ventilators – have vanished. Only the white-hot hull remains. If the ship had not been built of iron when it was called the *Dora* and was designed to haul cargo up and down the Elbe, it too would be gone.

Bereft of both anchors, the wreck of *The New Ilsebill* – with its paint it has lost its name – is now drifting in an easterly direction.

> Doomadosh!
> So many bills unpaid
> so many dossiers pending.
> Marriages that should have been concluded, divorces
> too, and separations of property.
> Cheated out of residual vacation.
> Before egg-yellow pudding was set on the table
> after the roast, because it happened on Sunday.
> In mid-sentence oath curse prayer,
> right after the dash, colon,
> jokes beheaded of their punch lines.
> As I was about to say . . .
>
> So much spoiled fun.

The Rat

Wherever the body's desire, just before the NOW NOW,
vanished for ever.
The royal flush obliterated,
or a Sunday afternoon nap
which found as it were no end.
And the rest of what failed to materialize:
the often postponed class reunion,
the next session, birthdays,
the annual income tax adjustment, baby's first tooth,
tomorrow's weather,
return visits and return matches,
bequests, the anxiously awaited laboratory results.
Due dates, the mail.
Ah, and the long-awaited shopping spree.

We'd have liked to change the wallpaper pretty soon,
We'd have liked to go to the theatre more often
as we used to do, and enjoy a good Italian meal afterward.
Under certain conditions we'd have liked
to start all over
and indulge again in this and that.
We had promised the children a vacation on the pony farm
and promised to be more considerate of each other.
We were saving up for a second car, for Grimms' Dictionary
and a complete camping outfit.
We thought we'd finally take a break
and stop aiming higher and higher . . .
We'd have liked . . .

Naturally the many minor wars ceased, and so did hunger
and socialism along with capitalism
and evil along with good and hatred along with love.
And brand new ideas that have not been fully worked out.
And school reform nipped in the bud.
The question of God unresolved, and so on.
Some of us may have been pleased with ourselves,
but wishes big and little remained unfulfilled.
And the price of gold dropped and would never again . . .
Because
One Sunday.
Doomadosh.

Only a few minutes later, and five minutes after the cuckoo clock next to the Sacred Heart print had called cuckoo twelve times, several bombs fall almost simultaneously – because the end programs are closely synchronized – in the south and north, in the west and east and hence on Gdynia and Gdańsk, on the former a common atom bomb and on the latter four or five neutron conservation bombs, as provided in the worldwide cultural pact, which the Polish government ratified only recently.

It is true that both urban centres are far from Matarnia, a village on the fringe of which Ann Koljaiczek is celebrating her hundred and seventh birthday, sitting in her rocking chair and telling her rosary in the midst of her guests – but not far enough.

Up until then she and her guests have been watching a video selection from her grandson's Post Futurum series. Despite a few inaccuracies – the hasty departure of the government officials from Warsaw, four peonies too many on the armchair – the film has been a success, applauded by all the guests, especially after the prelate from Oliva found divine providence and God's omnipotence confirmed by the new medium.

But while they are still celebrating and seeing themselves on the screen as birthday guests, lightnings rend the sky in Kashubia as everywhere else in the world, whereupon the guests rush out of the house and all, some quickly and mercifully, others painfully, die, perish, shrink with dehydration, because the Matarnia, Firoga, Zukow, Kartuzy area, where Bysewo used to be and where concrete runways have been situated for years – has been hit by two destructive systems, on the one hand by heat, blast and radioactive fallout, on the other by accelerated neutron and gamma rays.

The barn, including kitchen and bedroom, is blown off the house. The panes of the remaining windows are pulverised. The roof is carried away. The old chestnut tree, all the apple trees burst into flames, just as the woods north of Matarnia, which are all part of the great forest extending over hills to the sea, burn as if they had grown for that very purpose.

Some cars parked outside the garden gate are set on fire by the heat and transformed into scrap by the blast, while others, including the prelate's heavy limousine and our Herr Matzerath's Mercedes, burn slowly and quietly.

At first it looks as though only Anna Koljaiczek, in her erstwhile flower-bedecked armchair, had survived the end, blinded to be sure, but otherwise unharmed; then her grandson Oskar, lying under the rubble, is seen to move. When all the guests ran into the open and even Bruno the chauffeur followed the crowd, he stayed behind. Protected by the four walls of the parlour and spared by my will, which I impose against the She-rat and her *diktat*, they both survive.

And the screen remains animated. On it, though Anna Kol-jaiczek no longer sees them, birthday guests are still gathered, for the video film produced by our Herr Matzerath, who knew it all in advance, except that it would end in this way, wants to go on being entertaining. Once again we see Lady Bruns between Stephan Bronski's sons, once again the unctuous prelate. At last the cassette with the polka runs out and we see, after a close-up of the still chipper birthday child, the subtitle: 'End of the hundred and seventh birthday party of the venerable Anna Koljaiczek, née Bronski'. Then only the flickering screen. When the batteries give up, it too will go dead.

Missing the guests and relatives, Oskar's grandmother in her armchair cries out several times: 'Where have yuh gotten to?' She doesn't understand.

Near her on the table the porcelain horse lies in shards. And what's left of the *baumkuchen* is a mess. A roof beam has fallen on the electric barbecue. The cuckoo clock has fallen off the wall, the bronze head is buried, the naked ebony shattered, but intact the forged-iron Solidarność standard and the paper knife, amber handle and all. And everywhere, on the table and strewn around the armchair, lie gold ducats and cute little smurfs, among them the one with the drum. 'Oskarkins!' cries Anna Koljaiczek, 'I can't see, can't you tell me where you are?'

He, too, may be blind. Only smells can guide him. He has lost his voice, but he can crawl. Painfully, on all fours, he crawls out from under the kitchen rubble, through the parlour in the direction of the armchair and his grandmother's cries of 'Oskarkins!' Surprisingly, he still has gold-rimmed glasses on. His tie pin is missing. I have the impression that our Oskar, while the curtain was falling on the whole world and also on Kashubia, has got smaller; he seems to be visibly shrinking. Crawling over roof beams, he has reached the cute little smurfs; now he's at his grandmother's feet. Our abbreviated Herr Matzerath seeks refuge under her skirts as singlemindedly as if he had been looking all his life for this place.

He's gone and I'm rid of him. Never again will he. No more objections from him. Under the skirts he will go on shrinking awhile, and when, as our doctors say, death ensues, he will be completely dehydrated. Is Anna Koljaiczek, who has stopped calling out 'Oskarkins' but is mumbling her rosary, aware of Oskar's presence under her skirts?

> This end, we've seen it before.
> Moving images, showing how we evaporated,
> how shrinking we attained the ultimate ecstasy.
>
> That can be no surprise to us who anticipate
> dust storms and permafrost. Well informed,
> we shall cease to be well informed.
>
> We smile when we hear of groups in Canada,
> New Zealand and the mountains of Switzerland,
> who go in for survival training.
>
> Hard on themselves and others.
> Intent on continuity.
> Jump-up Johnnies, and Mabels, too, of course.
>
> It should, as agreed, start in Europe,
> which makes sense; most things began here
> and spread to the rest of the world.
>
> Thus all progress originates with us.
> Slightly weary of our historical burden, we date
> the end of all history.

Our Herr Matzerath said that, said it emphatically before starting on his trip to Poland; or was it the She-rat, whose sermon from the pulpit was addressed to the assembled rat nations?

The She-rat said: Find your way back to the one faith; or else it was he, commenting on an educational video film, who invoked reason by indicating the time – five minutes to twelve; whereas the She-rat spoke retrospectively. The world was out of joint, but the High Muckamucks of the human race put everything off from working lunch to working lunch; for which reason our Herr Matzerath, commenting on the film, spoke premonitory words: The world is out of joint, but everywhere the audible cracking is diagnosed as material fatigue, that we must learn to live with.

The Rat

The She-rat notes with regret that men saw their end coming but said: It's probably inevitable. But it made him angry too, as if he'd had a supply of hope. Can't you see, you fools, that it's in your power, now, on the brink of the abyss . . .

Ah, cried the She-rat, how devoted we were to you! Didn't we give you enough warning signs?

Didn't you, Oskar harangued the human race once more, didn't you see the rats running, warning you in broad daylight?

Other animals, too, cried the She-rat from the pulpit of Saint Mary's, showed fear. But man refused to be frightened.

According to the latest reports, said Oskar, the loquacious fish isn't talking, but swarms of jellyfish are beginning to sing over the waters.

But they saw and did not hear, lamented the She-rat to the rats at prayer; you see and you hear, cried Oskar, but you refuse to see the light.

If hens had laid cubical eggs as a warning, she scoffed, humans would have called the cubical eggs progress; and, he thundered as though eternity had supplied him with words: Must rivers flow uphill and mountains stand on their heads before you see reason?

Time and again the She-rat, speaking from the pulpit of Saint Mary's, reminded her congregation of man's madness. Meshuggalesh ballesseks! she cried. And indefatigably our Herr Matzerath, from end to end of his didactic video film, threatened the human race with destruction, for which reason he decided to put this cassette into production on his return from Poland. The She-rat, however, followed up her sermon with an admonition to all the assembled rat nations, not to let religious controversy divide them as the extinct human race had done, but to be reunited in the one faith and to pray all together for the last remaining humans.

She was referring to Anna Koljaiczek in her armchair and to me orbiting in my space capsule, for still down from the pulpit, but now in an affable rather than a preaching tone, she addressed herself to me; denying Oskar an opportunity to take the floor again, she supplied me with details of post-human history.

Now and then, she said, thunderous words still work wonders. Rejoice, young friend. We shall quarrel no longer. The religious controversy is dying down. The faithful are yielding, protesting that schisms are not deliberate, listening to reason. Offers are made, some worth considering. In other words, we Catholics have again

imposed ourselves. We have been helped by that minority which –
you remember? – broke away from the Orthodox creed, viewing
themselves as Early Christian Communists, whereupon they were
persecuted by other groups. It was probably the Protestant zealots,
if not the Orthodox themselves, who went to the worst extremes.
There was talk of torture. The heretics were said to have been
tormented in almost human ways. And then came the great act of
public deterrence. A persistent rumour has it that we Catholics
were the instigators. That is far from all higher truth, though it
cannot be denied that the event with its pictorial possibilities was
just what we needed.

That was how I heard about the crucifixion on Bishop's
Mountain.

She said: From that hill, you know, there's a fine view of the city.

I remembered panels of the Dutch medieval school, in which
Christ and the two thieves were undoubtedly crucified on Bishop's
Mountain, so much so that the towers of Danzig could be
recognized in the background. And behind them, alive with ships,
the Baltic sea.

A hundred and thirty un-Christian rats, said the She-rat, were
crucified on Bishop's Mountain.

I don't believe it, I don't believe it! I cried.

They lined up the crosses in three staggered rows.

But how did they crucify and what with?

With nails, of course, stupid.

Lies! Rat talk!

To convince me, the She-rat showed me the scene on Bishop's
Mountain that had brought about the unification, reconciliation, as
she called it, of the contentious rat nations. With the help of one of
those flashbacks that she can summon up at any time, I saw, neatly
gnawed, more than a hundred crosses with Early Christians
hanging on them. And just as Mary and John stood to the left and
right of the Crucified Christ over the main altar of Saint Mary's, so
two erect mourning rats flanked each of the hundred and thirty
crucified rats on Bishop's Mountain.

The crosses, the She-rat explained, were made of driftwood from
the river floods. And nails, from brads to steel spikes, can be found
everywhere.

The crosses were lined up so graphically on a knoll that the
background, the soot-blackened towers and turrets of the neutron-

ized city, seemed to follow of their own accord and behind them the sea, from which, however, all ships were absent as far as the horizon.

An effective example. We have been united ever since and have begun at last to strip the walls of those protective coatings with which the human race, shortly before the Big Bang, had covered all buildings earmarked for conservation.

As though to take my mind off the crucified rats, she faded in scenes of city life and in her commentary laid stress on the new hustle and bustle. And incidentally, the Protestant clans seem to have taken especial pleasure in removing the protective covering. Perhaps it's the need to do penance that makes them work so hard. Or perhaps it's only their German origin. See how methodically they uncover the masonry. They work in shifts. In addition, they've found a way to make use of those disgusting soot-black worms that we – remember? – call inedible. In any case, the steeple of Saint Mary's is again brick-red up to middle height. As is the magnificent decorative gable of Holy Trinity. Just see how well the masonry has been preserved under the covering.

I saw all right. Innumerable rats were peeling walls, with the help of finger-long soot-worms, removing the soot that had come with the dust storms. I even saw Protestant rats doing penance on secular buildings; they cleaned the Green Gate on the Mottlau and Long Market side, the façade of the Artushof and the Rathaus, going so far as to scale the tapering tower of the latter edifice, surmounted by a gold-plate King of Poland.

He's shining again, cried the She-rat. Isn't he beautiful? Isn't life worth living again? Thus, we say to ourselves, the sacrifice on Bishop's Mountain was not in vain. Once again we rats are united in faith. All of us together, we worship the last breathing human in her armchair, seeking strength in prayer as we do; incessantly the ancient one says her rosary. We hear her whispering: Blessed one, lady of sorrows.

What about me? I cried. Whom shall I implore? How am I to persevere in my space capsule when there's only a drifting wreck and my Damroka is gone . . .

You who have suffered for us . . . Unmoved, the She-rat repeated Anna Koljaiczek's prayers, until praying she faded from my sight.

Chapter Nine,

in which the women come to life again, the country is without a government, hunger gnaws, two mummies with accessories are delivered, whereupon agriculture begins, rat, bird and sunflower yield a picture, humans exist only as hypotheses, vegetation burgeons, twines, proliferates on all sides, Oskar butts in again, and after the first sound shift the harvest thanksgiving festival is celebrated.

ACTUALLY I should talk about painter Malskat, stop getting ahead of myself, follow his industry – then he painted the fourth and then the fifth vault – but whenever I start climbing high into the choir of Lübeck's Church of Saint Mary – it's cold, damp and draughty up here – the present calls me away from the scaffolding. Who cares about the phony fifties when at this very moment the forests are dying and with them the fairy tales; what interest can post-war years have for us in pre-war times, when my dreams by day and by night revolve around the Orwell Year? Furthermore, Anna Koljaiczek wants to die and can't. The wreck of *The New Ilsebill* is drifting out to sea. All these stories demand an end, whereas Malskat's story keeps wanting to begin all over again, as though it might be amusing to disinter old Adenauer and goatee Ulbricht and put them on pedestals, simply because to the painter's sacral forgeries the two founding fathers had added their own double forgery, which, as our Herr Matzerath said before going to Poland, it had been perfectly possible to live with up until now.

But what do I mean by now? The She-rat says: Now at last all dissension is behind us. With one voice the rat nations in the spacious Church of Saint Mary worship the last satellite, which is now orbiting the earth . . .

The Rat

In which I sit strapped. I in my space capsule. With panoramic view. Clear vision at last, now that the soot-black smoke has settled. Strangely distinct is the old earth's curvature, suggesting the coast lines of Vasco da Gama's days, when maps were still approximate.

The She-rat confirms my questions. Melting ice and tidal waves have corroded the shore lines. Not only have the Arabian Sea and the Mediterranean encroached on the land; my Baltic Sea has also expanded. Islands and islets washed away, every estuary widened. Seen from above, Danzig or Gdańsk looks to me like a city that has barred itself off with a wall of mud against the flooded Island. They say the Baltic is free from jellyfish now, says the She-rat, who complements my remarks whenever I start shooting off my mouth too panoramically in my space capsule.

When I ask her how those rats who have immigrated from Russia and were banished from the city proper have managed to settle in the once fertile lowlands of the Vistula estuary, which are all under water, she says: There are fragments of dikes, railway embankments, muddy knolls. We rats can get a foothold anywhere. Besides, the waters are receding. Like in Noah's times, when the Flood was abating.

Resisting my attempts to demonstrate human existence with quotations from the Third Programme or with actual facts, the exchange rate of the dollar, Olympic records, and so on, the She-rat jabbers away about post-human trivia. She speaks of successful litters which in turn produce flawless litters. Now and then I hear Anna Koljaiczek mumble: If only the end would come soon.

Only a short while ago my space capsule was over other continents, some elongated, others foreshortened; the Bay of Bengal and Calcutta, once so harrowingly crowded, were hardly more than a black spot when they entered my field of vision. But now, after a brief dream spell, I again see the Baltic Sea below me and the wreck drifting aimlessly in an easterly direction. I talk the human present into existence. How fortunate that the hedge of thorns is still growing in the dead forest and that the old Sleeping Beauty trick is still working. I escape into the fifties and watch Malskat's brush, which is now putting contours on the thirteenth saint out of twenty-one. To puncture the She-rat's post-human self-assurance, I say: Soon Chancellor Adenauer will be coming to Lübeck for the seventh centenary to see the miracle. Well, he's in for a surprise.

Günter Grass

Annoyed, and no longer in a conversational tone, the She-rat of my dreams says: Your five broads on the ship have just gone up in smoke . . . A lie! I cried out. I know better. Anna Koljaiczek isn't the only one who knows no end; there won't be any dying on the wrecked ship either. That's the way I want it. It's I, after all, who out of fear and helplessness manned the former freight barge with women. I loved them all. I was attached to them all by long threads and short ones. But over the years I lost them, and that's why I tracked them down and gathered them in a small space. I wanted them to get along with one another, to become sisters if all went well. So I thought up the ship and gave the women their sea-legs. That was easy enough, because they were all of a practical bent, capable of handling wrenches and spark plugs, yet conscious of a goal, which they long sought in the clouds and finally found under water. They were already within sight of it, they dressed up in preparation for their arrival; that, She-rat, was when you cried out end, finish, conclusion, your ratty Doomadosh. Now injured beyond help, they're crawling around on the deck, leaning over the side and trying to see the submerged city in the coastal water. And one of the five women, who no longer has lovely curls but is bald like the others, cries out, as though her mouth, now a bleeding hole, were still capable of crying out: There lies our Vineta! Below us. Never has the water been so clear. No seaweed, no algae to cloud the view. The streets and squares are still deserted, but the ladies of Vineta will soon enter the city in resplendent robes and greet us and beckon us to join them. They will bring us to their republic, which knows no violence, no coercion, but only gentleness and friendly games. And they will heal us, until we are smooth and curly-haired again. Look, sisters, there's movement in all the streets. A merry coming and going. We're there, there at last . . .

A painful daydream. Images crowded one another impatiently. I wanted to dream something pleasant, a harmonious round dance – a merry coming and going – but in Vineta there was nothing but rats scurrying through the streets, in and out of all the churches, banding together, rushing in opposite directions, across the bridges . . .

One of the women cried out from her bleeding mouthhole: they're bewitched, enchanted. An evil spell is upon them, we must set them free.

This is the Flounder's doing, cried another bleeding mouth. The Flounder must come and help to set the women free.

Flounder, they cried, hear us. Until ready to drop with exhaustion, they called upon the powerful flatfish to keep his promise, to rid Vineta of rats and make it a women's city again.

But no Flounder helped, spoke, set free. Not only devoid of jellyfish, but utterly lifeless except for the vermin running through the streets, the sea lay empty under an empty sky, over which from east to west moved churning clouds of smoke.

Is it true, I asked Anna Koljaiczek, groaning under the burden of life, that only rats are left, everywhere, even in Vineta, whose gates should be open to the women, as the Flounder promised below the chalk cliffs of Møn, and then time and time again, whenever he was called?

Then said Anna Koljaiczek, who actually wanted to keep silent and to die: There ain't no Flounder. And no fairy tales no more. And with people too, it's all over. They always grabbed and slashed. And always there was wickedness. And now there's nothing, everything's shot, because Our Father in Heaven has punished them. Oh, if only the suffering would end!

But even if I were to write: she is dead, dead, she couldn't die, any more than I could stop circling the earth time after time.

Jesus Mary and Joseph, cried Anna Koljaiczek. It's all over everywhere.

Answer! cried the man in the cosmic armchair. Have you, dammit, all gone down the drain? You can't all be dead and gone.

There aren't even any bleeding mouth-holes now. The women were at their last gasp. My will was powerless to keep them going. I couldn't think of any way to postpone their end. Only now – or once again – did the wreck of the *Ilsebill* drift out to the open sea.

Still softly Anna Koljaiczek: Dear Father in Heaven, if only it could be over soon . . .

And I heard myself lamenting. What have we done? What drove us to this end? No women, no Flounder, no fairy tales left, because the forests which cried out for help to the last, were reduced to smoke . . .

As though to comfort me, the She-rat said: But there's us. And the smoke settled long ago. The storms have disturbed all the ashes fairly, and now all life gets the benefit of the radiation. For a long time the earth had to turn without being warmed by the light. After the cold and darkness there were not very many even of us. But soon our numbers increased and everywhere life began to stir; in ponds and rivers, in offshore shallows. The old species in new forms, and species which had never been seen and came as a surprise even to us. Cheer up, my friend. Life will reach out again. The old earth will be renewed. And new fairy tales, in which the old ones survive miraculously, will be handed down from litter to litter.

Because it worked, because the spindle pricked Sleeping Beauty till blood came and released magic all about, whereupon the Chancellor and his ministers and all the experts and politicians, even the television crews and the clever newspapermen with their last scribbled words have fallen into a deep Sleeping Beauty sleep, no sooner is the hedge of thorns ready and dense than all the fairy-tale characters run away; they run from the scene of action in the dead forest, and from the stone monument to the healthy forest, until they come to their Gingerbread Boarding House, where Little Red Riding Hood's grandmother has been staying alone with the wolf.

Hansel and Gretel hold the Grimm Brothers by the hands. Rumpelstiltskin hops ahead on his one leg. In the old Ford ride the wicked stepmother holding the magic mirror and in the back seat Snow White with the sex-crazed dwarfs; the girl's chopped-off hands hold the steering wheel.

With her hair Rapunzel enfolds the weeping prince, who keeps turning round and making a rosebud mouth, as though he had only that one thing in mind, as though he could do only that and nothing else, as though that duty had been imposed on him, that obsession ingrained in him, as though, whenever Sleeping Beauty fell asleep he was constrained for all time to wake her with a kiss. He hesitates, stops, disentangles himself from Rapunzel's hair, determined to go to the hedge of thorns, part it with his frail sword, climb the ruined tower, and bend over the sleeper. But the witch has been waiting for him in the hollow tree. She grabs him by the neck and kisses him till his shoelaces come undone. Screaming, he runs after the others with the witch at his heels. Rübezahl follows hindmost, driving the melancholy pair before him, for time and again Jorinde and Joringel go stony with sadness and threaten to grow moss.

Refreshments are being served in the Gingerbread House. Rumpelstiltskin, now officiating as waiter, serves blue, red and green dishes. The Grimm Brothers are having woodruff flip. After downing his drink, the frog king makes the headache lady lie down beside the well, then jumps into it; a moment later, transformed

into a frog, he jumps out again and sits down on the lady's forehead.
Thereupon Gretel, as though her forehead were also in need of
cooling, lies down beside the lady. The frog, who only a moment
ago was breathing evenly, gets restless. He jumps from the lady's
forehead to the child's and back again, then repeatedly back and
forth. The witch looks on with eyes of flame. When the witch tries
lying on the other side of the lady, the frog starts jumping on the
witch's forehead as well. No rest between leap and leap. All three
foreheads are in need of cooling.

The boarders watch his breathless exertions with amusement.
The seven dwarfs punctuate the frog's jumps with obscene
gestures. Hansel is annoyed with Gretel. 'She hasn't got all her
marbles.' The Grimm Brothers are somewhat bewildered by these
jumpy variations. Wilhelm says to Jakob: 'You see, brother, our
fairy tales have a life of their own.'

Taking advantage of the witch's absence, the wicked stepmother
starts showing the Grimm Brothers through the museum. 'All in
perfect condition,' she says. 'The little bones, the poison apple, the
comb, the belt. Only the spindle is gone. I'm sure the gentlemen
can imagine where.'

Now all the female characters are making up to the Grimm
Brothers, especially Little Red Riding Hood and Little Red Riding
Hood's grandmother, who want to exhibit their fairy tale. The
magic mirror has barely started running the old black-and-white
film when they are both driven away by Rapunzel, who wants to
cheer up the melancholy prince with her Rapunzel film. After a
short squabble between Rapunzel and Little Red Riding Hood, the
wicked stepmother intervenes: 'We should really offer the prince a
bit of entertainment. Poor man. See how unhappy he is.'

Whereupon they all, along with the Grimm Brothers, who are at
once moved and puzzled, sit down to watch the flickering old film.

It is so sad that even the girl without hands can't help crying. She
bites the nails of her left chopped-off hand, which her right
chopped-off hand is holding. Rumpelstiltskin blows his nose.
Jorinde and Joringel are in tears.

Rather stupidly, Sleeping Beauty's prince watches the prince in
the film and laughs inappropriately at the prince's cry of 'Rapunzel,
Rapunzel, let down your hair,' which serves as a subtitle in the
magic mirror film.

Little Red Riding Hood runs out of the house in a temper,

followed by her grandmother, who barely has time to see where Little Red Riding Hood has taken refuge. The old women sits down beside the replete wolf, whose zipper is stretched tight, and from the Grimms' dictionary reads him words beginning with a: apologize, apology . . .

The prince is still hopping from forehead to forehead, though he is beginning to tire.

To one side of the house, Rübezahl is furiously piling wood.

In front of the house the seven dwarfs are playing cards.

No one is interested in seeing the happy ending of the Rapunzel film; only Rapunzel herself with her long hair sits lost to the world, looking on at her happiness.

The kissing prince runs frantically through the house; he just wants to kiss and kiss and kiss. When he gives the girl without hands a kiss, the chopped-off hands box both his ears.

The alarmed Grimm Brothers, supported by Hansel, plead with the wicked stepmother.

Jakob Grimm says: 'We can't let things go on like this. Think of it, the republic is without a government.'

Wilhelm Grimm says gravely: 'It could end in chaos.'

Hansel cries out: 'Exactly! I'll bet they're going nuts in Bonn. State of emergency, and so on!'

And Snow White's wicked stepmother says: 'We'd better take a quick look.'

Vigorously pressing a button, she shuts off the Rapunzel film shortly before the end and shouts: 'Listen. Everybody listen. We're switching to Bonn.'

Whereupon the grandmother opens the zipper, Little Red Riding Hood jumps out of the wolf's belly, Rübezahl stops piling wood and the dwarfs drop their cards. With his last strength the frog jumps off Gretel's forehead and into the well; a moment later, now king, he helps his lady, then the witch and finally Gretel, to their feet. He seems rather wobbly, over-exerted. The lady smiles indulgently. Gretel's smile is no longer childlike. The rest cure has done the witch good.

Again she is every inch the landlady, she wants to be boss. 'I will not have this interference,' she cries. 'In my house I decide when it's time to listen.'

After a short exchange of glances with the witch, the wicked stepmother cries out: 'When you people aren't doing nothing,

The Rat

you're playing cards or dallying with your boyfriend, while all over
Germany, in town and country, things are going haywire. There's
no government in Bonn. We, the fairy tales, have seized power.'

Since all look incredulous, unable to take credit for a real seizure
of power, they hear the wicked stepmother say: 'Mirror, mirror on
the wall, is Germany heading for a brawl?'

After a brief jumble of images, the magic mirror shows in rapidly
changing fade-ins excited crowds, demonstrations, looting,
soldiers and policemen in action, hooded figures, violent resistance.
Headlines are flashed on the screen; 'First the children disappear,
then the Chancellor.' Newsboys are seen hawking papers. –
'Chancellor and Cabinet lost in Forest.' – 'Federal Republic without
a Leader.' Water cannon. Free-wheeling truncheons. Panic shopping. Black flags. Symptoms of menacing civil war.

In the Gingerbread House the fairy-tale characters gathered
around the magic mirror have fallen silent. They are half proud,
half flabbergasted. Even the wicked stepmother can't believe her
mirror.

The Grimm Brothers are horrified to see what power fairy tales
still exert. Wilhelm whispers in Jakob's ear: 'This is our doing,
brother. As collectors and editors, we are the true instigators.'

Jakob replies in a whisper: 'Our simple household tales have been
taken too literally.'

At that Hansel and Gretel cry out: 'Our time has come. Show
what you can do. Cast your magic spells, bind or set free. Go on,
witch. Do your stuff.'

For the first time she laughs her blood-curdling witch's laugh:
'We will carry the forest into their cities.'

'That's the stuff,' cries Rumpelstiltskin. 'Everywhere it will
sprout, grow, take root, twine, burgeon, burst into bloom.'

The Grimm Brothers try to temper the enthusiasm of their
followers. 'Come, come. Let's not exaggerate. The written word
shouldn't be taken too seriously.'

The dwarfs, all seven of them, stand up to the Grimm Brothers:
stamping their little boots, they chant: 'No punches pulled!' and
'All power to the Fairy Tales!'

Meanwhile the witch has opened chests and cupboards, barrels,
caskets and flour canisters. Outside the Gingerbread House she can
be seen summoning, but without explanatory subtitle, because
those she summons appear from the forest, from the air: good and

bad fairies, crows and ravens, elves, goblins and other tinies, celebrated magicians and wild men, wood pigeons and rats. In the end, with imploring gestures, she calls her sisters, witches adept at flying on brooms and vacuum cleaners, all feminists to the fingertips.

Grandiose gestures, prolonged and cordial greetings. Merlin the magician stands out in this throng, most of whom, despite their fairy-tale character, are neatly, primly, well dressed. King Thrushbeard has a jovial greeting for the frog king, then for the Grimm Brothers, who feel rather lost in the crush and don't know what to do next.

With the help of name cards such as those used at congresses, we recognize Mother Holle and the brave little tailor, Cinderella and Siebenschön, Hans in Luck, and, because the camera singles him out, Tom Thumb, who has brought along a giant, in whose ear he is sitting.

Of course the seven kids are present along with the mother goat. But the assemblage is not restricted to those whom the Grimm Brothers, Ludwig Bechstein and Johann Karl Musäus have collected and fitted out with accessories. At the behest of our Herr Matzerath, who, were he not detained in Poland, would gladly have been there in the role of the Humpback Little Man, Hans Christian Andersen's pretty inventions – the steadfast tin soldier and the flying trunk, though empty – are also present. For the sake of the dying Black Forest, the little man of Schatzhaus out of Wilhelm Hauff's tale *The Cold Heart* might also be included.

Among all those summoned the witch now distributes bags, bottles and tins full of magic grains and magic juices. Stimulating ointments and miraculous elixirs are on hand. She fills the flying trunk to the brim. The good and bad fairies exchange tricks and secrets. The great Merlin generously outfits several esteemed though unfortunately impecunious fairy-tale characters with magic wands. Cinderella fills the crops of the wood pigeons with grains which are supposed to exert some sort of amazing action. The lower witches scatter magic food and the rats gobble it up so as to make it take effect somewhere else. Busily the girl's hands distribute bottles and bags to those who haven't got enough. Hansel and Gretel help with excessive zeal; they even slip an assortment to the pompous King Thrushbeard; and Tom Thumb in the giant's ear is given a sprinkler can so that he too can help.

The Rat

When all the boxes, chests, caskets, canisters and cupboards are empty, the Grimm Brothers' protestation – 'You mustn't do that! That kind of fairy tale will end badly!' – goes unheard, for the witch now sends all the assembled animals and goblins, Mother Holle with her feather bed, the magicians and fairies, tinies and wild men, away in all directions.

While dismissing them, she makes witch's signs, spits out witch's spells. The brave little tailor has provided himself with miraculous needles and magic thread. Replete with food and heavily laden, the seven kids and the seven dwarfs disperse. Some go on foot, some through the air. Merlin the magician dissolves into nothingness.

Jakob Grimm is alarmed, no, almost aghast: 'What are you people up to? This is insurrection, anarchy!'

Wilhelm says: 'Haven't we always known, brother, what power fairy tales have over people?'

Anxiously, the two of them follow with their eyes the characters, whom long ago – in Napoleon's time it was – they diligently collected and thought they had stowed safely away in their book of Nursery and Household Tales.

No, the kissing prince can't get away. The witch has a tight hold on him. The wicked stepmother stays behind too, but Snow White is allowed to put rouge on her cheeks and follow her dwarfs. Jorinde and Joringel disappear with Rübezahl and the ringleader. Rapunzel has to stay behind because of the prince. But the girl's chopped-off hands fly away, the right one holding a bag, the left one a bottle. The girl waves her arm stumps at her chopped-off hands. Little Red Riding Hood starts off with her basket over her arm. And Little Red Riding Hood's grandmother reads the Grimms' dictionary to the wolf, who has to stay behind . . .

> Witch, bewitch, bewitched.
> Neither three ground-up hairs
> nor henbane enters in.
> Neither sprouting grain nor excess droplets,
> neither the binding nor the liberating word
> is needed.
>
> We know and have learned
> to cross the pumpkin with the onion, the mouse
> with the cat.

Two genes here, four genes there: we manipulate.
What does nature amount to! Master of all skills,
we improve on God.

In old dictionaries, we find only
the lower sorts of chimera.
Soon the higher man will be produced;
our programme provides for him.
Stored in gene banks, he is daily enriched:
endowed with reason and then some.

More readily than any other
animal – even the pig –
the rat imparts itself to man,
to help him transcend himself.

Then came hunger. What was left after the Big Bang – their garbage, their accumulated tin cans, their shrunken leathery corpses – fed us for a time, until the first successful litters were born outside of escape passages and nesting chambers. Again we formed nations in marked-out territories; but there wasn't much to eat. It may have been penury that made us religious or, as you, our sardonic friend put it, Catholic.

As though wishing to embody hunger, the She-rat appeared shaggy, emaciated and unkempt in my dream, a picture of misery. I saw her eating tin, scrap iron, stones. There's nothing else, she said. Because of their teeth that keep on growing, they had to bite into something, if only a screwdriver or a remnant of barbed wire and, as you can see, chew it up. Here and there, a shrunken cadaver could be found, but that was hardly gourmet fare.

Then in my dream she was fat again, with sleek fur. Well fed, she told me about times of famine, but failed to mention the cause of recent prosperity. In those days, said the She-rat, when hunger taught us to pray, but piety brought us only bitter strife, one of our districts was rustic and desolate, yet unique, for in a cottage, whose walls were still relatively stable, there lived, breathing faintly and mumbling perpetually, that ancient crone, full of human years, who, thanks to tales that have echoed through the ages, is no stranger to you.

Be that as it may, we too revered her. How patiently she put up with our curiosity. Whatever she might mumble, however close we came to her, never an unkind word with regard to us. Once we heard: Mary and Joseph! If only the rats would help me . . .

But we couldn't do it, for apart from your remote existence, preserved in a space capsule, this ancient woman was the only human being we had left. We were determined to preserve her with tender loving care. After the era of cold darkness, when she stopped mumbling and scarcely breathed, we visited her cottage in groups. Not only the country folk, but the city nations as well sent delegations. When she sank more and more and though still breathing seemed dehydrated, we fed her liquids and pre-chewed food, which we could afford despite the shortages. There were always young rats at her service. We not only worshipped her, we coddled her.

I saw the days of post-human starvation that the She-rat was telling me about. I saw Anna Koljaiczek shrunk to diminutive proportions and floating in her spacious Sunday dress, I saw her surrounded by praying old rats, overrun by skinny young ones. I saw them feed her, saw her sunken, toothless mouth open as the young duty rats squirted liquid and pushed pre-chewed pap into it. Disgusting, I cried.

We've heard that before, said the She-rat.

But she wants to die.

She still enjoys it. Hear her smacking her lips.

But *what* is she enjoying? What?

We've had to sacrifice a few young rats, from healthy litters, it goes without saying . . .

Why don't you let her die, dammit? I cried, and heard my cry die away.

The She-rat's answer came slowly, as though to indicate the passage of time: Still alive, she was sacred to us. We worshipped everything in her cottage as we worshipped her, all the objects at her feet. Even more than the gold coins that seemed to have been scattered heedlessly around her chair, on one side a number, on the other an eagle or an erstwhile crowned head, we worshipped the little figures that were lying all about, over and under the wreckage. Figuring the manifold activities of mankind, they reminded us of the human race. When we cleaned them, they turned out to be blue and white. Freed from soot, their tools and other gear became red, green, brown, silver and yellow. What cute expressions they had. How adorably they displayed their industry. We'd have liked to play with them if every single figure hadn't been as holy as the ancient one.

That too provided a picture: rats in the midst of gold ducats and smurfs. Still other objects were lying around: a shattered porcelain horse, a wrought-iron inscription, the paper knife with the amber handle, the cuckoo clock that recorded the crack of doom at five minutes past twelve, this and that, the mangled electric barbecue, and Anna Koljaiczek's false teeth, which must have fallen out after the Big Bang; as for the rosary, she was still holding it.

Yes, said the She-rat, she gave us something to live for. She gave us unity, for the struggle for the true faith went on throughout the era of want. You remember, no doubt: we aped the human race, we persecuted, tortured, crucified our fellows, so much so that we rats might have been taken for heretic zealots and for zealotic persecutors of heresy. In the end, a not inconsiderable minority became such fanatical heretics that we had reason to fear for the ancient one's safety. If one were to search the religious conflicts of mankind for comparisons and human history for equally cruel aberrations, we should be driven to say that seven rat nations of Waldensians, Hussites, Anabaptists and Trotskyists attempted on several occasions to overrun the precinct we had marked off as sacred, and, as they put it, wipe idolatry off the face of the earth. Battles were fought, which sapped our strength. And hunger too may have maddened us . . .

Then I saw embattled, infuriated rats. Wars were fought over Anna Koljaiczek's ramshackle cottage, its garden and potato patch lay desolate, suitable for no other crop than hatred and war among rat nations, the war, let us say, between the Catholics and the Hussites.

In the midst of the nondescript rubbish outside the ruined house I managed to recognize the wreckage of our Herr Matzerath's Mercedes. The star on the mangled hood was absurdly unharmed. It was being fought over with exceptional bitterness. How those rats slashed and tore at one another. How their teeth, capable of chewing up sheet metal, closed on enemy throats, jaw locked with jaw, as rats bit one another to quivering death. Entangled in their own and the enemy's viscera, they were quite capable of blindly biting into their own hearts.

Then I saw rats fighting in Anna Koljaiczek's former parlour, evidently disputing the smurfs, for they too were bitten. When the battle moved to her manifo¹d Sunday dress, to her hands telling the rosary in her lap, and finally to her ruff; when one, then a second rat of the so-called Hussite party bit into Anna Koljaiczek's sweet shrivelled face, I screamed and banished the picture, but not my dream, which the She-rat reoccupied as if there had been no atrocities.

Eventually the war stopped, but not the famine. The majority won out. Again we were united in faith; reconciled at last, we worshipped her all of us together.

What? I cried. Was she still alive?

Patiently, said the She-rat, we healed a few wounds that had been inflicted on her in the heat of the battle. But from then on her left ear was missing . . .

And what else? I cried.

What is there to get so excited about? she asked reproachfully. A little humility, if you please. Soon the ancient one was dead. When we found her unbreathing after one of the last sand storms, we didn't relegate her corpse to the food supply, though there were still incorrigible splinter groups whose hatred and ravening hunger we were obliged to combat.

After a pause, her way no doubt of skipping over the last cataclysmic battles, the She-rat said: Anyway, she was parched, shrunk, diminutive, so light that removal seemed possible. Her poor cottage, we felt, was no longer the place for her. By majority vote, we chose an appropriate location. All the rat nations were agreed. We slid the ancient one off her chair, careful that nothing should bend, tear, break. And from under her multiple skirts, as we carried her, there appeared a desiccated child, which must have come into the world at the time of the Big Bang; oddly enough, his clothing and adornments were attractive but much too big, white-and-yellow shoes, any number of rings on his fingers, gold-rimmed glasses. The trousers and jacket suggested that the ancient one had given birth to a litte boy at the very last moment. We decided to transport the little fellow as well, and we had difficulty in fastening his rings and the frames of his glasses. Thus we rats took turns in carrying not only the light-weight saint, but her little boy, too, by many stages through the desolate countryside. It took time.

You seem incredulous, so I'll show you a picture. See how slowly and carefully they moved her.

And I saw relays of rats carrying the remains of Anna Koljaiczek and of our Oskar, reduced to the dimensions of a tiny child, through the hilly but totally vegetationless Kashubia. A long procession, for blue-and-white smurfs and even the shards of the Chinese porcelain horse were carried in the train of the two mummies. Actually the grandmother's grandson led the procession. The rats that followed at a distance were heavily laden, for they carried the cuckoo clock with its dial perpetually proclaiming the onset of doom and, most cumbersome of all, the wrought-iron standard. Other rats carried small articles in their mouths: a ruby ring that had fallen from Oskar's fleshless finger; the decoration which the Polish government had conferred on Anna Koljaiczek and which had dropped from her dress. Two rats carried the silver paper knife with the amber handle, her false teeth, her glasses; they even saw fit to transport that bone of contention, the Mercedes star. The rear was brought up by a long column of rats, each carrying a gold piece between its teeth.

There may have been some odds and ends left in Anna's cottage: the mangled Australian barbecue, the television set and the bronze head alleged to be a likeness of the American Joe Colchic, formerly Josef Koljaiczek. All in all, a difficult undertaking, an achievement in that era of post-human famine. Indeed, quite a few rats perished by the wayside and, as need dictated, were devoured on the spot. The procession was flanked by surveillance rats, whose incisors were held in awe by the beasts of burden. At last I saw the city's towers in the distance.

We made it, cried the She-rat. We got there. See for yourself, we mounted her on the plinth of the main altar of Saint Mary's. Under the cross anchored high up in the vault – that's where we put our saint. The Son of Man is hanging by three nails, and she sits at his feet, on a crate which in human times was called a tabernacle. Well she knows that her prettily clad little boy is under the hem of her skirt. And around the place where she sits – for she dried in a sitting position – we put everything that belonged to her and was worthy to be worshipped along with her: the gold coins and the little boy's ring, the wrought-iron standard and those dear little figures, which, sad to say, were badly chewed in the dark days of the religious wars. Look at them: still adorably blue and white. Still the droll replicas of the industrious human race, except that they manage with one finger less than the human hand numbered and that we are endowed with. Just look: How comical!

Yes, comical is right. On the plinth of the altar that elevated the mummies, I saw all the smurfs, singly and in groups. I saw those with trowels, saw the one with the monkey wrench. The one with the axe, seven reapers with scythes. The musical smurfs, including the drummer. The unemployed smurf and the one with the bottle to his lips. And this one and that one. I counted: not a one was missing; but all had tooth marks.

Then the She-rat reoccupied my dream. She said: We feasted our eyes on the saint and her first born, on the figures and coins, yet our ravening hunger remained unappeased. We were obliged to reduce our litters by half. It was beginning to look as though the rat nations, like the human race before them, were without a future. And then certain of the figures grouped on the altar gave us the salutary idea; or possibly what saved us was that a finger broke off the ancient one's left hand in which she held her rosary, fell from her lap, and came to rest where seven little fellows with their scythes were standing in a row, while other blue-and-white figures stood holding sheaves of grain. But though this ambivalent hint may have set our thoughts in motion, it was far from filling our stomachs.

Here she fell silent and let her whiskers play, as though to stress the prolonged gestation of the new idea. At length she said: No. Not an accident. We rats don't recognize accident. In any case the supplies we had accumulated in the deepest chambers of our escape passages at the approach of Doomsday included various assortments of seeds which, well packed and secure against dampness, had remained undamaged, for when we put a practical interpretation on the ancient one's hint and, emulating the blue-and-white figures, turned over here and there a plot of land which, because it was infested with hedge mustard and goatweed, seemed uncontaminated and fertile – when we had cleared these experimental fields of weeds, drilled them at intervals, sowed the seed and covered it with earth, then, when we no longer dared hope, the salvaged seed sprouted miraculously. And since the spring rains were almost free from noxious substances, since the dust storms had ceased and the post-human climate had become stably warm and humid, plants grew and fruits ripened.

The She-rat spoke as if rats had always been versed in agriculture. From late summer until mid-autumn we were able to harvest our first crop. We had planted lentils and corn, barley and turnips. A field of sunflowers was especially successful. Because sunflower seeds are rich in oil, this easily grown but uncommonly fruitful plant became our main crop. The new climate made it possible to garner two harvests a year. Not only the hills of Kashubia but equally the mud walls enclosing the urban districts were favourable to the sunflower. We who had formerly been active only at night became daytime workers. We inveterate nightwalkers took to raising sunflowers. Look, boss, at the expanse we covered with them . . .

> They come cheap from Hong Kong
> and have only four fingers
> on either hand,
> with which to hold tools or tennis rackets
> or for that matter, graciously, bouquets.
>
> Pressed from dyed plastic,
> they are durable
> and – this much is certain –
> will outlive the perishable human race in groups
> and as individuals.
>
> That's a comfort. For they were creatively modelled
> on us whose life is labour and sorrow.
> But smurfs are cheerful by nature
> and at all times playfully active
> with hammer and scythe and telephone.
>
> Nothing can dampen their spirits.
> Whatever may happen, their day begins cheerfully.
> Only their language, known in this country
> as Smurf language, may
> fail them in the end.
>
> Their silent grin, however,
> will remain, and round the clock
> their industry.

You've known the Kashubian hill country from earliest childhood: potato fields in the midst of woods and waterholes. Turnips, oats, barley and so on. As nothing was left of the forests and mere scrub – birch, alder and willow – was making a first hesitant appearance, but only in the vicinity of ponds and freshets – even the

Radaune sprang up clear and unpolluted elsewhere – we, hoping for forests, left the promising vegetation undisturbed. But from the hills of southern Kashubia to the Baltic sand dunes, and on all fertile mud slides as well, we farmed, here on clayey, there on sandy soil; the mud dikes of the low country would have been good for wheat, if seed had been available.

There she was again, tilling the soil while filling me in: No, no more potatoes. Those belly fillers passed away with the human race. But rotating our crops, we cultivated corn, turnips, barley and on a large scale sunflowers. See how they stand in rows, resplendent far and wide. Does it surprise you that we nocturnal animals have changed? To revive a distasteful turn of phrase: we no longer shun the light. In the interest of food supply we have made ourselves into day labourers.

She let me gaze and wonder. Then she said: You might think it was the luminous quality of the flowers, that egg-yellow crown of sunbeams that has weaned us from night life and given us a taste for the day? Nonsense. It was need that brought us to the light and changed us; whereas the human race was doomed to pass away because despite the crying need it was unable, unwilling to change. Whereas we changed.

The She-rat fell silent, but now I saw hilly sunflower fields amid Kashubian waterholes, ponds or lakes that mirrored the sky, saturated white clouds, but also groups of young trees, alders, birches, willows and densely growing rushes. And I saw rats working in the fields, row upon row, felling thick-stemmed, heavily laden sunflowers, gnawing wedges as though to bring down great trees. How quickly their teeth severed the stalks. How industrious they were, how perspicacious. Not a seed was lost. And how adroitly they beheaded the plants and lined up the capsules on the edges of the field to let them dry. Disciplined columns, but nowhere a forerat with a whip. They had posted guards, however, as though the harvest were endangered – by whom or what? – as though some alien parasites might benefit by their toil, as though, in addition to rats and supposedly mammalian bluebottles, some other animal worth mentioning had survived the Big Bang.

Yes, yes, said the She-rat. Of course those stories about flying snails, submarine spiders, and viviparous flies were devoid of truth. It was only for your amusement, because you like cock-and-bull stories, that we thought up such revolting vermin and unnatural monsters. But listen, young master, to that chirping and cooing. Not only sparrows, but wood pigeons as well, are present, as you know, in the post-human era. They are multiplying so rapidly as to become a plague, especially the sparrows. What else? The field mouse is with us again: stupid but tasty. And occasional rabbits. The sparrows are silvery white, the plumage of the pigeons is tinged with pink, and the mice are preposterously yellow. All that came with the Big Bang, just as we had to say goodbye to our old greyish-brown colour. Our litters are zinc-green. Later an earth-coloured tinge predominated. We older rats are clothed in umber. In any case, while the heavy seed flower heads are ripening on the stalk you see how cleverly our light-footed, still zinc-green young rats protect them from the birds.

And indeed I saw how the shadow side of every large ripening sunflower was occupied by a young rat; evidently this was a technicolor dream, for the zinc-green fur stood out just perceptibly from the green underside of the flowers. Then I saw time and again with what sureness of aim the young rats caught thieving sparrows between their teeth; they could even handle wood pigeons; grabbing the pigeons' throats between their teeth, they were drawn into the air by the fluttering pigeons and a moment later plunged to the ground with their exhausted prey. Several times I saw sudden flight, an aerial battle over the sunflower field, a plummeting as of a stone; saw how effectively the harvest was guarded. The slain pigeons and sparrows were lined up at the edge of the field along with the harvested sunflowers. Everything was due to be shared, for that is the way with rats. Indeed, while we humans were still pursuing our individual advantage, the rats became known to us as the sharing species, but we did not follow their example.

Rat, bird and sunflower have composed themselves into a picture ever since. The correlation that I saw in my dreams now strikes me as natural when awake. Never again shall I look upon sunflowers, as long as they continue to greet me as old friends from behind garden fences, as mere flowers; I shall always see the bird between the rat's teeth.

The She-rat of my dreams, however, took a more down-to-earth view: We weren't going to let our harvest of seeds be ravaged by spongers, such as we had been before the Big Bang, sometimes making off with as much as thirty per cent of the Indian wheat or the Mexican corn crop. Not to mention our raids on the warehouses where accumulation helped to keep prices up.

But then she exalted agricultural produce to the realm of mystical speculation: Even earlier than corn, barley or our number one belly filler, the swede, earlier than any other crop the sunflower took on importance in our lives, nay more, it transformed nocturnal light-shunning animals into heliotropic lovers of the light, and in our prayers we have attributed divine powers to the sun ever since; for which reason in Saint Mary's church, where we gather to mourn the passing of the human race, we find further occasion to be pious after the manner of rats.

Again the picture widened, became three-dimensional. From a distance, then close at hand, I saw, as though conjured into being, the plinth of the altar and what had adorned it of late. Henceforth it was not only the last resting place of the air-dried Anna Koljaiczek and her shrunken grandson; farm produce was now added. The new altar arrangement required the smurfs to crowd together. The gold ducats were as neatly stacked as if a cashier were in charge. The wrought-iron standard lay on top of the lifeless cuckoo clock. Reduced in format, dentures, glasses, ring and decoration were composed into a still life. The saved space was taken up with impressively swollen wreaths of fruit and choice game birds.

Only then did I notice that the outer parts of the plinth, which had formerly been empty, were also occupied: enormous turnips, bundled ears of corn, ears of barley contributed to the sacrifice. But what struck me as most significant was the full-grown sunflower that lay in Anna Koljaiczek's lap and covered her hands, one of which, the left, poorer by one finger, undoubtedly held a rosary. At her feet, beside the diminutive Oskar, I saw a pile of dried lentils.

But She-rat, I cried, what is all this? Where's your Catholicism? Don't you worship the crucified Son of Man any more? Have you come to look upon the old woman with the little boy as a fertility goddess? What has become of your reason?

She seemed somewhat embarrassed as, playing with sunflower seeds, she moved back into my dream.

Answer me, She-rat, I cried. Under her breath she hissed her ratgibber in which new, unfamiliar, unintelligible phonemes predominated.

I don't understand. Speak normally.

Oh, well, she said. We do our best. We are still devoted to humankind, and this for the present is our harvest festival. Possibly something else will take its place. Something different. Something sensible.

What? I cried. The superrat?

Certainly not, young master, she said. Her whiskers stood on end. Something higher. Something that has never been, but that might have been conceived in human times. A figure, no, several figures that will transcend ratkind as it has become and humankind as it was . . .

She listens with pleasure to Lute Music, to the Review of the Media with moderate interest, to Echo of the Day with indifference; during the actual News, she sleeps. What my Christmas rat still likes best is Educational Radio for All. Yesterday distinctions were drawn between taxes, fees and duties. And in another programme there was talk of historical levies, tithes for instance; we were told how the peasants groaned under the demands of the tax farmers, who exacted so much that there wasn't enough seed left for next year's crop. My Christmas rat scurried about in excitement, sniffed with interest.

Today Educational Radio expatiated on past and present farming methods. In play form it discussed clearing by fire, the three-field system, monoculture, biodynamic planting, compost, nettle decoction and so on. Quiet, as though contemplating, she sat facing the radio, pricking up her round ears, every whisker at attention. Even the signature tune, *The Merry Peasant*, aroused her interest.

At present the Third Programme is silent. Neither she nor I wants to hear along what lines the European Parliament in Brussels is planning to dam the milk flood or establish new cod-fishing quotas. We already know that according to the FAO statistics three point five to four children die of starvation each second. My Christmas rat agrees with me that all optimistic proclamations to the contrary – 'The situation is on the mend! There is reason to hope again!' – everything is running, slipping, sliding downhill, towards the statistically certain end.

But maybe the end has already been. Maybe we've gone out of existence. Maybe we're only living as if, a reflex and soon a terminal wriggling.

Or someone is dreaming us. God or some such higher being, some super-God, is dreaming us in instalments, because He loves us or thinks we're funny and can't get enough of our wriggling. In his flashbacks, thanks to the divine lust for publicity, we survive, even though the last show, or doomadosh, as the She-rat calls it, was put on ages ago; imperceptibly we passed away, because so inflexible is the human race that, even if men had happened to notice the end that took place one Sunday in June, our behaviour, our business as usual, our delivery and payment schedules, our lovable habits and terrifying obsessions could neither be changed nor done away with, neither renounced nor abolished.

As though we were still in existence, I said to my Christmas rat: Listen. Just before the twelve o'clock news the Third Programme often runs choral music. You like motets, don't you? So while you're listening to Schütz, I'll go and see Malskat, high up in his scaffolding. He did good work. After fifty and more figures in the nave, there will soon be twenty-one saints in groups of three in the choir loft, all casting Gothic glances.

I borrow scaffolding shoes. I visit him up there, flatter him, praise his powerful contours, laugh with him about stupid clergymen and garrulous art experts. But while I talk and talk, I have something else in mind, namely, to persuade him to paint, if not in the ornamentation of the capitals, then in the vacant fields, sunflowers protected by rats against the depredations of pigeons. This symbolism makes sense, especially because of the similarity between pigeon and rat: equally tough, both will endure into the future . . .

Malskat doesn't say no. I offer him a cigarette, a Juno of course. We talk about films featuring Hansi Knoteck, which we both saw in the days of our youth. Quite as a matter of course, we come back to pigeons and rats. He says: This late Gothic motif might easily be traced back to the Plague which, beginning in the middle of the fourteenth century, made itself at home throughout Europe with the help of the black house rat and a now extinct variety of pigeon. This scourge of God taught Christians to see that the end of the world was at hand – everywhere, including Lübeck, where of ten living inhabitants nine were snatched away . . .

No, no! I cry and climb down from the scaffolding. We can manage that without rats and pigeons. We need no plague, no scourge of God. Man has developed since Malskat's High Gothic times. By his own resources, self-sufficient, come of age at last, he can eliminate himself, and do it so thoroughly that no remainders are left to torment themselves. That is why even now he is out to destroy nature and all its excrescences. For before man dies, this forest with its mawkish undergrowth, King Thrushbeard's incalculable estate, must be wiped out . . .

While Little Red Riding Hood's grandmother is still reading the dictionary aloud – forgotten words which the wolf, who has been left behind, enjoys hearing – and while the Grimm Brothers are worried lest the present doings of the fairy-tale characters lead to excesses and uncontrollable lustiness; while Rapunzel plays dominoes with the kissing prince and the witch kills time over Parcheesi with the wicked stepmother; while the girl's thoughts dwell on her hands that have flown away, the good and bad fairies, ravens and crows sow magic seeds over town and country, over housing silos and concrete runways. And high over farflung industrial facilities the pilotless flying trunk unloads yet other seeds.

Industrial regions receive unexpected visitors from the ground as well. The seven dwarfs pour magic liquor – just a few carefully counted drops – into gas pumps. In Underground stations Little Red Riding Hood lets something fall from her basket. The girl's chopped-off hands are nimbly at work on the pylons of overland power lines. Goblins, elves and other tinies are seen in railway stations and under bridges – so busy, so eager. The seven kids deposit something under traffic lights; rat droppings bear witness in every switchbox; pigeons empty their crops in every loudspeaker.

Magicians hurry across busy squares. The great Merlin is everywhere. Now he is escorting King Thrushbeard and all doors and gates open to them. They visit power stations, coal-fuelled and nuclear, they visit the Hoechst and Bayer-Leverkusen chemical works. Like all-powerful bosses, surrounded by obsequious underlings, they visit conveyor belts in Wolfsburg, Cologne, Neckarsulm. They inspect the Leopard assembly line at the Krauss-Maffei Works; Merlin memorizes Celtic magic spells, and Thrushbeard sends out orders, dictates delivery dates.

Meanwhile attractively dressed witches and exotic-looking wild men have been mingling with the travelling public at the Rhine-Main Airport. We see them on escalators, at the check-in counters, disguised as flight attendants. In self-service shops Mother Holle lets downy feathers fly from flower-patterned pillowcases. From skyscrapers, on every floor of which he has strewn needles, the brave little tailor lets his big ball of thread unroll.

In short: wherever the profit motive stirs, wherever a market gap is discovered, wherever demand is tickled into life and the GNP promises to increase, here sowing, there trickling forces are subversively at work, every crack in the system is exploited. Rarely have the gears of the mechanism of the free-market economy been serviced so attentively.

Silently, with no need for explanatory subtitles, slogans are murmured and fingers crossed. In varying uniforms the steadfast tin soldier obtains admittance to the restricted areas of the Bundeswehr and of the Allied Protector Power. Having suddenly been promoted to high rank, he is saluted by the post commander. He caresses tanks, guns and rocket silos, is welcomed on board high-speed warships. He co-pilots supersonic planes. He is even authorized to leaf through secret documents and wherever he goes, even in the Defence Ministry, he leaves behind him certain trifles, no larger than grains of sand; he's an absent-minded tin soldier.

Already the counterforce is at work; at first hesitantly, as though the new springtime lacked self-confidence, then rapidly, explosively. At first only vegetative changes are to be wondered at; then unfettered growth draws crowds.

Plants sprout from chimneys and bridge piers, proliferate and spread. Superhighways spring cracks, making room for quickly twining plants. Greenery sprouts from conveyor belts, engines, escalators, elevator shafts, robots and department store cash registers. The cooling towers of nuclear power plants are infested with moss and lichens, as are armoured vehicles and supersonic planes. Algae cover frigates and missile-firing cruisers with a green coat that reaches halfway up their radar masts, as though all these ships had sunk years ago, as they are destined to do in any case. Creepers on high-tension pylons, up the sides of television towers. Budding, then leafy branches emerge from gun barrels; railway stations transformed into greenhouses. The Rhine-Main Airport teems with greenery run riot. The windows of ministries and executive office suites vomit greenery; green and nothing else is on the increase.

Growth. Everywhere nature is making trouble. It thinks up rare, hitherto unknown plants, including some that make concrete brittle, crack walls, bend steel pipes, eat file cards, even some with suckers that erase data. Mosses and lichens break the bank. Parquet floors sprout mushrooms. Enormous signs advertising giant corporations put out branches that make them illegible. Irresistibly nature gains the upper hand. Traffic in any direction becomes impossible. Smoke rises no longer from any chimney. No exhaust fumes, no polluted air. Frightened at first, people suddenly cheer up and have time.

Between shut-down industrial installations that have expanded into botanic gardens and on overgrown superhighways groups large and small are sauntering. Solitary strollers pick flowers or discover sinfully sweet fruits. Boys and girls climb clinging vines. Lovers bed down in giant strawberries. Everywhere this fruit invites to mysterious games. The garden of delights is open to all.

Gathered on squares overgrown with greenery, men and women, children and old people hold up banners and placards saying: 'All power to the fairy tales!' – 'Breathe deeply, it's worthwhile again!' – 'Let the Grimm Brothers run the government!' – 'At last the right kind of growth!' – 'We demand fairy-tale rule!'

While on all sides we see people happily engaged in idleness, the picture narrows to the size of the magic mirror's screen. Joy prevails in the Gingerbread House. Arm in arm, the wicked stepmother and the witch. For the first time in their lives, Hansel and Gretel are allowed to behave like children. Their task completed, some of the fairy-tale characters have come home. Not only the girl without hands, even Jorinde and Joringel are smiling. Only the Grimm Brothers shake their heads in doubt. (And as soon as our Herr Matzerath gets back from Poland, he too will undoubtedly give vent to misgivings.)

'This will result in chaos and immorality! There has to be *some* order. God-given or imposed by the state.' Jakob and Wilhelm Grimm take turns in crying out: 'This has to stop.'

After some hesitation the frog king and his lady, Snow White and the kissing prince voice agreement. Encouraged by Snow White, the prince says: 'I believe it is time for me to wake my Sleeping Beauty once again with a kiss.'

Rübezahl threatens to punch the prince on the nose. The witch and Gretel are disgusted with the frog king. When the prince tries to run away, Rumpelstiltskin trips him up. The witch and the bad fairies shape their hands into claws, but before they can grab him, the remaining dwarfs bind him with a strand of Rapunzel's hair and lay him down beside a doll made of straw, moss and leaves, which is supposed to resemble Sleeping Beauty and which he immediately starts kissing. The dwarfs then seize hold of Snow White and try to drag her into the bushes.

The Grimm Brothers are scandalized. They have always detested violence and mental cruelty. 'You ought to be ashamed!' cries Wilhelm. And Jakob: 'The next thing we know you'll stop *us* from leaving!'

The seven dwarfs let Snow White go, but stamp and shake their fists. Rübezahl puffs himself up into a furious mountain troll. The witch makes fiery eyes. Hansel and Gretel say: 'Let the Grimm Brothers go.' – 'They will form a new and good government.'

The fairy-tale characters, who have all assembled outside the boarding house, argue this point. The bad fairies and the seven dwarfs are opposed. The good fairies, the frog king and his lady, Mother Holle and King Thrushbeard are in favour. 'All power to the Grimm Brothers' reads a subtitle in the magic mirror, and thanks to the wicked stepmother's vote, a resolution to this effect carries a majority. Only Rumpelstiltskin, the brave little tailor, the dwarfs and the bad fairies are opposed. Many are still undecided. The girl's hands play stone paper scissors. The witch throws knucklebones. Rübezahl picks his nose. Bending over the Dictionary, Little Red Riding Hood's grandmother cries out: 'Here it says: Vote!'

'Let them go' wins by a small majority. The good and the bad fairies confer. In the end the three good fairies, with bleeding fingers, write the demands of the fairy-tale characters on lily pads: 'Good air! Clean water! Healthy fruit!' How simple it looks, how reasonable.

The fairies demonstrate their demands in a dance. The Grimm Brothers accept the lily-pad documents and promise to form a good government. 'From now on,' cries Wilhelm, 'the fairy tales will have a say!'

Led by the three good fairies, they leave the clearing and the Gingerbread House. Some of the fairy-tale characters wave to them as they go. The others have their doubts. The frog king dives into the well. The lady lies down. The frog king jumps on her forehead, then wants to move to the child's and then to the witch's forehead, but the witch is still throwing knucklebones and Gretel is standing gloomily off to one side.

Again the girl's hands start playing stone paper scissors with themselves. Little Red Riding Hood's grandmother reads the wolf words from olden times. All express the hope that this fairy tale will end well.

'I object! It can't end well. I'm pessimistic about this film. The story,' he cries, 'is taking a disastrous turn. Why all this unmotivated tolerance? We can't just let the Grimm Brothers go.'

There he is, butting in. He wants to be boss and director again. And his trip to Poland hasn't agreed with him. It has aged him. He no longer stands erect. He's bandylegged and keeps away from the mirror. There's sorrow in that sullen look. His clothes are still tailor-made, but he's swimming in them. What can have happened to our Herr Matzerath?

No sooner had he started back than his sufferings set in. When intense pressure on his bladder made him try desperately and painfully to pass water every fifty kilometres, and then at shorter intervals, whenever he sighted bushes to the right or left of the road, our Herr Matzerath had said to himself: 'It's just the excitement, the greetings, the good-byes, that kind of thing stimulates the kidneys.' But in the afternoon, as the Mercedes approached Poland's western border, the Oder river, when our Herr Matzerath's attempts to relieve his bladder became torture and, though the urge persisted, accomplished little – the barest drip – Bruno began to worry: 'Herr Oskar,' he said. 'As soon as we get to the West, say Brunswick or at the latest Hanover, we'll have to see a doctor.'

Though softly and comfortably seated, our Herr Matzerath suffered agonies all across the Democratic Republic. His forehead covered with sweat. His little fingers clutching, or drumming on, his trembling knees. The unbearable pressure, the fear of wetting his pants.

Then, to top it all, the frequent stops of the Mercedes on the open road, our Herr Matzerath's frantic but vain attempts, scarcely concealed by the shrubbery, to piss a little, if only a thimbleful, aroused the suspicions of the People's Police in the form of a patrol. Bruno braked to a stop; questions and answers necessitated an agonizingly long stay; the traffic cops failed to see how a man riding in a Mercedes – even one with the star missing – could be afflicted with so commonplace a disorder. They took meticulous note of every detail, even of the theft (localized in Poland) of the star symbol, and yet, when our Herr Matzerath invited the note taker to see for himself, the People's policeman did not hesitate long before wishing the sufferer a pleasant trip.

Fortunately the border formalities went off easily. Rather than wait until Brunswick or Hanover, the travellers, on reaching Helmstedt at a late hour, went looking for the municipal hospital and thanks to Bruno's innate sense of direction found it without too much wandering. The patient felt wobbly and weepy when the duty doctor palpated his abdomen and lost no time in calling in a urologist, who examined him rectally with sheathed finger.

I know all this at first hand. He has always been glad to expatiate on his mishap. No sooner back from Poland than he sought my ear. 'I thought I was in perfect shape. And now this. An old man's ailment. The urologist spoke of an extremely enlarged prostate gland. You know. Said it called for an operation without delay. Either with a catheter, reducing its size by scraping it through the urethra, or more radically by an abdominal incision.'

In Helmstedt they had merely inserted a temporary catheter; an unpleasant business, but it had relieved him enormously. His distended bladder had disgorged exactly one thousand four hundred and seventy millilitres of urine. The urologist – young but competent – had expressed amazement at the quantity, but had not accepted our Herr Matzerath's explanation: 'It was the excitement, Herr Doktor, my grandmother's hundred and seventh birthday, my emotion at seeing her after all these years.' 'No,' the doctor had said, 'it's not the usual reaction to festivities; it's a chronic condition; your prostate must absolutely be reduced.'

'Not before my sixtieth birthday,' our Herr Matzerath had protested. In the meantime he has been outfitted with an indwelling catheter. Since then, apart from the ugly, jiggling foreign body, he has had next to no trouble. All the same he has consulted a number of doctors – 'top specialists,' he assures me – in the vain hope of a reprieve. He gives me advice, tells me to give up coffee, liquor, and above all white wine and iced beer. But when I ask him for details of his trip to Poland, he becomes morose and monosyllabic.

What little I can gather is from random remarks. 'This Solidarność tragedy . . . Families are torn apart . . . Politics, politics . . . It's no good for Kashubians . . . It won't end well . . . They're always dragging the Virgin Mary into it. It's probably the condition of Poland that has affected my bladder.'

When I questioned him more directly about family matters: Oh, yes, my grandmother is fine. She was delighted with all the presents, especially the smurfs. Like a child. She's even considering – just imagine! – a trip. Her grandson's sixtieth birthday, she said, 'might tempt me'.

Of course I don't tell our Herr Matzerath that he doesn't exist any more; I let him go on acting as if he were the boss. Other people – even I myself – believe that life is somehow going on. So he doesn't need to know what has really happened in Kashubia. Bad enough that he's come back with a catheter.

So we talk about 'the Grimms' forests' and the phony fifties when with Malskat high in the scaffolding forgeries of every kind prospered. No, no! He must never find out that if he still exists it is only as a diminutive mummy adorning an altar serving the religious needs of rats. Because all the doctors say: No excitement. Our Herr Matzerath must not be upset.

Everybody knows we're musical; but it's not true, a silly superstition widespread before the Big Bang, proliferating like a weed and impossible to exterminate, that we are especially given to the sound of the flute, that the recorder no less than the transverse flute exerts an attraction on us, that someone with nimble fingers and trained lips need only come along and play his little flute, coax trills and quick runs from it, and we'll be ready to follow him, the often invoked Pied Piper, blindly to our carefully prepared doom, to drown miserably in the river Weser, for instance.

That was in the house-rat era. Dear little fellow, said the She-rat – she has taken lately to calling me master or young master, that kind of thing. Her new manner of speaking makes her ratgibber easier to put up with, takes the asperities off her usual hissing and gives her a broad, countrified pronunciation. Dear boy, she said, we'll talk about Hamelin and that sort of thing later. There's not a grain of truth in that legend. But it's true that we rats are able to produce a sound that has never been heard by any human being, is beyond the powers of any instrument, whether flute or fiddle, and can carry news over long distances. Its sequences were measured with the help of ultra-sound in the last years of the human era – in Boston, Massachusetts, incidentally.

The She-rat boasted a bit: Our info-system. Then she said: But if you like, young master, our sound might be likened to the singsong which your women – 'bags' was the word she actually used –

identified with the song of the medusas when they were out in their boat looking for a submerged city. True, they spoke of singing medusas, but there was also talk of a musical pope, as a model for singing jellyfish. So our music, if one wished to transpose it into audible terms, might suggest Gregorian chant, all the more so as the religious music of the human race has always been dear to us.

It seemed to me that I heard swelling psalmody as the She-rat went on: Even in the Early Christian age – though they didn't hear us – we sang with them in their escape structures, the catacombs. With them we developed our Kyrie. With them we worshipped. And for centuries we were despised and persecuted with them. If only that harmony had endured: we attuned to them and they to us. Ah, their well-rehearsed choirs. Ah, their polyphony. Until just before the Bang, the Poles living here sang with especial fervour; and that is why our singing, which more and more often fills the Church of Saint Mary from floor to vaulting, is not devoid of a certain passion that is often associated with the Polish people.

No, no, young master. There's no reason to fear nationalistic over-tones. True, we haven't forgotten that the Polish word for rat is *szczur*, we jokingly call each other *szczur*, or more affectionately *szczurzyca* – but obviously we're not Polish rats. There's no such thing and never was, any more than there are Portuguese or Hungarian rats or were in the human era; even though man, with his need to give everything a name, has seen fit – no one knows why – to call us *rattus norvegicus*. Still, there's something Polish about us, in this region undoubtedly. For instance, our taste for dill pickles and caraway seed can be traced back to what used to be the prevailing taste here, and that's why, side by side with our main crops, we grow cucumbers, squash and caraway seed, with considerable success; and that, too, is why there were seed packets in our escape passages. We also cultivate fungi and moulds. By adding mild rot, we produce sweet and sour dishes. There's something Polish about our character too. In contrast to the rat nations that have immigrated, or rather, have been resettled here from the West, who try to reduce everything to a system, we are more carefree, though not without a certain persistent, some say, pig-headed, seriousness. We hope for something. Our prayers are supercharged with longing. As though something higher that is not yet available – the Poles used to call it freedom – were almost within our reach . . .

No, that's nonsense! It's irrational! The She-rat interrupted herself. Obviously there can't be German and Polish rats. The differences are too slight. It's only on the surface that we sometimes show antagonisms, during the famine, for instance, when we became so fanatical in matters of faith. Yes, those German rats are spoiled, it amuses them to list all the things they had in the prosperous West and have now lost. They deplore and praise our modesty too loudly and too often. They're so restless, so hyper-active. Also, they always think they know better, in that they're incorrigible; but there are some things they do know better, such as techniques for storing seeds. Since freedom doesn't mean too much to them, they are more orderly than we are, they can be downright crotchety about it. They've begun to take an informed interest in our shipyards; all right, why not, but when they start sorting screws and ball bearings, nuts and bolts, and painstakingly removing the rust, or worse, when they start bragging about their supply of spare parts, they sound just absurd, all the more so as they ridicule the playful but not unskilful work we do with metal objects we find, and have often wantonly destroyed the rather artistic compositions we display in front of the Artushof or on the porches of Lady Street.

You shouldn't take that so seriously, I objected. Actually, the German rats suffer from their obsession with order. They admire your light touch, your gift for improvisation, your innate artistic sense. Those scrap-iron figurines of yours are really worth looking at.

Nonsense! said the She-rat, a mere pastime. Play. But our serious efforts aren't appreciated either. It has to be admitted that we take an interest in old buildings, whose condition leaves them indifferent. If not for our method of mixing a weatherproof mortar from lime that we make from sea shells we find in the alluvial sand and the sand which the constant wind blows into the streets, the historical buildings of the Right City and Old City of Gdańsk would decay even more quickly than they're doing now. But that doesn't stop them from claiming possession of our Danzig. If it were not for the rat nations that keep trickling in from Russia, where to judge by all reports things are still looking bad, our local conflicts, or why not admit it, our German–Polish antagonisms, might easily get out of hand. How fortunate that the Russians are here, that it's not just them and us. Well, we know what that led to in human and in early post-human times; for when we rats flew at one another during the famine, it was not only with zealotic references to the true faith; we also reviled one another as You Polacks and You Prussians!

Oh, how fortunate, young master, that since we've been tilling the soil, since we've ceased to shun the light of day, a phonetic shift has united us. Our language has adapted itself to our new activities and habits. Haven't you noticed, young master, that our speech has become softer, more palatal, of late? We don't squeak, we don't hiss any more. We even manage to produce deep, broad sounds. Previously unaccustomed words like seed, manure, cucumber, grain and not least sunflower are being pronounced with sonorous fluency. The sharp, hissing sounds we used to make have become fuller, but also flatter, one might say broader. That's because we talk so much about the harvest, about planting, and time and again about the weather. In country regions the pronunciation has become especially broad. In urban districts intermediate sounds are developing, the A, O and U are coming out more euphoniously.

And I heard the rats chatting away with city accents and country accents, recollecting the past and speaking of current activities.

They called the Ancient One Olshe or Olshke. It sounded cosy and warm, as though Anna Koljaiczek's manner of speaking had guided town as well as country rats through a phonetic shift. The She-rat said: Well, young master, wouldn't you like to hear what we sing in church at the harvest festival?

After showing me a number of scrap-iron sculptures inspired by the human countenance, which had been on display in the Long Market, and calling my attention to columns of workers whose function it was to stabilize the crumbling walls of the Old City with lime mortar, the She-rat drew me into the interior of Saint Mary's Church, as if it were my destiny to be led over and over again into that Gothic soul barn, in which every word takes on higher meaning.

So close pressed were the assembled rat nations that the stone floor of the church and the inset tombstones of the old Danzig patrician families were hidden from view. The deep organlike chant, sorrowful at first, then jubilant, silvery on the high notes, must have been carried by several choirs, for the voices were skilfully interwoven. It filled the church from the floor to the fan vault of pillars striving toward their lofty keystone.

The rat mass in Saint Mary's had already begun; or was it without beginning or end? From the west portal to the distant main altar, on which, as I knew from earlier dreams, lay those venerable objects of worship, Anna Koljaiczek, shrivelled and leathery but still recognizable, and at her feet, amid tattered, cloudlike skirts, her grandson Oskar, rat nations moved to the rhythm of the song. The congregation arose as one rat. They stood up on their hind legs, tilted their snouts and tremulous whiskers toward the vault above them. They did not, however, clasp their forepaws in prayer; instead, they extended their finely articulated, clawed hands as though overcome with the yearning of their polychoral song. Even their tails stood erect, pointing heavenward. Then they stood again four-legged on the floor, displaying round rat humps throughout the great three-naved church. All had tucked their tails away. They were practising humility before rising once again, a rat nation of many thousand heads, with a gesture of yearning and supplication.

And when I saw them in prayer and supplication – the old earth-green rats hindmost, the young, still zinc-green rats closer to the altar – it seemed to me that they were no longer praying like Catholics, I detected a pagan undercurrent; just as the farm produce that lay heaped on the altar obscured such devotional objects as Anna Koljaiczek's rosary and the wrought-iron standard. Only the smurfs and the gold ducats were still recognizable. On this I saw cucumbers and squash in addition to the usual farm produce. But sunflowers predominated. And even the cross suspended over the altar was so covered over with heaping baskets of fruit that the presence of the crucified Son of Man could only be guessed at.

No! I cried. You can't do that. It's pagan, it's idolatry, sacrilege . . .

The She-rat whispered: Hush, young master. Can't you see how fervently they are imploring the sun?

But really, She-rat, don't you want to be Christian again, or if not Christian, at least Catholic . . .

Your vast churches, she said, were intended for many faiths and might have been made to order for us . . .

But I won't have it, I cried. I can't stand any more of that whining and whimpering. Faith was never my forte. I don't give a damn about your hopes. Besides, it must be hard on our Herr Matzerath to be a measly desiccated altar ornament for you rat nations, when actually he has just come home safe and sound from Poland. The trip has taken a good deal out of him, seeing all those people again, the goodbyes. Excess pressure that doesn't want to drain off is giving him trouble. He's been wearing an indwelling catheter ever since. It gets in his way, embarrasses him. But his grandmother means to visit him soon, when he turns sixty. Hear that, She-rat, she is planning to visit her Oskar in the flesh.

Sure sure, she said, you're still spinning out your story.

And then and then?
Then came the currency reform.
And after that, what came after that?
What had been missing before came miraculously, piece by piece,
Most of it in instalments.
And what happened then, when everything was present?
We acquired children and what goes with them.
And what about the children, what did the children do then?
They asked stupid questions about what had gone before
and then and after that.
Well? Did you come clean?
We remembered
the bathing weather in the summer of '39.
And what else?
Hard times after that.
And then, and after that?
Then came the currency reform.

Chapter Ten, in which a storm breaks out during an official ceremony, our Herr Matzerath asserts himself, the She-rat imputes secrets to the drifting wreck, the prince runs away, news is reported from Hamelin, the densely crowded rats are full of expectancy, no mail brings news from Travemünde, but the bells ring at the onset of the new era.

IT'S MY sea, it has shores in many countries, from Reval and Riga in the east to its western bays and bights, with the churches of Saint Mary in Lübeck, Stralsund and Danzig, the cathedrals of Schwerin and Schleswig, likewise with the Church of Saint John in Stege on Møn and the white-washed churches in Elmelunde, in many Danish towns, then along the Scanian beaches, the Swedish skerry coasts, in Ystad and Stockholm, up as far as the Gulf of Bothnia, along the shores of Finland, as far north as the Baltic Sea extends, on the islands of Bornholm, Gotland, Rügen, also in the flat or hilly back country, wherever bricks were baked, rich in cathedrals and three-nave churches, town halls and arsenals, blessed moreover with Holy Ghost hospitals and guildhalls, with Cistercian and Franciscan monasteries, all of which, and not only the buildings of the Hanseatic League in the Wendish district are classified under the head of brick Gothic and line the shores of my sea, the gentle, treacherous Baltic with its low salt and high jellyfish content. Furthermore, all these buildings are chockful of art treasures. In one the choir loft, in another the guild silver is said to be significant. Stupidly arrogant inscriptions under patrician coats of arms lay claim to humility before God. Madonnas, though skinny, look pregnant. Winged altarpieces and wood-carved crucifixion groups are worth visiting, as are the torture chambers and their instruments; and one is sometimes surprised at traces of astonishing mural painting.

I've told you about the cathedral in Schleswig on the Schlei, where, even including the cloister, painter Malskat restored paintings on lime mortar to their Gothic past. To this day there are some who deny that he created High Gothic frescoes under the choir screen of Lübeck's Holy Ghost Hospital. But it is certified that he worked ably first in the clerestory of the nave, then in the choir loft of that church of Saint Mary which, though presenting the dimensions of a French cathedral, is held to be the mother of all brick Gothic churches and which was about to celebrate its seventh centenary.

Malskat had to hurry. Dietrich Fey his employer was pressing him. The scaffolding had already been removed from the nave. An official ceremony had been planned. Printed and sold by the millions, special stamps in two denominations – fifteen pfennigs dull green, twenty-five pfennigs reddish-brown – both figuring the rapid painter's Annunciation group, added to the prestige of the impending centenary celebration and brought profit to the Lübeck church.

The blackskirts took in a hundred and eighty thousand shiny-new marks, and yet those stamps which today, I presume, bring outrageous prices from collectors brought not a red cent to the painter, who, high in his scaffolding while the business was in progress, was afflicted with a perpetual cold. He, the creator of the Annunciation group, praised by all the assembled art experts for its expressiveness, came off empty-handed.

Remote from all business considerations, Malskat, in such seclusion that he might easily have been forgotten, pursued a nagging thought that could no more be deflected than a power drill. And on 1 September 1951, when the ceremony finally took place in Lübeck's Church of Saint Mary, our sure-footed painter, though he had worked hard for three years first in the nave, then in the choir, was not at the centre of the celebration, sitting with the dignitaries and guests of honour, as was of course his boss, but was seated far back among the common people. That's how I see him and I wonder whether his thought, once conceived, was still tormenting him. And thus, far in the background, did he appear to his one and twenty choir saints, standing on painted consoles in seven groups of three, some in splayed pointed shoes, some barefoot.

Closer to Malskat, sitting motionless in his back pew, were the numerous saints in the nave. Every vault of the clerestory bore witness to him. From vestiges of paint that crumbled to dust when touched ever so lightly, following what traces were still discernible, but more from within himself, he had exhausted his inner treasure for a pitiful wage. Empty, drained, Lothar Malskat sat in the back pew. He sat there in Dietrich Fey's old suit, which Fey had worn in the Schleswig cloister days. The trousers were too short, the jacket too tight at the shoulders. He felt squeezed, hemmed in. All those saints looking down from on high must have regarded him as a pathetic scarecrow; and from far off, from the front wall of the choir, his Virgin with Child must have seen him as a late confirmand. She had grown famous in the meantime, her likeness was featured in the luxury volume in which a group of art historians, without mentioning Malskat, praised the murals in Lübeck's Church of Saint Mary as a miracle.

He laughed inwardly. For though she was sprinkled with white islets of mortar and her contours were eroded as though by centuries, this Virgin had a particular expression: it was wild, harsh, of a veiled sweetness. He had conceived the now-famous Madonna with Child during a coffee break in May 1950 – that was when the last edibles were exempted from rationing – deep in thoughts of a movie actress who had appeared to him the night before – *The Merry Petrol Station* was showing – unblemished by time, as though the war had never been.

While Malskat was still laughing inwardly, Bishop Pantke spoke from the pulpit to all those assembled but especially to Chancellor Adenauer, who sat there as though carved in wood; it was not the bishop who, beguiled by the Devil, had given the vault a keystone in the shape of a swastika, but a little old man, who spoke to the guests and dignitaries, and also no doubt to the common people on the back benches.

I can't claim to know everything that made Malskat laugh inwardly while the bishop was speaking and can only surmise that it must have been the movie actress in the role of madonna or else his persistent thought. Nor do I know what Chancellor Adenauer was thinking while Bishop Pantke's sermon was falling on his ears. The guests and dignitaries seated around him in obese innocence can hardly have troubled his mind, but it may be presumed that he was thinking about rearming the recently disarmed Germans and was mustering thoughts of divisional strength. Or did he merely listen with Catholic impassivity to the Bishop's Protestant sermon?

The Bishop praised and thanked God, cramming him into short and long sentences. He spoke of God's grace and God's goodness, of God's love, which is assured even to sinners, and of the miracle God had wrought in dark times; further, as was timely, he spoke of the defeated, to whom God had given a manifest sign.

When Bishop Pantke struck up 'Now thank we all our God', Lothar Malskat sang in a loud voice. Others who sang were: Malskat's employer, Dietrich Fey, church architect Fendrich, church councillor Göbel, curator of monuments Münter, under-secretary Schönebeck, who from his office in Bonn had financed the Lübeck miracle, and various provincial and federal politicians. The common people sang as they have always sung. And so did the first Chancellor of the freshly hatched state, like Lothar Malskat a talented wonder worker, beside — or across from — whom the founder and wonder worker of the other state might with a clear conscience have sat down and joined in the singing, if only with secular words. For our Herr Matzerath rightly sees the three of them, Adenauer, Malskat and Ulbricht, as an active triumvirate. He maintains that even before the onset of those years that he designated as the phony fifties they had begun to create the old anew from crumbling nothingness and to hoodwink everyone in masterly fashion, each in his own way.

It makes sense. But I do not support our Herr Matzerath's proposal that today, at a fitting distance and now that the swindle of the fifties has at last been exposed, large format postage stamps should be printed and circulated throughout Germany, showing instead of the now so appallingly expensive Annunciation group, the trio perched on the tops of columns: the top-hatted Rhenish Chancellor should stand on the right of the East Prussian painter in his matted woollen cap and on his left the Saxon First Chairman in a vizor cap. The flank men might display emblems, such as toy-size tanks of American or Soviet make; paint brushes and wire brush would be appropriate for the middle man. The triune forgery of those days could be elevated to the rank of a postage stamp, just as Germany's present prosperity is undoubtedly based on that for-gotten swindle.

'And on hard work!' cries our Herr Matzerath. 'Indefatigably they fashioned their forgeries, faithful in every detail. The one and

Günter Grass

the other swindled; the one in Saxon accents, the other in tones of piety, each lied and conjured up his Germany in order that the third, in Lübeck, where Germany borders on Germany, might create a Gothic roof arching over them. How can these three help becoming symbolic, if only in a perforated rectangle? On letters and posters, in the lowest denomination even on postcards, I see the three of them making their way from here to there, from hither to yon. What politics could not achieve is accomplished by the postal service. An all-German stamp, authenticated and postmarked. A triumph of philately!'

My objection cuts no ice with our Herr Matzerath. If there must be stamps, I say – but he listens only to himself – then only stamps coupling Ulbricht and Adenauer, side by side like the two poets, or profile half hidden by profile like the Grimm Brothers. For the fact is that soon after the centenary celebration Malskat, having thought it over carefully, seceded from the trio of forgers.

On the afternoon of 1 September 1951 he was enjoying an extra celebration with some construction workers at Fredenhag's Beer Hall. Dietrich Fey, his employer, still in his Stresemann hat, dropped in just for a second and stood them all beer and schnaps. Then he was due at the Town Hall, where not Malskat, but he, the handsome Dietrich Fey, was to be introduced to the Chancellor. According to the local press, Adenauer said: 'Well, you've left a fine job for the art historians.' The unauthenticated legend has it that after saying these words the Chancellor winked at Fey.

Later Malskat and some of his friends went to the café Nieder-egger. He had definitely made up his mind to expose the fraud. Driven by that persistent thought. For during the ceremony, just as a dated and sealed honour scroll was being handed to pretty boy Fey, a storm from on high came down on Lübeck: a direct hit. This unmistakable reproof from heaven terrified the painter in the next to last pew. As pious as his painting, he knew the meaning of thunder and lightning. Time and again, a sudden flash lit up the fraudulent pictures in the nave and choir. Besides, it was sacrilege to hold this ceremony on 1 September, the day when twelve years ago war had been declared on Poland . . .

Moreover, the lightnings followed by God's eternally thunder-ing word reminded him of Palm Sunday 1942 when British planes had emptied their bomb bays over the Inner City of Lübeck. An incendiary bomb had penetrated the roof of Saint Mary's Church

[276]

and set the brick building so thoroughly on fire that the big bell came tumbling into the nave and the finger-thick whitewash, laid on layer after layer, which since the Reformation had kept the interior of the church soberly Protestant, cracked off the walls, revealing the contours and coloured fields of Gothic murals: fragmentary hints, no more, the crumbling afterglow of spent beauty. And from these remnants, which had become more and more scant since that fiery night, not Fey, who had received the honour scroll and at whom the Chancellor may have winked, had created the Lübeck miracle, but Malskat; he and no one else.

His saints. Three metres high in the choir, two in the nave. In the nave mounted on columns, in the choir under canopies. Yes, indeed. Romanesque, Byzantine, even Coptic trappings were decidedly becoming to them. Under straight hems, on finlike feet turned upward and outward, the saints face one another in silence and yet they are eloquent, when for instance the Resurrection in the fourth vault makes answer to the Crucifixion in the south vault. The St Bartholemew in the third vault, the one with the knife, earned the special praise of the art historians who in June 1951, when the whole project was almost finished, climbed the great scaffold under Fey's guidance.

On the occasion Malskat had slipped away to one side of the scaffolding. Unseen, he laughed at Fey's orotund explanations: He, he and no one else. He had done, he knew, he was certain of all the details. Fey attributed certain flaws, details which Malskat in his haste had forgotten to execute, such as the wound in the left hand of the resurrected Christ or the stigmata on both St Francis's hands, to omissions by the High Gothic master of the choir and nave; even in those days, it seems, artists had been pressed for time.

Tall, gaunt and stocking-capped despite the summer weather, Malskat had listened to these erudite lies. He laughed to himself, as he had early learned to do. It was then that he first decided to divulge his scaffolding secrets.

But when the painter ran to the curator of monuments and to every possible church official, no one would believe him. The protectors of monuments thought he was bragging, the clerics were afraid of scandal. The seventh centenary celebration was coming up. The Chancellor had let it be known that he would attend. This truth-loving Malskat with his wire brush story was a nuisance. 'How can he speak of forgery!' cried the blackskirts. 'A hundred experts, who all say genuine, authentic, epoch-making, can't be wrong.'

That was the era of winking, of appearances, of whitewashing. In the decade of innocent lambs and clean bills of health, of murderers holding public office and Christian hypocrites on the government bench, no one wanted to know too much, regardless of what had happened.

Malskat was about to give up and let well enough alone. If the storm hadn't descended on Lübeck with lightning and God's thundering words, he might have kept his peace. But now that heaven had addressed him directly, the painter gathered up his sketches and models, his diaries and other evidence, hired a lawyer and by denouncing himself brought the untimely truth to light.

Much as his indwelling catheter inconveniences him, he is visibly contented. Striding briskly back and forth, he intones his speech. This time in patent leather shoes. He won't let go. What his head conceives has to take form. Next to the blackboard, on the windowless back wall of his exaggeratedly spacious executive office, a vastly enlarged black-and-white photograph has been affixed; it represents in vertical format the group of three by Malskat's hand which still occupies the seventeenth bay in the clerestory of the nave in Lübeck's church of Saint Mary; only the saints of the choir were expunged after the trial.

With his pointer he points out details: 'The first is holding a sword. The one in the middle a paint brush. The third has a goatee.' Oskar is trying in schoolmasterly fashion to convince me. 'Don't make me laugh!' he cries. 'Call them saints! Sure, sure, I know what you'll say: Scatterbrained Malskat, careless because he was under-paid, forgot to draw those three circles. Just as he neglected here and there to paint a shoe, just as he left out the Lord's wounds and St Francis's stigmata, he simply forgot those haloes. But if we look closely – which not everyone is capable of doing – we recognize a deeper purpose. Those three men, I say, are not incomplete apostles, they are portraits, or if not portraits then idealized representations of our clever painter and two statesmen, or High Muckamucks, as your Rat calls them. No, not at all! I don't mean to say that Malskat decided one day on his high scaffold to say: Hoopla! Now I'm going to paint myself between old Adenauer and Ulbricht, the goatee. No, I prefer to suppose that the spirit of those times dictated that group of three. In a sudden illumination, he saw himself between those two. Or else he unconsciously, innocently as it were, added this profane constellation to his community of saints. I'll go and see him, I'll join Malskat at the Café Niederegger. Over tea and pastry, in a frenzy of enthusiasm, we'll remember who and what contributed to the fraud that was everywhere prevalent in those days. If I didn't have this catheter sticking into me, I'd be on my way right now.'

Lucky he had that trouble. If not for this foreign appendage, he would already be taking consequences as he tends to after a long speech. Our Herr Matzerath is silent. Evidently the past has caught up with him. He pads about uncertainly, looks for a first word; he's found it, for his ring finger – the one with the ruby – beckons me to come close, closer. I have to bend down, smell his cologne, because he wants to whisper. 'You wanted to do away with me, didn't you, to kill me, no less. Your plan to wind up my story in far away Poland, under my grandmother's skirts. A plausible end, but too obvious. Maybe I've outlived myself, but Oskar can't be eliminated like that.'

After granting himself and me as well a pause, our Herr Matzerath says from out of his deep executive chair: 'I can appreciate your tendency to round things out in rather too much of a hurry; besides, I'm aware that my existence bothers you, you'd like to stop me from interfering. You want to get rid of me. So that in the future no one can point at me when he means you. In short, if it were up to you, I'd already be written off . . .'

This of course I deny. But despite my protests he continues to impute homicidal intentions to me. 'Why deny that you were planning to celebrate my impending birthday with a cleverly anticipated obituary? A fatal case of uraemia would have suited you; just the right death for yours truly. Luckily my chauffeur foiled your plan by leaving the autobahn at Helmstedt and taking me straight to the best urologist in town. Think of it: one thousand four hundred and seventy milligrams of urine in my bladder . . .'

Which brought our Herr Matzerath, decidedly alive, back to the familiar details. Since it became necessary to fit him out with a catheter, his ego has taken on new substance. Nothing can divert him from the helpful little tube and its stopper. 'What a simple, what an ingenious invention!' he cries, and never wearies of explaining how thanks to the special type of catheter that has been introduced into his urethra, a cherry-sized ball can be blown up near its tip, which retains it in the bladder and gives the wearer a sense of security. 'You see,' he says, 'that's characteristic of man. However desperate the situation, he manages to help himself.'

He dismissed my objection that his present condition, which, as no one, not even he would deny, tends to be degenerative, was beyond the powers of any helpful catheter to rectify. 'Cassandra!' he cried. 'All around me I hear Cassandras. Look at it this way: my demise was meticulously planned, and yet I've returned, though ailing, from the fields of Kashubia. Admittedly, an operation will be inevitable as soon as I reach the age of sixty, but you may be sure that I run no risk of being removed from this world; on the contrary, it is you who have vanished and are flying around as if some magician – if only as a joke – had hexed you into a space capsule . . .'

Was it necessary, She-rat? Was it necessary that a Big Bang should put an end to everything that was going on? And must I now take the most niggardly care of the diminutive Oskar, now shrunk to the size of an altar ornament, in order, with scarcely a time lapse, to listen to the drivel of this Herr Matzerath, who goes on making plans and giving signs of life all over the place? Will nothing, not even the Third Programme, stop? And is there nothing for me to do, while you rat nations bring in harvest after harvest and heap up sunflower seeds, but to report on the drifting wreck, because the women had hardly caught sight of Vineta below them when they were extinguished? Am I to think up nothing but obituaries?

Quickly diverted, brought close to them; for women have sometimes favoured me with their feelings: one affectionate, as though thinking of herself, the second violent and impatient, the third on special occasions, the fourth persistent, the fifth took full possession of me and holds it to this day: Damroka . . .

You will admit, She-rat: something has always been missing, or else some residues have been complaining. Never have I been at home as I wanted. My ball has always had a dent in it. That is why I thought up a ship manned with women. Just as an experiment – just to see what would come of it – it pleased me to send them all harmoniously on a voyage, though they were all deadly enemies and avoided one another with care. That's women for you, as people used to say. But you, She-rat, put a sudden end to my attempt to see them all as sisters. Ah, if I could only be expunged along with them, leaving no trace.

But you want me to write. So I write: The wreck is drifting in an easterly direction.

Once the Baltic Sea is spread out under my space capsule, you say, I should keep an eye on the drifting wreck.

But the wreck matters only to you, I wrote it off long ago, just as I wanted to write off our Herr Matzerath. What does he want now? Why is he always butting in? What am I supposed to do with the damned wreck?

The women, along with the black-bordered, blue-painted super-structure, vanished in flame. How I miss them. With them I was pathetic and magnificent. Love! That, She-rat, is something you know nothing about. That feeling of too-much and never-enough. All you rats want is to live and survive. Keep an eye on the wreck, you say. Something is moving on it, young friend, something is moving.

Yes, planks are rattling. Remnants of rail bend and fall over-board. What else is supposed to be moving? Ghosts? Mirrored wishes? Or would tapes be playing themselves on the tape recorder?

I don't hear a thing. No medusas singing. The sea is sometimes smooth and sometimes rough and no longer darkened by dust storms. It glitters rejuvenated, maybe it smells as it did when I was a child and summer after summer . . .

Maybe the sea is new, maybe it's breathing, alive again, inhabited once more by plankton, herring larvae, medusas and strange fish, fish that will one day become land animals. Maybe in the depths of the sea the Flounder is rising from his bed of sand, as you rats rise from your holes. Maybe something will come along. But only the wreck is left. Drifting lifelessly. Though always on an easterly course, even when the current runs the opposite way.

The She-rat has advised me to think back. Remember, she cried, what happened on Gotland just before Doomsday, when your broads went ashore in Visby. All five together, so enterprising. Their exaggerated sailor's gait. Come on, young friend. Re-member!

At first the daintiest of them, the Old Woman, the grey-haired one, who was always cooking and washing up, wanted to stay on board and guard the ship. But then – yes, I remember – it was decided that all should go ashore. They wanted to stir up that tourist museum, that collection of ruins. What do you mean stir up? First a bit of shopping: Swedish frozen food. Aquavit nowhere to be found. But plenty of processions. The protest marches usual in those days. Well, against this, that and the other, and for peace. Very young and fairly old Gotlanders in gym shoes and rubber boots. Was it raining? Drizzling. A lousy summer. But perfectly peaceful behind painted slogans. Well rehearsed and only half awake, the Gotlanders plodded through the town. Against all sorts of things that were described as dangerous on placards and sandwich boards. Sure, She-rat, I don't mind remembering what was timely just before Doomsday. Oil pollution and pauperization, the armaments race and the dying forests. Just as I said: against this, that and the other. And some were for Jesus. Oh yes, another thing: one group was against experimentation with animals.

That's it! said the She-rat. At last! And what happened then? Did they just run around?

My five women, who had dressed fit to kill for their shore leave, joined this not very long procession which in addition to placards carried over-lifesize dummies representing hand-painted dogs and rhesus monkeys – some even wore rat and mouse masks. One of my women was wearing something long and golden yellow, another a turban and baggy Turkish-style trousers, the third a black silk . . .

The She-rat told me to stick to the subject. When I made fun of the women for running around with the protectors of animals when only yesterday they had been netting and measuring jellyfish, she again interrupted my report, which, I have to admit, was getting rather personal.

That is of no interest! she cried. No battle of the sexes can interest us today, only what happened in Visby.

Okay. There was a riot. In the outskirts, in a research institute. A branch of Uppsala. I don't believe any of the Gotland people, young or old, started it. Probably the engineer or the Old Woman threw the first stone. And then the helmswoman started in. In any case Damroka, who was ordinarily the slowest, was the first to go inside. Followed by the other women and then by the Gotlanders. Later it was said they'd behaved like Vandals. Smashed some rather expensive instruments in the laboratories. And then before you knew it the cages opened. A liberated monkey was said to have bitten a Swedish librarian, and that had consequences, because the monkey . . .

No digressions. Keep going, the She-rat insisted.

Rabbits and dogs, all the rhesus monkeys and guinea pigs, even a few mice were caught later on. Naturally the women went back to their boat when the blue-blinking police car arrived. They cast off quick and beat it for Vineta. They didn't want any trouble. Because it seems that two dozen rats, especially interesting ones, had escaped and were last seen on the waterfront by a Finnish sailor, but he was drunk . . .

There we have it! cried the She-rat, her whiskers standing on end. Then she ordered me to keep on observing the drifting wreck. It had long vanished from sight, she said, hiding itself even from me, the man with the panoramic view. You remember, young friend, just after the Big Bang, the thick layer of soot-saturated smoke that lay over land and sea. The Earth was without light. Neither you nor we rats can say how long the darkness lasted. Or what happened to the drifting wreck in those days – or was it months or years? – of cold. Did it drift about coffined in blackness? Or did it get stuck in the permafrost? Had there been life, any form of life in the hull of the ship, we rats often wonder, how could it have survived?

Exactly! I cried. Nobody could have come through, not even a bedbug. That wreck should be written off. There's nothing more to be got out of it. So should our Herr Matzerath. Away with him. All that is ancient history. Tell me instead, She-rat, how your agriculture is doing. Has the spring been too wet? Have the last harvests been good? Have you been rotating your crops?

Natcherly, young master, cried the She-rat, in her broad rural accent. And I saw fields reaching out to the horizon, turnips, corn, barley, sunflowers. How heavily bowed were the flower heads. I saw seeds in orderly lines. I saw bright-coloured birds above the fields. A beautiful dream.

No sooner have the Grimm Brothers gone than Rumpelstiltskin, the waiter, cries out: 'Kindly have patience!' He's serving drinks outside the house. Cheerful and receptive to little jokes, groups stand about chatting, as though the witch had invited the characters of widely known fairy tales to a cocktail party. They exchange old-fashioned courtesies, yet tensions carried over from times gone-by make themselves felt. The bad fairies can't refrain from making nasty remarks about the good fairies. The brave little tailor tries to pick a fight with the Wild Men. Quarrelsome dwarfs and woodsprites are everywhere under foot. The witch and the wicked stepmother look daggers at each other. Rübezahl has offended Mother Holle. Little Red Riding Hood tries to vamp Hansel. When the frog king refuses to plunge into the well, Gretel tries to take refuge inside the wolf, but his zipper gets stuck. Little Red Riding Hood's grandmother reads archaic words from the dictionary, but no one is listening. There are greater attractions. Merlin the Magician and King Thrushbeard hold court. Dwarfs and woodsprites try to push their way in. The lesser witches want to be there too. 'Even I,' cries Thrushbeard, 'would have no objection to Jakob Grimm as chancellor.' Merlin, who had just been talking about intrigues at King Arthur's table, concedes: 'Yes, our people would always be willing to tolerate the Grimm Brothers.' All laugh and drink to the health of the new government.

Only the girl with the chopped-off hands is sad. Her hands hang listlessly on the string around her neck. She shuffles from one chatting group to another, declines the drink Rumpelstiltskin offers her, takes no interest in Rübezahl's boasting about the days when he frightened poor charcoal burners and glass blowers, looks on with dismay as one dwarf after another drags Snow White into the bushes, becomes sadder than ever each time she runs into Jorinde and Joringel, and finally slips away into the Gingerbread House, where Rapunzel, with whose hair the prince is tied, is sitting on the window ledge beside the wicked stepmother, and the curtains are blowing.

The prince is still kissing the doll copied from his Sleeping Beauty. Rapunzel and the wicked stepmother are playing cat's cradle, a tricky game played with string. For a long while the girl with chopped-off hands looks on.

At last she plucks up courage and says: 'Could I see my father striking the two axe blows?' When the wicked stepmother consents, the girl's hands, to be helpful, take the cat's cradle, so enabling the wicked stepmother to press a button on the magic box. When the screen starts to flicker, the wicked stepmother takes back the cat's cradle and holds it out to Rapunzel, who modifies it in taking it.

The magic mirror now shows one fairy-tale scene after another. We see the seven dwarfs around Snow White's glass coffin; Rumpelstiltskin in a rage pulls his leg off; the kids escape, one into the clock case; the golden ball of the child who will grow up to be the lady with the perpetual headache falls into the well; finally, the magic mirror shows the girl with the chopped-off hands.

Huddled on a stool close to the mirror, her tied hands in her lap, the girl sees her father, at the bidding of the Devil to whom in his distress he has sold himself, strike two axe blows, how she then, her chopped-off hands dangling from a string, wanders forlorn and aimless through the world, how in the end a prince helps her to embrace a particular tree in love, whereupon her hands grew again and she lived happily with the prince.

But in spite of the cat's cradle the wicked stepmother keeps an eye on the fairy-tale film and, since it's her nature to be wicked, manipulates the plot with her little finger. From then on the scenes change quickly: the father swings the axe twice, the prince helps the girl to hug the tree, again the terrible father, again the helpful prince, again the axe; brief happiness and horror without end.

As in the film the hands of the girl on the stool grow again, then again lie severed on her knees. Over and over again, with no relief.

Meanwhile the cocktail party goes on and on. Some of the fairy-tale characters play their roles. A wolf's face appears under Little Red Riding Hood's grandmother's nightcap. The witch makes brooms dance. Rübezahl bends iron bars. As though sleepwalking, the frog king's lady carries her frog from group to group on a tray. Hansel and Gretel get the last beech nuts and hazelnuts out of the slot-machine in the Gingerbread House. The good and bad fairies change one another into scarecrows. Cinderella and King Thrushbeard, the steadfast tin soldier and Mother Holle are also in love with their roles. They forget themselves completely in playing themselves. Snow White refuses to go into the bushes with one dwarf after another and prefers to be a thousand times more beautiful, regardless of for whom. Thus fairy tale merges with fairy tale. Jorinde lies with the tin soldier. Joringel lies with Cinderella. Only the witch remains true to herself and Hansel: bedded between her enormous tits, he dreams of what goes on behind the hawthorn bush and of other things as well.

The wicked stepmother and Rapunzel are also immersed in their game. While taking the cat's cradle from each other time and time again, they fail to see the kissing prince throw off the trammels of Rapunzel's hair, jump out of the window, and, as the forest is just behind the house, escape with a few leaps.

Nor does the girl with the chopped-off hands notice, for she is still watching her film, into which another prince has just brought happiness, which, however, is shortlived; the wicked stepmother is still manipulating with her little finger.

Outside, the cocktail party is breaking up. Violent gusts of wind. Those who have bedded down in pairs suddenly feel cold. They rush distraught into the house. While continuing to serve tea and fruit juice, waiter Rumpelstiltskin says: 'I wonder if the Grimm Brothers have formed a good government.'

The fairy-tale characters are startled back to reality. The girl, whose hands have again been chopped off in the film and lie severed on her lap, is roughly pushed away by the dwarfs. The wicked stepmother stops playing cat's cadle and switches the magic mirror to Bonn. All, including Rapunzel, now with long hair, crowd together in their eagerness to see what is happening far away.

In Bonn greenery is still proliferating. Ivy and vines creep into the windows of the chancellery and the council chamber where the Grimm brothers are holding the first meeting of their emergency cabinet, consisting of bishops, generals and professors. They pass around the lily pads inscribed with the demands of the fairy-tale characters: pure air, clean water, wholesome fruit. The bishops and professors nod thoughtfully, cautiously. The generals sit motionless at the conference table, annoyed by the greenery assailing them on all sides. The industrialists are indignant. They gesticulate and pound the green felt table top. Arguments and secret whisperings. Under the table, where a thicket is growing, banknotes are slipped to the professors and bishops.

Now all are talking except the Grimm Brothers. Even the bishops, though regretfully, oppose the three demands, simple as they look, modest as they are. For the first time, Jakob Grimm pounds the green table angrily. Only his brother is startled. The industrialists and generals put on an expression of condescending surprise, the professors of dismay.

Jakob cries out: 'I am still Chancellor, I and no one else.'

Wilhelm backs him up: 'And don't forget it!'

The response is laughter, in which the bishops join, though with restraint.

The group in the Gingerbread House see Wilhelm Grimm telling the amused cabinet about the three good fairies. All are spellbound by what is going on in Bonn. Alarmed, they see how little weight the words of the Grimm Brothers carry.

Suddenly Gretel cries out: 'The prince. Where's the prince?' Dismay, confusion, mindless searching. Rübezahl hits the seven dwarfs. The witch grabs Rapunzel by the hair and reaches for her scissors. But then the wicked stepmother says: 'He can't have gone far.'

She switches off the Bonn programme, in which Wilhelm Grimm is still raving about the good fairies, and turns the dial until the running prince appears on the screen.

The witch, Merlin and the wicked stepmother take turns in hurling curses and magic spells after the fugitive. The prince stumbles, falls, somersaults, but runs on. He grows a long nose, bat's ears. And still he runs and runs. The spells increase, outdo one another, cancel one another out; he turns into a deer, a unicorn, a rubber ball, and still he leaps, trots, rolls onward. And now a prince again in every way, he reaches the edge of the woods, finds his way to the overgrown autobahn and, after stripping the greenery from a road sign, runs on to Bonn.

In the Gingerbread House Merlin the magician and the wicked stepmother are arguing. (Herr Matzerath wants the furious fiery-eyed witch to reach for her scissors after all, but the idea of a bald Rapunzel doesn't appeal to me, and I rescue her long hair by playing Hansel off against the witch.) As though he had grown to manhood behind the hawthorn bush, he takes the scissors away from her, saying: 'That won't get us anywhere.'

Gretel cries out: 'While there's life there's hope.'

At Hansel's order, the wicked stepmother switches the magic mirror back to the cabinet meeting. Supported by his brother, Jakob Grimm is still resisting the corrupt emergency government. Industrialists are whispering with generals. Under the table, professors are counting thousand-mark notes. Above the table bishops smile as only bishops can smile, while twiddling their thumbs or leafing through their breviaries.

Jakob Grimm shouts: 'I still set the policy here.'

The industrialists tear up the lily pads. One of them cries out: 'But we have the say!'

Another: 'No one can stop us!'

All shout: 'Down with fairy tales!'

We see Wilhelm Grimm in tears. Jakob sits down exhausted. One of the generals presses a button, which brings the police into the room. The Grimm Brothers are arrested. Quickly another general takes the Chancellor's chair.

Though the professors have their doubts, the Grimm Brothers are handcuffed. Wilhelm says: 'You see, brother, such disrespect has always been our lot.'

Jakob says: 'We shall resist nevertheless. I shall write a memorandum.' Both are to be led away by the guard.

The kissing prince runs in breathless. Throwing kisses into the air, he reports: 'I've been, I was, but I ran, ran, and now I'm here!'

Seeing the Grimm Brothers in handcuffs, he makes a courtly bow and says: 'Gentlemen, I dutifully offer you my help and support. But I must insist that you release the esteemed Grimm Brothers at once.'

When the generals and industrialists seem undecided, the prince explains. 'Let us understand one another. Without me and my kisses Operation Wake Sleeping Beauty cannot succeed. Have I made myself clear?'

While the generals confer with the industrialists, one of the bishops, on instructions from the fresh-baked General-Chancellor, removes the Grimm Brothers' handcuffs, while the other smiles benignly. The new Chancellor says: 'Let us be merciful and content ourselves with house arrest. That will enable our friends to rest and to write whatever they please. Fairy tales for all I care.'

Obligingly, the professors give the Grimm Brothers their hats. Jakob and Wilhelm take their hats and leave the room, saddened but unbowed.

As I agree with our Herr Matzerath that unhappiness in the Gingerbread House should not be faded in at this point, the scene belongs to the kissing prince. On a large map of the forest, he shows where the hedge of thorns has imprisoned the sleeping Sleeping Beauty, the sleeping Chancellor and his soundly sleeping entourage.

Immediate burst of activity. 'Alert stage three!' 'Order to special troop!' 'Focus on Sleeping Beauty awakening.'

Telephones are hidden under the proliferating greenery. Commands are issued. In anticipation of his happiness, the kissing prince kisses both bishops, then tosses kisses into the air. (Our Herr Matzerath says quite correctly: It's a disease. Nay more: In kisses lurks death.)

> Don't touch it.
> Woe, someone is bending down,
> casting a shadow, taking action.

Never again shall some stupid prince
play his part to the end
in order that the cook may give the kitchen boy
a resounding box on the ear
and that further consequences inevitably.

One kiss suffices to undo.
After that all who were asleep
continue more horribly than ever
as though nothing had happened.

But Sleeping Beauty's sleep still
holds captive all those who
if released would warrant fear.

In the Third Programme, as in all other radio programmes, a number of air raid drills were announced today. The wailing of the sirens is to be modulated so as to have different meanings. Crescendo and decrescendo, sostenuto and so on. These things must be learned. All are therefore requested to switch on their radios at certain hours and tune in on important instructions. These instructions must be followed. Those of us whose ears are still ringing with warning and all-clear signals from the last war are called upon to refresh our fears.

Later on, my Christmas rat and I hear a significant wailing of sirens. The shipyard nearby is equipped for peacetime conditions and for emergencies. We distinguished pre-alert, alert and all clear. It came off as announced. Now we know.

Strangely enough, the graduated wailing gave one a sense of security by making it appear that someone was caring for us. We won't be taken by surprise.

Then we listened to Educational Radio: something about coping with traffic, then something about behaviour modification of violence-prone children, then 'People Talking'. At the start of the news, we were told to regard the failure of the Brussels summit as no more than a temporary setback; toward the end of the news a success was reported; scientists in Uppsala, Sweden, had succeeded in isolating genes derived from Egyptian mummies two thousand four hundred years old and reproducing them in tissue cultures: progress!

My Christmas rat and I agree: These news reports are a fake. It's true that things are still happening, but nothing functions any more. The Third Programme, whether dealing with Brussels or with Uppsala, has run out of steam. Such happening is mere reflex, deferment, desecration of mummies. But while I curse the Brussels knights of the expense account and the Swedish gene-iuses – just imagine, they transfer mummified information to brand-new live cells! – my little rat curls up sleepily, as though from her point of view there was no cause for her whiskers to take notice.

So I tell her what I learned recently in Hamelin, when, deviating from the festival programme, I visited the crypt of Saint Boniface.

Now, little rat, I know the truth. That was after the children's crusades and a good sixty years before the Plague. The people were pretty mixed up in those days. No one knew right from wrong. For years there had been no emperor, only murder and assault. Everyone did as he pleased and grabbed what he needed. And everywhere there was ground for fear. Fear of things to come. Just plain fear. Young men and women roamed in all directions, through town and country, up the Rhine. They danced like maniacs, they lashed themselves bloody. Their songs, their flagellants' howling frightened the Jews, because driven by fear the flagellants killed the Jews.

But other young people, more sensible and less fearful, travelled eastward, to Moravia and Poland, to Kashubia and the land of the Vinetans, where they settled the shores of the Baltic Sea. In Hamelin there seem to have been a hundred and thirty young men and women, who on St John's Day, which fell on 26 June 1284, followed a recruiter who was said to have played the flute beautifully.

Believe me, Ratkin, there's not a word about rats in any chronicles. No scholar has ever been able to prove that the flautist was a ratcatcher on the side. And even the philosopher Leibniz was only speculating when he suggested – as was only too plausible – a belated children's crusade. One thing is certain: the rats were a fiction, tacked on to the story because people said that anyone who leads our children away – even to a more prosperous foreign land – is a ratcatcher; anyone who catches rats catches children as well and leads them away.

But since visiting the crypt of Saint Boniface cathedral, I am convinced that something entirely different happened. Hamelin has always been full of mills and storehouses, and of rats as well.

Obviously people who lived by the grain trade were no lovers of rats. Every miller, grain dealer, and master of the related guilds looked upon rats as an unmitigated plague. But, because the times were so topsy-turvy, their children began to play with rats. Perhaps it was largely to annoy their parents that they fed the rats and carried them about, as some misbehaved children do today. And like today's punks the Hamelin children carried their pet rats on their shoulders, embedded in their hair, or under their shirts. Rats could be seen peering out of pockets and sacks.

That led to bad tempers, to family quarrels. The aldermen voted a law forbidding anyone to play with rats, to feed them or carry them about on one's person. For fear of punishment a few children and young people complied. But a hundred and thirty Hamelin children and young people did not. They defied the law, banded together with the rats, and paraded up and down Baker Street, down Cathedral Street to the river Weser, past the watermills, through the Wendish Quarter to the market and Rathaus, which they occupied for several hours and blasphemously renamed Rat House. They even took their rats with them to mass and vespers services in Saint Boniface. The rats, said the official reports, had made them mad.

A child or two was whipped in the marketplace and put in the stocks, but as the incorrigible rat lovers included children of the most respected citizens, even the sons and daughters of aldermen, the magistrates could not resort to torture, such as racking, pinching and scorching with red-hot tongs.

But when there were rumours of black masses and a rat cult, and the cathedral crypt was mentioned again and again; when the hundred and thirty began to dress rat style; when, putting on naked tails, they looted bakeries and butcher shops in broad daylight; when they grew wilder and wilder and more and more like their rats, the tanners and porters began to grumble about parental permissiveness. Seditious talk was heard at guild meetings. Dominicans thundered from the pulpits against the human rat rabble.

Finally, under clerical pressure and also no doubt for fear of the rebellious guilds, the aldermen and magistrates, meeting in secret session, decided on a drastic countermeasure. A piper unknown in the town, skilled in playing the flute and bagpipes, was paid earnest money to come and make himself popular with the perverse children. One day – St John's Day it was – playing the flute, he led them through the West Gate as though to a happy outing. He led them to a deep cave in the nearby Calvary Mountain, and there he staged a lavish party for the hundred and thirty Hamelin children and their pet rats. Pork sausages were grilled and barley beer drunk. The rats are said to have joined in dancing the round. The singing, it seems, was hellish.

But when the party was at its height and the barley beer had steeped the children in lethargy, the piper crept out of the cave. Then the entrance, as wide as a barn door, was sealed by the town constable, walled in by masons, covered over by peasants with cartloads of sand, and sprinkled mercilessly with holy water by priests. It appears that not much screaming was heard from the cave. Rumours that circulated later spoke of a single escaped rat.

Great was the lamentation over the lost children. Nevertheless, the piper was paid in coin of the realm. And the town was soon richer by a legend. The ambiguous word 'exodus' was entered in the town chronicle. Ever since then a reputation for perfidy has attached to Hamelin. There will be vengeance, little rat, there will surely be vengeance.

The children are more and more afraid.
They dye their hair loud colours.
They paint their faces mould-gray
or chalk-white
to frighten fear away.
Lost to us, they scream silently.

My friend, grown older with me
– we seldom see each other, exchange greetings from a distance –
the one with the flute, whose cadences
never come out twice the same,
often came close to losing his son
and now lost him for good.

Sons raised biblically or some other way
run away young.
No one wants to be around any more when his father dies,
wait for his blessing, take guilt upon himself.
Our increasingly rebated forgiveness moves no one but ourselves.

Such a life isn't worthwhile.
For this stretch of the way – made to our measure –
they have no time.
What we endured, encouraging one another with jokes,
seems to have become unbearable.
They don't even feel like opposing an angry no
to our conscientious yes.
They simply switch off.

Ah, dear friend, what taught us
such longlived doubt?
Since when have we been straying so consistently toward goals?
Why are we possible without the slightest meaning?

How I worry about my sons, about myself;
for even mothers, practised in all-understanding,
are at their wits' ends.

It's drifting, no, keeping to its course. No longer due eastward despite the headwind. No, the wreck of the onetime sailing barge, then coastal motor barge *Ilsebill*, lastly the research ship *New Ilsebill*, puts about off the Hela Peninsula, circumnavigates the peninsula, which the flood reduced to a mere spit of land, but which is now growing, transforming the bay into a lagoon, takes a southerly course into the lagoon, and heads, if that can be said of a wreck, for the breakwater and harbour of the city of Gdańsk, which with the towers of the old Hanseatic city of Danzig is still recognizable from afar and exerts an irresistible attraction; how otherwise would I, time and again, and why would this helpless wreck be drawn to it now?

The wreck is moving at half speed. This I see from my space capsule, under which the Baltic Sea shimmers from time to time. What other places lie below me on my prescribed orbiting course, the Nile delta or the Bay of Bengal for instance, or the Greater or Lesser Sunda Islands, reveal nothing through the veils of mist, but when coming from the north I pursue my orbit and the coast of Sweden takes form, then the Baltic Sea, my sea lies like a pond, clearly outlined at my feet. True, Gotland, Bornholm, and the rest of the islands are there no more, but above Scania I discern agricultural structures, cultivated fields.

I am able to bring the wreck, which is no longer drifting but keeping its course, very close. This I can do thanks to my system of lenses. It's summer. In the back country ripening sunflowers and other crops give evidence of life. Already I'm tempted to call: Earth, come in, Earth, answer me, Earth. But I know there's no one left to call back: Roger. And: What's up, Charlie? She alone can answer. She entertains me with news, claims to know more than I can see with my own eyes, ferrets out sensations. She even hears . . .

Listen! cries the She-rat. Chugging. Listen carefully: that's a ship's engine chugging. You ought to be pleased, young master. Your *Ilsebill* is manned. How, otherwise, could the engine? If it's not your broads, someone must have. It was a total wreck. And now it's running. That good old diesel engine. Just listen. Like clockwork.

I'd never seen her more excited, running around the harbour basin. Now on the island, now back and forth on Long Bridge, now in the shipyard area, now on top of the quay wall. Finally she jumped up on a bollard, cast about for words, couldn't finish a sentence. Young master, young friend, she cried. Is it possible? In spite of the cold, the ice, the darkness? In spite of the dust storms and those damned rays that even we can hardly. And yet, because some time ago. Inconceivable. Possibly just a few specimens. See how expectantly we. Full of hope. But also of fear . . .

Not only the She-rat on the bollard, whole nations of rats have occupied the waterfront. Dense crowds of them everywhere, on every crane, on the slipways of the Lenin Shipyard, atop the silos of the sulphur port, which they normally avoided, on the towering walls of the drydock. In every spot that offered a view; on the Island where the Mottlau and the Dead Vistula converge, on both banks of the Mottlau. In Neufahrwasser, which used to be called Novy Port and whose residential quarters as far as Wrzeszcz are submerged by walls of mud which, now planted with garden crops, sunflowers for the most part, form a green belt enclosing the harbour as far as the breakwater. Rats, everywhere rats, restless, driven by curiosity, piled high, tied into thick knots.

And when the chugging of the 180 hp engine could no longer be doubted and ceased to be a mere wish, when, because silence prevailed, this one sound filled my whole dream, because the rats kept rigidly still; when rumour became news that what was left of the erstwhile research ship would not put into the modern Overseas

Port but was heading for the old, historic port, by whose Long Bridge only two excursion steamers, which had formerly been white, had been moored since Doomsday; when finally the chugging wreck, whose bare deck remained uninhabited, stopped beside the ruins of the warehouses dating back to the Second World War and the rebuilt warehouses of the interwar period, and docked with flawless seamanship across from the Long Bridge; when among the rat nations the news circulated that the Awaited Ones had at last made fast to Warehouse Island, formerly known as Spichlerze, the rats poured from the shipyard and harbour section of the New City, from Neufahrwasser and the mud walls to the Old City and Right City, through their streets to the Mottlau port, so that, soon after the wreck docked, Lady Gate, Bakers' Gate, Green Gate and Holy Ghost Gate were clogged, the waterfront overflowing, the windows and gables of the Gothic buildings facing the Mottlau festooned with rats.

The rusty excursion steamers were overloaded. Every place offering a view was taken. The observatory tower was overrun with rats. The charred remains of Crane Gate were full up. The figures adorning the broad-beamed Green Gate were unrecognizable. Only the shore of Warehouse Island, lined with rats only a short while before, had emptied when the wreck landed. And empty it remained as though to leave room for the coming event.

Call it respect or fear; in either case distance was in order. Yes, we sensed that something was coming, but we didn't know what it would look like. Collective prayer had summoned up images, but too many of them; they cancelled one another out. Although our singing in Saint Mary's – you've seen us often enough gathered in our devotions – aimed at the return of humankind – and we included the Ancient One and her shrunken little boy in every prayer – we had no clear notion of the form in which man would be resurrected for us, we had not so much as an inkling of his outline.

No wonder, the She-rat went on, that speculation ran wild. What will he be like? Of normal size as we knew him? Outsized? One-eyed, or peering about him with four eyes? Even though we had decorated the high altar of our principal church with lifelike groups of those blue-and-white dwarfs, those toys in human form that were mass-produced toward the end of the human era, we hoped that man would not be given back to us in diminutive form. Our expectations had remained vague. And yet we should have known or suspected what was in store for us. Tested, subjected to long series of experiments. Treated to poisons and antidotes in the interest of human-oriented research, and toward the end actually honoured and awarded a prize, we knew what the human mind had finally thought up in its determination – that was their declared purpose – to improve the human race. But eagerly as we had looked forward to it, what turned up, what came to light so to speak, horrified us.

As soon as the wreck came alongside between two bollards, we brought sunflowers, extra-large turnips, ears of corn, plucked wood pigeons and sparrows, and arranged them around the bollards – hurriedly, because we didn't want to be there when they emerged. Have I already told you that hordes of rats, bundled together in the ringing chambers of Saint Mary's and of other churches, managed to get the bells ringing? Hundreds of stout old rats clung to the ropes. Anyway, when the awaited ones appeared and we froze in expectation, the bells rang as in human times.

I saw them emerging from the forecastle hatch, climbing upright, striding, then standing. I saw them negligently exchanging free-moving leg with supporting leg. They must have been about the size of a three-year-old child. Hairy only in places, both sexes showed human proportions. But though I was unable to detect so much as the stump of a tail, they showed oversized rat heads on long necks.

The She-rat had her place across the way, on the roof cornice of the Green Gate. At first, she said, they acted as if they hadn't yet noticed us. The bells went on ringing. Moving up and down the deck, they limbered up, stretched, shook themselves. Only then did they wave casually in the direction of the throng on the opposite shore and on the gables and towers and gates of the city. Though up until then we had been pushing and shoving to get a better view, we now froze. Believe us, my boy. Not a single restless tail. No sign of emotion except in the whiskers. Horror? No doubt. But also disappointment and a slight desire to laugh, to laugh at the Awaited Ones when they had hardly arrived. But the horror predominated. Thank God, the bells died down little by little.

I saw what the She-rat showed me. I was rather amused. I laughed in my dream. When the hairy rat-men – or hominid rats – there were five of them, then seven, and finally twelve – made the wreck fast to the bollards and two or three of them went ashore, they saw what the hospitable rats had piled up for them. Without ceremony they set to and gobbled up turnips, corn and sunflowers, cobs, flower heads and all. They didn't touch the pigeons and sparrows. Evidently repelled by the raw meat, they tossed the plucked cadavers into the Mottlau.

It was then that the last of the bells stopped ringing. Throwing off their trancelike rigidity, the rat nations withdrew from windows, from gables and gate turrets, from the shore installations of the Long Bridge, from the excursion steamers at the foot of the ruined Crane Gate. A soundless retreat, which I interpreted as disappointment. No doubt they gathered in Saint Mary's, where they went to pray and ponder.

Later, when I would have liked to dream something else, the She-rat said without entering into the picture: And for this preposterous product of human science – you can't have forgotten, pal – we were awarded the Nobel Prize. For achievement in the field of genetics! And this, as you see, is what came of it: rat-men or hominoid rats. The Awaited Ones. A caricature of our hopes.

At first we called them the Newcomers. For a time we spoke of Manippels, or Nippels for short. Then finally we remembered those two honoured gentlemen, who toward the end of the human era revealed the DNA structure, split the cell nucleus, elucidated chains of genes; their names were Watson and Crick and since then we've called the Newcomers Watsoncricks. Having a longer period of gestation – eighteen weeks – and smaller litters – four or five infants – they reproduced more slowly than we did. Incidentally, five of the twelve Watsoncricks who came ashore were females and pregnant. We should have destroyed them all, destroyed them at once.

I've told our Herr Matzerath about the landing of the rat-men. He thinks their small size is adequate and speaks of them as all in all a successful project. Too much mail on my desk, but no news from Travemünde. Lately I've been dreaming repetitions and variants. Quick as a flash the witch cuts off Rapunzel's long hair with a pair of scissors the wicked stepmother has handed her; unasked, the She-rat keeps projecting that one scene on my monitor: how first the women's hair – Damroka's curls! – catch fire, and then they go up in flames altogether. No. What seems more likely is that the women turn paler and paler, until nothing remains of them but traces of paint on crumbling lime mortar, which painter Malskat, now on orders from our Herr Matzerath, wipes away with a scrubbing brush, before putting in, with a sure hand, five women, all of whom, however, look like the movie actress Hansi Knoteck and not one the least bit like my Damroka.

Still no postcard from Travemünde. In the Third Programme life goes on, and as promised my Christmas rat gets fresh straw each week. In Hamelin the festivities come to an end uneventfully. On the other hand, I dream, in instalments, the news from Uppsala that the cloned isolated genes of Egyptian mummies are beginning to reproduce. This gives the Watsoncricks, no sooner landed, ancient Egyptian profiles; as in the days of Ramses I, they stand or stride like statues, with square shoulders and stylized hands, feet and navel; and even their rat heads seem to have originated in the Nile Delta.

This our Herr Matzerath finds unacceptable. He wants to give the newcomers a Swedish imprint. But he agrees with me when of the twelve I make special mention of four or five, because they wear jewellery. No sooner have they decided on their first shore leave than I see them wearing silver pendants, necklaces with ivory, onyx and gold links. That, I cry out in my dream, is a belt wrought of fine silver wire, which I last saw in the midst of the bric-à-brac in Damroka's sea bag; and it's not too tight around the waist of that exceedingly pregnant Watsoncrick. And long ago I gave the oceanographer that coral chain adorning the neck of another Swedish Manippel – though she had probably forgotten it – when we were still on loving terms, I also recognize various pieces from the helmswoman's jewel box, which she never wearied of wearing, though it didn't last long between us. Earrings! One of the female rat-men – pregnant as they all were – is wearing earrings with big rocks on them; if I only knew to whom I gave these treasures when – I haven't forgotten the prices – for her birthday, for Christmas or for Mother's Day . . .

On this subject the Rat of my dreams says: The world may end, but your womanizings will go on for ever. Look a little more closely, Pops. Rings that you picked up at junkshops, bought after brief bargaining and were at all times ready to give away, are now being worn by male Nippels – on their thumbs, oddly enough.

Again the witch picks up the scissors to make the shorn Rapunzel cry. Then I see Malskat, once again at work high in the scaffolding, impose Egyptian severity on his Gothic murals without fear of incongruity; what he accomplishes with swift brush strokes is a self-portrait: young, with a bit of the Eulenspiegel about him, he squeezes himself between two ready-painted elderly gentlemen, who benefit by the Egyptian touch. Then I dream of mail, postmarked Travemünde. Then I see our Herr Matzerath giving the Grimm Brothers a contract. Then the cuckoo clock strikes twelve times. And now Watsoncricks are landing again, and again the bells are ringing . . .

Chapter Eleven, in which the Awaited
Ones settle down, the Sleeping Beauty sleep ends
disastrously, triplets come as a surprise in Hamelin, a
verdict is handed down in the Lübeck art forgery trial,
Warehouse Island is too small, once again our Herr
Matzerath has known it all in advance, the Watsoncricks make order and — because the mail brings good
news — music consoles.

OUR DREAMS cancel each other out.
Wide awake, the two of us
confront each other
to the point of fatigue.

I dreamed of a man,
said the Rat of my dreams.
I argued with him until he thought
he was dreaming about me and said in his dream: The Rat
of my dreams thinks she is dreaming about me;
we read each other in mirrors
and question each other.

Could it be that both of us,
the Rat and I
are being dreamed, that we are the dreams
of a third species?

In the end, once words are exhausted
we shall see what is real
and what is only humanly possible.

They are blue-eyed. Slowly they take shape. They cast shadows and have qualities, some of them comical.

We have just said that despite their heads and partial pilosity, they have human proportions and walk decently erect. Now we say: Their furlike hair is blond; accordingly, their blue eyes do not seem out of place in their oversized rat's heads; the admixture of Swedish genes has had such typical consequences both in white-haired and in red-eyed laboratory rats that the Scandinavian origin of the newcomers cannot be held in doubt or be adulterated with exotic admixtures. They are clearly a product of that branch of the University of Uppsala – the geneticists there corresponded with their colleagues in Boston, Bombay and Tiflis – which began at an early date to store cultures of cell nuclei. Scientists the world over worked together. Thus the landing greeted with church bells must be regarded as a continuation of human history. The relatively brief interruption created by the Big Bang has been bridged over. One more invasion. For just as long ago Goths arrived by the shipload, gained a foothold in the Vistula estuary, settled for a short while without great enthusiasm, then moved on to the south to play their part in the migrations, those rats liberated in Visby must be seen as a force which – as is already evident – will make history.

Who said that? The She-rat of my dreams? Or did I say what had been dictated to me? Or did she say what I had put into her mouth? Or did she and I speak synchronously in my dream?

We were both surprised by the looks of the Manippels, by their intense blue-eyed blondness, even though the She-rat had longed for the arrival of the Awaited Ones and I had feared it. At first we took refuge in laughter: Aren't they funny, aren't they a scream? Those protuberant arms, that stilted, stiff-kneed gait. The way the males cover their sex and the females crouch down when pissing. Their elaborate greetings, their solemn gestures. Yes, they're really weird.

Since they landed, we've seen them grab land, unobstructed by the rat nations. In occupying Warehouse Island between the two arms of the Mottlau, that area fraught with history, in aiming their urine and placing their dung on the bridges leading to the Right City and the Lower City, in other words, marking out their territory in the manner usual with rats, they acted as if their claims had been authenticated.

In roughly the same way, said the She-rat, said I, the Teutonic

Knights must have obtained the right of settlement for their order. Yet because they had so decidedly taken possession of Warehouse Island, the Awaited Ones were not only tolerated by the local rat nations, but respected as agents of a higher power – at a suitable distance. No, there was no contact, no playful measuring of strength. Nor after the initial ringing of bells was there any show of deference. At the most, we have begun of late to approach one another on the bridges and sniff: alien.

We're playing a waiting game. We see them every day and we can't make head or tail of them. But the She-rat and I are agreed about one thing: these Swedish-manipulated rat-men – she says emphatically, hominoid rats – emanate a self-sufficient, possibly stupid, phlegmatic-seeming power, that has no need to prove itself; one believes without being told that they are prepared if necessary to act quickly, intelligently and decisively, but never immoderately, always commensurately with the provocation. They embody power, but never blind, raging violence. An easy-going discipline is innate in them. They maintain implicit, inconspicuous order without having to be bitten – as is unfortunately the case with rats – by overseers.

The She-rat says this; I confirm: once the comical aspect of their appearance has worn off, the Awaited Ones are beautiful, of a terrifying beauty. Not as seen from a distance, but close up, on the bridges, they show individual features. They are not identical clones; no, each male and each female is beautiful in a different way. The blue of their eyes ranges from a light watery or milky blue to a cold, metallic blue and that dark, suddenly blackening blue which in the human era was attributed to the heroic gaze. In between, time and time again, moments of radiant cerulean, of the blue-eyedness that moves us.

The She-rat and I see them wheaten-blond, gold-blond, red-blond, pacing off Warehouse Island, casually taking possession of territory. Here they stand musing before the ruins left over from the Second World War; they have no way of knowing that once upon a time the last Jewish ghetto was bounded by Munich Street, which runs parallel to Adebar Street. This story is no concern of theirs. They have no past to cope with. They enter the stage, programmed to start from zero and burdened by no guilt. We see that with envy.

There's something clumsy about them. There they stand,

slightly bowlegged. They are not all identically hairy. Some have curly patches on their backs, upper arms, thighs. Even on their finger and toe joints – yes, they grab things, stand and support themselves with human hands and feet – they have light curly hair. Those with straight head hair wear it long and parted. And there are blond lashes on their light to dark blue Swedish eyes.

That, in my opinion, is beautiful. But the She-rat says that side by side with ratty components she sees elements of the domestic pig. When she points out the absence of a long tail, I notice that the rat-men's spinal column ends above the coccyx in a stunted, but unmistakable curly tail. The She-rat says this without acrimony, as though the combination of human genes with those of pigs and rats were preferable to a program confined to ratty and human genes.

That weird little curly tail is indeed an argument. My attention has been called to it a number of times, and I can't overlook it. But I take a different view of these reduced curly tails. I refuse to call them pig's tails, point to the possible caprices of manipulated nature, and continue to identify the new species as rat-man or hominoid rat. This enrichment suffices. Only the ratty can or should be made manifest in man. Since we no longer exist in our old-accustomed form, we have at least become possible in this new conception. Only the rat, I contend, could enhance and improve man. Only this particular chain of genes could outdo nature. This was the only possible way of extending the process of creation. I should find it hard to speak of a porcine component – really, She-rat, I ask you.

They live in couples. One is struck by a not excessive, but discernible female dominance. The female hominoid rat does not content herself with rearing her litters. Once her triplets or quadruplets have been fed, we see the female strolling thoughtfully about, while the male hominoid takes care of the offspring. Apparently, equality between the sexes has at last been achieved. What in human times never worked out and time and time again brought strife to kitchen, living room and bedroom, what, however great the love, could not be bridged over, has here found a natural, harmonious, if perhaps somewhat boring solution. Eager as I am to find tensions, incipient quarrels in their daily life, nothing crackles, no sparks fly, it's all convincingly tedious.

No sooner landed, they began to multiply. Of course, they will not for some time be as numerous as the local rat nations, but the first young couples have already begun to mate, the Swedish Manippels are already an extended clan and will soon be a nation. The She-rat and I have counted over a hundred blue-eyed rat-men, who have established their territory on Warehouse Island and are eager to expand. Two of the five-storey half-timbered houses, which were rebuilt after the Second World War, are occupied from cellar to attic by children and adolescents. Thus far food has been no problem because all the warehouses are filled with the provisions of the local rat nations: ears of corn, heaps of grain, lentils and sunflower seeds.

The She-rat whom I think I'm dreaming about has her misgivings about this, and I, whom she – so she says – is dreaming about, am worried too: supplies always give out sooner or later. Some day there will be problems.

She, however, deplores omissions: We should have exterminated them the moment they landed. They were only twelve then. It would have been child's play.

In principle, I agree with her and in all likelihood it was I who, out of concern for the rat nations settled in the Danzig area, demanded the immediate elimination of the Manippels. In any case we agree that the present peaceful situation is deceptive. Already the fourth generation of the blue-eyed rat-men has reached the age of puberty. In the storehouses the sunflower seeds are sinking from storey to storey. Obviously the supplies in the former Raiffeisen Warehouse – barley used to be stored there – are exhausted. More and more gnawed-off corn cobs are floating in both arms of the Mottlau. True, the rat nations are not starving, especially as the last harvests have been more than abundant. Still, the rats are worried. What will happen when everything has been gobbled up? Where will they go when they are hungry and too many?

Their social life still looks peaceful. In the evening when they stand in groups or saunter back and forth arm in arm, they seem harmless, concerned only with themselves and their reproduction; the males rather gentle, the females domineering. They occupy Warehouse Island in good order, as though that were room enough for them. They blow the whistle briskly when any of their children in playing run out on the bridges and jump over territorial markings, heading for Green Gate or, passing the Milk Pitcher Tower, for the Lower City, where our Russians have settled behind mud walls.

Their offspring are obedient. In early childhood they learn to vote by raising their hands. They try to be good neighbours and make no attempt to rush things. Neutrality is innate in them. There's something gratifyingly Scandinavian about their behaviour, as if a certain social democratic quality were embedded in their genes. We reassure ourselves with such observations.

Thus far no Watsoncrick has shown himself in the Long Market or in front of the Rathaus or Artushof. Devoid of curiosity, they content themselves with their territory. While we worry about their future and our own, they seem unconcerned, sublimely contented. Dwindling provisions and cramped quarters do not deter the blond, blue-eyed Manippels from becoming more and more numerous. Their beauty multiplies menacingly; from every warehouse window it shimmers smooth and curly.

We still take pleasure in their charm, but it has come to our attention recently that the full-grown Nippels congregate for exercises. From across the Mottlau, the She-rat and I see them in columns and wedge-shaped formations. Erect, they practise keeping in step. Oh God! They're marching. Column left, right, about turn; they mark time, they freeze on command, eyes right, eyes left, forward – march! Across the quiet water the She-rat and I hear their commands. A palatal, one might say, reassuring accent, I'm reminded of the mumbling of those creatures that our Herr Matzerath imported into Poland for the poor Kashubian children. The Watsoncricks seem to be shouting: Right – smurf – face! About – smurf! Forward smurf! Smurf two three four, smurf two three four. Smurf . . .

They're coming! All those in the Gingerbread House are crowded around the wicked stepmother's magic mirror, which shows vehicles with caterpillar treads, of a type never seen before, bursting from the open gullets of underground concrete silos. With hinged grabs, jutting cowcatcher, spike, battering rams, jointed lateral suckers, they resemble the dragons of legend; and, just as tanks are named after wild beasts, they are called dragon bulldozers, or dragons for short.

Now the dragons are rolling over the autobahn, crushing the greenery, coming closer and closer. (Herr Matzerath wants these vehicles, which hitherto have been used only in India and South America for clearing widespread slum areas, but are now driving away all those who only a short while ago were cheering the Grimms' fairy-tale government, to be equipped with flame throwers. I am opposed to such old-fashioned weapons, but Oskar's early imprinting is bound to win out in the end, so profoundly was he affected by the flame throwers used in the battle for the Polish Post Office.)

Panic grips the Gingerbread House. King Thrushbeard is frantic about his property. The good fairies weep, the bad fairies writhe. Jorinde and Joringel are petrified. Rapunzel, as though suffering from the cold, wraps herself in her long hair. The horrified frog jumps from the lady's forehead into the well, and the frog king, trembling with fear, jumps out. Unable to bear the sight, the girl covers her eyes with her chopped-off hands. And Little Red Riding Hood's grandmother reads disaster-related words from the Grimms' Dictionary to all who wish to listen: Dire disaster dismal distress . . .

At first only Rübezahl with his club stands prepared to resist. Then the brave little tailor and the steadfast tin soldier. At the urging of the dwarfs, several of the lesser witches piss into hurriedly collected empty bottles, which the dwarfs cork. The girl's chopped-off hands practise mechanical manipulations.

Off to one side, Snow White and Little Red Riding Hood advise the Chancellor's children to run away. 'You'd better go home before it's too late!' But Hansel and Gretel refuse: 'We stand shoulder to shoulder with you.'

The magic mirror shows that the dragons have left the autobahn. They approach the forest, assault it, eat their way through, spit out kindling, chewed-up moss, chopped roots. From the turret of the first dragon, the kissing prince shows the General-Chancellor of the emergency government the way. He throws kisses in the direction of the thorny hedge, behind which he knows his Sleeping Beauty sleeps.

Everybody in the Gingerbread House is still furious at the defection of the treacherous prince. Rapunzel is ashamed of herself. The witch, Merlin the magician, and the wicked fairies try to stop the dragons with curses and magic spells. But the curses rebound in a shower of sparks or provoke only superficial changes. The dragons grow dragon's teeth, rolling eyes make their appearance, cleft fiery tongues shoot out between spike and cowcatcher; thus the dragon's armament comes to include our Herr Matzerath's flame thrower.

The Rat

Only the prince is undismayed by all this. As though in a trance, he throws orientational kisses. Now the column, whose last vehicle is carrying a commando equipped with shields and visor helmets, reaches the clearing in the middle of which stands the stone statue of the Grimm Brothers.

With horror the fairy-tale characters see one of the dragons projecting its battering ram, taking a run, ramming the monument, ramming the pedestal, and, taking a fresh run, overturning the stone Grimm Brothers, who break into pieces. Other dragons stamp them into the forest floor, including the heads we know and love so well, now so cruelly shattered.

At the sight of this ruthless violence, the fairy-tale characters in the Gingerbread House feel themselves sinking into the ground along with the Grimm Brothers. The good and bad fairies cry out: 'Woe to the sons of man, they know not what they do!'

The kissing prince, who was at first aghast at the destruction and then pulled his cap down over his eyes, points in a new direction. The dragons, however, do not follow his instructions, but head in the opposite direction. Their violence is not directed at the Sleeping Beauty behind the hedge of thorns; another account must be settled first and without delay. Deeper and deeper the column eats its way into the healthy forest.

'Alas!' cries Snow White. 'My story will soon be over!'

Jorinde and Joringel lament: 'Our grief will be no more.'

Little Red Riding Hood, the silly little thing, cries out: 'Maybe they've only come for a visit.'

Rapunzel knows: 'Without fairy tales mankind will be poor.'

'Aw, go on,' says Rumpelstiltskin. 'It's a long time since they've missed us.'

Ignoring these lamentations (in which our Herr Matzerath joins: 'This unhappy ending has me worried!'), Rübezahl calls for assistance. 'Follow me,' he cries, brandishing his club.

All leave the Gingerbread House. The wicked stepmother takes her one and all, the magic mirror, which only a moment before was mirroring the rampaging dragons. Outside, the wolf's chain is taken off. The wicked fairies remove all the magic spells from the enchanted ravens, swans, and deer, whereupon a horde of raffish, embarrassed young princes stretch their legs, then band together; at once anxious and defiant.

The dwarfs distribute the bottles of witches' piss. King Thrushbeard can think of nothing cleverer than to make the steadfast tin soldier a general. The wolf drags his tail and wants to be chained up again. The frog king would like to escape into the well, but his lady and the witch stop him. The girl with the chopped-off hands is first to hear the noise of the approaching dragons. She stops her ears. Hansel clutches Gretel's hand.

Now they come bursting out of the forest, six of them widely fanned. One sees their grabs, spikes, and suckers. Battering rams threaten, and cowcatchers. Between cowcatcher and spike they have cleft fire-spewing tongues. Terrifying rolling eyes. Behind the dragons special troops, protected by shields and visors, secure the cleared ground. Looking out from one of the dragon turrets, the prince smiles insipidly and waves at the brave but lost fairy-tale characters. He even throws kisses, until the commander's fist pushes him down inside the dragon. From other turrets the bishops bless the coming action. (I have a feeling that our Herr Matzerath, as though from long habit, has, if not allied himself, at least made common cause with the enemy; I have a hunch he's, no, I *see* him among the industrialists.) 'Down with fairy tales!' cries the General-Chancellor.

The seven dwarfs, wood sprites and goblins throw their Molotov cocktails – bottles full of witches' piss. The bottles explode, but the dragons, now painted over with grotesque figures, plough right on, sticking out their cleft, fire-spewing tongues.

Rübezahl, who goes to meet the dragons with his club, is to be crushed first, then the steadfast tin soldier, then all the dwarfs, wood sprites and goblins, who thought too late of digging in. Next to go are the raffish princes, who only a short while ago were swans, ravens or deer. The wolf finally leaps at one of the dragons, rebounds, and is torn to pieces. The good and bad fairies, King Thrushbeard, the shivering frog king, his lady and the witch, all the lesser witches, Snow White, the wicked stepmother, Little Red Riding Hood, Jorinde, Joringel, Rumpelstiltskin, Mother Holle, the wild men and the brave little tailor, all are crushed or, like the flying trunk and the broom-riding witches, seized by grabs and suckers, set on fire by cleft tongues, sucked, shattered, burned – or, as the Germans put it, eliminated: and the dragons spit out behind them what they have seized in front.

Merlin the magician is spitted on the spike. Rapunzel's long hair is caught in a dragon's tread. The girl with the chopped-off hands goes up in flames, while her hands fight to the bitter end, stuffing something or other into a sight slit, trying to loosen a screw. Until she too is seized and ground to bits, Little Red Riding Hood's grandmother resists the roaring violence by reading aloud from the Grimms' dictionary: 'Mercy, merciful, merciless . . .' But nothing can stop the dragons.

As though in passing, the Gingerbread House is destroyed. The magic mirror, Rumpelstiltskin's leg, the dwarfs' caps, the wolf's burst zipper belly, Little Red Riding Hood's cap lie all about, shattered, smashed, crushed, torn to pieces. The girl's hands are maimed, Snow White's coffin shattered, the Dictionary in tatters, each volume . . .

Ah, how sad, how pitiful! (And if he hadn't deserted to the enemy, says our Herr Matzerath, he too would have met the same dismal end.)

Only Hansel and Gretel escaped. That's their forte: running away before it's too late. Pursued by the dragons, they run hand in hand from the healthy forest to the dead forest, until they come to the dense hedge of thorns, behind which the all-encompassing Sleeping Beauty sleep is still in force.

Hansel and Gretel hide behind fallen trees. The kissing prince shows the General-Chancellor, bishops and industrialists, who are looking out of the turrets of the other dragons, the new direction. From their hiding place the children see how the standard governing clique – capital church army – crush and level the hedge of thorns, clearing the way to the ruined tower, the Sleeping Beauty, the benumbed Chancellor, and his benumbed retinue.

Now (while our Herr Matzerath sneaks away through a side porthole and once again, as though pretending to be a child, chooses to play innocent) one of the commanding dragon's grabs seizes the kissing prince, lifts him out of the turret, lifts him higher, still higher, lifts him up to the roofless chamber in the ruined tower, where instantly, without a qualm, he clutches his Sleeping Beauty, kisses her as never before, madly, desperately, hopefully, as though there were something to hope for, and wakes her with a long passionate kiss. With the kiss-awakened Sleeping Beauty in his arms, he is lifted by the grab and swung to one side of the ruined tower, whereupon little by little the awakening Chancellor and his awakened retinue enter the picture.

Ah, this fairy tale still comes out right. Immediately the

Chancellor bites into a piece of Black Forest cherry torte which he
had in his hand all through his Sleeping Beauty sleep. No sooner
awakened, the experts and ministers start bickering as usual over
details. In the same moment, the policemen ready their submachine
guns. The journalists continue the sentences they had begun. Film
footage resumes. Everyone knows his cue. Everything gets back to
normal, as though nothing had happened.

And while still munching his last bite, the Chancellor cries out:
'Children! My dear children! Everything is back to normal. The
bad dream is over. Come home. Your father and mother beg you to
come home, where everything is shipshape, just as it was before.'

Hansel and Gretel now leave their hiding place and run away
again. (Disengaged from the action, our Herr Matzerath wants this
development, which is after all conceivable, and I agree with him.)
Not at the command of the Chancellor, who thinks he can simply
go on governing as if there were no generals, clerics, industrialists,
the grab of the commanding dragon hurls the kissing prince and his
Sleeping Beauty to the ground where both are broken to pieces.

Now the dragon rolls over the lovers, who in death are still
kissing. Now it wants to follow the Chancellor's children, wants to
grab them and crush them, but they are already far away . . .

> We didn't want this,
> say dismayed persons
> to others who are profoundly dismayed.
> So much dismay has statistical value.
> Never have the ratings been so high.
>
> We are shaken, say choruses
> to other choruses, which are profoundly shaken.
> We the majority, which can be counted,
> are profoundly dismayed and shaken.
> Afterward there will be talk of newly won stability
> and losses which, sad as they are,
> we must learn to live with.
>
> The new majority has plucked up courage again
> and will not be easily downed.
> Nevertheless, say the editorials,
> a man should be able to show dismay,
> at least after the evening news, now and then.

The Rat

I promised my Christmas rat not to let things end with this running away, but to look for another ending, if possible something better and nobler, as our Herr Matzerath recently, when as usual we called on each other, suggested, with a slogan or two: 'Give them hope! Never dismiss the possibility of a miracle.' Nevertheless, she's listless and stays in her little shack, showing only the tips of her whiskers. Nothing can tempt her: no concert of sacred music, nor the water levels of the Elbe and Saale, certainly no Echo of the Day; and even the bla–bla of 'Educational Radio for All', which can ordinarily count on her interest, can't get a rise out of her; the daily proof of our existence, the Third Programme, pulls a blank.

So I try Hamelin. Get a load of this, Ratkin, they've been celebrating there for weeks. They're making speeches and showing pictures with rat motifs. I myself have submitted pictures inspired by you, that reflect my dreams. Rats practising the upright gait, rats digging in, rats fleeing, rats praying. A scurrying rat against a backdrop of Danzig-Gdańsk and its many towers. And the rat-man or hominoid rat. Painted with deep-black brush, drawn with Siberian charcoal, or outlined, gouged, finely hatched on copper plates with an engraving tool . . .

Actually I'd rather have told them in Hamelin what really happened there seven hundred years ago. But those people have no desire to hear about the Gothic punks who made common cause with their pet rats. That sad truth has no place in the festival programme. It might be bad for the hotel and restaurant business. Present-day punks might suddenly get the idea of coming from distant parts with their rats that they've dyed pink or arsenic-green, to honour the memory of their Gothic predecessors on the banks of the river Weser; shrill, horrifying the townspeople with their tinkling chains, their deathly pale makeup. Once again chaos would make itself at home in Hamelin. And once again it would be necessary to call for order, to create order. Telexed from Hanover and Kassel, police would arrive, armed with chemical truncheons and water cannon. The cops would carry shields for protection as in the Middle Ages and visors. Nobody wants that. Truncheons at the ready! Street battles. The seventh centenary celebration could get out of hand and make banner headlines: 'Hamelin called – and the punks came!' That sort of thing.

No, this story is not what the programme needs. Its truth is too

Günter Grass

naked. Because, Ratkin, to make matters worse, it seems that the hundred and thirty Gothic punks, who were shut up in Calvary Mountain and buried alive, included burgomaster Lambert Rike's singularly lovable youngest daughter and her rat. A quiet, thoughtful girl of sixteen by the name of Gret, who with her wheaten-blonde pigtails was engaged to the son of rich miller Hornemule, and who was in the habit of praying beautifully, imploringly, and at great length, until, like other girls and boys before her, she fell in love with rats in general and with one particular rat. This Gret, the burgomaster's youngest daughter, seems to have called her rat Hans; she may have done it with this Hans and may have let him time and time again.

Why do I say seems and may have. She did it, she let him time and time again.

Up until then her twatlet had been above suspicion. With the help of other-worldly prayers, she banished every thought of finger-length intrusion. The rich miller's son had only been allowed to come within shouting distance. And even on the way to church nothing more titillating than an exchange of glances had been countenanced.

The rat, however, had been countenanced. At first Gret permitted only playful admittance, then Hans was permitted more and more, culminating in the whole hog and that again and again. Whereupon the burgomaster's daughter found herself with child and after an inappropriately short time gave birth to triplets, which though small were proportioned like other Hamelin babies, and altogether human except for their dear little, cute little rat heads.

What rejoicing among the hundred and thirty Gothic punks! As the canon's son, whose name was Hinner, had the key, the whole lot of them slipped into Saint Boniface at night through the sacristy door and descended into the crypt, where the three little sons were baptized in the names of the three Kings of Orient and henceforth bore the names of Caspar, Melchior and Balthazar. Devoutly, the boys and girls in their heavy metal stood around the stone baptismal font and forbade the bells sewn on their rags to tinkle. The rats which they carried on their matted head hair or on their bare skin under their beggar's rags were also as still as mice. The canon's son, Hinner, said the words that the sacrament of baptism requires. Under the low vaulting, the others piously professed: Credo in unum deum . . .

The Rat

After that they celebrated until morning on the bank of the river Weser. But the burghers had no wish to share the joy of the Gothic punks. The words nucleic acid and genetic code were not yet in use. Animalized humans and humanized animals occurred only in fairy tales, artist's fantasies, or – not so good either – in the witches' sabbath, but not in Hamelin by broad daylight. Indignant whispers made the streets narrower. Grey monks and white monks preached hellfire. The lower trades were beginning to agitate against the patrician aldermen. When not only tanners and porters, but also millers and pastry cooks talked sedition, rebellion was to be feared.

But when the bailiffs went into action and tried to liquidate the young mother's babes, the hundred and thirty formed a redoubtable protective ring around the cute little things. They threatened first to sabotage all the watermills, then to set fire to the diocesan tithe barn and to the granaries outside the Thy Gate.

In the end it was burgomaster Rike in person who, because of his youngest daughter's disgrace and at the urging of the aldermen, the church warden and the agent of the Hanseatic League, sent for a piper from far-off Winsen on the Luhe, who was credited with the gift of producing very special sounds. In return for a written promise that he would be rewarded with silver after turning the trick, he came to Hamelin and with his variously pitched lutes made himself popular with the hundred and thirty. He played them music to dance by whenever they wished, and taught them new dances. They soon made him acquainted with their hiding places and refuges, including the spacious cave in Calvary Mountain, whither Gret the young mother had fled with Hans the rat and her three unusual babes from the arms of the town bailiffs and the clubs of the brutal miller's men.

And on Saint John's Day the piper, who also knew how to keep bagpipes inflated, led the remaining hundred and twenty-nine out of the town in order, as he said, to give a party for Gret, the sweet young mother, her Hans and her three babes. He led them across fields and meadows, through underbrush and hazel bushes to the cave, where they were to regale themselves on barley beer and flatbread, smoked bacon and honeycomb.

Of course provision had also been made for the rats, which had been brought along. They were fond of cheese rinds and sunflower seeds. Clad in rags and hung with bells, the hundred and thirty danced with their rats until long after midnight. The sons of merchant Amelung, the daughters of pastry cook Stencke, the children of the knight Scadelaur Jörg, of numerous guild masters and master brewers, jiggled and contorted themselves. Dance-mad in their midst, Gret and her Hans. Hop, stamp, shake. All this, remember, happened in a period that was wild about dancing. So enamoured were the dancers of one another that in the early morning hours they did not miss the piper. When the joy was at its height and other maidens opened up to their rats, he slipped away.

He seems to have climbed a tall tree and waved his feathered cap, whereupon things happened according to plan. The cave – as we know – was sealed up, covered over, and sprinkled with holy water. Thus – counting the babies Caspar, Melchior and Balthazar – one must speak of a hundred and thirty-three children of Hamelin, who on 26 June of the year 1284 vanished ino Calvary Mountain and were never seen again.

To my Christmas rat, who had stepped out of her house and whose whiskers bristled as I told the story, I said: And by the way, it was at about this time, if not the art historians but the past life of the painter Malskat is to be believed, that the murals of Lübeck's church of Saint Mary were painted. Not only those of the nave and choir, but also those of the window openings and arcades. That was when the drôleries of the fairy-tale windows came into being. They show an ass and a hen; the ass is plying needle and thread, while the hen is sitting on eggs from which evil will undoubtedly hatch out. We see crayfish playing chess together. The fox-monk is preaching to the sheep and the goat. Why is the stag sitting at the spinning wheel? The flying birds in the upper trefoil and between the ogives of the fairy-tale windows may be pigeons. But in one window, opening over a virgin's head framed in a medallion, we see, in a medallion of the same size, an animal with a long, smooth tail and a bearded human head. The identity of this animal admits of no guesswork. The influence of Hamelin on the master of the Lübeck choir and naves is unquestionable.

In any event, the mother of Gothic brick churches bore witness in its murals to an age of horror. And when roughly six hundred and eighty years later a painter once again climbed high in the scaffolding, he remembered miracles and omens, St Vitus dances and dances of death, all the foreordained evils and horrors. Before long, so the story goes, the rats came and with them the Plague and its agony . . .

The art forgery case resulting from Lothar Malskat's voluntary confession dragged on for two years and the East Prussian defendant's appearances were always a big success with the public. Nevertheless, sift through them as I may, the proceedings at the Lübeck provincial court yield little but empty talk, because, though both Malskat and Dietrich Fey his employer were sentenced, the one to eighteen months, the other to two years in prison, the real forgers remained honourable men in the eyes of the judges and remain lying, cheating, sanctimonious hypocrites to this day. Nor were the political forgers ever put on trial. They left the stage unpunished; when they died of old age, the one was buried with official honours, the other was half forgotten.

For that reason we still look upon that fraud of the fifties, which, abbreviated, we call GFR–GDR, as authentic, whereas a good part of Malskat's art, those twenty-one saints in seven vaults of the choir, was obliterated with scrubbing brushes in 1955. But since the scrubbers neglected to cover the now art-free surfaces with Protestant whitewash, dark spots and smudges still bear witness to the desecration of Malskat's testimony.

Ah, if only his pictures had been left in place, especially as he brought the truth to light, and the real fraud, which was never confessed, the handiwork of the two founding fathers, had been wiped away. He, who made a clean breast in court, was sent to prison, while the two master forgers were permitted unscathed to go on playing their unsavoury game of state against state. Countering lie with lie, setting forged money against forged money, and soon – while Malskat's Gothic paintings were being zealously destroyed – sending divisions of soldiers, once again German soldiers, into each other's field of fire; and this, the old men's heritage, remains in force to this day, with more and more soldiers, with more and more precise purpose, and with the well-drilled intention of carrying it through to the end.

Ah, Ratkin, Educational Radio can help us no longer. What can the Echo of the Day do for us, if it drowns out the echo of past horrors and crimes with adventitious prattle? The programmes cancel one another out. Nothing must be allowed to cling and give pain. Sievelike we remember: Yes, there was something, yes, something, something . . .

Only traces remain. When, by order of the Lübeck church council, the twenty-one saints in the choir were more smudged than washed away, at the very same time as the military alliances of the two states against one another were contracted, then, along with the major works, many lesser ones were lost, some of which Malskat produced out of caprice and others, true to his Gothic spirit, he had woven into this or that drapery or capital, smuggled into some ornament, painted almost without thinking, or scratched into the mortar base.

Obviously contemporary material: beside the pointed shoes of a saint in the fourth vault, I read traces of an engraved map, on which, between the island of Rügen, here called 'Rugia', and the mouth of the Peene, a cross has meaning, because it is connected with the name of the submerged city – scratched in: 'Winneta'. And in the middle capital of the sixth arch there is a miniature showing three little men with sharp-nosed animal heads, playing the flute together, combined in an ornament which would flow quite naturally toward the arabesques of the capital, if the words: 'This happened on Saint John's and Saint Paul's Day in Hamelin' were not scratched into the mortar to one side.

Clearly, the flute players are three little boys. They are seated and naked. I have no hesitation in calling the little boys' heads rat heads; but this late discovery, which – admittedly – is based on blurred photocopies, is not meant as belated new evidence for the Lübeck art forgery trial, especially as Malskat's conviction had the force of law and as he did his time cheerfully.

He was even released a few months ahead of time. Mail came in heaps. His fame glittered in a dull period. He took his sketchbook and some coloured chalk to his cell with him, but produced nothing significant. Never again did he bear witness to past horrors. The Gothic glow was gone. All that was water under the bridge.

She speaks. Or does she, in dreaming me, allow me to go on thinking undismayed that I am dreaming her, and in order to keep me quiet, that she has once again definitely taken the floor in the person of the She-rat?

And is the space capsule still my residence? Am I destined to remain for ever in this orbit? Dreaming ellipses, longing for slight deviations or simply to get out, as if I weren't strapped in?

She sits on the dome of the observatory beside Lady Gate, which leads to the Mottlau. She says: This old building, where the astronomer Johannes Hevelius sat long years ago with his big quadrant, observing the phases of the moon, allows us to take a cautious look around and to look back as well. We should have struck long ago. It will soon be too late.

And I saw what the She-rat said as she looked back: United as we rat nations had been after the Big Bang – nothing matters but survival! – we quarrelled fiercely once the Watsoncricks seized their territory. Our services in Saint Mary's never recovered the simplicity that made you, our dear friend, suppose that we rats practised religion in the Catholic manner. Once again we were disrupted by a fanatical Protestantism enacted before and behind the altar, dragged up the pillars to the fan vault – this human bickering about the right way, this nose-crinkling self-righteousness, this all-too-human either-or. So fundamentally divided we could have torn one another to pieces. Some demanded: Away with the Nippels. Kill them this very day! And others on the contrary: Not yet. Wait and see. Let's not be in too much of a hurry.

She lamented: And yet we had all been united in our hope for the return of the human race, in any form whatsoever. Despite our gratifying survival and well-fed increase in numbers, we missed mankind. And if we addressed our prayers to that ancient woman, so shrunken she was easy to transport, and to the wizened little boy huddled at her feet, the source of our piety was our longing for the return of mankind. We even included the blue-and-white midgets in our prayers, in the hope that they would help us, teach us to till the soil. Our song, in which you, young master, were prepared to hear a Gregorian quality, had no other purpose than to bring man to us, to make him, the redeemer, come and relieve our manless loneliness.

Oh well, said the She-rat, true enough, we were not so utterly alone. Other animals turned up; some of them, such as the mammalian bluebottles, disgusted us, and others we preyed on in connection with our farming – pigeons, sparrows, field mice – but nature couldn't think up anything human. Then when they got here – Oh, young master, how we had longed for that ship, what intimations we had of it in our daydreams – great was our disappointment.

Not like that! cried our first horror. We didn't want him so indeterminate. Such a monstrosity, even with blue eyes, is neither fish nor flesh. We can't regard this ghastly, ridiculous hybrid, to which moreover a porcine component has been added, as our counterpart, and besides it offends against the image of man that we still bear intact within us. It's not for this, for this – as you'll have to admit – human botch that we've survived. Because when we dream about you in your space capsule, or keeping us company, we still look upon you as glorious and exemplary.

Maybe, said the She-rat in the dome of the observatory near Our Lady's Gate, which offered an incomparable view of Warehouse Island, maybe our party were too quick to cry out Eliminate! Exterminate! Maybe we radicals were too spontaneous in trying to convert our sound insight into a collective will to destroy. In any case, contrary voices made themselves heard without delay: Wait. Keep an eye on them. Draw cautious inferences from their habits, find their weak points.

Others hoped and speculated. Maybe they'll move on. Maybe their litters will sicken and die. Maybe they are merely products of poor planning, and that would make them thoroughly human.

So we took up observation posts, here in the old observatory, across from the west bank of Warehouse Island and in the embrasures of Milk Pitcher Tower, which face the east bank. For weeks, for months we've been mounting guard, but nothing happens. You see how their numbers have been steadily increasing, while our dissensions have been getting more and more ferocious. Not only in the city, but in the country as well, we have split into parties. Our turnip, corn and sunflower fields have been divided. New and hostile territorial boundaries have been marked off. Quarrels about seed have reduced our barley and lentil acreage. The two parties keep separate storehouses. We attend Saint Mary's in shifts.

It has recently been decided that all streets leading left from Baker Street and Doublet Street towards the Mottlau should be confined to our party, and those leading right to the Outer City Ditch to the appeasers. They keep bla-blaing about hope: maybe we'll learn to get along with them in the end. Maybe, if we humour them, the hominoids will get used to us. After all, they're dependent on us. They lived on our garnered provisions, the surpluses we've been storing for years. Let's just provide them with what they need. Call it indemnity, tithe, or tribute. In any case, they shouldn't be made to go hungry. Hunger might make them aggressive. We rats ought to know what hunger means.

The She-rat laughed bitterly, as though the experience of a

thousand years stuck in her craw. Listen to this, young master. The same old saws, mouthed by incorrigible optimists and appeasers. We, however, see clearly, only too clearly. They'll demand more and more. In the end, they'll be allotting their surplus to us. They'll put us on rations. We'll be the victims of their greed, their acquisitiveness. That is the one human thing about the Nippels. Kill them, we shout, but we don't kill them; instead, we fight tooth and nail with our own people. In Weaver Street, around the Stockturm and behind the Arsenal, there have been street battles; in the country only slight excesses so far.

And I saw them tear one another to tatters. Bite one another to death. The undiminished sharpness of rats' teeth. The She-rat took me to all the places where their quarrel degenerated into warfare. In the neighbourhood of Warehouse Island we observed strict decorum lest our discussions become known to the Manippels, but nothing inhibited our hostilities in the city centre. Groups of rats hauling sunflower heads and ears of corn from the arsenal, which like the theatre has been used as a storehouse of late, intending to take them via Weaver Street, Long Street and Green Gate to the Warehouse Island bridge, there to deliver them as tithes, were set upon by hordes pouring in through Doublet Street. Hand-to-hand fighting ensued. Decimated and weakened, only a few of the appeasers fought their way to the bridge. Not much food for the Manippels.

I cried out: That's meagre tribute.

She-rat: Much too much, all the same.

I: Anyway, they'll suffer want.

Serves them right, she cried, all they do is eat and fuck, fuck and eat.

Warehouse Island looked overpopulated. It's true that without striking a blow they had occupied the adjoining island on the Straw Dike side between Kielgraben and the Mottlau, and found additional quarters in the former pumping station and in Bleihof. And yet there were Watsoncricks, children as well as adults, looking out of every warehouse window and skylight. Dense crowds on the waterfront and on Chmielna, as the Poles had renamed Hops Street. Congestion at the approaches to the bridges, especially the wide overpass across Leningradska, the former Suburban Ditch, the boundary of the Right City. On all sides they pressed, now emaciated and bony. Their original Scandinavian-seeming com-

Günter Grass

posure, their Swedish social democratic stolidity, had given way to a contagious restlessness, an almost uncontrollable activism. Across the water we heard them: their crude, but hitherto amiably palatal, smurfish speech had now developed guttural curses and threats.

Then the She-rat and I saw them draw up in formation. No, they were not armed, with the iron bars, for instance, that can easily be broken from cellar windows. Unarmed, they formed an offensive wedge, which moved at the double across the bridge, passed through Green Gate and debouched on the Long Market. Columns followed: blond, blue-eyed, their rat's heads distended, as though concerned with nothing to the right or left of them, as though driven by one concentrated will. Needless to say, the sexes were on an equal footing. Meeting with no resistance, female and male Watsoncricks occupied the Long Market as far as Matzkauschen Street. Guards of both sexes were posted on the porches of the richly gabled patrician houses. Impassive as though it were no concern of theirs, they allowed the rat families to escape from the scent-marked buildings, from the Artushof, which they had converted into a warehouse for corn, and from the lofty-towered Rathaus, where they stored barley, the Rathaus cellar being devoted to sunflower seeds and sugar beets. They advanced no further. Right behind the lion-adorned portal of the Rathaus, from which stairs lead to Long Street, they blocked the way with concrete buckets which had served as flowerpots during the human era, when the Inner City was a pedestrian zone. At the same time they pissed and shat new markings.

After that all was quiet. No more violent movements. They stopped to eat at their leisure. Then there were shifting groups, looking thoughtful in a phlegmatic Nordic way, standing around the Neptune fountain, apparently trying to figure out how to teach the imposing bronze figure, a muscular naked man with a trident, how to spout water as he used to; one or two of them did silly imitations of the sea god.

Look sharp, said the She-rat. They won't keep quiet for long. They won't be satisfied with what they've got. For a while, until new litters are born to them, they'll leave us alone, but then it will be the turn of Long Street as far as the Stockturm, and then the district from the hippodrome to Anchor-maker Street. They may leave the suburbs to us. But they'll take the whole Right City

[320]

around Saint Mary's as far as Old City Ditch; we'll be left with Stare Miasto, as the Poles called the section of the Old City around Saint Catherine's. Then we'll squeeze into the already overcrowded Lower City, until we're driven out of there too. And after that, want to bet, rats will be tolerated only in the country, forced to till the soil under overseers from the Vistula lowlands to the Kashubian hills so the Watsoncricks have enough to eat.

When I silently watched the bustling activity between Warehouse Island and the Long Market and saw not without pleasure several extended clans moving from the Raiffeisen warehouses into richly gabled patrician dwellings, dragging pieces of furniture resembling chairs and tables with them, the She-rat said over-eagerly, as though to divert my attention from other human characteristics of these clones: By the way, our people are on the move again. More rats have come to us from Russia. And not so long ago the first immigrants from India arrived. They bring interesting news. Of course the cities of Kiev and Odessa aren't there any more. But there too hominoid rats seem to have arrived on foot and by sea. And we've had similar reports from the Malabar Coast. Even if only half these reports are true, it would be a mistake to disregard them. Now at least we have some idea of what's going on elsewhere. The Indian Nippels seem to be built like ours, but in addition they have wings, yes, wings like angels. As to the Russians, they are reported to have four tits and to multiply faster than our Swedes. Ah, cried the She-rat, if only we had settled their hash on the spot, just as the Russian rats liquidated their Watson-cricks, who were said to be of Georgian origin, the moment they landed. Our people hunted them down amid the ruins of Odessa and killed them. The ones in Kiev, however, grew powerful. Incredible as it may sound, they seem to have been US products, smuggled in shortly before the end of the human era; including some hefty black ones.

Our Herr Matzerath would have liked to work all that into a video film. So there's a distinct possibility that his firm will soon present the miraculous survival and ulterior development of the rat-men in pre-produced cassettes; just as Oskar, with detailed foreknowledge of the hundred and seventh birthday celebration of his grandmother Anna Koljaiczek, produced it with the help of the Post Futurum company and showed it to the birthday guests except for the concluding sequence.

He knows how to capture the future. With discrimination he pre-tastes things to come. He films the anticipated manifestation of which Bloch speaks. But our Herr Matzerath must embed everything in history, not only himself and his well-dressed questionableness, but everything that has ever happened, is happening or will happen, including the part played by the rat-man in post-human history.

In his video film which – as announced – is expected to be distributed in large numbers and to flood the video market, *The New Ilsebill* does not sail directly around the Hela Peninsula and head for the mouth of Danzig harbour. No, the wreck must wait for the Goths, who more than fifteen hundred years ago moved out when the lots were drawn, to start migrating. Our Herr Matzerath follows them from the mouth of the Vistula to the shores of the Black Sea. To remote Spain and the boot of Italy he accompanies them. And everywhere rats clean out one encampment after another; everywhere, on battlefield after battlefield, rats play their part.

The landing on 26 June 1630 of Swedish King Gustavus Adolphus, sometimes known as the 'Lion from Midnight', must also help to prepare the way for the advent of the rat-man. Since our Herr Matzerath, as though to compensate for the small stature of his early life and the hunchbackness of his later existence, must repeatedly devise grandiose panoramas, and since he prefers prolixity to concise, in-a-nutshell episodes, he has commented on the Swede's landing on Usedom – who wants to count ships, who wants to count sails? – with cascades of sentences from Grand Master Döblin's novel *Wallenstein*; by reaching out with both hands, the video film on the one hand culls tatters of history from the past, and on the other robs the future of its bold plan.

Needless to say, rats were present on Gustavus Adolphus's ships. The rat that decided the fate of Europe was still the black house rat and not yet the brown rat. And of course rats went ashore with the young Swedish and Finnish peasants, so as to become gravid with history at Nordlingen and Lützen, or at Wittstock for that matter, wherever war was prolonged.

Having Russian admiral Rodhyestvenski's Baltic fleet drop anchor in 1906 in the harbour and roadstead of Libau to show us how quickly the rats left his ill-reputed ships may strike some viewers of the video film soon to appear on the market as superfluous, but the producer of the cassette was determined to omit nothing. That's him all over. Always wanting to put in one more little thing. He even makes the Russian sailors sing melancholy songs on their ratless tubs. But now, well prepared for by roughly and precisely dated history, the Manippels at last go ashore. Or is it still too soon? Must the credits be followed by more credits? Is a last bit of historical background needed?

Our Herr Matzerath didn't want to curtail the period in which Oskar's existential break occurred. So we see the burning city of Danzig, we see refugees plodding overland and fleeing across the water. Overloaded ships are expected to carry civilians, party bosses, wounded or still unwounded soldiers away from the approaching Soviet armies to Western Baltic ports. We see the *Wilhelm Gustloff* on 30 January 1945 with more than five thousand persons on board sinking twelve sea miles west of Stolpmünde and the *Steuben* on 10 February with more than three thousand. The *Cap Arcona* makes three trips, after which twenty-seven thousand fugitives consider themselves saved, then goes down in flames off the coast of Schleswig-Holstein with five and a half thousand ex-inmates of Neuengamme concentration camp on board. British bombers had got their orientation wrong. This happened on 3 May, five days before the end of the Second World War.

But here again the rats knew what was what. Not one wanted to sail on the *Wilhelm Gustloff*'s last voyage. No sooner has the *Cap Arcona* taken concentration camp inmates on board than we see more than a thousand rats hastily leaving the doomed ship, as the history books call it.

He omits nothing. Our Herr Matzerath shows us everything, people and rats on the last ferryboats and coastal steamers – among them the freight barge *Dora*. In getting ahead of himself and, with the launching of the research ship *The New Ilsebill*, fading in the brief period before the Big Bang, he follows his video dramaturgy, which knows everything simultaneously.

In his film we finally see the five women outside Visby's Institute for Genetic Research. We hear shouts, we hear the smashing of glass panes. Cages are opened before our video-maddened eyes. We rejoice with the liberated animals. At first it looks as if only normal animals were set free, but on closer scrutiny we notice that in addition a good dozen, for whom innumerable experiments are scheduled, are liberated: man and rat, rat and man, linked together through genes, perfected Watsoncricks, which quickly find their way to the harbour.

In his film, which incidentally has the deliberately sober title *Before and After*, our Herr Matzerath shows all this: how the rat-men, each one of them barely a metre high, reach the docks; how they find a coast guard cutter closely guarded, how an excursion steamer strikes them as inappropriate, and how at last *The New Ilsebill* strikes their fancy; how they steal provisions from warehouses, go on board with bundles and find a companionway open; how eighteen or nineteen of them crawl through a porthole and take refuge between the floor boards and the iron hull of the former freight barge.

The rat-men in the film look as if I had dreamed them. And when the five women man the ship a moment later, I see that our Herr Matzerath also thought the captain beautiful. She resembles my Damroka. Nor are the other women in the film unknown to me. We see the ship casting off and putting out to sea.

From this point on the video story runs straight ahead. What Gustavus Adolphus did in his time, *The New Ilsebill* wants to repeat; she heads for Usedom. What Gustavus Adolphus neglected is for the women promise and destination. They drop anchor over Vineta Deep and submit to the inspection of the GDR coast guard, who find nothing. A pretty little scene in the film: the women primping, putting on jewellery, sauntering around the deck and playing their favourite roles: all queens.

Of course our Herr Matzerath could, or possibly should, have outdone himself with historical fade-ins. But just as he simply drops the episode of the talking Flounder, who in conversation with Damroka forecasts the imminent end, then omits the polychoral song of the medusas, so, in line with his rejection of 'all irrationality', as he puts it, he also suppresses the story of the submerged city and the promised republic of women, and goes straight to the last gasp of human history.

Possibly Oskar regarded the talking Flounder and his visions as a diversion from his own existence. Possibly the song of the medusas reminded him too painfully of the glass-annihilating screams of his childhood years. Possibly the women's will to rule was suspect to the undersized but emphatically masculine gentleman. In any case, he dropped, omitted, suppressed and denied. He forbade his film exorbitant special effects and allowed the Big Bang to descend as though from a clear sky.

The Rat

It comes as inexorable fate. No one has willed it, no one has prevented it. Questions of guilt are not asked. References to rats at work in the central computers are also absent. It all just happens. Lightning flashes and appalling glare are simply the last word in cinematic technique. We see the mushrooms familiar to us from other films sprouting over Peenemünde, Stralsund and beyond. We could interpret the whole thing as a mere natural catastrophe if our Herr Matzerath's voice did not blare trumpetlike over the final catastrophe.

We hear him shouting: 'Thus what was long in the making happened. Thus what men had long been promising one another was fulfilled. Mankind had long been in training for this event. So ends what should never have begun. Oh, Reason! Oh, Immortality! Nothing was completed, but now all is consummated!'

As is only logical, the women go up in smoke without having found their Vineta. Couldn't our Herr Matzerath's pre-vision have dreamed up a gentler, equally conceivable fate? Something comforting. The dramatic effect would if anything have been enhanced if shortly before the end he had allowed the Flounder to swim flatly over Vineta, to open his crooked mouth and to call all five women, beginning with my Damroka, from shipboard into the depths. Under water, to be sure, but far from all post-human events, a new history could have begun with the founding of Femina City, which might have softened the end of the other history. But no! To be logical and strictly consistent: their beauty had to come to nothing. Not I, but Oskar wanted it that way. Since then I've missed the women painfully.

So the wreck drifts forlornly eastward. But in the forecastle manipulated life stirs. For seconds, the video film shows figures in the black hull of the ship. They too have suffered losses. Six, no seven specimens of the new species perish and are thrown overboard. Twelve are left. One makes out shadowy outlines of human limbs and ratty heads. Four or five of them, obviously of the feminine sex, do seaman's work like professionals; they keep the wreck on course. Then suddenly they escape below deck, because a dust storm has come up.

Even the Watsoncricks fear the worldwide fallout. Fade-ins show how bad it is everywhere. Not only Moscow and New York have been turned to dust, not only the Donetz basin, the Po and Ruhr valleys are now scorched earth; Zurich and Bombay, Rio and

Cape Town have also had it. Hong Kong. That, you say, was Hong Kong?

One can hardly list what Herr Matzerath's anticipating cinematic art spirits away, flattens out, transforms into lunar landscape, or in special cases, where it was permissible to spare cultural monuments, preserves as backdrops: Florence for instance, Kyoto and – as we know – Gdańsk. But though the shut-off is worldwide in our Herr Matzerath's film, though nothing stops dust storms and unbroken cold and darkness from eradicating all life, nevertheless the wreck, though shadowy, remains in the picture, until at last the sun is no longer darkened and dust storms give way to life-giving winds. We see a few Nippels stretching their limbs on deck.

I admit this section of the Matzerathian film drags in places. After all, cinematic treatments of catastrophes are known to us from numerous movie-house films, current during the final phase of humanity. Once again full of ideas, Homo ludens anticipated his end. And yet, despite these failings, the Matzerathian creation differs from the usual eschatological productions. Its anticipation of a carefully planned afterlife shows perspective.

Illuminating is the film's finale, which deals with post-human history in its transition to neo-human history: even more than in the dream, which the She-rat has commented on from an anxious rat's point of view, the beauty, the charm especially of female rat-men is evident. Time and again the camera revels in reddish-blonde, in wheaten-yellow pilosity; fuzzily flattering, it coats arms, thighs and breasts; dense and furry, it covers shoulders; fleecelike, it embeds odd-looking curly tails just below the coccyx; and don't forget the head hair. From the rat heads downward – ha, their white-lashed blue-eyedness – it descends, smooth but also curly, over the back, so that, thanks to this cinematic treatment of glorious curls, my Damroka has again been accessible to me in dreams.

Slowly, almost hesitantly: it's she with her lovely curls. And now she's wearing Damroka's amber necklace. Ah, dear Herr Matzerath, how I long for the victory of the Watsoncricks over the inferior rat nations! And my wish is already coming true, giving ground for timid hope . . .

In any event, the She-rat goes on to tell me what the video film, thanks to its familiarity with the locale, was able to prevision: After landing to the ringing of bells, they occupied district after district, the whole Right City between the Suburban Ditch and the Old City

The Rat

Ditch – without violence, by the way, thanks to a calm display of authority. Instead of destroying the rat nations, they merely thrust them aside in pursuit of their own needs. Casually, without stopping to demand, they take a share of the barley, corn and sunflower stocks. They help to organize and plan the storage and distribution of the municipal, centrally stored supplies.

The She-rat admits: Supplies are distributed fairly, though after longer and longer waiting periods. The rat nations are still allowed to attend the church of Saint Mary, as well as Saint Bridget, Holy Trinity and Saint Nicholas. In general, one is struck by the tolerance of their legislation, which is promulgated in palatal, almost guttural, but also in heartwarmingly smurfish tones. The Catholics no longer have the last word; all rats are allowed to practise what religion they please. Again they worship in different ways. Thus, a regulated urban life goes on behind mud walls covered with greenery; apart from occasional rounds of inspection, the country districts are disregarded. The hominids have set up branch offices in Kartuzy, Tczew and Novy Star, the former Neuteich.

All in all, the Swedish Manippels and the Kashubian rats, as well as the newcomers – some African clans have immigrated recently – lead a congenial, harmonious life, which our Herr Matzerath, who on the one hand lies shrunken at the feet of his shrunken grandmother and on the other hand goes on living with his indwelling catheter, is pleased to relegate to the future.

After treating me to an exclusive showing of his video film *Before and After*, he said: 'When we celebrate my sixtieth birthday, as we shall before long, I hope to see your charming wife with you among the guests.'

As though the telephone had not yet been invented, I was informed by postcard of the ship's arrival in the port of Travemünde: 'Letter follows.'

The letter that followed is full of affectionate concern: in addition to the woollen blanket for the double bed, a sweater for me has been finished. Further, I read: the trip went off according to plan. Even the coastal waters of the GDR were navigated without great difficulty. True, they were allowed to land neither in Greifswald nor in Peenemünde. 'Too much canned goods. Many evenings spent listening to a cappella choral music.'

The letter goes on to say that the research project has been more or less carried out. A further increase of jelly-fish is to be feared, but it would be premature to speak of a medusification of the Baltic. With a continuing increase in algae, however, the danger of regional pollution cannot be excluded; the sea stinks in shallow spots. 'Anyway, I'm fed up with counting jellyfish.'

In the letter that followed the postcard I read: Of course tensions on board could not be avoided. 'As I foresaw, the barge is too cramped.' Needless to say, old grievances had been warmed up. In retrospect, the behaviour of the helmswoman, who always had to play first fiddle even when it squeaked, was especially irritating. Despite violent arguments with the engineer – 'during our shore leave in Visby, where she dragged us all to the movies, they were playing some American tripe about monsters, half animal, half human' – she was bearable. The oceanographer was disappointing: 'All she knows is her work.'

All three, says the letter, went ashore in Kiel. 'The helmswoman has appointments at the provincial courthouse: terribly important! The engineer has another exam coming up. Naturally the ocean-ographer is urgently expected at the Institute. All of a sudden, the ladies were in a hurry. Only the Old Woman stuck it out until we tied up in Travemünde; in the end she even scrubbed the deck and the forecastle.'

The letter also mentions unusual cloud formations and a rainy summer. Not a word about Vineta Deep. Møn's Klinten and the chalk cliffs of Rügen Island are termed 'more beautiful than one can imagine'. They had even had a party on board: 'Just ourselves, of course. It was fun.' And without transition: 'Interesting as the trip has been in spite of everything, the *Ilsebill* will have to be sold.' A number of incidents had shown that the women had not learned to get along at close quarters. 'I don't know why. Bad vibes all along. It even got on my nerves to have all these women on board.'

At the end I find, after kisses suggested by small circles, some more affectionate remarks and the announcement that my Damroka would soon be chucking everything else and going back to music.

> I dreamed, not of my rat
> but of a black piano which, overgrown with cactuses,
> wanted to be taken to Europe where
> it was forbidden to keep pianos.

The Rat

And I in Europe dreamed
there was one last pianist,
who couldn't take her fingers off
the cactuses etcetera.

It wasn't a piano, it was a Bechstein grand
which, black but now overgrown with green,
cried out for a pianist
of the traditional European school.

With scissors she disengaged
the lid over the keys
and both pedals from
the thicket below.

She played only briefly in my dream,
something by Bartók; allegro andante allegro.
Then the cactuses started growing again, and everything
was green, as it had been in Brazil.

The next time I dreamed the She-rat,
I told her about it. The cactuses, she said,
are only imagination; the Bechstein grand, however,
is an organ that has survived.

Then I heard Bach in Saint Mary's: forte piano fortissimo.
The nave was full of rats.
The organist, however,
had beautiful long curls over her shoulders.

Chapter Twelve, in which a carriage drives into the past, two old gentlemen talk about the good old days, another Damroka has beautiful curls, museum pieces are collected and rats fed, sad news darkens a birthday party, Solidarność conquers, but nothing is left of mankind, and the last hope crumbles.

ONLY HANSEL and Gretel escape. The dragonlike vehicles have crushed, mangled, shattered every fairy tale that promised to end well or badly, and spat it out behind them. In the end the prince, who had awakened his Sleeping Beauty with a kiss – whereupon sleep released the Chancellor and his retinue – was stamped into the forest floor along with his Sleeping Beauty, so that all we, who in the film as in life are always the losers, have left is a pair of detached rosebud lips. Never again will anyone kiss like him. No everlasting sleep will come over us. From now on all dreams will be daydreams.

The soldiers' laughter. 'Everything, kaput!' They slap each other on the back.

No wonder everything goes on as before; no, worse, because now there's no hope. But while the experts bicker as if there were nothing else to do, while ministers and industrialists carry on with their deals in perfect security, for the submachine guns are again at the ready, while the bishops, who can think of nothing new, give the generals their blessing again, and the Chancellor, for the benefit of the television crew and to the delight of the journalists, shouts at the top of his lungs: 'Hansi! Margarethe!' – Hansel and Gretel cut and run.

That's how our Herr Matzerath wants it. I agree with him. Someone has to get away. Nobody wants to be entirely without fairy tales.

That's what people are saying all over the country, but when the journalists ask, 'Mr Ex-Chancellor, do you miss your children very much?', it's not their father but the General-Chancellor who answers with a helpless shrug: 'We must learn to live with such losses.'

Though no one is following them, the horrified Hansel and Gretel keep running through the unchanging rigor mortis of the dead forest. Not a single backward glance; only away, away, away . . .

When the television men hold a microphone up to the industrialists and ask: 'And now what's to be done about the forests?' one of the industrialists answers: 'Write 'em off. We'll do to the forests what we've done to the fairy tales.'

That stands as a subtitle while Hansel and Gretel keep running.

In response to questions, the bishops represent all happening, whether good or bad, as the will of God. 'The Lord giveth and the Lord taketh away,' says one. And another: 'God's will be done.'

As written on the clapperboard which an assistant strikes before every interview, the television documentary will be titled: 'Witch dead – fairy tales finished.'

Asked finally for their opinions, the ministers and experts all reply at once: 'New expertises will be needed.' – 'Independent ones of course!' – 'It's time to establish priorities!' – 'Let others talk about forests. We ignore them!' – 'What's dying isn't the forests, but the spirit of the enterprise!' – 'That's all a lot of childishness, pure childishness.'

Hansel and Gretel laugh and keep running. As they run hand in hand through the dead forest, saplings sprout and burgeon. Leap after leap, the dead branches change and so do the laughing, hopping and skipping children. As though moving backward in time, Hansel and Gretel are wearing old-fashioned clothes. Running in knee breeches, laced shoes, knitted stockings and long skirt, they show bobbing braids and flying curls under cap and bonnet. They are designed by the hand of the graphic artist Ludwig Richter; and the forest turns as green as the pious Moritz von Schwind painted it: dark firs, towering beeches, oaks, elms, age-old mixed forest, so dense and deep that no charcoal burner can penetrate it.

They run as though fairy tales were still in existence, as though, before you knew it, the unicorn would, as though, where jays flush, the woodpecker taps, and mushrooms grow in a circle, the witch cannot be far off. Something is moving in the underbrush. Again the anthill. As in the beginning, when there was still hope, it's a golden hair, which the wood pigeon carries in its beak to show them the way, through variegated filtered light, through ferns and moss and carpets of pine needles, for they are going somewhere.

And where two paths cross in the middle of the forest, Hansel and Gretel are not in the least surprised to see a carriage harnessed to four white horses. With no coachman on the box, studded with silver nails, as though the lord of the castle had obligingly sent it.

The horses snort. Their harness gleams. The carriage door opens. Glad to see the children again, Jakob and Wilhelm Grimm greet them with friendly smiles. They too are in Biedermeier dress: high hats, frilled collars, velvet jackets, pockets and sleeves bordered with braid; just as they are known to us from yellowed prints made long ago when they collected fairy tales in Hessen and elsewhere, in the days when forests were still forests.

Our Herr Matzerath thinks there's not much more to say. Nevertheless I leave Wilhelm Grimm the sentence: 'Come and sit with us, children.' And Jakob Grimm's invitation can serve as a subtitle: 'This present day is no place for us. We are no longer welcome.'

Hansel and Gretel might curtsy graciously and say in unison: 'We had a hunch that we weren't lost for ever!'

Then they get into the carriage, which is guided only by the four white horses, not forward but back into the past, with the horses trotting behind it. An entertaining journey; the travellers meet all sorts of simple folk.

To the left and right of the bumpy road, which soon emerges from the forest but leads between meadows and grain fields to another forest, we see people striding along in old-fashioned costumes, in rags and uniforms, striding jauntily or struggling under heavy loads: the little old woman bent under her bundle of faggots, the man carrying the beehive, the woman with the wicker basket, the peasant, the calf led by a rope, two itinerant journeymen, the goose girl, the beggar boy, but also handless peasants and heavily guarded prisoners in chains.

But because the carriage in which Hansel and Gretel are riding with the Grimm Brothers is going backwards, all the people they pass are going backwards step by step; as though the old woman were being pulled by her bundle of faggots, the man by the beehive, the potter's wife by her heavy back basket, and the peasant by the calf on the rope. Singing, the young journeymen walk backwards. The geese drive the maid back into the barn. The little boy tries to beg from the people behind him. And once they've dragged and driven one another far enough into the land of Once-upon-a-time, the landless peasants and prisoners, along with the soldiers guarding them, start hoping that they will finally find land, get better pay and be free from chains. So full of promise is the past.

Here the silent film *The Grimms' Forests* might end. And anyone who finds the regressive ending of the silent film about the dying forest and the death of the fairy tales too encouraging, too embellished by hope and not angry enough, need only, our Herr Matzerath advises, open the newspaper and read, until overcome by anger, what the Chancellor's experts have to say. The story of Hansel and Gretel, in any case, is over and done with.

Ah, Rat, Ratkin. What, apart from the Third Programme, have we left? Where is there any hope? In whose presence might I, when I dream, say: We still exist. We are still here. We want to and we will . . .

True, Malskat exists. Affected by so much past present, he lives on an island in the Deepenmoor near Lübeck and not far from the dead-sure border between the two states which to each other impersonate a different Germany. As an honest forger, he has survived his contemporaries who remained swindlers to the end, in poverty to be sure, but respected by all, while the old fox and the goatee with the Saxon accent stick bitter in our craws.

And when, Ratkin, I maintain that not only Malskat but also our Herr Matzerath is still in existence and (in his case) producing marketable video cassettes, you can believe me, for I too am still here and only occasionally in my space capsule. I've brought the crumbled cheese that you're fond of. To you I demonstrate my existence by caresses, kind words, and fresh straw. And Damroka, who again exists, drops in now and then with her coffee pot and watches us as we converse.

It remains only to confute the thesis that all is mere illusion and afterglow. According to this thesis, we no longer exist; we are only seemingly active, dreamed by rats, who alone are real and who keep inventing us who used to be, because they are reluctant to lose the concept of man. They deliberately dream me, you, your open cage, your crumbs of cheese, Malskat on his island in the Deepenmoor, Damroka's brief visits, the media-mad Herr Matzerath and the Third Programme, whose brave speakers contend that life goes on, that it's worthwhile to go on living and listen to Educational Radio for All. That there is hope, if only in crumbs. That all dangers can be averted by reason, self-discipline and exhaustive rethinking. That where there's a will there's a way. That it's possible to plan for the future. That for all our scepticism the year two thousand will definitely come. We are even told that protective coverings will be thrown over what forests we have left; that glass domes will provide fresh air for large settlements; that genetics will provide an answer to hunger; that a way will soon be found of making mankind peaceable for ever more; that little by little time will consent to be turned forward and backward; we must only, says the Third Programme, have the will to will, and to rethink as soon as possible . . .

And so we live on, dreamed by rat nations who alone are real and making progress. The Watsoncricks, says the She-rat, are taking over more and more. What our Herr Matzerath's video film held out as a prospect has become well-organized fact: in the Danzig-Gdańsk area they have developed a system of taxation which guarantees superabundant food to the humanoid rats and landed property to all the rat nations that engage in agriculture.

Whichever way power is organized, property is obviously indispensable, an insight that has carried over into the post-human era. Could it be that we, dreamed by rats, are acquiring a constructive influence on the rat-men that we are dreaming? It would seem, after all, that in former times God, seen as a bearded man, had no objection to any of the images man made of him.

She's growing. My Christmas rat is growing perceptibly. I'm amazed. Yet it's known that ordinary brown rats and laboratory rats grow throughout the three years of their lifetime. I observe her growth with alarm. One day she may cease to be, lie stiff on her back. What shall I wish for at Christmas, when there's no more ratkin, but only Malskat and his outdated story, our Herr Matzerath and his video market, Damroka once in a while and, while the Third Programme goes on rumbling, my own self, fallen out of everyone's dreams, only me?

The She-rat claims that the Watsoncricks have succeeded in

getting the Neptune Fountain and organ in Saint Mary's back into working order; and, no sooner back from Poland, our Herr Matzerath is planning to put his pre-produced cassette, anticipating his grandmother's hundred and seventh birthday, on the market.

The organ of Saint Mary's was destroyed by fire toward the end of the interbellum, but shortly before the end of the human era a new organ was built into the saved organ screen of Saint John.

Now our Herr Matzerath is planning to produce a serial on the Adenauer–Malskat–Ulbricht theme. Its working title might be *Forgers at Work*, or possibly just *The Phony Fifties*.

The She-rat says the rat nations enjoy the organ concerts that the Watsoncricks put on for them every Sunday.

He seems to have visited Malskat recently on his island in the Deepenmoor. Needless to say, our Herr Matzerath arrived in his chauffeur-driven Mercedes. 'Ferry!' he cried when he saw there was no bridge to the island. Malskat ferried the humpback little man across in a rowboat. The chauffeur had to wait with the Mercedes.

The Third Programme, which is always up to date, is doing Bach at the moment: Toccata and Fugue in F Major. But, the She-rat tells me, the clones also know their Buxtehude. There's no reason for secrecy about what the two aging gentlemen had to say to each other on the island.

While the one paced the floor of the tiny room, as though that were all the exercise he needed, gesturing eloquently with his hands, the other, his everlasting woollen cap drawn half over his ears, listened. The one said: 'Actually I should put *The Dying Forest* into production, but your story takes precedence.' The other said nothing.

'All that, the destruction of the choir saints and of the Grimms' forests, must be regarded as a logical unit,' said the humpback little man on his way back and forth. Few words escaped the painter under his woollen cap, a few technical details at the very most.

From time to time, as though to gain perspective, they both spoke of their childhood. They called Danzig and Königsberg unforgettable. 'What was crucial for me,' said the one, 'was that on my third birthday my poor mama gave me a tin drum, lacquered red and white, whereupon I decided to stop growing.' 'Even as a child,' said the other, 'I painted a lot. My paintings were modelled on the old masters in my father's antique shop.' Then, after skipping over their youth, disposing of the war years in a few sentences, terming the ensuing black market period ghastly but enjoyable, they felt at home in the fifties.

'An American song,' said the one, 'sung ad nauseam by a quartet calling themselves The Platters, and titled most convincingly *The Great Pretender*, might, in the plural, of course, have been taken as a national anthem by the two German states.'

'We are the Great Pretenders,' sang the one, while the other proposed a street song of the fifties, the words of which raise the question of payment.*

'Our film,' said our Herr Matzerath, 'will make use of the new medium, the video technique of fluid transitions, and is intended to open the eyes, most particularly of the young and unsuspecting, and to make them acquainted at long last with the era of the great forgeries.'

'I, at least,' said Malskat, 'exposed my part in the big swindle. All of a sudden, I stopped thinking it was funny.'

And then our Herr Matzerath, ignoring Malskat, launched into a long speech:

'We start in the late fifties with the scaffolding; shifting from one scene of action to another, we show the big scaffold going up in the interior of Lübeck's church of Saint Mary. We fade in the preparations for the proclamation of the two states, on this side, let's say, the zeal of the parliamentary council, on the other the busy comings and goings between Pankow and Karlshorst. Then we show the all-German forgery at work on three levels. The Russians, the Americans and the art experts all suspect the forgeries from the start, but fail to realize how credibly real every swindle becomes if it lasts long enough.'

Because the only evidence of early mural painting in the church of Saint Mary is a trickle of pulverized paint, an East Prussian painter is hired at starvation wages to create Gothic saints from nothing, or rather from the painter's treasure trove, which since his childhood has become more and more richly endowed. In the same way, early dreams, on this side of a Rhenish-clerical, on that side of a Saxon-Prussian stamp, are made to come true. Those statesmen,

* Who's going to foot the bill?
  That's what I'd like to know?
  Who's got so much money?
  Who's got so much dough?

the one with the features of an Indian, the other with those of a German petty bourgeois, have had to wait a long time for the opportunity; never has the painter with the Gothic cast of mind been offered so large a surface. The political forgeries are given the name of Republic; the murals are called the miracle of Lübeck. True, on this side and that side, and in the vaulting of the choir loft, swastikas are chiselled away; true, on this side and that side a message on the one hand democratic, on the other Communist, is spooned out like pudding, but yesterday's screams are long heard behind the new façades; however carefully the cellars are sealed, the smell of corpses cannot be hidden; the shit-brown reputation of certain Lübeck clergymen makes it hard for them to be pleasing to God in new innocence. But the fraud is successful! On either side the defeated, who only a short while ago were begging for indulgence, have curried favour with the victor power. Flies in the ointment? Already they are militarily reliable. Build! Build! they shout and things are looking up again! They talk about guilt, as if it were a matter of debts and instalment payments. Soon the ones are less poor than their exhausted victor power, while the others are firmly convinced that they will soon be richer than their victor neighbour; and the murals in Lübeck's church of Saint Mary amount to a lot more than was ever there before. All the Gothic anyone could wish for. And everywhere people stand, lie, kneel in wonderment before all-embracing phoniness. And the whole world is amazed at how quickly a defeat can be turned into the opposite. Risen from the ruins! We sing, we shout, we slap each other on the back: We're somebody again. We defy anyone to do the same. Yesterday the lowest of the low. And today? Oh well, a gloomy rainy uprising of the workers over there, a more mumbled than shouted count-me-out protest against rearmament over here. Quite a few embarrassing scandals, but they happen everywhere. So long as we behave and go on being the big victor's pet, keep unauthorized persons away from the scaffolding, speak often enough of the first German workers' and peasants' state, of our free democratic constitution, and of the seminal power of North German Gothic, the forgery will be consecrated on all sides. As happens in Bonn, Pankow and Lübeck, where during the seventh centenary celebration even master forger Adenauer is taken in; or did the Old Man suspect the fraud and admire only the way it was put across? 'They've done a good job,' he is said to have said in his Rhenish dialect, and given a Catholic wink . . .

Our Herr Matzerath paused. He took short steps in Malskat's low-ceilinged room. With sparse gestures he added a few more touches to his *Phony Fifties* video film: we must show the taste and fashions of those years. Not only the inevitable kidney-shaped tables and the yawningly empty large-format abstract paintings, not only the Messerschmitt bubble car and various Borgward limousines, but also the growth of the two armies. In song, the evening perpetually sinking into the sea off Capri, Fritz Walter on the soccer field, and on both sides murderers in public office. 'Oh yes,' he cried, 'every crime, the clock that cannot be turned off, ticking incessantly behind the façades. Tell me, my dear Malskat, I've heard that you sometimes concealed rats, singly or in pairs, in the ornament of the capitals and in the drapery of your saints . . .'

Malskat denied it. Lots of fabulous animals – the turkeys in the Schleswig cloister had been by his hand – but rats, never, he had never so much as dreamed of . . .

Recollection settled between them like dust. They thought back. Especially our Herr Matzerath must have enjoyed running off his life in reverse, station after station. He removed his gold-rimmed glasses, revealing the blue eyes that saw through all miracles, invited the painter to his forthcoming birthday party, and said: 'My dear Malskat, you should have let the fraud take care of itself.' To which the painter replied: 'Maybe so. But I just happen to be honest.'

As at church the Amen,
Everything is predetermined. Therefore,
in numerous books and in exciting films, our end
has already come off and is now legend,
like that Hamelin story, which was also predetermined.

For when the lost children with their rats
were shut up in Calvary Mountain and the time
refused to pass, they whispered
to one another: This isn't the end.
They'll look for us and
surely find us.

The burghers of Hamelin, who had immured their children,
rats and all, in the mountain and
sealed it, decided to look for

their children, and pretended to be really looking.
They went out to look and cried:
We'll surely find them.

Just one of the children said to his rat:
They will not find us, because no one is looking.
That, I know, was predetermined.

I can draw her on white paper: the She-rat of my dreams wears
her hair in curls and is becoming more and more human. When she
says in passing that the rule of the Neo-Swedish Watsoncricks in the
Danzig-Gdańsk area has proved to be mild and gets along without
harshness, she is speaking *pro domo*. No Christmas rat, and no
longer the bare-tailed She-rat enlivens my dreams by day and by
night. No, this ratty human with the beautiful curls reminds me of
Damroka, who in reality, when the human race came to an end,
dissolved with other women in a research ship, but then, because I
dreamed a postcard, which a letter promised to follow, was
suddenly here again: at home.

She listens to me patiently. She understands my complaints, my
denial of her reality. Her hair keeps getting new ideas. Dearest, she
says, aren't you content to be dreamed, to be dreamed only by me
and to be relieved of responsibility from now on, because outside of
my dreams you do not exist?

It's pleasant to be dreamed by her who says I. She shows me
everything. The Neo-Swedes walking erect in the streets of
Danzig's Right City. Couples with their broods – the hominoid
rats' children are really cute – saunter back and forth between Long
Street Gate and the Long Market. No sign of normal rats. Only
when hominoid inspectors – always in pairs – visit the surrounding
country, the Vistula estuary and Kashubia, do normal rats enter the
picture.

Amiably and attentively the Neo-Swedes oversee the agriculture
of the rat nations. They give knowledgeable advice. Barley and
corn are still the staple crops; spacious, rolling sunflower fields still
gleam in the sunlight. Young rats, hidden behind flower heads, still
catch pigeons, sparrows and other pests.

They say: We proceed cautiously. After all, it was unmanipulated
rats, who took care not only of themselves but also of us, who could
have exterminated us when we were weak and few in number. But

they accepted us. Rang their bells in welcome. They recognized us as human beings in an improved version. Their fervent wish, my dearest, was not for your return; no, all their singing and praying was for our coming. You told me about masses, you said, and thought, that the prayers of the rat nations were Catholic. That's nonsense, superstition. We have given their congregations a new order, a Reformation as it were.

And I saw the changes in the interior of the church of Saint Mary. The mummy of Anna Koljaiczek with the shrunken Oskar at her feet, the altar decorations, the gold ducats and blue-and-white smurfs, the eyeglasses along with their case, the paper cutter, the false teeth, the wrought-iron Solidarność standard, the decoration conferred by the Polish government, all that and Oskar's rings had disappeared. Cold severity and Protestant bareness predominated. Two male Neo-Swedes officiated at the altar, stiffly and meticulously, as though checking upon each other. But down from the pulpit my curly-haired beauty spoke over the heads of the assembled rat nations. In countless variations she spoke only of labour and sorrow.

A gloomy solemnity emanated from the altar and pulpit, oppressed the congregation, humbled them, kept the rats so subdued that they could not stand erect. And there was nothing Gregorian about their singing. They sang stanzaic hymns. I believe I heard: A mighty fortress . . . and Do not despair, ye precious few . . . But the familiar words all sounded totally besmurft; every third word was corrupted by the palatal mumbling of the Watson-cricks. I felt tempted to join in the singing.

That's the second sound shift, said the manipulated Damroka, though not in a shifted accent; if anything, she rolled her R's, as they have been rolled from time immemorial in western Pomerania. I found her on the organ bench which, like the music stand cut to the measure of the Manippels, seemed tiny in comparison with the huge organ pipes. She improvised with her hands and feet, as though playing the organ came as natural to her as inhaling and exhaling; all this had been made possible by the magic three-letter word DNA.

While Damroka was doing variations on Jesu, Joy of Man's Desire, I heard her report: Actually we have not eliminated that gruesome mummy and her mummified gnome. You'll find them both in the farthermost corner of the organ loft, where no one pays much attention to them. As you know, we manage without violence. We favour slow, painless transitions. Our conduct is guided by rational insight, and that is why we have not forbidden the worship of the two mummies; on the contrary, we tolerate it and on certain days even encourage it. Year after year, for instance, on the anniversary of the Big Bang, we celebrate it by allowing the rat nations to worship the two mummies, as we do on the anniversary of our landing. Since then these last two concrete exemplars of humanity have exerted a deterrent effect, a late insight which can only be beneficial. Look at them! I say time and again from the pulpit. Never again must this happen. See to what it has reduced mankind. Let these mummies be a reminder and a warning to us. See how abominable!

And to me, too, the curly-haired hominoid rat spoke words of enlightenment. Still playing the organ with hands and feet, she said: By saying Yes to the rat component in us, we are becoming truly human. And because we are aware of our human component, the ratty component has become essential to us. Though originally the work of man, we point beyond our creators, with whom we sympathize in retrospect. They were their own downfall, whereas we, because of the ratty component in us, have a future.

She stopped playing, turned to me with her rat's snout but also her magnificent curls cascading on both sides, and said: One more reason to take a sympathetic but also distanced view of the rats when groups of them worship the last orbiting satellite in which you, my dearest, whom time and again I have dreamed at close quarters, are preserved for ever. We hear your grumbling. Your complaints and demands are known to us. Your screams of Come in, Earth. Answer me, Earth, tempt us at times to crack jokes at your expense. Your encapsulated dream that human beings still exist, still active and brimful of ideas, communicates itself to us. We understand your anger well. Your belated remorse strikes sympathetic chords. And I am moved to hear you grieve for your Damroka.

I would gladly have buried my head and all my loneliness in her curls; only her laughter upset me. Still seated at the organ, but now with her hands in her lap, she said: Sometimes, I admit, we smile when you keep claiming reality for your human machismo and your dreary sexploits, whereas I, your loved one after all, and all the Swedish Manippels, and all the rat nations entrusted to our care, are the product of your dreams, which are interchangeable with other dreams.

Suddenly stern, she said: This must stop. We tolerate no evasions. It might occur to us to forget you, to stop thinking you funny, to start dreaming something other than you, mammalian bluebottles for instance. I hope you catch my little hint.

We quarrelled. I cried out: Your preposterous bluebottles. There's no such thing.

She stood up to me: Pretty soon you'll cease to exist. I gave in. All right, Damroka. But kindly stop threatening me.

Still stern, she pulled out organ stops: Just a warning, my dear, to let you know what emptiness you would fall into if I should . . .

The rest was drowned out by the roar of the organ. Softly, perhaps too softly – but she heard me all the same – I said: No, I beg you. I still think you're beautiful. What's more: I dream you physically. I'm really wrapped up in you, crazy about you, even if you Nippels are a bit too small. I'm getting used to it, adapting myself. Even your ratty face can't scare my love away. We should come closer, still closer together, if only the organ bench weren't so small and your twatlet so narrow . . .

I heard myself loud over Bach and Buxtehude, over all the organ stops: Yes, it's you and you alone that I want. My love, I've never felt it so strongly; I want to be everything possible, your spouse, your fool, your heavenly bridegroom. I love you so I could nibble you, eat you, devour every bit of you . . . But oh, my dearest, stop contesting my wretched bit of reality. It's mine and I won't let anybody, see? You can make up to me as rattily as you please. The moment I wake up I'll twist the knob and the Third Programme will confirm my existence. The Third Programme always knows the answer, it consoles, it relies on reason. It tells us in advance what will be decided in Brussels tomorrow. It teaches us to put hope, if only the teensie-weensiest, in long-winded talks scheduled to be held soon. Something is always happening somewhere. Interest rates are going down. The Pope has no end of travel plans. End of season sales will stimulate the economy. And our Herr Matzerath will be celebrating his birthday, he's going to be sixty; a party to which we, please, Damroka, are cordially invited. But you remain unmoved, as though all that – the Pope, Brussels, the end of season sales – were pure imagination, mere fiction . . . Neither she nor the tiny organ bench were within my reach. Strapped into my space capsule again, I heard her. Painfully remote, her image filled my monitor. My stammering: But all I wanted was a bit of medium-term data . . .

Those rolled R's. Her voice imprinted in western Pomerania: Don't talk nonsense. Will you ever get it through your head that the whole lot of you, including the Third Programme, exist only in our dreams? Or – quite apart from love – to make myself plainer: as long as we and the rats entrusted to our care are willing to remember you, the godlike self-destroyers, there will be human movement, in other words, you too will exist as a gradually diminishing reflex. To tell the truth, we regret our loss of memory, that paling of once distinct images. We combat it, we are not idle. First in the Artushof, then in the Rathaus, we mean to set up a museum; educational exhibits of the human era will be on display. A good deal can still be learned from your garbage. And all sorts of impressive objects were left in your buildings and basements: typewriters, telephones, a movie camera, an intact Volkswagen, spare parts and accessories, a reasonably well preserved Bechstein grand. And the ancient woman with her brat won't be left any longer to gather dust in the organ loft; at last they will come to rest as an exhibit in our collection. And needless to say, we, like the rat nations before us, will do everything in our power to preserve the crumbling buildings of Danzig–Gdańsk. Sorrow and labour enough, God knows.

After considerable begging and wheedling, in which no end of time was lost, she let me unbuckle myself and approach her again. Under her guidance I visited the Museum of Late Human History. And I saw groups of rats, led by Watsoncrick instructors, climb winding stairways, hurry through the Rathaus rooms. All in perfect order. Everything in its case. And how much there was to see!

Look, cried my loved one, who to celebrate was wearing an amber necklace under my Damroka's cascading curls, see how much is left of you humans.

I saw a dentist's chair and beside it the instruments that went with it. A mini-computer next to an old-fashioned storekeeper's scale. Plenty of art, including some Gothic pieces. And imagine: porcelain. But also light and heavy weapons. Ground-to-air missiles. Next to these a tempting toy department with a sprinkling of smurfs, singly and in groups: the one with the axe, the ones with scythes, the two with tennis rackets symbolizing leisure, the one with the signalling disc regulating toy traffic, the idler, the fruit vendor, a number of smurfs operating an expertly constructed miniature railway or waiting on the station platform; all as cute as ever. I saw kitchen utensils, mixers and toasters; I saw police accessories, truncheons, handcuffs, visor helmets. I saw a few leftovers from human history, most of them with German–Polish implications: amid decorations and badges Solidarność, the wrought-iron standard, the fourth letter from the last still holding the white and red flag.

Oh! And this too. What I didn't want to see. Look! she cried. Look at this! And I saw a piece of my childhood: between the lagoon and the Baltic Sea, a model of the Stutthof concentration camp, which had been only one of more than a thousand six hundred camps, displayed as a witness to human history, forgetting neither the crematoriums nor a single one of the barracks.

On the way back, I saw a globe which the visiting rats would have liked to touch and set in motion, if they had been allowed. And in the book department, which like the musical instrument room was extremely crowded, I discovered, amid large, rather unstable piles of books, quite a few Polish masterpieces, *Pan Tadeus*, *Ferdydurke*, etc., and there I looked about for him and his grandmother. But it wasn't until I visited the Red Room of the Rathaus, where the Tribute Money painting had been, that I found the mummies of Anna Koljaiczek and her grandson. Finally at rest. Half covered by some crumbling fabric. He at her feet. But something was lacking.

I whispered to my dearest. She smiled. Yes, my curly-haired guide, in whom I recognized my Damroka, smiled and allowed a tin drum, in passably good condition, which I couldn't help seeing on my visit to the toy department, to be moved into the Red Room of the Rathaus. This was done by two Neo-Swedish attendants. Oskar was given what he lacked. My dearest said with a laugh: What was it they used to say? Everything in its place.

Later, moved elsewhere, or rather, shut up in my capsule, I heard her, though the picture didn't show her manipulated charm: You see, we spare no effort. Many of the pieces were found in the city; others, such as shards of Kashubian pottery, were brought in from outside. We felt that the memory of man should not be allowed to pale and die. Thus the rat nations are actually taught to remember human greatness and human hubris; I admit, you see, that we hominoid rats are sometimes obliged to exercise coercion. We impose visits to museums. Since we control the stocks of seed and grain, we have no difficulty in enforcing our regulations. The fact that we allot land titles makes the rural, agricultural rat nations if not totally dependent on us, then at least eager to please. And this has consequences. From the mouths of the rivers to the hill country the land has already been distributed. All the rat nations supply transport columns, for all stocks are centrally stored. Only in the city is surveillance possible. Distribution takes place here. And we are in charge of it. Under this system no one need go hungry. It is based on tolerable shortages.

Here she broke off. She had talked herself into a contemplative mood. After a pause, which left me time to toy with other realities – I evoked deadlines, a forthcoming birthday party – I heard her say in tones of anxiety: It is not without misgiving that we observe this development. The danger of relapse into a brand of human behaviour that is only too well known must be recognized, all the more so as we had learned to strike flame, which will have, no, already has had, consequences. We hominoids simmer, boil, roast our ears of corn, as well as the farm rats' game, all of which they have had to hand over, because of our almost insatiable passion for meat cooked over the coals. Yes, they do what is expected of them. But it's far from sufficient, less and less so. Our efforts to relieve the meat shortage by planning are making slow headway.

Her report was worse than I had feared: Since in some regions, especially in rich marsh land, the populations have increased disproportionately, it became necessary to thin out the rat nations by selection, first in the Vistula estuary, where immigrants from Russia and India are settled; later on, the measure will be extended to the Kashubian hinterland, where old residents, intermingled with rats of German extraction, have their plots of land. We concentrate strong young animals in particular territories . . .

Right! she cried, you've guessed it. In the place where we landed, where the wrecked ship is still tied up and can be visited on holidays, on the so-called Warehouse Island, we feed selected young rats selected seeds and grains, until they are crammed full and ready for slaughter. As we have succeeded in producing edible rats of far above normal weight, we shall soon be adequately provided with roasting meat; even pigeons, you know, are in short supply outside the harvest season. Since we introduced soup kitchens, we have no real shortages even now. There's always something braising or frying. We ought to be content with what we've got. And yet, as the last barley harvests were over-abundant, we've started brewing beer, an innovation opposed by the council of Neo-Swedes. It's served on Arsenal Alley, on certain porches on Lady Street, and in the Rathaus Cellar. In moderation, of course, and always under state control. Group booze parties must be approved, and suitable supervisors must be present. But when Big Bang Day was celebrated recently – the seventy-fifth anniversary it was – our people offered the rat delegations present a spectacle that can only be described as deplorable: hordes staggering up and down Long Street, the Neptune Fountain overflowing with vomit . . .

All that worries me, my dearest, she said, and was close to me again on the tiny organ bench. She was improvising. It sounded sad. Like a Passion. Oh, Damroka!

In the search for differences between man and animal,
love is often mentioned as
a faculty peculiar to man.
Meant here is not
love of fellows, which is more frequent
among animals than among men,
but that of Tristan and Isolde
and other exemplary couples,
which even among swans
are inconceivable.
Little as we know about the whale and his cow,
scenes such as those between Faust and Gretchen
would be alien to those large mammals,
if not unnatural.
Higher than the stag's rutting is Solomon's Song of Songs.
Nothing the apes do can equal the lovers of Verona.
No nightingale or lark, only man
loves at all costs, in and out of season, to the point of madness
and beyond the grave.
As we know, lovers would even like
to eat each other up.
That is true, dearest: at once, bones and all.
But first – to a lute accompaniment –

let us roast
a juicy loin of pork and eat it.

Please, please let's accept his invitation. Look, he's had cards printed, kind of silly, in Sütterlin script. There won't be a big crowd, only close friends. He mentioned you especially in a handwritten note. '. . . and do bring Damroka . . .' We can dress as we like. He asks for an answer. (Malskat seems to have declined. Too bad.)

We got there too early. Only a few guests at the start. A few of the long-legged ladies he goes in for. They always look like nurses in civilian clothes. Tired from so much caring. He hadn't made his appearance yet. Damroka was wearing her golden yellow dress. The present I had brought was a translation of his memoirs, illegally printed in Poland, a rarity in two volumes on unspeakable paper. (The legal edition was published only recently, and was soon out of print.)

Only a few gentlemen from his firm, his lawyer, the ladies from his sales department, two Japanese business friends and several big-name film producers who are more or less under obligation to him, among them an eternal youth in dinner jacket and Alpine boots, who liked best to exercise his genius in tropical jungles and sandy deserts or – like Luis Trenker in his day – on excessively high mountains. Further, an eminent professor and an unshaved poet who never stopped glaring, though the childlike lady who was with him looks something like Maria Truczinski, who as a young thing, before becoming Frau Matzerath, often wore a necklace of wooden beads. Maria, however, who actually turned up wearing pearls with her severely tailored suit, took no notice of her youthful likeness, but reserved her concern for her uncouth son Kurt, who headed straight for the buffet.

The host had not yet made his appearance. In an undertone I filled her in on the guests, who by then had almost all arrived. She knew the professor. 'That headwaiter serving the sweet champagne,' I said, 'is his chauffeur Bruno. A jack of all trades.'

Early September. Indian summer outside. Evening sun trickling in through the veranda windows. Damroka took a dislike to the genius in Alpine boots: 'He's always admiring himself in the mirror.' Over the loosely grouped gathering hovered the voice of the professor, who spoke as though addressing a far larger audience. Referring to the still absent host, he recalled his seminal remarks about the role of the outsider. One of the film makers who, in doing a film of his own a short while ago, had become closely acquainted with the birthday child's early years, declared: Exactly. He had focused on Oskar's exemplary outsiderness.

Then he made his appearance. Our Herr Matzerath approached his guests, not as expected through the French doors, but through a hidden side entrance. Belatedly discovered, he was applauded.

We saw he was embarrassed. Reluctant to join any of the little groups. All in large checks. Were his glasses misty? With a look of irritation he surveyed the gathering, overlooked me in spite of Damroka, seemed to miss someone or other, Malskat undoubtedly, suddenly drew himself up and, before concerning himself with any of the other guests, greeted Maria, who had to bend down to be kissed on the cheek, something which his early love, now a matron, had always detested. Little Kurt was feeding far off at the buffet: smoked salmon canapés, cracklings.

From then on our Herr Matzerath was besieged. Congratulations and more congratulations. (He took more interest in the film producer who at the professor's suggestion had recognized him as an outsider, than in me, to whom he owes his indwelling catheter.)

And what a lot of presents! On a long table lay small parcels and even big ones. He took only fleeting notice of them, but the Polish edition of his memoirs seemed to give him pleasure: 'Better late than never.' When I introduced Damroka, who even towers over me, he tilted back his bald head, looked up at her and managed the smile that makes everyone to whom it's addressed turn suddenly hot and cold. 'I understand,' he said. No more. Then he was besieged again.

A lot more might be said about the beginning of the birthday party. For instance: The buffet, which was not long in opening, had been supplied at bargain prices by Maria's delicatessen department. Or: How when the terrace doors were opened, the Japanese guests were quick to snap group photos including the birthday child, one of them showing Oskar between Damroka and myself. Or: How little Kurt, addressing our Herr Matzerath as 'brother dear', importuned him with news of his debts. Or: A late summer evening, no mosquitoes, merriment, golden . . . But relaxed and only marginally artificial as the party promised to be, something impels me to cast a shadow on it.

The Rat

It was Bruno who brought in the telegram on a silver tray. He had piled other telegrams and special delivery messages of congratulation on the gift table. This one he handed his employer in person. It may be that Bruno's way of delivering special messages, sluggishly, as though reluctantly, imposed increasing silence on the birthday guests; after me the film maker, who had occasionally been close to Oskar's moods, took notice; then the professor; at length all realized that something staged by another director must have happened.

Have I already said that our Herr Matzerath takes his glasses off in reading? He held them to one side, arching his little finger. He read, look around, was wholly in possession of his all-penetrating blue-eyedness, motioned sparely to little Kurt to come closer, said: 'My son,' then: 'She was your great-grandmother,' and asked him to read the telegram aloud.

Dispatched in Matarnia by the priest of the like-named parish, the telegram announced the death of Anna Koljaiczek, who had passed away at a biblical age. Little Kurt was unequal to the task. He stuttered, broke it down into syllables. It ended with: 'We grieve with you.'

Bruno must have suspected how our Herr Matzerath would take his grandmother's death; he refilled glasses all round so adroitly that Oskar's wish that all might drink with him to the memory of Anna Koljaizcek could be fufilled without delay. Oskar then requested that there be no condolences and begged the guests to carry on with the party just as the deceased would have wished, despite the shadow that had fallen on it.

So the guests stayed. Only little Kurt left. All stood in groups and talked in muffled tones. When our Herr Matzerath asked leave to sit down, Maria stood beside him. How lost he was in the spacious armchair, with his patent leather shoes a considerable distance above the floor. Damroka said: 'Look, she's holding his hand.' There was nothing casual about Maria's gesture. As long as he remained seated, she stood by him.

I don't remember who, other than myself, asked the professor to say a few words, probably the film producers and the poet; in any case he spoke extemporaneously, yet as comprehensively as if his obituary on Anna Koljaiczek could be expected to explain the world and the state it was in. 'We all know,' he said, 'what she embodied,' and proceeded to divulge what all of us knew. 'How

[349]

she endured a century and more of horrible, nay more, barbarous history. True, she lived on the fringe; she suffered the times. It was her grandson who participated, who shared in the action, yes, and the guilt as well. But without her, who spent her whole life where she had started out, on the Kashubian land, which – as we now know – signifies the world, he, our outsider and dubious hero, would have been rootless, lost as it were.'

Then the professor reminded us of Oskar's thirtieth birthday and said with the air of one who knew even the most obscure details: 'At that time he thought he could get away from us.' He went on to call our Herr Matzerath's further existence typical of the fifties, spoke also of himself and his own outsiderness, and mentioned the Matzerathian video production only briefly, but not without critical implications. 'Our friend just seems to have this thing about the media.' He concluded after a subordinate clause about me and a reference, heard and approved by all, to Maria: 'But now Oskar is all ours.'

And so the shadowed birthday took a cheerful turn after all. The speaker was congratulated. If my Damroka had not drawn him into a lengthy conversation about early Baroque church music, the professor would in the end have been feted more than the birthday child. Then she took him prisoner with an account of her Baltic voyage, no station of which she omitted – Møns Klint, Visby, Greifswald Bay . . . 'But now,' she said, 'I'm fed up with jellyfish.' Finally Oskar, at first still hand in hand with Maria, mingled again with the guests.

I learned, incidentally, that for the present a production of *The Grimms' Forests* was out of the question. This I was told by the manager of the Post Futurum company. They would soon, if that was any comfort to me, take up the Malskat case. Herr Matzerath, it seems, was convinced that the key to our success must be sought among the vestiges of the fifties.

The film producers named their forthcoming productions. For reasons that were not evident, the poet's countenance darkened. Maria left without saying goodbye to me. Like an idiot I got involved in an argument with the genius. Luckily the professor, and with him Damroka, remained in a good mood. They even taught the poet to smile though unshaven. How kind it was of our Herr Matzerath to clap his little hands and ask for attention.

As though to give the party an appropriate end, he announced a screening of what he called a 'largely private production', to which, however, the sad news had now given general interest. So it was that we all saw a Post Futurum production, which now dealt with past events. Bruno drew curtains to shut out the evening sun, moved chairs into a relaxed seating arrangement, pushed a wide screen into the middle of the room, refilled glasses all round and fed the cassette into the VTR. The film was entitled: *The Hundred and Seventh Birthday of the Venerable Anna Koljaiczek née Bronski.*

How fortunate that this rustic fête was put on display. For if Oskar had pre-produced his urban sixtieth birthday party, I should now have to report how faithful his premonitions are in every detail: everything, Maria's buffet, every counted slice of salmon and goose breast, all the guests, even the poet's beard stubble, my Damroka's golden yellow dress, the Alpine boots worn with the dinner jacket, finally, the telegram on the silver tray, little Kurt spelling it out, the professor, urged to speak, launching into a speech that started with Adam, and he himself, diminutive in large checks, everything, I say, would have been previsioned, snatched away from the future, including Maria's hand on his little hand; but he spared us, and let his birthday party end in Anna Koljaiczek's parlour.

When Damroka and I, along with the last guests, crowded into the cloakroom, our Herr Matzerath called me back once again: 'Let's talk about realities!' he cried. 'Have you counted those Watsoncricks' fingers, really counted them from one to five? Do it, do it soon.'

At the next opportunity I did so. Like all the smurfs that Oskar took with him on his trip to Poland to make the Kashubian children happy, all the Neo-Swedes, when I dreamed them at close quarters, including my curly-haired beauty on the organ bench, had only three fingers each on each hand, in addition to the thumb. And yet, like the smurfs they are adroit. I saw them manipulate skilfully, until every human implement – the wrench, the hammer, the wheel, the compass – remembered its function. It was not only in tones of command that their language sounded besmurft; when I listened carefully, the syllable 'smurf' occurred in every third word, as a prefix or suffix or middle part. Instead of eating, they smurfed it down. And true to their Scandinavian origin, they indulged in smurfic silences.

Our Herr Matzerath thinks it must have amused the Gotland

gene manipulators not only to endow their chimaeras with four-fingered hands but to program them with the plastic gibber whose infantile quality must have been familiar to the late-human scientists from infancy. It even seems likely that there was a serious purpose behind this linguistic inspiration of the Uppsala scientists, namely, to reconcile the colloquial speech of the rat with that of man in his final phase.

And true enough, it cannot be denied that the Watsoncricks, at the time of their landing and settlement of Warehouse Island, exerted a certain moderating, call it social-democratic influence. Their political and business debates went on and on, concepts such as social-smurfic order and smurfocracy were in the air. And the rat nations listened, keeping their distance to be sure, yet eager to learn. Thus it should not surprise us that their language as well during the second sound shift assumed a smurfic character, and that our Herr Matzerath, who was familiar with smurfic ways long before smurfs came into existence, should want to give his video production about post-human developments such subtitles as: By virtue of the smurfic soul, this ailing world will be made whole.

Unfortunately, the world did nothing of the kind. Once again everything went wrong. To my Christmas rat I said after Educational Radio For All: 'You see, now the Neo-Swedes are eating fat rats off the spit.' It was bound to happen. There's too much of the human in them. The She-rat of my dreams doesn't want to resemble the common brown rat any more; she wants to have beautiful curly hair like my Damroka.

Or was it I, who no longer wished to dream you, Ratkin, who, if it had to be a rat, wanted a manipulated one? Whichever way I dream, these Nippels must not have a future. Away with them! Come out, little rat. Say: We'll get rid of them. They'll destroy themselves. And we'll help. They've turned out too human.

It wasn't until the Third Programme announced the water levels of the Elbe and the Saale, that she came out of her shack. She stretched, sniffed the air as usual, stopped awhile between feeding dish and baby bottle, and didn't go back to her dark home until the start of Politics at Noon: Nicaragua and more Nicaragua.

How adult she is, though she's still growing. We agree: those Manippels must be exterminated. And even our Herr Matzerath, whose video film actually aimed at securing the future of the hominid rats, expressed misgivings in a last speech soon after his sixtieth birthday.

'You see,' he said, shifting his free-moving leg to one side, 'I've been influenced by the media from early childhood. I vastly overestimated the power of a tin object – and failed miserably. Yes, my voice was piercing, the public gave it credit for more acts of violence than I could vouch for. But I lost my protective medium at a bad time. Then, when things began to look up and the phony fifties created hope for more and more, it turned out that I had lost my voice for good, so I was obliged to go back to the tin drum of my childhood. By breathing life into an obsolete instrument and evoking the past with it, I succeeded in filling concert halls until everyone was sick of the past. Thus I lived after a fashion on simple and compound interest and on memories. I refused to give up and let the ever-present blackness have the last word. Then new media came to my help. The intimate video cassette has a special appeal for me. It's suited to home use. In short, I found my market gap and turned out slightly above-average educational porn. When the end of all human history became easily foreseeable, I discovered a field of activity suited to my talents. According to a last look backward, which I owe to myself and to painter Malskat, our demise will be documented and the course of post-human history anticipated by the sailing of *The New Ilsebill*. True, I'd have preferred the Neo-Swedes to have more rat instinct and less human reason. In all likelihood, the development augurs a short process. The subject rat nations have been seized with unrest. Unfortunately, the whole thing will go its predetermined course. To venture a prognosis in the words of my late grandmother: There won't nothing be left.'

It begins in Kashubia, not on the Island. The paired Nippels disappear from the edges of the corn and barley fields. In extensive sunflower fields, they perish. Suddenly attacked by rats, more and more rats. And that's the end of the overseers. It looks like child's play. Like a game of cops and robbers. They could have done it ages ago. Rats, which only yesterday might have been fattened and roasted over a corn husk fire, can now be seen gnawing manipulated flesh off the bone.

No, that's wrong. Before it begins in Kashubia and then on the Island, something else happens. The wrought-iron standard, which was recently a museum piece in the Rathaus, has vanished. The Neo-Swedes notice its absence, but attach no great importance to the theft – other things have been stolen now and then, a smurf or two for instance – but this time they're making a mistake: too sure of their power, they underestimate the message of the standard and its significance, harking back to the human era. In any case, no sooner have the iron words been removed and put to work in the underground, than the whole Watsoncrickian system collapses.

Of course new overseers are appointed. But they too vanish in the fields and stay vanished; nothing is found of them but their skeletons. Shipments of corn and sunflowers, barley and lentils are delayed, disorganized, arrive more and more seldom at the Great Mill, the Central Municipal Warehouse, the Hotel Hevelius, the Arsenal, the Municipal Theatre, and the Lenin Shipyard canteen; in the end they stop completely. Punitive expeditions accomplish nothing; they get lost, bog down in the alluvial mud of the Vistula estuary, in the hilly fields of Kashubia, and turn back exhausted and decimated. When the forward posts of Kartuzy and Novy Staw, and near the coast the closely guarded field of ruins once known as Oliva become endangered and untenable, the Neo-Swedes withdraw into the city, behind the green-clad mud walls. The casemates of Mount Hagel are evacuated. Bishop's Mountain is abandoned.

Only now do they start searching in earnest for the lost museum piece. The sacristies as well as the cellars of the shipyard canteen are under suspicion. The stolen standard is reported to have been sighted in various places. On Warehouse Island, where fattened young rats are densely concentrated, search parties fail to find the standard, but clashes occur. Massacres are ordered by way of deterrence. Similarly in the Lenin Shipyard area and in those churches that have become notorious as secret rats' meeting places – Saint Bridget's, for example – the search for the word is unsuccessful. But the accursed, unutterable word, which it is forbidden to utter, is in the air, it is whispered from mouth to mouth. Even the besmurfed communication of the four syllables is prohibited. Because the word was repeatedly shouted in a state of drunkenness and because no barley was being delivered anyway, the brewing of beer was stopped.

How bewildered they seem, those double rows guarding the Arsenal, the Mill, the high-rise hotel, all the buildings where supplies are stored, for they have not yet begun to suspect that their stocks of grain and seeds are seeping away from below, through secret passages, as though some powerful suction were at work underground. None of the storey-high heaps can be preserved; they vanish downward. At this point, the gigantic fatted rats revolt and occupy first their fattening installation, then the whole of Warehouse Island, lastly Bleihof. In the end, the Neo-Swedish administration of the centralized meat-storage plant has nothing left but bones and blond wool; hunger sets in, the hominids begin to starve.

I see them insecure, anxious. No more Scandinavian phlegm or Gotland daring. They creep away into the houses of the Right City and Old City. Their usual promenades, up Lady Street, down Long Street for instance, have become dangerous. By way of the sewers, which were still open at that time, the rat nations are able to infiltrate every house, old and new. Rat after rat squeezes through the water pipes until the situation of the Neo-Swedes, even indoors, becomes untenable. Their last refuge is Saint Mary's. The order 'To Saint Mary's' is passed from house to house.

I see the haste with which, though in marching order, they withdraw from the Wood Market and Coal Market. Stockturm, Rathaus and Long Market are evacuated. Flight from Dog Street, through Bagmaker Street. From the Stockade and the former Polish Post Office they flee in wedge formations and head for the Mottlau via the Fish Market, Long Bridge and Holy Ghost Gate. Crowding through narrow arches. A headlong rush for Saint Mary's, where they will all – they may have numbered barely twenty thousand at the end – starve unless a miracle happens. But the spacious three-nave church offers them no escape, let alone a miracle, for every upward glance reveals new dangers: from every buttress, from every vault, all the way up to the keystone, hang clusters of young rats, waiting patiently.

Panic is averted with difficulty. In addition to hunger, the clones are soon attacked by a plague. Gene seems to be warring with gene inside them. At the slightest pretext, they fly at one another's throats, biting and strangling. Bodies are piled high in the centre nave. Soon the clones are obliged to abandon the altar area, then the organ loft, from which until then consoling music was heard from time to time, lastly a passacaglia. For fear of being cut off from all the exits, the vanishing remnant assemble at the north portal. There are less than a hundred of them, and each day their number dwindles. They try to eat one another, but can't, they shrink back in disgust. In the end, the last Neo-Swedes summon up courage – there are five, no, I count nine, twelve – and leave the house of the dead.

They try to escape by way of Lady Street. They drag themselves past porches occupied by rats. Every cornice, every doorway, every window is crowded with rats. The twelve are not attacked, and yet there are only nine of them now, then eight, then seven, who make their way through Lady Gate to the Long Bridge. Five, one of whom is my emaciated Damroka, try to make their way from Green Gate across the bridge to Warehouse Island. And they make it, all five, but when, Damroka in the lead, they reach the other bank of the Mottlau and are about to board their ship, they see *The New Ilsebill* manned from bow to stern by rats.

Couldn't that have been foreseen? And how could they have made the wreck, which had long been a popular sight visited by tourist groups, seaworthy? And even if the engine had started, where could the last of the Nippels have sought safety?

The deck and the midships companionways leading to the forecastle are occupied by young fattened rats, said not so long ago to be tasty. Three of the Swedish Manippels are still standing erect. They stagger, hold one another up. It's touching to see the feeble gestures with which they summon the fattened rats to leave the wreck. Their wheaten blond hair, now a dull clay colour, is shaggy and matted. But the once zinc-green rats have become greyish brown and then black. Since the start of the uprising, they have grown darker, blacker. Thus the rat nations have come closer, as though in reverse, to the species which in human times was called *Rattus rattus* and which – so rumour has it – brought the plague to mankind.

The last to give out is my Damroka; her hair falling in strands, she sinks to her knees, then collapses on top of the others. Instantly all five are assailed by black rats. Their flesh dwindles. They are still twitching. But not a whimper, not a moan. I seem to hear a ringing of bells, but fainter, much fainter than when the Watsoncricks arrived.

I dreamed that I could take hope,
barely a crumb or whatever is left
on plates eaten clean, and hope that something,
not an idea, more like an accident,
supposedly friendly, was on its way,
unobstructed by frontiers,
that it was spreading, contagious,
a salutary plague.

The Rat

I dreamed that I could hope again
for winter apples, Martinmas goose,
strawberries year after year,
for my sons' incipient baldness,
my daughters' greying, my grandchildren's postcard greetings,
for advances and compound interest, as though mankind
had unlimited credit again.

I dreamed that hope was permissible
and looked for words to justify it,
dreaming to justify my hope.
So I tried, I said good,
new, small hope. First cautious,
then sudden, I thought. I called it
treacherous, begged it to have mercy on us.
The last hope I dreamed
was consumptive.

I dreamed: A last hope is permissible; there's
sympathy and understanding.
People leave their ignition keys lying around,
They trust one another and leave their doors unlocked.
My hope did not deceive me; no one
ate his bread unshared; except that the merriment
I had hoped for, though all-embracing, was not
our kind of merriment: rats were laughing at us
when the very last hope was forfeit.

Well, have you seen the iron writing? Have you spelled it out?
Quadrisyllabic, it stood amidships, legible when we threw them off
the deck.

There she is again, laughing. One of the young black rats who
were selected and concentrated in the Vistula lowlands to be
fattened is my She-rat. We have the say again. Nothing is left of
them, not the slightest particle. Only we, you see, in future nobody
but us rats.

I see multiplying nations. Free from humans at last, the earth
provides space. Again there will be plenty of fish in the sea. On the
hills behind the city there will be dense forests. Birds will make use
of the sky. New, undreamed-of animals will appear, among them
mammalian bluebottles. But the old Danzig is falling apart. The

richly ornamented façades are crumbling. Towers are falling asunder. Gothic gables sag, collapse. Slow decay. Every brick, Saint Mary's, all the churches give up.

And as she draws the bottom line, the She-rat says: Thus mankind's foulest idea has been expunged. Its last monstrosity has been exterminated. What those iron letters say, we have practised, man has not. Nothing capable of survival bears witness to him.

My usual No. Please, She-rat, couldn't it be that we humans . . . but one last hope . . .

Oh yes, we'd forgotten all about you, going round and round in your capsule. What's this, new plans, new projects?

Giggling, she says: Why not! Seeing he's gone out of existence, man should be entitled to go on hoping, to give us rats something to laugh about, if we should dream about you again sometime . . .

The rest is swallowed up by laughter, which swells into earth-encompassing merriment. Innumerable multi-tailed litters and litters of litters, whom I provide with entertainment.

Nevertheless, I say, there's still hope that not you dream creatures, you rats, but in reality we . . .

We rats are more real than anything you could dream.

Yet, in spite of everything, there must . . .

Nothing must, not any more, nothing.

But I want, I want . . .

What do you want?

Only assuming that we humans are still . . .

All right. Let's assume.

. . . but this time let us live for one another and peacefully, do you hear, gently and lovingly, as nature made us . . .

A beautiful dream, said the She-rat, before dissolving.

William Burroughs
Queer £2.95

Almost thirty-five years after it was written, the publication of a legendary novel by one of the greatest living American writers.

For more than three decades *Queer* has remained in manuscript form – at first due to the reluctance of publishers to touch a book with such a candid homosexual content, and later, due to its author's own reluctance to make public the painful events it recounts. Now, at the zenith of one of the most notorious and influential careers in American letters, *Queer* will finally reach the avid public that has been waiting for it.

Queer is a love story – the account of William Lee's painfully circular seduction of Eugene Allerton in the Mexico City of the 1940s, and the romantic agonies he suffers. It marks the first appearance of Burrough's coruscating style of humour, which was later to flower so spectacularly in *The Naked Lunch*. In his introduction Burroughs discusses frankly and courageously the shattering event that happened after the occurrences described in *Queer*; and how this event has haunted his life and affected his work. The publication of this book is a major literary event – the most revealing work ever by a unique artist.

'The only American novelist living today who may conceivably be possessed by genius' NORMAN MAILER

Tama Janowitz
Slaves of New York £3.95

'If there were a literary equivalent to a new *Talking Heads* album, *Slaves of New York* would be that book' MADEMOISELLE

'Tama Janowitz is a clever writer. She draws trendy New York popartsies to a T. These New Yorkers are slaves to high rents, migratory relationships and, most significantly, their own contagious modishness . . . Janowitz's imagination is vivid and she can invent truly memorable situations and details . . . (She) can be laugh-out loud funny and wonderfully sharp . . . A talented writer' WASHINGTON POST

'So savagely witty, so acerbic, so piercingly accurate . . . Tama Janowitz has a merciless eye for absurdity which she trains primarily on Greenwich Village "artistes". She traps them in self-conscious postering and serves them up as metaphors for her sardonic and quirky view of *au courant* urban life' LOS ANGELES HERALD EXAMINER

'Janowitz is a fearless writer. Her details are quirky, her language is lean, and her sentences sprint along with deceptive ease. The protagonists in her stories share with her a shyness and a sense of always being out of place. Although they try in earnest to fit in, they put on the wrong clothes or say the wrong thing or fail to grasp the subtle messages other people send their way . . . With the publication of *Slaves of New York*, Tama Janowitz could become the most talked-about writer of the year' NEW YORK

'With the younger generation of writers already buried under a mound of volcanic hype, it is remarkable that Janowitz, unsmothered by the critical acclaim for her novel *American Dad*, can write with such freshness' ELLE

'The shrewd observation, the skewed invention . . . are the gifts of a singular talent' JAY McINERNEY, AUTHOR OF BRIGHT LIGHTS, BIG CITY, IN THE NEW YORK TIMES

FIRST BRITISH PUBLICATION

Vladimir Nabokov
The Enchanter £2.95

The literary treasure of the season. This work — long believed to be lost
constitutes the 'first little throb' of a fascination with tormented compulsion
that Vladimir Nabokov developed further in *Lolita*.

Paris, 1939. Vladimir Nabokov's imagination is titillated by a newspaper
report of an ape coached by scientists into drawing the first picture ever by
a captive animal: he draws the bars of his cage. In the ensuing months,
Nabokov translates the notion into a study of the terrible cage that
madness can be, and then tries to view it through the eyes of a madman.
The result is *The Enchanter*.

The unnamed protagonist of the story is, outwardly, a respectable and
comfortable man, a jeweller: inside, he churns at the sight of the pointy
knees and dimpled elbows of 12-year-old girls. Not just any little girl but
that one whose graceful awkwardness embodies the delicate balance of a
rose on the very threshold of full blossom.

Sitting on a park bench one day he is captivated by the tremblingly
beautiful form of just such a girl, roller-skating over crushed stone paths.
His desire to be near this beauty burns in him and drives him to begin a
courtship of the girl's pitiful mother — a path that can only end in the
splintering of his life.

In searing prose, Nabokov delves into the dark corners of the soul that
obsession can lead to. Forces play with this poor man in *The Enchanter*,
now frustrating him, now leading him on, now pulling him just to the edge
of madness. As the story unfolds, the reader cannot know when disaster
will strike but knows full well that it is inevitable.

Vladimir Nabokov himself mislaid the original manuscript of *The Enchanter*,
and only now, ten years after his death, has it been found and translated by
his son Dmitri Nabokov, who has added an introduction to his father's two
forewords.

All Pan books are available at your local bookshop or newsagent, or can be ordered direct from the publisher. Indicate the number of copies required and fill in the form below.

Send to: **CS Department, Pan Books Ltd., P.O. Box 40, Basingstoke, Hants. RG21 2YT.**

or phone: 0256 469551 (Ansaphone), quoting title, author and Credit Card number.

Please enclose a remittance* to the value of the cover price plus: 60p for the first book plus 30p per copy for each additional book ordered to a maximum charge of £2.40 to cover postage and packing.

*Payment may be made in sterling by UK personal cheque, postal order, sterling draft or international money order, made payable to Pan Books Ltd.

Alternatively by Barclaycard/Access:

Card No.

Signature:

Applicable only in the UK and Republic of Ireland.

While every effort is made to keep prices low, it is sometimes necessary to increase prices at short notice. Pan Books reserve the right to show on covers and charge new retail prices which may differ from those advertised in the text or elsewhere.

NAME AND ADDRESS IN BLOCK LETTERS PLEASE:

....

Name ——————————————————————————

Address ——————————————————————————

——————————————————————————————

——————————————————————————————

——————————————————————————————

3/87